When
HOPE
Blossoms

Books by Kim Vogel Sawyer

FROM BETHANY HOUSE PUBLISHERS

When
HOPE
Blossoms

Kim Vogel
A Novel by
Sawyer

BETHANY HOUSE PUBLISHERS
a division of Baker Publishing Group
Minneapolis, Minnesota

© 2012 by Kim Vogel Sawyer

Published by Bethany House Publishers
11400 Hampshire Avenue South
Bloomington, Minnesota 55438
www.bethanyhouse.com

Bethany House Publishers is a division of
Baker Publishing Group, Grand Rapids, Michigan

Printed in the United States of America

Library of Congress Cataloging-in-Publication Data
Sawyer, Kim Vogel.
    When hope blossoms / Kim Vogel Sawyer.
        p.   cm.
    Includes bibliographical references.
    ISBN 978-0-7642-1035-8 (hardcover : alk. paper)
    ISBN 978-0-7642-0787-7 (pbk.)
    1. Mennonites—Fiction. I. Title.
PS3619.A97W43 2012
813'.6—dc23   2012000969

Scripture quotations are from the King James Version of the Bible.

The internet addresses, email addresses, and phone numbers in this book are accurate
at the time of publication. They are provided as a resource. Baker Publishing Group
does not endorse them or vouch for their content or permanence.

Cover design by Lookout Design, Inc.
Cover photography by Aimee Christensen

12   13   14   15   16   17   18   7   6   5   4   3

For *Connie, Lisbeth,* and *Sheila,*
who had to say good-bye
but know they'll see their children
again someday.

"For there is hope of a tree,
if it be cut down,
that it will sprout again,
and that the tender branch thereof
will not cease."

Job 14:7 KJV

1

"Momma . . . is this home?"

Amy Knackstedt looked up from the box of linens at her feet. The uncertainty in her daughter's blue eyes pierced Amy. There'd been so much upheaval in Adrianna's short life—how would it affect her view of the world? Amy held her arms wide, and the little girl dashed over for a hug. "Yes, sweetheart, this is *home*." Amy emphasized the last word, savoring its meaning. She planted a kiss on Adrianna's tousled brown hair, then set her aside. "Go ask Bekah to brush and braid your hair."

With a dimpled grin, Adrianna skipped around the corner and up the stairs to where Amy had put her eldest child to work cleaning and organizing the farmhouse's single bathroom. Bekah had scowled—an expression that appeared more and more often since she'd passed her thirteenth birthday—when given the task, but she hadn't argued. Amy sighed, remembering her daughter's reaction. She supposed she should be stricter concerning Bekah's sour moods. Dad had even called

Bekah disrespectful, which was grounds for severe punishment in their Old Order Mennonite sect. But Amy couldn't find it in her heart to scold. Bekah carried more responsibility than most girls her age. She deserved a little leniency.

Balancing the stack of folded sheets and pillowcases in her arms, Amy headed for the enclosed stairway in the kitchen that led to the three bedrooms. When she'd learned she and the children would occupy a century-old farmhouse, she'd hoped for four bedrooms so each of the children could have their own room. But three bedrooms was one more than they'd had in her father's house. Adrianna and Bekah would have to pair up, but at least Parker no longer had to share with his sisters. Could he be eleven already? As big as the children were getting, they needed their own spaces. And this house and property offered them room to grow.

Thank You, Lord, for Your provision. The prayer formed automatically—the result of years of talking to God. But the emotion behind the simple statement was far from rote. The Lord had nearly moved mountains to bring Amy and her children to this place, and she sensed in the deepest part of her soul they would find healing here.

As Amy passed the smallest bedroom, she peeked inside to see how Parker was coming along in putting away his clothes. Her son stood in front of the four-drawer chest, a puzzled expression on his face. All four drawers hung open, and he rested his fingertips on the edge of the highest drawer. Affection rose within Amy's breast, followed by the persistent silent question of what-might-have-been, as she gazed at her only son.

"Doing okay, Parker?" She kept her voice low to avoid startling him.

Slowly, as if his neck joint was rusty, he shifted his head to peer at her. "Huh?"

Amy didn't respond to the single-word query. He'd heard her—he needed time to form a reply. After a few seconds, he gave a jerky nod that made his thick brown hair bounce on his high forehead. He looked so much like his father. "I'm okay. My socks and underwear go in the top drawer . . . right?"

Amy offered a reassuring smile. "That's right. Top drawer for socks and underwear. Then shirts in the middle ones. And pants in the bottom." She paused between sentences to give Parker time to absorb her instructions.

Parker scrunched his face. "It's all backwards."

"Backwards?"

He nodded rapidly, clinging to the drawer to hold his balance. "You wear your shirt on your middle, your pants under that, and socks clear at the bottom on your feet. So socks should go in the *bottom* drawer."

Amy stifled a chuckle at his reasoning. "That makes a lot of sense, but look at the drawers. See how the very top drawer is the smallest one?"

Parker examined the drawers with one eye squinted shut.

"Would your shirts fit in that drawer?"

The boy heaved a sigh, his skinny shoulders rising and falling. "Not all of them."

"But your socks and underwear will fit, right?"

He peeked inside the drawer, as if measuring it. "Uh-huh."

"So that's where they go."

"Okay, Mom."

Amy waited long enough to watch him pull out a cluster of socks from the box on the end of his bare mattress and drop them in the top drawer before she turned toward her own bedroom. She entered the room, paused, and drew in a deep breath, testing the air. She'd opened all of the windows in the house upon her arrival yesterday evening, and now a dew-laden new-day scent wafted in. After sitting unoccupied for over a year, the house had acquired a musty odor. But the stout Kansas breeze, combined with open boxes of baking soda that Adrianna had cheerfully planted in a corner of each room, was creating the desired effect. The house smelled fresher already.

She used her elbow to bump open the closet door and then stepped inside. She wrinkled her nose. The small space smelled like a dead mouse. She hoped she had another box of baking soda. Or two. Ducking her head, she moved to the shelves that lined the short back wall of the wedge-shaped closet. Earlier, she'd washed the shelves with soap and water, then covered them with plain paper. She was grateful for the shelves, even if they were tucked under the eaves. They provided a nice storage space for extra sheets, towels, and blankets—going-away gifts from the fellowship members in Arborville, Kansas.

Handling the fresh items brought a rush of memories, faces of people she'd known her entire life flashing through her mind. If Gabe hadn't died, she'd still be with them. But he *had* died, taking away her security. She needed a new security. How she prayed Weaverly, Kansas, would become her and the children's promised land.

Amy finished arranging the items neatly—even if they were tucked out of sight in a closet, she wouldn't do a slipshod job—then stepped back into the bedroom. The sun pouring through the uncovered windows highlighted the faded flowered wallpaper and scuffed wood floor. The room held a tired, worn appearance, but once she'd hung curtains and spread a pretty quilt on the bed, it would feel more homey. Before she started decorating, though, she needed to finish giving the house a thorough scrubbing from top to bottom and get all of their belongings put away.

There'd only been time for a cursory dusting and sweeping yesterday evening before they moved the furnishings into the rooms because the Mennonite men from the fellowship in Ohio needed to return the rented U-Haul trucks first thing this morning. So they'd dragged everything into the house and departed, leaving Amy and the children to organize things on their own. Although she might have appreciated some extra helping hands, she liked being able to choose how to arrange the furniture in the rooms of *her* house. She hoped God didn't see her delight as selfish, but she couldn't deny a sense of freedom in being the one making decisions rather than following Dad's or Gabe's directions. Thirty-three years old and marching into a future of her own making. Her heart skipped a beat. What kind of future would it be?

Fear tried to wiggle its way from the depths of her soul, but she pushed the unwelcome emotion aside. This was not a time of fear, but of celebration. Of gratitude for open doors and new beginnings. Dropping to her knees, Amy spent a few moments in prayer, placing the niggle of doubt into her Father's hands and requesting discernment to do what was best for herself, Bekah, Parker, and little Adrianna.

"Amen," she finished and pushed to her feet just as clattering footsteps pounded across the floor. She turned toward the door, and Bekah rushed in, her face flushed and the trailing ribbons of her white head covering bouncing on her shoulders. Panic shone in Bekah's brown eyes. She must have encountered another mouse. With a light chuckle, Amy said, "Honey, I know Grandpa packed some mousetraps, but I still haven't found them. As soon as I do, I'll—"

Bekah gasped out, "Mom, Adri and Parker . . . I—I can't find them anywhere. They're gone."

✧

Tim Roper turned off the riding mower's engine. The machine bucked a couple of times, spluttered, and finally died. His ears rang in the sudden silence, and he tipped his head, waiting for the buzz to clear. Slowly the sounds of the orchard filled his ears. He smiled. He'd never tired of the wind's whisper in the trees.

He climbed off the mower, his muscles stiff from holding his balance in the backless seat, and reached to pinch a plump pale-pink bud on a Golden Delicious apple tree. His gaze roved to the nearest tree, then shifted down the row. Buds—some as small and round as peas, others as fat as hazelnuts—peppered the slender branches. Over the past days of mowing, he'd noted the Red Delicious, Gala, and Jonagolds were equally laden with buds. If all went well—no late frosts, no insect infestations, no hailstorms to rob the branches of blossoms—he'd have a bumper crop this year. He needed one after last year's dismal harvest. Yet, despite the uncertainties of his profession, he wouldn't trade operating his apple orchard for any other job in the world.

His boots flattened the mounds of cut grass as he wandered between the rows, checking for broken branches, signs of decay, or troublesome insects. While he walked, his mind tripped over other pressing springtime tasks. He still needed to trim the grass beneath the trees—the grass near the trunks stood at least twelve inches tall, creating a good hiding place for critters. He also needed to make arrangements for the delivery of the rented bee colonies to ensure adequate pollination. If the harvest was good this year, maybe he'd purchase his own hives at the end of the season so he wouldn't have to bother the beekeepers in Osage County again. There'd be costs involved in setting up the hives and getting started, but he could bottle and sell the honey, so in the long run he'd be money ahead. He liked that idea.

He ducked between trees and made a loop toward the waiting mower. He preferred mowing in the morning hours, before the May sun got so high and hot, but once the bees arrived, he'd have to mow later in the day.

The bees were busiest in the morning, and they didn't like the mower's noise. They wouldn't do their job if he disturbed them. But until they arrived, he'd continue to take advantage of the cooler morning hours.

Tim squinted upward, noting the sun high in the cloudless blue sky. Morning was close to gone already—he needed to get a move on. He'd ride to the house, load his little trailer with the push mower and weed-eaters, then come back out. His stomach growled. Or maybe he'd eat lunch first. With late spring's longer days, he could afford to take a half hour of rest—still plenty of work hours remaining. And plenty of work to fill the hours.

Whistling, he plopped into the mower's seat and reached for the ignition. But as his fingers connected with the silver key, a sound reached his ears. An out-of-place sound. Laughter—high-pitched and carefree. He froze, his body breaking out in a cold sweat. Without warning, time rolled backward half a dozen years. In his mind's eye, he pictured Charlie galloping in his unique, awkward gait between the dwarf trees, his face alight with joy, laughter pouring from his lips.

Tim shook his head hard and the image faded, but the tinkling laughter rang again. Not from his imagination, but in reality. Frowning, he searched the area. Was a family picnicking nearby? It wasn't uncommon for Weaverly families to drive out and picnic under the trees—the orchard's former owners had allowed it, and he hadn't brought an end to the practice.

Another burst of laughter, followed by a childish demand: "I want a big, big, *gigantic* bouquet."

Scowling, Tim leaped off the mower and trotted in the direction of the voice. At the far edge of the band of Golden Delicious trees, he spotted a little girl. He slowed his pace, taking in her twin brown braids and simple knee-length dress with its attached modesty cape. *Mennonite.* His heart lurched, his feet stumbling to a halt. But she couldn't be. There weren't any Old Order Mennonites in Weaverly.

The child's arms overflowed with bud-heavy twigs, and she looked into the thick branches of a tree. "A *big* stick this time."

A *big* stick? She wouldn't be able to remove a large branch from the tree, and she could do some serious damage if she tried. Tim jolted into motion once more, waving one hand over his head. "You there! What do you think you're doing?"

The child spun, a few sprigs falling from her arms. Her gaze fell on Tim, and a smile lit her pixie face. "Hi, mister. Look! I'm getting flowers for my mama."

Up close, Tim realized just how many branches had been stripped of their buds. Buds that wouldn't become blossoms. Blossoms that wouldn't become apples. He balled his hands into fists. "These flowers aren't meant for picking." He barked the comment more harshly than he'd intended.

The child blinked up at him, her mouth forming an O of alarm.

Tim drew in a deep breath. He glanced around. "How did you get here?"

She tapped one tennis-shoe-covered foot on the grass. "I walked."

Tim frowned. Walked? How much distance could a little kid like her cover? Not much, he'd wager. "Where is your mother?"

The girl rocked gently to and fro, her skinny braids swinging with the motion. "At my house."

The reply was less than satisfactory. "Where is your house?"

Twisting her head, the child squinted over her shoulder toward the west. "Over there. Somewhere."

Tim looked in the same direction, pondering possibilities. The only house close enough for a child to manage the distance was the old Sanford farm. He'd heard some scuttlebutt in Weaverly about people from Ohio purchasing the Sanford acreage as well as three or four houses in town, but he hadn't paid much attention. His focus was always on his orchard. Now he wished he'd listened more carefully to the town gossips. If he'd had any idea the newcomers from Ohio were Mennonites, he might have—

He shook his head. Would he have sold the orchard and moved? Not likely. He loved this place too much to leave it, even to avoid contact with Mennonites.

He turned to the girl, who stared into the tree again. She was a cute little thing—innocent-looking with those big blue eyes and shabby braids. But she didn't belong on his land, picking the buds from his trees. "I want you to go home. And from now on—"

A startled yelp sounded from behind Tim's shoulder, followed by a scrambling noise. A second child—a boy, older than the girl—fell from the branches with a wild flailing of arms and legs and landed flat on his bottom in the thick grass beneath the tree.

2

A loud cry escaped the boy's mouth, followed by an intense intake of air that indicated the wind had been knocked out of him. The little girl squealed, "Parker!" She dropped her armload of twigs and scampered forward.

Tim got to him first. The boy had curled up like a giant roly-poly bug, holding his stomach and gasping as desperately as a fish on a creekbank. Tim dropped to his knees next to the boy and pressed him flat, advising in a sharp tone, "Calm down. Breathe through your nose." The boy stared at Tim with wide brown eyes, his mouth flapping open and closed. Tim gave him a little shake. "I said breathe through your nose!"

The boy's shoulders jerked spasmodically, but he clamped his jaw closed and took short, uneven breaths. Slowly, his red face faded to a muted pink that closely matched the tree buds. When he appeared to be breathing normally, Tim took hold of his shoulders and helped him shift to a seated position.

The boy grimaced, planting both palms on his lower back. He groaned.

The little girl folded her arms over her chest and clicked her tongue on her teeth. "Parker, you were s'posed to climb down from the tree, not jump."

The boy—Parker—hung his head. "I'm sorry." His voice, low and soft, held shame. "I didn't mean to do it wrong." His face lifted, his repentant brown eyes meeting Tim's. Something in Parker's expression tugged at Tim's heart. He swallowed hard, unable to tear his gaze away from the boy's pleading face.

The girl stomped her foot. "An' you made me lose my buttons. Now we gotta pick more." Her dirty hands lifted to the drooping branches above her head.

"No!" Tim jolted to his feet and swept the branches out of the girl's reach. "You can't pick those."

The child tilted her head, her brow all puckered. "But why? The little buttons are so pretty. Like pink marbles." Her infectious giggle rang. "Momma's most favorite color is pink. I wanna take them to Momma."

Tim wanted to take the children to their mama. He turned to Parker, who had rolled to his hip and was struggling to stand. Concern tickled the back of Tim's mind. Considering the short fall—the lowest branches were barely as high as Tim's chin—and the cushioning grass beneath the tree, he hadn't expected the boy to be hurt. But his slow movements indicated pain.

Tim caught the boy's upper arm and lifted him to his feet. Upright, he stood as high as Tim's armpit. Tim judged him to be between ten and twelve years old, but his mannerisms made him seem younger. "Are you okay?"

"Huh?" Parker stared at Tim for a moment, openmouthed.

Had the fall knocked the kid senseless? Tim repeated, "Are—you—hurt?"

Parker bobbed his head. "My rear end hurts."

Tim held back a snort of amusement. Served him right, climbing up in the trees and picking the branches clean of buds. "Can you walk?"

The boy shuffled forward with his back shaped like an apostrophe and his face pinched into a frown. "Ow. Ow."

He'd intended to put the children on the other side of the fence and send them on their way, but it would be cruel to make the boy walk the quarter-mile distance to the Sanford farm with a sore back. Besides, maybe he really had jarred something. Tim might be held accountable if the kid suffered some kind of long-term effect. Not that Mennonites would sue, but . . . Tim sighed. It meant losing work time, but he could transport the children to the Sanford place in the rusty golf cart he used to get around the orchard.

"Stay here." He pointed at the little girl and scowled. "And don't pick any flowers . . . er, buttons. I'll be back in a few minutes."

Like an obedient puppy, the little girl plopped down on the grass and crisscrossed her legs. Parker hovered over her like an old man with osteoporosis. Tim doubted Parker would sit. He trotted to his mower, climbed aboard, and rode the thing as quickly as he dared to the house. From there, he unlocked the shed, hopped into the golf cart's seat, and muttered a warning—"You better start, you crotchety old thing." It started, and he grinned.

Less than ten minutes after leaving the two kids sitting beneath the Golden Delicious apple trees, he returned. They hadn't budged. He shifted to the edge of the cracked vinyl seat and patted the empty spot beside him. "C'mon. Get on."

The little girl bounced up, grabbed the boy's hand, and pulled him to the cart. She clambered in, but the boy hesitated. The girl hunched her shoulders and giggled. "Get in, Parker. It'll be fun." She shot Tim a bright smile.

Tim rolled his eyes. "Parker, you can walk or ride. It's your choice."

Finally, Parker grabbed the iron armrest on the seat and heaved himself into the cart. He fell into the narrow space next to the girl, releasing a yelp when his backside connected with the seat. Tim sucked in a sharp breath. Not that he held any fondness for these two little urchins who'd robbed his tree of the potential for a good three dozen apples, but he still didn't want the boy to be seriously hurt. He'd try to avoid bumps on the way to the Sanford place.

The little girl chattered as they drove slowly along the dirt road, but Tim didn't reply. No sense in encouraging the kid to think of him as a friend. In fact, he intended to inform their mother to keep them home where they belonged. Most Old Order moms were diligent when it came to supervision. Unless things had changed a lot since he was a boy. His own mother had never let him venture far from her sight. He ground his teeth. Now these kids had him thinking about Mom.

They reached the lane leading to the Sanford farm, and Tim slowed the cart to make the turn. As he aimed the nose of the cart for the house, he spotted another child wandering between the house and the barn. Her white cap and trailing ribbons as well as the simple dress let Tim know without a doubt the family who'd claimed the farmstead was definitely Old Order Mennonite. He gritted his teeth so hard his jaw ached.

The girl held her cupped hands beside her mouth. He assumed she was hollering, but he couldn't hear her over the cart's rumble. She came to a halt and turned to look in his direction. Her eyes flew wide. Then she took off at a run, disappearing behind the house.

Tim pulled up the cart next to the house and shifted it into park. "Hop out," he ordered the pair on the seat, "and go get your mom or dad for me." He'd have a firm talk with the new owners, and then he'd leave them be. For good.

✢

"Mom! Mom! Some man is here! He has Parker and Adri with him!"

Bekah's shrill voice reached Amy's ears, and she nearly collapsed with relief. Having been warned about an abandoned well in the pasture behind the house, she'd left Bekah searching the outbuildings around the house and headed out to the pasture herself. She'd found the well and its wood cover, but there was no sign of the children. She was planning where she should look next when Bekah's call came.

Amy waved both hands over her head. "I'm coming!" She broke into a run, the uneven ground and her wind-tossed skirts slowing her pace despite the sturdy tennis shoes on her feet. The stout breeze loosened the pins holding her cap, and she clamped one hand over her head as she ran. She rounded the house, her heart leaping for joy when she spotted all three children standing next to a rusty, open-sided cart. A tall man wearing a baseball-style cap similar to those worn by the Mennonite men sat in the cart's seat with one leg extended to the ground. Apparently he'd been the one to bring the children home. Gratitude swelled in her chest, and she ran directly to the little group.

21

Throwing her arms around both Parker and Adrianna, she kissed their sweaty heads and then aimed a smile at the stranger. "Thank you so much, sir. I've been so worried!" She shifted her gaze to her son and youngest daughter, searching their dear, dirty faces. The fearful worry that had held her captive for the past half hour abruptly switched to aggravation now that she knew they were safe. She frowned at the pair. "Shame on you for wandering off that way. From now on you stay right here on our property, do you hear me?"

They both nodded, their expressions contrite, and her irritation melted. She hugged them again. Parker let out a yelp. Amy pulled back. "Parker, honey, what's wrong?"

"He jumped out of a tree and fell on his bottom," Adrianna said, her bright voice devoid of concern.

Amy gawked at the boy. "You were climbing trees?"

"We were getting you flowers." Adrianna answered for her brother again. "But that man"—she pointed a dirt-smudged finger to the man who remained half-in, half-out of the sorry-looking cart—"wouldn't let us bring 'em to you."

The man slowly straightened, rising to his full height, which was intimidating up close. His frowning countenance added to his unapproachable appearance. "I caught these two on my land, snipping branches from one of my apple trees."

Amy turned toward the children. "That was very, very dangerous. Parker, I want you to promise me you won't climb any more trees."

Parker gave his customary "Huh?" Then he blinked twice and nodded. "Okay, Mom."

Amy took hold of Adrianna's shoulder. "And you should never pick flowers without asking permission first. Tell

Mr.—Mr.—" She blew out a huff, turning again to the man. "Your name, please?"

"Roper. Tim Roper."

Amy turned Adrianna to face the man. "Tell Mr. Roper you're sorry."

"I'm sorry, Mr. Roper." Very little repentance colored Adrianna's tone, but Amy decided to address the issue more fully later—after he had departed. Adrianna pulled on Amy's skirt. "I'm thirsty. Can I have a drink?"

Bekah stepped forward. "I'll take them in and help them wash up."

The trio headed for the house. Amy watched them go, noting Parker's stiff gait. Maybe she should make a doctor's appointment for him, just in case. Falls could be dangerous, as she knew far too well.

Eager to return to her children, she gave Mr. Roper a smile. "Thank you again for bringing them home. We're new here, and I'm sure their curiosity carried them away. It won't happen again." She started for the house.

"It better not."

The man's disparaging tone halted Amy. She slowly turned to face him.

He scowled, folding his arms over his chest. "Those trees are my livelihood. I can't have your kids over there, picking the branches bare. All my other neighbors respect the boundary. I'd appreciate it if you'd keep your kids on your own side of the fence."

Mr. Roper's blunt, condescending manner of speaking raised Amy's hackles, but a biblical admonition winged through her conscience: *"A soft answer turneth away wrath."* She drew in a slow breath, giving herself a moment to pray for patience before replying. "I apologize, Mr. Roper. If there's anything I can do to make up for the damage to your tree, I—"

He waved a hand in dismissal. "No need. Just keep them home from now on. It isn't safe to let kids run wild that way."

His words cut Amy to the core. How many times had she berated herself for the long-ago day when she'd let Parker run after Gabe rather than keeping him close to home? If she'd made a different choice, maybe he'd be whole. Maybe Gabe would still be with them. Her chest constricted, hindering her breathing as tentacles of guilt wrapped around her heart.

"Now that we're clear, I need to get back to work." Mr. Roper whirled on his bootheel and slid onto the seat of his cart. He gave the key a twist, and the engine coughed. With a scowl, he twisted the key again. A stuttering *click-click-click* came in response. He slapped the steering wheel, then let his head drop back, releasing an aggravated grunt.

Although Amy preferred to escape to the house, she couldn't leave the man sitting in her driveway in a dead cart without offering assistance. She took a hesitant step forward. "Can I—"

"Does your husband have an extra can of gasoline sitting around?" His gaze whisked across her cap and the black dangling strings. "Or maybe a vehicle—a truck or tractor—he could use to tow this thing to my place?"

Amy gulped, taken aback by the brusque question. "I . . . I'm a widow, Mr. Roper."

His face flooded red. He grabbed off his hat, leaving his short-cropped brown hair standing in sweat-stiffened spikes. "I beg your pardon. I just assumed, since you purchased a farm, that . . ."

Amy understood his confusion. Dad had questioned the

wisdom of her choosing the farmhouse rather than one of the houses in town, but she'd grown up on a farm. She'd loved the open space and feeling of freedom in living away from town.

She explained, "The land will be used to grow corn, wheat, and soybeans. But I won't be the one planting and harvesting. Some families who've also moved into the area will make use of the land. With help from my fellowship near Arborville, I purchased the house; a brother Mennonite fellowship in Ohio owns the acreage."

Had he grimaced at the words *Mennonite fellowship*, or had she only imagined it? Trepidation sped her pulse.

He pulled his lips to the side, as if chewing the inside of his cheek. "I . . . see."

"I don't have a tractor or truck, but I do have a car." Amy gestured toward the small ramshackle garage at the rear of the house. "It has a hitchball for towing. I'd be glad to pull your cart to your property if you'll give me a few minutes to check on my children."

He nodded—one abrupt bob of his head—then returned the hat to his head. He stared across the ground, his expression grim.

Amy trotted to the house. All three children were in the kitchen, seated around the table in the middle of the room. Parker wore a milk mustache and Adrianna's cheeks were smeared with peanut butter. Amy glanced at the half-eaten sandwiches, crumpled napkins, crumbs, and empty glasses on the table's Formica top.

"They were hungry." Bekah sent her mother a sidelong look. "I guess I should have asked first before fixing sandwiches."

Amy gave Bekah a one-armed hug. "I'm glad you took care

of lunch." She moved to the sink and washed her hands. Her time in the pasture, hunting for Adrianna and Parker, had left her sweaty and dusty. "I'm going to use our car to tow Mr. Roper's cart to his house. Girls, make the beds while I'm gone. The sheets are in my closet. Parker, I want you to put the books on the shelf in your room." She wiped her hands on her apron skirt, satisfied the tasks would keep the children occupied for the length of time she'd be gone.

Adrianna wriggled down from her chair. "Can I come with you, Momma?"

"No." Amy ignored her daughter's crestfallen expression. "All of you stay in the house until I get back. If someone knocks on the door, don't answer." She grabbed the car keys from a nail pounded into the back doorjamb and charged out the screen door, letting it slam into its frame behind her. She backed the car from the garage and pulled it close to Mr. Roper's cart.

Leaving it idling, she hopped out. "Mr. Roper, would you position it correctly? I'm not adept enough at backing to do it right." Gabe had always done the driving. Amy had been forced to learn to drive following his death, but she'd often deferred to her father. Better a stranger drive her car than risk backing into his cart.

Wordlessly, he strode forward and slid behind the wheel. With a few whirls of the steering wheel and some short jaunts forward and back, he angled the car so the rear bumper of the car and the cart's nose rested a mere eighteen inches apart. Then he turned off the ignition and got out. "Got a rope?"

"Um . . . I'm not sure."

"Mind if I check in the barn?"

Amy nodded, and he headed in that direction, his stride

long and his arms swinging. Amy fidgeted, waiting for his return. She'd lost an entire week between packing and moving, and she still needed to set up her sewing room so she could get busy on the quilts she'd been hired to create prior to moving to Weaverly. How she hoped her quilting business would flourish. Without Dad's financial assistance, she needed the income desperately.

Mr. Roper returned, a length of chain dangling from his hand. "This'll do." She stayed out of the way while he looped the chain through the cart's frame and connected it to the hitchball. Brushing his hands, he rose, his knees cracking. "That's it. Let's go."

Amy stifled an amused snort. Apparently all men were short on words and long on action. She'd surmised it was a Mennonite trait, but this man was clearly not Mennonite. He climbed into his cart, and she slid behind the steering wheel. Sticking her head out the open window, she called, "Are you ready?"

He waved his hand in reply.

Gritting her teeth, Amy started the engine and put the car in gear. She'd never towed anything before. What if she hit a bump and bounced Mr. Roper right out of the open cart? Sweat broke out across her back and trickled between her shoulder blades. Her hands tightened on the wheel, her knuckles white. *Lord, be with me. . . .*

3

Bekah swept a damp rag across the tabletop, sending the crumbs onto the linoleum floor. "All right, you guys, you heard Mom. No more running off." She'd never admit how scared she'd been when she realized her brother and sister were missing. But now that they were back, safe and sound, she was just plain mad. Shouldn't she feel relieved rather than angry? She wished she could make sense of her up-and-down emotions. "Parker, go get busy on those books. And, Adri, get sheets for our beds from Mom's closet."

Parker looked at the floor, where bread crumbs lay scattered next to his tennis-shoe-covered foot. "Mom puts the crumbs in her hand and then puts them in the trash. She doesn't throw them on the floor."

Bekah flopped the rag over the edge of the sink. As many mice as seemed to live in this old house, they'd eat the crumbs in no time. "Don't worry about it."

"Crumbs belong in the trash," Parker insisted, his scowl

deep. He stared at the crumbs as if he expected them to jump from the floor into the waste can on their own.

Bekah huffed. Unless she swept up the crumbs, Parker wouldn't be able to think about anything else. She stomped to the corner and retrieved the broom. "All right, all right, I'll get rid of the crumbs." She gave the broom a vicious swipe. Crumbs flew in every direction.

Parker sucked in a huge breath, the gasp almost comical with his wide-open mouth and disbelieving stare.

Adri squealed and leaped out of her chair. "Bekah, you're making a mess! Momma *never* sweeps like that!"

"Well, I'm not Momma." Bekah slapped the bristles at the floor again. The crumbs scooted around the floor like a nest of disturbed ants.

Adri grabbed the broom and tried to wrestle it away. "Stop it, Bekah."

"*You* stop it!" Bekah yanked hard, gaining ownership of the broom.

Adri fell backward and landed on her bottom. She set up a wail. Parker stood beside the table, wringing his hands. His dark eyes reflected fear more than worry. He muttered to himself—the words indistinguishable. Bekah wanted to scream at both of them to shut up and go do their chores. Hugging the broom to her chest, she wished her anger could be swept away as easily as those crumbs.

God, what's wrong with me? Am I going crazy, like Daddy did? The thought scared her so much, tears spurted into her eyes. She threw the broom aside and reached to help Adri to her feet. Adri pulled away, refusing her help. Blinking away her tears, she decided to let her sister sit there and cry if that's what she wanted to do.

Bekah turned to Parker. "Budger . . ." She used the nickname Dad had given Parker—his teasing play on Parker's name. "I didn't mean to make a mess. I'll clean it up."

Parker gazed at her, unblinking. "You promise?"

"Yes, I promise." Parker needed so much reassurance. Why couldn't he be normal, like other kids' brothers? Why did everything have to be *so hard* with him?

"All right." He turned and shuffled for the stairway, his movements even slower than usual, and plodded upstairs.

Bekah folded her arms over her chest and frowned down at Adri. Even though her sister was far younger than Parker, there wasn't any reason she couldn't behave normally. Then again, maybe sitting on the floor and howling was normal for a five-year-old. Even so, Bekah's patience was spent. "Are you done yet?"

Adri sniffled, rubbing her eyes with her fists. "You hurt my feelings, Bekah."

Bekah crouched down to Adri's level. She knew she should apologize—she'd been rough with Adri, and she was wrong. But she wasn't really sorry, and she wouldn't add lying to her list of wrongdoings. Still, she gentled her voice. "You ready to help me make those beds?"

Adri drew in a shuddering breath. Her lower lip poked out, and tears trembled on her thick lower lashes. Her blue eyes—Adri was the only one of the kids to have Mom's eyes instead of Dad's—looked even bluer with all the tears. "I'm tired."

Bekah grabbed Adri's hand and pulled her up as she rose. "If you'll put sheets on your own bed, then you can take a nap."

For a moment Adri stood, shoulders hunched and lower

lip hanging in a pout, but then she heaved a deep sigh. "All right, Bekah." She trudged upstairs, too.

Bekah grabbed the broom and quickly swept the crumbs into a neat pile. She couldn't find the dustpan—so many things were still in boxes—so she pushed the crumbs onto a piece of paper and dumped all of it into the waste can. Then she put the broom in the corner and headed upstairs. She glanced into Parker's room. He knelt in front of the bookshelf, his face puckered in concentration. As she watched, he carefully lifted out one book from the box beside him and placed it just-so on the shelf. Bekah considered telling him he could stack more than one at a time, but she knew he'd say "huh?" and then need her to show him what she meant. And she didn't feel like showing him. So she moved on to Mom's room instead.

Apparently Adri had been in the closet riffling through the sheets, because the stacks were all askew. Mom wouldn't leave them like that. Mom did *everything* right. Bekah took a few moments to straighten the stacks of sheets, towels, and pillowcases before removing the pink-striped sheets that belonged on Mom's bed.

She smoothed the bottom sheet into place, wondering why Mom needed such a big bed. All of the kids had twin-sized beds, but Mom's was a queen-size. Wouldn't the big bed make her miss having Dad on the other side of the mattress? But maybe Mom didn't miss Dad as much as Bekah did. Mom never talked about him. Neither did Bekah. But she couldn't help thinking about him.

With a flick of her wrists, she flipped the top sheet over the mattress. She knew how to tuck the bottom corners so the sheet would hang neatly, and she performed the task without conscious thought, her mind skipping through memories from way back. Before Adri was even born. When Dad was alive, and Parker was normal, and they all lived in their own house instead of with Grandpa, and nobody in town looked at them with pity or—worse—with blame. Bekah *hated* those looks. That's why she hadn't put up much fuss when Mom said they were moving to another town. But now that they were here, away from everyone and everything familiar . . .

Bekah stuffed the pillows into matching cases and plopped them onto the bed. Then she moved to the window and looked across the landscape. In lots of ways, the view reminded her of Arborville. Square patches of farmland stretched to the horizon, resembling a giant quilt. Lots of open space. Clumps of scraggly trees here and there to break up the expanse of farmland. Except the trees east of their new house weren't scraggly or clumpy. They stood in neat rows, like a king's forest from a storybook. The tips of the branches all met each other, creating a lacy canopy of green. It looked like a good place to hide away with a book.

With a dramatic sigh, Bekah turned from the window. She didn't have time to sneak away and read. Work awaited. She grabbed sheets for her bed and Parker's bed and headed for her brother's room. Mom would be back soon, and she'd expect things to be done.

⁂

Sweat trickled down Tim's forehead, stinging his eyes. His stomach growled, reminding him he hadn't eaten since early that morning. Couldn't the Mennonite lady hurry? He could pedal a bicycle faster than she was currently driving her old blue Buick. Through the back windshield, he watched the black ribbons of her mesh cap dancing on her shoulders.

An uncomfortable twinge unrelated to hunger crept through his stomach. When he'd seen those black ribbons, he'd assumed she was married. To discover there was a widow—a widow with children—living next door brought long-buried admonitions to the surface. *Care for widows and orphans.* Hadn't the biblical mandate been drilled into him along with so many other rules and regulations? He'd fled that life, eager to escape the never-ending lists of *do* and *do not.* But now, without warning and without invitation, the old teachings pricked his conscience.

The Buick's brake lights flashed. Again. How she loved the brake. Tim tapped the cart's brake in response. By inches, the Mennonite widow eased the car into the lane leading to Tim's double-wide trailer house. Dust swirled as they made the turn, but as soon as they entered the lane, the dust settled. Trees on either side of the dirt road blocked the wind. Sweet scents filled Tim's nostrils, removing some of the unsettledness of the past minutes. His tense shoulders relaxed, and he released a breath of relief. He was home again—his place of security. His place of refuge.

The woman stopped the car midway between the house and the huge, ancient barn. The Buick's engine stilled, and she stepped out of the car. Tim hopped out and crouched next to the bumper to untangle the chain connecting the cart to the vehicle. Her shadow fell across him. Gooseflesh broke out on his arms. Julia used to stand so close her shadow touched his, but unlike this woman, Julia was never silent. She even talked in her sleep. Sometimes at night, Tim still listened for the mumble of his wife's voice. Squatting in the Mennonite woman's shadow, only the whisper of the trees and clank of the chain in his ears, Tim found himself wishing the woman would speak to chase away the memories of Julia's cheerful, endless speech.

"There." Tim jerked the chain free and rose, holding the thick lump of links toward the woman. "Thanks for the tow." Then, almost without conscious thought, he added, "But I meant it when I said keep your kids away from here. My trees . . ." His gaze swept across the nearby row of apple trees, full and lush and green. "I won't have them damaged."

"I understand." Her voice, devoid of condemnation, brought Tim's focus back to her. A small smile tipped up the corners of her lips. "I'll do my best to keep the children at home. I'm afraid having an entire forest of trees so near will be a huge temptation for them." She whisked a glance around, her eyebrows high. "This seems a delightful place to play."

"This is a working orchard, not a park."

She nodded, appearing unruffled by his curt statement. "I'll have a firm talk with the children." She started toward her car.

Tim took two stumbling steps after her. "There are lots of summer activities for kids . . . in Weaverly." Now why had he blurted that out? It opened a door to conversation. Wouldn't it be better to send this lady back to her old farmhouse and get to work? But if her kids had things to do, they'd be less likely to come pester him. He tucked his fingertips into the pockets of his Levi's and leaned his weight on one hip. "Everything's listed on a board outside the library doors. Might check 'em out. That is, if you don't mind your kids mixing with non-Mennonites." Unbidden, a hint of sarcasm had crept into his tone.

Her smile didn't flicker. "Thank you, Mr. Roper. I'll

certainly take the children to town and check into the activities after we've put the house in order." A light chuckle escaped her lips. "The children will enjoy meeting others from town before school starts in August."

Tim drew back, startled. "You're sending them to public school?" He hadn't been allowed to mix with non-Mennonites during his growing-up years. Maybe things had changed some in the past two decades.

She raised her shoulders in a delicate shrug, the attached cape of her pale pink dress shifting slightly with the movement. "In Arborville, the children attended public school. I see no reason not to allow them to do so here."

Why had these Mennonites chosen to move here? Several years back—the year before he'd purchased the orchard from his wife's uncle—a group of Mennonites had driven over and picked apples. Had they scoped out the area then and begun planning to purchase land? The thought unnerved him. He blurted, "It's a good school. Small classes, caring teachers." He recalled her son's slow movements and delayed speech. "They've got a good special ed program, too."

Pain momentarily flickered in her blue eyes. "I need to get back. The children are alone, and I have a lot of work waiting for me." She'd left the car door open, so she slid into the seat and curled her hand over the door handle. "Thank you for bringing Parker and Adrianna safely home, Mr. Roper. I appreciate your kindness." She gave the door a slam, sealing herself inside. The engine ignited, and she turned the car around then aimed for the road. As she rolled past him at a snail's pace, she lifted her hand in a brief wave. Then the car headed down the lane and around the corner, disappearing behind the trees.

Tim remained rooted in place, staring at the spot where his lane emptied into the road. A heavy, stifling feeling filled his chest. He recognized the feeling: loneliness. But why? He'd been alone amongst his trees for four years now, ever since the accident stole Julia and Charlie from him. He'd filled his days with work and had discovered a sense of purpose, if not the joy he'd experienced prior to their deaths.

Yet, undeniably, standing in his driveway with nothing but trees for company, he felt alone. He shook his head, redirecting his thoughts. Go inside. Eat some lunch. Fuel up the cart, hitch the flatbed, load the hand mower, and get back to work. The plan established, he thumped his way toward the house. But the firm plod of his soles against the ground couldn't quite eradicate the loneliness that nibbled at his insides.

4

Amy stacked the last of the supper dishes next to the sink while Bekah ran hot water. Suds billowed, sending up a clean, lemony scent. Amy paused and inhaled deeply, absorbing the fresh aroma. Somehow the essence revived her even more than the canned soup and grilled-cheese sandwiches had. Maybe she'd conjure enough energy to set up her sewing machines before bed.

Turning from the counter, she aimed a stern look at Adrianna and Parker, who remained at the now-empty table as she'd directed. She put her hands on her hips. "All right, you two. You have a job to do."

Adrianna groaned. "Momma, we've been jobbing all day. I'm tired." She emphasized her statement with a broad yawn.

Amy's lips twitched with the effort not to smile. Her daughter's invented word and the exaggerated slump to her shoulders invited a chuckle. But when the children needed discipline, she couldn't relent. These were the moments she missed Gabe the most—when she wanted to share a moment of amusement or needed someone else to be the rule-enforcer. "I know we've all worked hard today putting the house in order, and you'll be able to go up to bed soon, but before you do I want each of you to write a note of apology to Mr. Roper for climbing in his trees and destroying several branches."

An image of the man's frowning countenance flashed through Amy's memory. When at all possible, they were to live at peace with their neighbors. She'd gotten off to a rocky start with their nearest neighbor. It would do them no good to make an enemy of the man whose land bordered hers. She prayed that an apology, along with a promise to keep their distance, would be enough to repair the damage the children had done.

Parker hung his head, but Adrianna gazed up at her mother, her bright eyes blinking innocently. "But, Momma, I don't know how to write yet."

From the sink, Bekah released a little snort. Of amusement or derision, Amy couldn't be certain. She chose to ignore her older daughter and focused on the younger one. "You can draw a picture to say you're sorry." Shifting her gaze to Parker, she said, "There's a writing tablet and pencils in the desk in my room. Bring them down, and you and Adrianna get busy."

Parker nodded and pushed away from the table. His plodding steps carried him upstairs. Amy moved to the other side of Bekah and reached for a dishtowel to dry the dishes Bekah had washed thus far.

Bekah nudged her with her elbow. "Leave them. There's not much. I'll dry, too." She didn't lift her gaze from the sink but continued washing, rinsing, and stacking, her lips set in an unsmiling line.

Amy appreciated Bekah's willingness to do the task alone,

but she wished her daughter expressed more pleasure in offering assistance. As a child, Amy had gloried in being her mother's helper, knowing she was relieving a burden from the woman she loved. Bekah relieved much of Amy's burden, but her sullen expression and negative attitude made it difficult for Amy to appreciate her daughter's help.

Even so, she slipped her arm around Bekah's waist and pressed her cheek to her daughter's temple. "Thank you, sweetheart. If you're okay here, I'll get started setting up the sewing room."

Parker trudged back down, paper and pencils in hand. He sat gingerly and pushed two sheets of paper across the table to Adrianna. He lifted his puzzled face to his mother. "What should I write?"

"Tell him you're sorry for trespassing," Bekah said.

"Huh?"

Amy sighed. She'd had a firm talk with the children after returning from Mr. Roper's house about staying on their own property. She hadn't used the word "trespassing" because she didn't feel the younger two would understand it. "Tell him you're sorry for bothering his trees."

"And promise we'll never do it again," Adrianna sing-songed, swinging her feet. She busily scribbled a short, fat tree trunk with a huge ball perched on its top.

Parker leaned over his paper, his tongue poking out one side of his mouth in concentration. With all three children occupied, Amy moved to the room she'd claimed as her sewing room. Standing in the middle of the scarred wood floor, she turned a slow circle and surveyed the large space designed by the original owners as a formal dining room. Despite their intentions, the room couldn't be more perfect for sewing.

Built-in cupboards flanked the door to the kitchen on the north wall, providing ample storage for her baskets of fabrics and sewing notions. A bank of windows faced west, allowing in the evening sun. The wide doorway opposite the windows, which led to the airy sitting room, promised a flood of morning light, as well. She could set up her sewing machine in front of the west-facing windows, and her quilting machine would fit neatly in the southeast corner. The room was large enough to accommodate her cutting table, too. She planned to leave it up in the middle of the floor, ready for use at a moment's notice.

A tower of boxes currently filled the center of the room, with the cutting table folded and leaning against the wall. Amy stifled a groan. So much to do before she could set up the machines and sew. The children had helped organize the other rooms, but this room she would take care of on her own.

She fingered the plastic file holder on top of the stack of boxes. Inside, the sketches for six different projects awaited her attention. Those orders would carry her through the next three months, but what then? Her business, Threads of Remembrance, which specialized in creating one-of-a-kind keepsake quilts, had provided a secondary income for her and the children in Arborville, but she hadn't needed to rely on it completely. Now, away from Arborville and her father's financial support, she'd need a steady income.

"Momma, we're done!"

Adrianna's voice carried from the kitchen. Amy stepped around boxes and returned to the table. She picked up Adrianna's drawing of a well-dotted tree—the child's attempt at drawing apple buds, no doubt—with clouds floating overhead and a line of shaggy grass stretching across the bottom. Amy hid a smile. Adrianna had signed her name in the upper right-hand corner. It read "Abri."

"Very nice," Amy said and reached for Parker's paper. He handed it over. Amy's heart ached as she read Parker's simple message, scrawled in his oversized block print. *Mister Ropper I am sory I climed in ur Tree and boke ur branch pleese Forgiv me Parker.* One long, painstaking sentence absent of punctuation and sporting many misspellings. Amy battled with herself. Should she correct the paper and have him copy it over?

She turned to Parker, ready to make suggestions for improvement, but he looked so hopeful she didn't have the heart to tell him he'd not done it right. His message was sincere. If Mr. Roper couldn't see beyond the errors to the sweet apology, then it was his problem, not Parker's. "Tomorrow morning, before we go into town and see what kinds of activities are available for you during the summer, we'll go by Mr. Roper's and deliver your apology letters."

"Um, Momma?" Adrianna made a face and pointed at her paper. "Mine isn't a letter. It's a picture. Of a tree."

Bekah turned from placing the last of the plates in the cabinet and caught Amy's eye. An amused smirk twitched on her lips. The unspoken communication between mother and daughter lifted Amy's heart. She winked at Bekah and then fixed a serious expression on Adrianna. "We'll deliver Parker's letter and Adrianna's drawing of a tree. Now head upstairs, you two. Wash your faces, brush your teeth, and get into your pajamas. I'll be up soon to read our verses, and then it'll be time for sleep. We've had a busy day."

The two scampered upstairs, Adrianna's giggles competing

with Parker's huffing breaths. Bekah hung the dishtowel over a little silver bar above the sink, then leaned her hips on the edge of the sink. "Want me to go make sure they get ready for bed?"

Amy tugged one of the white ribbons trailing from Bekah's cap. "Wouldn't you rather take a book onto the back porch and read before the sunlight is all gone?"

Bekah straightened. "Really?"

"Really. You've done plenty today."

Bekah dashed to the enclosed stairs.

Amy called, "Bekah?"

Her daughter paused on the little landing, peeking over her shoulder.

"Thank you for all your help in the house and with your brother and sister. I don't know what I'd do without you."

Bekah sucked in her lips, her brow furrowing. Then she gave a quick nod that sent her ribbons bouncing on her shoulders, turned, and trotted out of sight. Amy sank into the nearest chair, looking after her daughter. She'd hoped her compliment might elicit an answering smile, a sweet "You're welcome, Mom." Over the past year, it had seemed Bekah drifted farther and farther away. What had happened to the smiling, happy little girl who'd dogged her steps and begged, "Let me help you, Momma. Please?"

The clatter of feet on the stairs intruded upon her thoughts. Bekah trotted around the corner with a book in her hand and slipped out the back door without so much as a glance in her mother's direction. Tears pricked Amy's eyes. Might she, in this place of new beginnings, find her sweet Bekah again? *Father, bind us together once more. Please, dear God.*

⁑

"Adrianna Amelia, stop kicking the back of my seat!" Bekah spun to glare over the backrest at her sister. Adri grinned, one finger in her mouth.

Mom sent a disapproving look in Bekah's direction. "Season your tone with kindness."

Bekah huffed and faced forward. Couldn't Mom scold Adri instead? Bekah wouldn't be fussing if Adri would just keep her feet down instead of bouncing them on the back of the seat. Last night, when Adri had leaned against her arm while Mom read from Psalms, she'd felt so close to Adri and to Mom. But now all those good feelings had fled, leaving her grumbly. She stared out the window at the passing landscape to keep from scowling at her mother.

Mom slowed the car and turned into a long lane lined by trees. Another bump on the seat's back sent Bekah sitting straight up. She gritted her teeth and planted her hands on the dash, looking ahead. Instead of a tall, square two-story farmhouse with a spindled porch like theirs, Mr. Roper's house was one story with some kind of up-and-down brown siding and an almost flat roof. A rickety-looking iron platform served as a porch. The yard in front of the house was bare of flowers, but flowering vines crawled up the side of the huge barn, framed the doorway, and wriggled their way all along its rock foundation. Bekah decided the red-painted barn looked a lot more inviting than the house.

Mom parked the car, then looked into the backseat. "All right, you two. Hop out and deliver your apologies."

Bekah bit the inside of her cheeks to keep from laughing when Parker and Adri gaped at Mom. Parker offered his customary, "Huh?" Adri launched herself forward and hung her arms over the high back of the car's front seat. "Aren't you comin', too, Momma?"

Mom shook her head, her black ribbons swaying beneath her chin. "No. You wandered onto Mr. Roper's property by yourself. So you can apologize by yourself."

Bekah almost felt sorry for her brother and sister as they slowly slid out of the car and walked hand in hand to Mr. Roper's front door. Parker let loose of Adri's hand to knock, and then the two stepped back and waited on the corner of the rusty iron platform, flicking worried glances over their shoulders to the car. Bekah sneaked a look at Mom's profile. Mom bit down on her lower lip, her brow all puckered as if she was worried, too.

Bekah said, "If it bothers you so much to send them up there alone, why not just go with them?"

"They need to do this alone. It's part of growing up, being accountable for your actions. If I do their apologizing for them this time, they'll expect me to make amends the next time they make a mistake. That isn't what's best for them."

Bekah shrugged. "I don't think it matters much. I don't think Mr. Roper is here." At that moment, someone tapped on the passenger-door window, and Bekah yelped in surprise. She turned to find the orchard owner staring through the glass at her. She quickly rolled down the window.

Mr. Roper looked past Bekah to Mom. "Did you need something?"

"The children have something to tell you." Mom gestured to the front of the house.

Mr. Roper strode around the car. Adri and Parker clambered down the wobbly steps and met him halfway across the yard. Adri thrust her drawing at the man, then locked her hands behind her back, swaying as she stared up at him. Parker lifted his letter more slowly, his head low. Bekah saw his lips move, but she couldn't hear what he said. Mr. Roper looked at the papers in his hand, then reached out and patted Parker's shoulder. It looked like an awkward gesture, but Parker lifted his head. A crooked smile appeared on his face.

Bekah discovered she'd been holding her breath. She let it out in a whoosh and looked at Mom. Relief shone on Mom's face, too. Mom rolled down her window. "All right now, children. Get in the car so we can let Mr. Roper get back to work."

Adri and Parker dashed to the car, Parker's ambling gait cumbersome next to Adri's nimble spryness. A wave of protectiveness rose within Bekah's breast as her brother nearly fell into the car. She was glad Mr. Roper accepted their apology. It would have broken Parker's heart to be treated rudely. And it would've broken hers, too.

Mr. Roper followed and stopped next to the car, leaning down to peer in at Mom. "I told the kids 'no hard feelings.' " He shook the papers. "I appreciate them setting things right."

" 'If it be possible, as much as lieth in you, live peaceably with all men.' " Mom quoted Romans 12:18, a verse Bekah had memorized when she was very young. She had a hard time remembering it sometimes when it came to living with her little sister.

Red streaked across Mr. Roper's cheeks. He balled his hand into a fist, crumpling the papers. "Yeah. Well, like I said, no hard feelings." He started to straighten.

"We're goin' to the li-barry," Adri chirped from the backseat, bouncing on her bottom. "Momma says there's programs for us there."

Mom sent Adri a silencing look over the seat. Then she turned to Mr. Roper. "I'm taking your advice and checking into summer programs. You said they were listed at the library?"

"That's right." Mr. Roper began naming the various activities available in town.

Listening in, Bekah clamped her teeth together. Everything sounded so babyish. Did she want to do arts and crafts or get involved in reading races with other kids?

"You'll find the library on the east edge of town, right across from the high school. You can't miss it." He pushed off from Mom's windowcase. Before Mom had the car out of park and into drive again, he'd trotted back into the barn.

Mom angled the car down the lane and turned west onto the dirt road. She smiled at Bekah, but Bekah thought she looked a little strained. "Here we go, getting acquainted with our new town."

Parker and Adri cheered from the backseat, but Bekah's stomach gave a nervous flip. In Arborville, half of their neighbors had been Mennonite. The non-Mennonite people in town were used to them and they'd all lived peaceably together. But this new town wasn't used to Mennonites. Would the kids point and stare? Would they make fun of her dress and cap? Worse, would they torment Parker because he was slow? Bekah gulped as the car rolled past the farmhouse on its way to Weaverly, their new home. She hoped Mom hadn't made a mistake by bringing them here.

5

Amy whispered to her daughter, "Keep an eye on your brother and sister. I'll be back at noon to pick you up."

"Okay, Mom."

Bekah, hunkered into a strange chair resembling a huge half-filled beach ball, barely looked up from the book in her hands. With her ankles crossed, her dress smoothed precisely over her knees, and the rumpled ribbons from her cap crunched against her shoulders, she looked younger than her thirteen years. Tenderness welled in Amy's breast. "You'll be all right until then?"

Bekah gave a long-suffering sigh. "We'll be fine."

Amy bit down on her lower lip, contemplating the wisdom of leaving the children for nearly three hours. The friendly librarian had assured her that parents often sent their children unattended to the library, but it still felt uncomfortable to leave the children in an unfamiliar place on their own. However, the children didn't seem at all uneasy about spending their morning in the cheerful, air-conditioned library. Amy set aside her apprehensions and reached down to squeeze Bekah's shoulder. "All right, then. I'll see you later."

Waving to Parker and Adri, who sat cross-legged on the floor in front of a plastic tub of puppets, Amy set off for home. "Lord, forgive me. I need to let loose of my fears that something ill will befall them when I'm not looking. I know worrying means I'm not trusting You to keep watch over my children." She spoke the prayer aloud as she pulled the car onto the highway. Her prayer was sincere, but even while she uttered the words, she realized Parker's accident had impacted her deeply. Now that she knew what kind of harm could befall a child, would she ever be able to completely release the burden of worry?

She rolled down the window and let the warm air caress her face as she drove. Only a short distance—a little more than two miles from town to the farmhouse. Once the children were familiar with the entire town, she could let them ride their bicycles to the library or the park now and then. The highway wasn't heavily traveled. How many people needed to visit Weaverly? The town, with its population of less than one thousand, was as sleepy as her former hometown. She'd been comfortable allowing the children to ride their bikes all over Arborville. They'd probably appreciate the same freedom here.

"Roots and wings," she murmured to herself, recalling her mother's philosophy for child rearing. A mother's first responsibility was to give her children roots; the second was to let them grow wings. Amy found the first half much easier than the second.

In the rambling house by herself, she made good use of her time and set to work on the sewing room. By eleven thirty she was hot and sweaty—she needed to purchase an additional box fan to put in the window—but she couldn't deny a sense of pride in having everything neatly organized and ready for use. This afternoon she would start stitching the trio of quilts she'd designed for three siblings who'd lost their mother to cancer. Hopefully the wall hangings created from patches of their mother's favorite items of clothing would bring happy memories.

She washed her face and hands, changed into a fresh dress, then returned to the car to drive into town and retrieve the children. Adrianna was waiting at the window, and the little girl raced out and met her mother on the sidewalk. Bekah pounded after her. Amy captured Adrianna in a hug while Bekah scowled.

"You were supposed to stay with me." Bekah folded her arms over her chest and released a huff. "Mom, she's been complaining for the past half hour about being hungry. She even asked the librarian if she had anything to eat! I was so embarrassed."

Amy placed on a kiss on Adrianna's head and took the little girl's hand. "Maybe next time you come in, we'll send some crackers or fruit. Then if you get hungry, you can sit on the bench outside the library and have a snack."

Bekah snorted in reply as she followed Amy back into the library. Amy stopped at the librarian's tall desk and thanked her for letting the children stay.

The woman smiled brightly. "It was no problem at all, Mrs. Knackstedt. They're very polite. And they got to meet a few of our town's children who came in to borrow books or use the computers. In fact"—she bobbed her head toward the row of computers on the far wall—"Parker seems to have made a friend. The two of them have been playing Number Munchers for almost an hour."

Amy's heart caught at the sight of Parker side by side with another boy, their heads nearly touching as they manipulated images on the screen. The other boy was smaller and obviously younger, but it was more likely a younger child would choose to befriend Parker. Even the boys Parker's age in Arborville who'd grown up with him sometimes abandoned him due to his clumsy gait and inability to easily grasp the concepts of their games. So far, Parker hadn't expressed sadness at being overlooked by his peers, but she knew eventually he would recognize the slight. She prayed she'd find ways to ease her son's pain when the day came.

Adrianna tugged on Amy's hand. "Momma, what did you make us for lunch?"

Amy smoothed stray wisps of hair from Adrianna's face. "I haven't fixed lunch yet, sweetheart. I was very busy. But I'll fix us something as soon as we get home."

"Then let's go *now*." Adrianna gave Amy's hand a firm yank.

Amy frowned at her daughter, then offered the librarian another smile. "Thank you again. I guess I'd better take these children home and get them fed." She handed Adrianna off to Bekah. "Take her to the car." Then she headed to the bank of computers. "Okay, time to go, Parker. Say good-bye to your friend."

In typical Parker fashion, he muttered "Huh?" but offered no word of complaint. He set aside the gray controller and unfolded himself from the plastic molded chair. "Bye, Lance."

Lance tipped his freckled face toward Parker. "See ya." Then he spun on his chair, meeting Amy's gaze. "Can Parker come to my house? My big brother's got a Nintendo. He lets me play games on it sometimes. They're a lot cooler than the games on this thing." He jammed his thumb at the computer screen.

Parker gave Amy a pleading look. Amy slipped her arm around Parker's shoulders and smiled at the younger boy. "We'll have to talk about that at home. But I imagine Parker will see you again here at the library. Do you come in often?"

Lance shrugged. "Sometimes. When there's nothin' good on TV." He slapped his controller onto the table and bounced up. "I gotta go. See ya later." He darted out of the library.

Amy and Parker followed more slowly. Although Parker hadn't mentioned his back hurting this morning, his stiff motions made Amy believe he was still a little sore from his fall from Mr. Roper's apple tree. She wouldn't rush him. They reached the car, where Bekah and Adrianna sat with the doors open and their feet dangling out. Adrianna shot to Amy and threw her arms around her mother's waist.

"I smell somethin'."

A pleasant aroma reached Amy's nostrils. Her stomach panged in response.

Parker sniffed the air like a hound dog on the hunt. "Mmm. Hamburgers."

Adrianna bounced up and down while still clinging to Amy's middle. "I want a hamburger for lunch! Please, Momma? Please?"

Parker added his pleading look to Adrianna's open begging. Amy pondered the amount of cash in her purse. Surely she had enough to purchase hamburgers. The children had worked hard the past week getting ready for the move and settling into their new home—they deserved a treat. She looked at Bekah. "Does a hamburger sound good to you, too?"

Bekah offered a slow, disinterested shrug. "Whatever." She pointed up the street to the next block. "The café's over there. We can just walk."

Adrianna immediately released Amy and began trotting in the direction of the café. Amy caught up to her and captured her hand. The little girl giggled, swinging their joined hands and making giant strides to match her mother's. Parker and Bekah trailed behind, talking softly about the kids who'd come into the library. Although the walk was short, the sun beaming from overhead heated Amy's scalp through her mesh cap. She welcomed the rush of air from the café's window cooling unit as she and the children stepped inside.

Even though it was noon, only one of the tiny café's tables was filled. Amy led the children past the group of retirement-age men who surrounded a rectangular table near the front window. Plastic open-weave baskets of half-eaten burgers and crispy fries sat in front of each man. Their conversation ceased as they watched Amy and her children parade past, then resumed when she settled the children around a square table at the back corner of the dining area.

A teenage girl with shaggy-cut, streaked blond hair and silver braces highlighting her smile bustled from behind the counter and ambled to their table. Her gaze flicked across Amy's head covering. "Hi. Welcome to the Burger Basket. You some of the new folks who moved in?"

Amy noted the men at the rectangular table angling their heads in her direction, obviously listening. "I'm Mrs. Knackstedt, and these are my children."

"I'm Adri," Adrianna said, her bright smile aimed at the girl. "What's your name?"

The girl beamed back. "Tara. I have a little sister named

Trista who's just about your age. Betcha you'll be in kindergarten in the fall, right?"

Adrianna nodded enthusiastically, her braids bouncing. "Uh-huh. An' Parker'll be sixth grade. An' Bekah'll be eighth grade." She pointed at her siblings by turn before squinting up at the girl again. "What grade are you?"

Tara laughed, her braces flashing. "Eleventh grade. That sounds pretty funny, doesn't it?"

Adrianna responded with a trickling laugh.

Amy supposed she should discourage Adrianna from talking to everyone she met, but she found it difficult to curb her daughter's friendly nature without squelching her. Thus far, most people had responded positively to the little girl's overtures, including the men at the other table, who grinned, bumping one another with their elbows.

Tara whipped a little pad of paper and a pencil from the pocket of her apron. "But I guess you all didn't come in here to talk. You prob'ly wanna eat, right?"

"Yes!" Adrianna crowed, and Bekah rolled her eyes, clearly embarrassed by her sister's exuberance.

Tara pointed to a chalkboard near the front counter, which bore neatly written items. "Menu's printed on the wall over there. Today's special is BLT on toast with chips and a pickle—two ninety-five. Want me to bring you something to drink while you decide what you're gonna eat?"

"We'd like iced water to drink," Amy said, "and a hamburger and fries for each of us, please."

"Want those burgers with everything? That'd be pickles, onions, ketchup, and mustard," Tara said.

Adrianna made a face, earning another laugh from the young waitress and a round of snickers from the other table.

Amy said, "Everything for all but Adrianna, who doesn't care for onions."

"I got it. Coming right up." Tara spun and breezed around the corner into what Amy surmised must be the kitchen. As soon as she'd disappeared, the man seated at the end of the table tipped his chair back and fixed Amy with a steady gaze.

"Hey. Knackstedt, did you say?"

The children all looked to Amy to reply. Amy offered a nod. "That's right."

"I heard somebody named Knackstedt moved into the Sanford place. That you?" He peered at her from beneath the low-tugged brim of a battered cowboy-style hat. His gray eyebrows were so thick they seemed to give him a perpetual scowl, but his grin was friendly.

"Yes."

"A farmer, are you?"

Before Amy could respond, the café door opened, and her neighbor, Tim Roper, stepped in. He glanced at the table of men, then at Amy.

Parker and Adrianna chorused, "Hi, Mr. Roper!"

Although she could hardly call the man a friend, Amy couldn't deny the rush of relief that swept over her at the sight of a familiar face. Without thinking, she said, "How good to see you again."

Mr. Roper yanked the billed cap from his head. "Good . . . good to see you, too."

Adrianna wiggled out of her seat and held her hands toward the table. "Wanna sit with us, Mr. Roper? We got room."

Laughter blasted from the table of men. The one who'd questioned Amy sent a teasing smirk in Mr. Roper's direction. "Yeah, Tim, go ahead and join 'em. You'd fit right in with the Mennonites, seein' as how you used to be one."

The muscles in Mr. Roper's jaw clenched, and something akin to anger—or was it desperation?—flashed in his eyes. "That was a long time ago, Ron." He gave Adrianna a weak smile. "I can't join you, but thanks for asking." He stepped to the counter, turning his back on the other café patrons. Tara scurried out to take his order, and the men at the table went back to chatting with each other.

Adrianna tugged at Amy's arm, demanding attention, but Amy couldn't tear her eyes away from the tall man who leaned on the counter and spoke softly with the café's waitress. His bitter comment echoed through her mind. *That was a long time ago.* He'd been Mennonite and had left the fellowship, and his tone intimated it hadn't been an amicable parting.

"Momma?" Adrianna's fretful voice carried over all the other café noise. "How come Mr. Roper won't sit with us? Is it 'cause he's not a Mennonite?"

Mr. Roper's face blanched. He slapped his ball cap into place. "Forget the burger, Tara. I'll just grab a sandwich when I get home." He stormed out of the café. The moment the door slammed behind him, uneasy laughter rippled across the rectangular table. The one named Ron slapped the nearest man on the back and chortled, seemingly pleased with himself. But Amy found nothing amusing in Mr. Roper's behavior. The man apparently carried a deep resentment toward Mennonites.

And he lives right next door.

6

Tim slammed the door of his truck, curled his hands over the steering wheel, and forced himself to calm before he started the ignition. That Ron. Tim snorted, shaking his head. The older rancher didn't mean to be derogatory—he just liked to dig at folks. It wasn't as if Ron hadn't dug at Tim before.

Last July at the annual Fourth of July citywide celebration, Ron had jokingly told a young man who'd lost a back-alley boxing match he could regain his dignity by taking on Tim—since he'd been raised to be nonviolent, he wouldn't lift a hand in defense and it'd be an easy victory. Tim had joined the others in laughter at the outrageous statement. And only three weeks ago, when Tim wore his cowboy hat to church, Ron had asked why he wasn't wearing a black flat-brimmed hat instead. Teasing. Always teasing.

But this time he'd teased in the wrong company. Tim hadn't wanted Mrs. Knackstedt or any of the other newcomers in town to know about his background. Folks in Weaverly wouldn't even know he'd been raised Mennonite if Julia's aunt and uncle hadn't used his religious upbringing to assure the townspeople the homeless young man with the pack on his back wasn't a threat to the community when he started working for them.

Shortly after his arrival in Weaverly, he'd gone to the county courthouse and legally changed his name from Rupp to Roper, intending to erase all vestiges of his former life. But how could a person completely erase the first half of his life when others knew it had existed and used it as a topic of jest? Now, thanks to Ron, Mrs. Knackstedt knew about Tim's background. And she'd surely tell the other Mennonites who'd taken up residence in Weaverly. Would they all go on a mission to return him to the fold?

Tim stifled a groan. He needed to get home where he could work off some of this frustration. He reached to start the ignition, but before the motor revved to life, the café door opened and Ron ambled out, a paper bag in his hand. He trotted to the open driver's window and jammed the bag in at Tim. "There ya go."

The scent of hamburger and onion wafted from the bag. Although he was hungry, the aroma didn't entice him the way it usually did. Tim set it on the vinyl seat beside him and reached for his wallet. "What do I owe you?"

"Nothin'. Call it a peace offering." Ron propped his elbow on the windowsill and smirked at Tim. "You sore at me?"

Tim blew out a breath. "Nah."

"You sure? You took off like somebody lit a fire under your feet. When a fella moves that fast, anger's usually propelling him."

"I'm not mad." Although fury had initially coursed through

his middle, Tim was more worried about the changes that might come into his life than truly angry. "I know how you like to rib a guy."

Ron blasted a short, "Ha!" He waggled one bushy eyebrow. "Only do it to folks I know can take it."

"I suppose you think that makes it a compliment, huh?"

The older man laughed loudly. Then he tipped his head toward the café, his expression turning serious. "Whaddaya think of having Mennonites moving in to Weaverly? Think it'll be okay?"

"What do you mean?"

"Seems odd to me, is all. Them buyin' up empty houses and a whole passel of land. They won't, you know, try to take over the town or anything, will they?"

"They'll probably keep pretty much to themselves—grow their crops, raise their families." But why had they chosen Weaverly? Of all the farmland in Kansas, why had they come to the town where Tim had decided to settle? He continued in a deliberately light tone. "They'll be friendly enough, but they won't force themselves on you." Although they might force themselves on Tim, seeing him as a wandering sheep.

Ron patted the truck door and stepped back. "Yeah. Guess you're right. I mean, you're Mennonite and you never tried to push your beliefs on anybody in town." A sly grin crept up the man's grizzled cheek. "Matter of fact, we seemed to have converted you pretty good, gettin' you into the Community Church and all—when you come, that is."

Weaverly folks hadn't converted him. He'd made the decision to never again be Mennonite when he'd left his father's house. "Yeah, I guess so. Thanks for the burger, Ron. I need to get back to the orchard. Crazy deer broke down a section of the west fence." Which was probably how his little human visitors had crossed onto his land. He gestured to the roll of barbed wire in the truck's bed. "I need to get it repaired before they do any more damage." He meant both deer and roaming children.

"If you need extra hands, gimme a holler."

Tim drew back in mock surprise. Ron enjoyed his retired status and frequently bragged about how he "didn't do nothin' and that suits me fine." "You wanna help run wire?"

Ron waved both hands in the air as if fending off a swarm of bees. "Not me. My grandson Brandon is fifteen now, plenty big an' needing a job. He'd be a dependable worker for you. He's run wire fence at my ranch before."

"I'll keep that in mind," Tim said. "Bye now." He started the truck and backed into the road, watchful for kids who were out of school and running free. He'd developed the habit of careful watching when Charlie was little. The boy's poor hearing didn't always warn him of moving vehicles. It didn't seem to matter how much time passed, he still possessed the habit of caution. But he supposed he could have worse habits.

He rolled up his window and turned on the AC as he headed on the highway toward home. The chilled air hit him full in the face, reminding him of how many worldly habits he'd adopted over the years. Wouldn't Dad scowl if he knew his son kept a cell phone strapped to his hip, hosted a Web site to bring in business instead of trusting God to meet his needs, and wore Levi Strauss britches and western-style shirts with ivory-faced snaps instead of work trousers and homemade button-up shirts? Dad wouldn't approve any of those new habits. But mostly Dad would frown about the habits Tim had deserted—reading his Bible, praying, attending every church service instead of only when he wasn't too tired. . . . Those things from his childhood and youth lay long abandoned.

Tim slapped the steering wheel, forcing his thoughts elsewhere. Hadn't he left his home so he wouldn't have to worry about pleasing his impossible-to-please father? So why think about him now? Because that woman moved in next door and reminded him, that's why. Well, a half mile separated them. So next door or not, he wouldn't have to see her. Or talk to her. Or anything else, for that matter. It wasn't as if *he* needed to take care of widows and orphans.

The truck approached the Sanford house and Tim took his foot off the gas, letting the truck coast by. He'd long admired the century-old house with its gingerbread trim and sturdy corbels gracing the roof's eaves. He'd even looked into buying it when the Sanfords put it up for sale two years ago, since it was right next door to his orchard. Nothing wrong with his little double-wide except for the ghosts hiding in every corner. A new house would've been a good way of starting over for him. But old man Sanford wouldn't sell just the house—he wanted someone to buy both the house and the acreage. Tim couldn't afford the entire property.

Now, looking the house over, he decided Mr. Sanford had done him a favor. The house had needed a paint job for several years already, and it looked like a few shingles had blown off. Mrs. Knackstedt didn't have a man on the place to see to those needs. Who would take care of the painting and shingling and anything else that needed doing?

"Here you are fussing about widows and orphans again," he groused aloud. *Keep to yourself. You don't get hurt that way.*

He stomped the gas pedal, and the truck leaped forward.

His orchard kept him plenty busy. Let those Mennonites take care of their own.

✦

While Amy and her children ate their burgers, which were delicious, other townsfolk came and went. Although none of them spoke to the little family at the corner table, Amy sensed no animosity, only the mild fascination often associated with something new. She smiled in response to curious gazes and received several shy smiles in return. Apparently rebuffed by Mr. Roper's quick departure, Adrianna focused on her food and didn't attempt to engage anyone else in conversation.

They finished, and Amy paid for their lunch. She pressed two dollar bills into Tara's hand for a tip, and the young woman rewarded her with a bright, silver-graced smile. "Thank you. You all have a good day, now." Her gaze dropped to Adrianna, and she tweaked the little girl's nose. "Betcha you and Trista'll be good friends."

Adrianna giggled, and Amy herded the children outside. The unseasonably hot sun—they'd seemed to dive from winter right into summer this year, skipping the pleasant days of spring entirely—felt unbearable after enjoying the air-conditioning. Amy sped her pace, eager to get out from under the blasting sun. No shade-providing trees lined the two scant blocks making up the business district, but several trees stood tall and proud on the library's lawn. When they reached the sidewalk in front of the library, they all slowed, heaving sighs of relief.

Bekah tugged at the collar of her lightweight dress. "Ugh. It's so hot. I wish we had a pond at our house so we could swim." She cast a sidelong glance at her mother. "There's a public swimming pool at the city park. It usually opens the first week of June, but they opened it early this year 'cause it's been so hot already. The librarian told me."

Amy opened the back car door and ushered Adrianna and Parker inside. She kept her voice light, even though an odd trepidation tiptoed through her middle. "Is that right?"

"Yes. And she said most of the kids in town hang out there during the afternoons. If we wanted to meet kids, that'd be the place to go." Bekah slid into the passenger's seat.

When Amy settled herself behind the steering wheel, Bekah spoke again. "It'd be nice to use the pool, but we'd look pretty silly in our long shorts and T-shirts when everyone else is wearing swimsuits." She stared out the window at two children—a boy and girl—ambling side by side on the sidewalk, their flip-flops slapping the cracked concrete. Both had towels draped around their necks. The boy was bare-chested, wearing baggy, flowered swim trunks, and the girl wore a two-piece suit in shimmery lavender.

Adrianna bounced to the edge of her seat, throwing her arms over the back of the front seat. "How come we wear shorts and T-shirts 'stead of suits?"

"Swimsuits aren't modest." Bekah's voice held a hit of sarcasm. "We have to be modest." She pinched the cape of her dress and wiggled it. "That's what this is all about."

Adrianna crinkled her nose. "What's modest?"

"What's modest?" Parker echoed.

Amy started the engine. "We'll discuss the definition at home." She sent a firm glance in Bekah's direction. "But for now let me say being modest is important because it's pleasing to God, and we always need to try to please God before we please ourselves."

"Oh." Adrianna flopped into the backseat, apparently satisfied. Bekah turned her head to gaze out the side window. She didn't say anything more, but Amy noted her daughter's jaw was set in a stubborn angle. Shifting her focus to the road, Amy decided she'd have a talk with Bekah after the younger two went to bed that evening. Now that Bekah would be attending the public high school with more non-Mennonites than Mennonites, it was more important than ever for the girl to hold to the convictions of her faith. Amy's heart would break if she lost Bekah to worldly temptations.

When they reached the house, Adrianna lumbered upstairs for her afternoon nap. Parker asked permission to play in the barn. After warning him to be careful, Amy gave approval. Then she looked at Bekah. "I'd like you to wash the curtains we brought and hang them on the line out back. When they're dry, you can iron them and then put them on the rods."

Bekah sighed, plopping the stack of books she'd checked out from the library on the corner of the kitchen counter. "Yes, Mom." She scuffed toward the kitchen, where Amy had left the box of folded homemade panels. Amy watched her go, debating with herself about whether or not to sit Bekah down for a chat. Even though she expressed no open rebellion and moved to obey, her attitude smacked of defiance. By the time Bekah scooped up the box and stepped out the door to the back porch, where Amy had set up their sect-approved wringer washing machine, Amy decided to let the girl work off some of her frustration. They'd have their talk at bedtime, and she'd address Bekah's attitude.

Opening the cabinet in her sewing room, she withdrew the basket of cut pieces for the three remembrance quilts, then put her machine to work. The afternoon flowed, the back door opening and closing as Bekah went in and out, a breeze drifting through the open windows carrying the sounds of wind in the trees and birdsong. Lost in her task, Amy was hardly aware of the hours slipping by until a small hand tapped her arm.

Amy stopped the machine and turned to pull Adrianna into a hug. The little girl, still drowsy, tumbled into her mother's lap. Amy scooped her close, savoring the scent of Adrianna's sleep-sweaty hair. The child nestled, and tears stung the back of Amy's nose. She wished she could hold Bekah this way again. Children grew up too quickly.

Adrianna yawned, toying with the ribbon dangling from her mother's cap. "I'm hungry. Can I have a snack?"

Amy glanced at the clock. Three forty—still plenty of time before supper. A snack wouldn't ruin Adrianna's appetite. "Sure." She kissed her daughter's head and set her aside. "Bekah's probably outside. Go find her and tell her I said you could have a banana and some graham crackers." Adrianna dashed for the back door. Amy called after her, "And get Parker from the barn." He'd apparently lost himself in a make-believe world or had fallen asleep out there—Amy hadn't heard a peep from him all afternoon. "He'd probably like a snack, too."

"Okay, Momma." The door slammed behind Adrianna.

Amy turned back to her project, taking a moment to examine the partially completed quilt top. She smiled, pleased by the progress made. If she continued at this pace, she would have the first quilt top all pieced by tomorrow evening. She pressed her foot to the pedal, ready to stitch the next row of patches together. Just as the needle penetrated the joined fabric squares, a frantic cry of "Momma!" sounded from outside. Nearly toppling her chair, Amy jumped from the machine and ran through the kitchen to the back porch.

Adrianna, her eyes wide, leaped onto the porch and grabbed her mother's hand. "Bekah says come quick!" She dragged Amy toward the barn.

7

Tim pounded the U-shaped staple into place over the string of barbed wire, then gave the wire a tug. It released a subtle *ting* but vibrated for less than ten seconds. Good and tight. He glanced down the fence line, wishing he had the funds to put up galvanized mesh fencing at least three feet higher than the current five-foot-tall post-and-barbed-wire fence. No deer could clear a fence like that. But the more protective fence was another expense beyond his reach at the moment. Maybe after this year's crop?

He slipped the hammer into the loop of his work jeans, then snagged the water bottle he'd dropped in the grass at his feet. The water had turned tepid, but the moisture felt good draining down his parched throat. He glugged the bottle dry, then crumpled the plastic, flattening it as best he could before jamming it in his back pocket to throw in the recycle bin at home. Patting the box of staples in his shirt pocket, he turned his attention to the next post.

"Hi, Mr. Roper."

Tim nearly jumped out of his skin. He spun around to find

the neighbor's boy, Parker, standing less than ten feet away. Why hadn't he heard the kid approach? Feet on dry grass weren't exactly quiet. But somehow Parker had managed to sneak up on him. The situation left him unsettled. "What're you doing here? Didn't your mom promise to keep you home?"

The boy cringed, hunching his shoulders. "Mom said to stay on our land." He rocked his head back and forth, reminding Tim of a clock's pendulum. The boy's lips twisted into a grimace. "I'm not . . ." He straightened, throwing back his skinny shoulders. "Traipse-passing."

Tim had to bite down quick on his tongue to keep from laughing. The boy was obviously proud of his big word, but he had no idea he'd gotten it wrong. Besides, he was definitely traipse-passing—traipsing right along Tim's fence line.

Parker pointed, one shoulder hunching again as he squinted into the sun. "Whatcha doing?"

"Fixing my fence to keep pests out." Tim presented his back to the boy. Parker's mannerisms—the self-conscious shrugs, word confusion, and questions—reminded him too much of another boy. Thinking of Charlie always brought pain. Tim walked the line, checking each post to be certain the barbed wire was securely fastened. Trying to refocus.

The rustle of Parker's shuffling footsteps followed. "Pests . . . like bugs? Mom calls flies and spiders pests."

Tim located a loose staple low on a post. He pulled his hammer free, stooped down, and aimed its head at the post. "Stop and think for a minute, Parker. Would a fence like this keep out bugs?" *Bang! Bang! Bang!* He glanced over his shoulder. Parker was crouched down, imitating his pose. He jerked upright and moved on. To Tim's chagrin, Parker trudged along behind him, faithful as a puppy dog.

"I guess not. Bugs could fly straight through the wire."

"Now you're thinking straight." Tim heard the undercurrent of ridicule in his tone, and he shook his head hard. He had no cause to be mean just because the boy brought up memories Tim would rather keep buried. He turned, intending to apologize, and caught Parker extending his finger toward a pokey barb. "Don't do that!"

The boy jerked. He clutched his hands together and stared at Tim. "I . . . I wasn't gonna hurt it. I just wanted to see if it's sharp."

Tim stomped to Parker's side, his hands curled into fists. If Parker broke his skin on the barb, he might need a tetanus shot. "Let me save you the trouble of testing it. Those barbs are *very* sharp."

Tears swam in Parker's eyes. Tim gritted his teeth, more affected by the boy's reaction than he cared to admit. But he remained stern. "Barbed-wire fence is dangerous. You need to stay away from it. Promise me you won't try to climb on it or put your hands on the barbs."

The boy blinked several times, biting down on his lower lip. Finally he nodded. "I promise, Mr. Roper."

Tim blew out a breath of relief. "Good boy."

A lopsided smile replaced the boy's crestfallen expression. Tim's heart gave a leap at the transformation. Automatically, a smile tugged at his own lips. Then he whirled, once again turning his back on Parker. What was he doing, making friends with this Mennonite kid? No good could come of it. He clomped in the direction of his truck, which he'd left parked alongside the road. "You better get on home now. Your mom's probably wondering where you are."

As if on cue, the cry came from a distance: "Par-r-r-r-ker-r-r-r? Where are you, Parker?"

Both Tim and Parker turned toward the sound. Tim offered a grim bob of his head. "See there? Told'ja."

Parker repeated his turtle routine, the lower half of his face nearly swallowed by his hunched shoulders. "I'm in trouble, huh?"

"Could be."

The boy aimed an innocent look at Tim. "But I didn't climb your trees or go on your land. Right?"

Tim stifled a chuckle at Parker's reasoning. Wasn't it just like a kid to try to turn things around to his own favor? He decided it was best not to answer. Instead, he cupped his hands beside his mouth and hollered, "Mrs. Knackstedt! It's me, Tim Roper. I've got Parker."

Moments later Mrs. Knackstedt's capped head appeared above the gentle rise of weed-spattered ground. Her worried face pinched Tim's conscience. He should've sent Parker straight back the minute he'd discovered the boy following him. Parker stayed rooted in place until his mother reached his side. Tim expected her to wrap the boy in a hug, the way she had the last time he'd wandered, but she grabbed his arm and shook it.

"Parker Gabriel Knackstedt, I am not happy with you at all. What are you doing out here, bothering Mr. Roper again?"

Parker ducked his head, and Tim surprised himself by coming to the boy's defense. "I imagine he heard the hammer banging—I've been working on my fence—and he got curious."

Parker nodded so hard Tim was surprised his head didn't come loose. "I thought somebody was building something, like Dad used to do. I wanted to see what he was building. In case I could . . . help."

Tim gave an involuntary jerk at the boy's words. Didn't every boy need a man to show him things? Before his relationship with his dad had gone sour, he'd trailed his father, watching, imitating, learning. So much of what he knew about fence building and mechanics—even though he'd grown to resent the brusque way Dad taught him—he'd learned from his father. They were lessons he'd used again and again. Of course Parker would seek out a man's teachings. It was only natural.

The woman kept her frown pinned to her son. "That's not an excuse. I gave you permission to play in the barn. I did not give you permission to go across the pasture to Mr. Roper's place."

"I didn't climb his trees," Parker whispered. "I didn't go on his land."

Mrs. Knackstedt closed her eyes for a moment, as if gathering her patience. Tim understood. How many times had he failed in communicating something important to Charlie? As hard as he tried, sometimes Charlie just couldn't grasp what Tim wanted him to know.

He stepped forward and curled his hand over Parker's shoulder. "Listen, Parker." He waited until the boy turned his woeful face upward. "Wandering around out here by yourself isn't a good idea. There are all kinds of things that can happen to a boy. You could step in a prairie dog hole and hurt your ankle. You might surprise a snake." The boy's eyes flew wide. So did his mother's. Tim swallowed a chortle and went on. "As hot as it gets, the sun can make you dizzy and sick. So your mom is smart to want to keep you close to home. Remember you promised me not to touch the barbed-wire fence?"

Parker nodded slowly, his eyes glued to Tim's. "Uh-huh."

"Well, I want you to make me another promise. That you'll never, never go farther from your house than your mom's voice can carry. If you stay within what we call around here 'shouting distance,' you'll be safe. Okay?"

For long seconds Parker stared into Tim's face, his dark eyes unblinking. Then his head bobbed in another slow-motion nod. "Okay."

"Good." He looked at Mrs. Knackstedt. Gratitude shone in her blue eyes. He turned quickly away. "I've got chores waiting—" He intended to say he needed to get back to his house. But other words tumbled from his lips. "But let me drive you to your place. Looks like you're just about worn out from traipsing around out here in the sun."

She pursed her lips, and for a moment, Tim thought she would refuse. He held his breath, his emotions seesawing back and forth on whether he wanted her to accept his help or not. At last she offered a weary smile. "Thank you very much for your kindness, Mr. Roper. I believe we would appreciate a ride."

The two of them followed Tim to his truck and climbed in, Parker in the middle straddling the gear shift. They didn't speak on the short ride, which suited Tim fine. He couldn't figure out why he'd offered the ride in the first place. The sooner he could let them out and get back to his own business the better. He pulled up close to the house and put the truck in park. "There you go."

Without warning, Parker threw his arms around Tim's neck in a stranglehold of a hug. "Thank you for talking to me, Mr. Roper. You're a nice man. I like you."

Tim's heart thumpity-thumped in his chest. He sucked

air, not because Parker's arms were so tight, but because the boy's spontaneous action was so much like Charlie's. Tim wanted to grab the boy and hold on forever just to relive the feel of his precious son in his arms. But it wasn't fair to use Parker that way.

Very gently, Tim disengaged Parker's gangly arms. "You're welcome. I like you, too." His dry throat made his words come out growly. "You . . . you listen to your mom, now, okay? Keep yourself safe." Real regret filled his chest as he gave Parker the directive. If the boy stayed safe on his own land, Tim wouldn't see much of him.

"Thank you again, Mr. Roper." Mrs. Knackstedt leaned past Parker, her hand on her son's knee. "Parker has made you some promises, and I intend to see he keeps them. We'll do our best not to bother you anymore." She popped open the door and slid out. Parker clambered after her. She pushed the door closed, then slung her arm around Parker's shoulders and guided him toward the house.

Tim backed out of the driveway at a snail's crawl. He blinked several times, trying to erase the image of Mrs. Knackstedt walking with her arm tucked protectively around her son's shoulders. But it remained imbedded in his mind's eye, and it brought a wave of memories of his own boyhood, his mother, her unconditional love. So different from Dad's, which demanded immediate, unquestioning obedience. For the first time in more years than he could recall, Tim experienced a longing to see his own mother. But seeing her would mean seeing Dad. And the day he'd packed his bag, Dad had growled, *"If you walk down that road, remember it doesn't go both ways. You won't be welcome here ever again."*

No, no matter how much he might like to see Mom, Tim

couldn't go home again. He had a new kind of home—his trees, his apples, his business that filled his every waking hour. As long as the Mennonite woman honored her promise and kept her distance, he'd be safe from the memories that swelled at each encounter with her or her son.

❖

Bekah held the chair steady while Mom stood on the vinyl-covered seat and clipped the final curtain rod into place. The rod secure, Mom gave the snowy white curtains a few deft flicks with her fingertips to even out the gathers, then stepped off the chair. Her gaze whisked around the room, a smile tipping up her lips. "Curtains make such a difference."

Bekah raised her eyebrows. It would take more than curtains to brighten this dreary old farmhouse. Their house in Arborville had been old, too, but soft white paint on the walls and honey-colored stained woodwork had given it a comfortable appearance. This house's chipped, blue-painted woodwork and faded wallcoverings just made it seem tired and run-down. But Mom wouldn't want to hear her thoughts.

Wordlessly, Bekah lifted the chair and carried it to the kitchen. She sensed Mom following her, but she slid the chair into place at the square table that filled the center of the room without glancing back to see. The moment she released the chair, hands descended on her shoulders and turned her around.

Bekah stiffened, fully expecting Mom to scold. After all, she'd instructed Bekah to wash, iron, and hang the curtains, and Bekah had dawdled. Now it was past her bedtime. Mom had spent the entire day working and she'd still had to finish Bekah's job. Deep down, Bekah knew she'd been disobedient, and guilt tried to take hold of her heart, but she stubbornly refused to accept it. She was still a little mad at Mom over the talk they'd had after Adrianna and Parker went up to bed. Mom was so set in her old-fashioned ways.

To Bekah's surprise, instead of scolding, Mom folded her in a hug. "Thank you for your help, honey." After a squeeze, Mom released Bekah. Something flickered in Mom's eyes. A kind of pleading Bekah really didn't understand. "Is the house starting to feel like home to you now with all our furniture arranged and curtains on the windows?"

Bekah angled her face to look at the ruffly curtain gently lifting in the evening breeze that poured through the kitchen window. Just like in Arborville, the wind here in Weaverly never seemed to cease. The pink-dotted fabric billowed and collapsed, billowed and collapsed, much like Bekah's emotions of late. "I guess." Then she jerked her face to look into her mother's eyes. "Mom, can I ask you something?"

Mom tipped her head. One black ribbon crunched against the shoulder of her rose-flowered dress. The gloomy color looked out of place amid the spatter of cheerful blooms. "Of course."

Bekah gulped, gathering her courage. "You said moving to Weaverly would give us all a fresh start. Right?"

Mom's lips pinched briefly, but she nodded.

"So why can't that mean a fresh start in more than just where we live? Why can't we do something else new, like wear shorts when it's hot outside? Or buy a swimsuit—it doesn't have to be a two-piece—and go swimming in the public pool like other kids? Or maybe even cut our hair instead of piling it under these scratchy caps?"

As Bekah spoke, her voice rose in both volume and speed.

Bottled up questions poured out fast before Mom could interrupt and tell her to stop fussing. "We moved away from Arborville and all the people of our fellowship. We're in a brand-new place where nobody knows us. Not even the Mennonites who came from Ohio really know us—just a little bit from helping us carry our stuff into the house. Do we have to dress this way and . . . and live in an old house to make God happy?"

Bekah ran out of words. She plunked into the nearest chair, exhausted. She peered up at her mother, who stood silent and unsmiling before her. Another thought filled her mind, and she spit it out before she lost her nerve to share it. "Why is it so important that we be Mennonites? Mr. Roper isn't Mennonite anymore, and he seems okay. Wouldn't we be okay if we decided not to be Mennonites, too?"

8

Amy silently prayed for guidance as she pulled out a
kitchen chair and seated herself across from her daughter. She should have known this conversation was coming.
Amy's dad had grimly predicted shortly after Bekah's eleventh
birthday, "You watch. That one's going to give you heartache.
She thinks too much." At the time, Amy had discounted her
father's words, secretly proud of Bekah's ability to reason
deeply and ask difficult questions. It meant the girl had intelligence, and intelligence was a good thing.

But now the questions threatened the foundation of Amy's
faith. Perhaps she should have taken Dad's warning more
seriously and better prepared herself for this moment. Closing her eyes to calm her raging emotions, she pleaded with
her heavenly Father to let the Holy Spirit speak words that
would reach Bekah's questioning heart.

"You asked why we can't take off these caps and cut our
hair." Absently, Amy smoothed her fingers down the ribbon
of her own cap. "Tell me why you began wearing your cap."

Bekah traced squiggles on the table, her head low. "Because the church said I had to when I got baptized. It means I'm part of the fellowship of believers."

Amy frowned. Surely Bekah knew the deeper reason the women of her sect donned the mesh caps that covered their hair. "Why else?"

"And the Bible says a woman should cover her head when she's praying, and we're supposed to be in prayer all the time." The girl grimaced, making Amy wonder what thought trailed through her mind. "So we wear the caps all the time." Bekah's head shot up. "Does that mean women who don't wear caps never talk to God?"

Amy swallowed, seeking an appropriate response. "I think there are some people—both women and men—who go through life never talking to God. They're too busy looking at themselves to realize there is a God in Heaven who loves them and wants them to be His children. To me, those are the saddest people, because they're always trying to fill something inside of them that can only be filled one way, and they miss the way."

Bekah listened intently, no hint of defiance in her face.

Drawing in a steadying breath, Amy continued. "And then there are people who do know God. They aren't Mennonite, but they believe Jesus is their Savior and that God is their Father. They hold their faith in their hearts, but they don't feel it's necessary to clothe themselves differently to show it on the outside."

"But the Mennonites think they need to show it on the outside, too."

Amy nodded in agreement. "The Bible teaches us to be separate, not of the world, so our clothing lets others know that we are a separate people, living for God rather than for self." Amy took Bekah's hand. "Sweetheart, I know it's hard to dress differently from others your age. It will be even harder here, with so few Mennonites and all of them strangers to you right now. But God gives us strength to do what He calls us to do."

Bekah stared long and hard into Amy's face. Her sober expression gave away nothing of her inner thoughts, yet Amy sensed the girl was rolling things over in her mind, searching for her place of peace. So Amy sat quietly, allowing her daughter to process what she'd shared. While she waited, she prayed for Bekah's understanding and acceptance.

Finally, Bekah looked away, her shoulders rising and falling. "Okay, Mom." She spoke with her face aimed at the kitchen window, seemingly entranced by the play of the wind in the curtains. "I think I see why you want us to keep living the same way we did in Arborville, even though we aren't in Arborville anymore. But there's still one thing I have to figure out for myself."

"What's that, honey?"

Bekah pulled her hand loose and rose. "Whether God really called me to be a Mennonite." She turned and darted for the stairs. Her clattering footsteps faded away, but Amy's heart continued pounding in her ears.

She folded her arms on the table's smooth top and let her head drop into the bend of her elbow. The brief conversation in the comfortable kitchen had sapped her energy even more than her walk across the pasture in the late-afternoon sun. "God . . ." The name groaned from her lips. "You promised to give Your children strength to stand firm through every one of life's challenges. I need Your strength now. Without the support of my fellowship, I feel the way Bekah must feel—as if I'm standing alone. Give me strength and wisdom to guide my precious daughter to the truth. Strength, dear God, please give me, and my daughter, strength."

On Saturday morning, Amy assigned cleaning tasks to each of the children. She delegated laundry duties to Bekah, put Parker to work sweeping and mopping all the floors, and instructed Adrianna to chase every bit of dust from the baseboards and furniture with a feather duster. While the children worked on the house, she worked on piecing the second wall hanging for the family of grieving siblings. Although in Arborville she'd never sewed quilts on Saturday, reserving that day for housecleaning, baking, and preparing for Sunday's dinner, she'd lost time with the move and needed to make it up.

Smoothing the fabric into place beneath the silver needle of her machine, she experienced a rush of joy. She'd always loved quilting, and she believed God had given her a special ability to create patterns and color combinations that pleased the eye. Using the articles of clothing given to her, she had planned a trio of similar yet distinct thirty-six-inch-square quilts. By combining texture and color with information the children had shared about their mother's likes and dislikes, she felt certain she'd captured tiny pieces of the woman's life in art.

The sewing machine whirred and she thought ahead to next week when she would use her automatic quilting machine to bind the decorative tops to the plain backings. All three sisters had chosen the same stitching pattern for their individual quilts—a series of interlocking hearts. The pattern was Amy's favorite, the perfect choice for any remembrance quilt.

The machine's hum drowned out the sounds of the children's soft banter. She was so caught up in her work, she almost missed the thump of someone knocking on the front screen door. In their six days in their new home, no one had visited. The knock brought both elation and curiosity. Who might it be?

Tucking stray wisps of her hair beneath the edge of her prayer cap, she hurried toward the door. Parker and Adrianna also came running. She shook her head, shooing them back to their tasks. They scurried around the corner, giggling together. Amy looked through the screen door. One of the men from Ohio who'd helped her move into the house stood on the porch with his black Sunday hat in his hands. He offered a nod of hello as she squeaked the door open. "Good morning."

"Good morning, Mrs. Knackstedt." He peered past her into the front room. "I see you have your house all in order already. Those of us who settled in town do, too."

"I'm so glad." Amy searched her memory for the man's name. Mr. Schell? Mr. Mischler? Both men were big-boned with dark hair, so she couldn't be sure which one stood on her porch. Somewhat embarrassed, she held out her hand in invitation. "Won't you come in? I have some cold lemonade in the refrigerator. I'd be glad to pour you a glass."

He stepped over the threshold but remained near the door, twisting the brim of his hat. "No, thank you. I just came to ask . . ." A sheepish look crossed his face. "If you would rather say no, we'll understand, but . . ."

Amy's curiosity increased with each second that ticked past. She laughed softly to cover her unease. "What is it?"

"Tomorrow, as you know, is Sunday. We don't have a meetinghouse in Weaverly yet, but we'd like to hold a service. One of our men is asking about using one of the empty businesses in town until we can get a proper meetinghouse built. In the meantime, we need a place to come together for worship." His gaze bounced around the spacious sitting room. "We noticed when we moved you in how large this room is. I believe it would accommodate all of us. We wondered if you would consider hosting our service tomorrow."

Amy glanced at the room. Considering only around twenty-five people would attend the service, she certainly had the space. "I'd be happy to host the service tomorrow. As a matter of fact, we can hold services here for as long as we need to until we have a building available." She grimaced in apology. "But a few people might need to stand and the children might have to sit on the floor. I have the sofa and chair, and four kitchen chairs, but—"

He waved one of his big hands in dismissal. "Don't worry about seats, Mrs. Knackstedt. One of our men, Christian Hunsberger, has a pickup truck. He said he could carry chairs out for us to use if you don't mind him coming a little early to get the room set up."

Amy smiled, relieved. She'd been so busy getting herself and the children settled, she'd forgotten about Sunday services. Now the promise of worship with like believers—even though they came from a fellowship in Ohio and she from one in Kansas—gave her heart a lift. "Tell him he's welcome to come anytime after eight o'clock. The children and I will be up and ready to help him arrange the room."

The man beamed. "Thank you so much, Mrs. Knackstedt. My wife, Lorraine, is eager to meet you. I told her about your big sewing machine, and she would like to see it sometime."

"I'd be delighted to show it to her." Although Amy hadn't

yet met the woman, she already imagined them becoming friends.

"And I think our children are close in age to yours," the man said. "Of course, ours are all boys, but it will do them good to get acquainted before school starts. They can be support to one another, yes?"

His tone carried a hint of a German accent, reminding Amy of her grandfather's deep, seasoned voice. Her smile grew without effort. "Yes, that would be good for all of them."

"Well, I'll go then and leave you to your day." He plopped his hat on his head and stepped back onto the porch. "We'll see you tomorrow morning."

An idea struck. Amy darted after him, letting the screen door slam into its frame behind her. "Why don't you tell the others to each bring a little something for lunch, and we'll have a meal together here afterward. Then we can all get better acquainted." For the past two nights she'd lain awake, praying and fretting over her conversation with Bekah. Being accepted into this circle of Mennonite believers from Ohio would surely help Bekah feel at ease with her own heritage again.

"I'll tell everyone," he said, inching backward toward his waiting vehicle.

Amy stood on the porch and waved as the man pulled out of her driveway. She turned to go back inside, but then she paused, her gaze drifting effortlessly to the stand of trees east of her house. Mr. Roper's orchard. Her heart gave a funny half-skip. Would the man see all the cars in her yard Sunday morning? Would he hear their songs of praise drifting across the prairie from her open windows? Might their example of coming together for worship minister to his soul and restore within him the faith of his fathers? *God, if it be Your will, use us to draw him back to Your fold.*

The prayer complete, she stepped back into the house, a smile forming on her face as she imagined tomorrow's visitors filling the sitting room. Then she clicked her tongue on her teeth. If this sitting room was to serve as the temporary meetinghouse, it needed a much more thorough cleaning than the children would give it. She also needed to prepare extra food so she could share with her new fellowship.

She'd intended to spend the afternoon sewing, but she rapidly changed her mind. Preparing for this service—a service she prayed would aid in bringing understanding to Bekah's soul and perhaps reach the heart of the man next door—was more important than sewing. She hurried to the kitchen and called, "Children? Come here, please. I need to talk with you."

9

Amy swept the back of her wrist across her forehead. Even with all the windows open and a box fan whirring from the corner of the kitchen, the room was unbearably hot. But the heat wasn't solely due to the Kansas sun—she'd left her oven on low all morning to keep the casseroles carried in by the other women warm until mealtime. Although she'd turned off the oven nearly an hour ago, warmth still radiated from its cast-iron sides. The oven's ability to hold heat would be a blessing during the winter months.

Adding to the stove's warmth, steam rose from the sink of dishwater. Since they'd used her house and mostly her dishes, she'd assumed the task of washing the stacks of dirty plates, bowls, cups, pots, and pans. And of course, having seven women crowded into the room made things feel tight and sticky. But Amy didn't begrudge their presence. How she'd enjoyed their morning together! Already she felt the stirrings of oneness with these people. She prayed Bekah was experiencing the same feeling with the young people her age who clustered on the back porch.

Cheerful cries filled the backyard—children at play. Amy easily detected Adrianna's melodious giggle and Parker's lower-toned guffaws in the mix. The low rumble of men's voices drifted from the sitting room into the kitchen, where the women jostled together. The combined sounds created a sweet song of unity.

Ellie Hunsberger, the youngest of the women, brushed her elbow against Amy's arm as she reached to return the clean bowls to the cupboard. She laughed softly, sending a shy smile in Amy's direction. "Maybe next time we should buy a package of paper plates. The cleanup would go faster, I think."

From behind them, someone *tsk-tsk*ed. "Shame on you, Ellie." After only one morning together, Amy already recognized Margaret Gerber's somewhat abrasive tone. Perhaps the older woman didn't intend to be condescending, but of all the women, this one struck Amy as the most critical. "Paper items are a waste. Only lazy people use them. Doesn't it say in Proverbs, the fourteenth chapter and twenty-third verse, 'In all labour there is profit'? We should take joy in our given toil, not look for ways to simplify."

Ellie dipped her head. She continued stacking the clean, dry dishes in silence.

Apparently the other women feared the sharp side of Margaret's tongue, because they too stopped the cheerful chatter of moments ago and focused on completing the cleanup tasks. A half hour after they'd begun, Amy's kitchen was in order and everything sparkled. She gathered the sodden dishtowels and carried them to the little area beneath the stairs where she kept a laundry basket. The opening to the hidden storage area was next to the door leading to the back porch, and Amy couldn't resist sneaking a quick peek outside to see how her children were getting along with the others. She smiled at the wild game of tag taking place in the backyard, Adrianna and Parker in the middle of it. But her smile faltered when she spotted Bekah leaning against a tree by herself at the far corner of the yard. The handful of other children near her age remained in the shade of the back porch. Why had Bekah left the group?

Amy reached for the screen door, intending to go out and check on her daughter, but Margaret Gerber called, "Amy? Do you have more lemons to mix another batch of lemonade? The pitcher is empty again." Amy changed direction, retrieved lemons from the refrigerator, and gave them to the woman.

Margaret bustled to the counter and began digging through Amy's kitchen drawers, talking all the while. "I'm puzzled why you would choose this house away from town, since you have no husband to see to chores." She flicked a curious glance over her shoulder as she withdrew a knife from the drawer. "Wouldn't a house in town be more sensible?"

Amy loved the openness of the acreage—it gave her children room to run, and by secluding them somewhat she could limit the influences that might come from any unchurched townsfolk. But she sensed no matter what reason she gave, Margaret would find something at fault. She handed the woman a small cutting board, one Gabe had crafted from strips of oak for a Christmas gift the year Bekah was born, and said, "I realize I don't have a husband to see to things, but I'm not concerned. With the men of your fellowship farming the land around the house, they'll be close by should a need arise. I'm certain they'll be willing to offer assistance if it's needed."

Tamera Mischler bustled to Amy's side. "Of course they

will! They've already discussed the importance of checking on you when they come out to work. And now that all of our places in town are in order, the men will put their hands to work preparing the ground for soybean planting. You'll have someone close by every day."

Warmth flooded Amy. How wonderful to know these people—these strangers quickly turning to friends—cared about her well-being.

Margaret sniffed, pushing the cutting board back into Amy's hands. "This is too small. I'll just use the countertop." She whacked one lemon in half. "But what about at night? There's no one here at night." She aimed a speculative look at Amy, her double chin emerging with her head-tucked-low pose.

Was the woman trying to frighten her? Amy hugged Gabe's gift to her middle. Without conscious thought, she quoted a portion of Deuteronomy 31:6. " 'Be strong and of a good courage, fear not . . . for the Lord thy God, he it is that doth go with thee; he will not fail thee, nor forsake thee.' " She smiled at Margaret, who continued to pinch her brows in silent censure. "The children and I are never alone."

Margaret returned to slicing lemons.

Lorraine Schell leaned against the counter on the other side of Margaret and used a dish rag to mop at the juice spritzing the countertop. "Besides, Margaret, Amy has a close-by neighbor—the orchard-owner, Mr. Roper. If she has an emergency, surely he'd be willing to offer a helping hand, considering he was raised a Mennonite."

A variety of murmurs—Margaret's reproachful, the others' regretful—filtered through the kitchen. Before Margaret could openly condemn Mr. Roper for abandoning his faith,

Amy said, "He's been very neighborly." An image of the man caught in Parker's embrace filled her memory. Many people would have pushed Parker away, but Mr. Roper treated the boy with kindness. How she appreciated his kind response to her son. "He's quite busy with his orchard, though, so I don't want to impose on him unless it's an emergency. I'm glad the men will start coming out each day. And if they ever need anything from me while they're working—something to drink or eat, or to use the facilities—they're more than welcome to come to the house."

Approving nods went around the small circle of women. Margaret snatched up two lemon halves and began squeezing the juice into a tall plastic pitcher. "I intend to make sure Dillard has a good lunch and a jug of water in his truck before sending him out. That's my duty as his wife. And you might as well know, I've instructed him not to come to the house except to check on you." She bounced an imperious look across each of the women in the room before looking directly at Amy. "There's no need for the men to be pests just because you're here and available during the day. You have your quilting business. The men coming and going would keep you from focusing on your work." She squeezed the last lemon half and then tossed the rind into the sink with other squeezed-flat shells. "Besides, one needs to avoid creating fodder for gossip. Men coming and going from a widow's house might be construed as inappropriate dealings."

Lorraine Schell gasped, and the others gaped at one another, but none of them voiced an argument. Amy, as the newcomer to the group, didn't believe it her place to let Margaret know she found her comments offensive, but she couldn't stay silent in the face of unwarranted criticism. She lifted the pitcher with trembling hands and held it beneath the faucet. Her gaze on the flow of water, she said quietly yet firmly, "I know the men will be responsive to me in case of an emergency. I will be responsive to them, as well. That's what members of a fellowship do for one another."

After placing the full pitcher on the counter, she slid the sugar canister next to Margaret. "Would you like to add the sugar? I'm sure you have a preference for how much sweetening to use. The wooden spoons are in the drawer near your hip."

Margaret pursed her lips, but she began scooping sugar without another word. Amy left her to the task and crossed to the table where Lorraine, Tamera, Renae Stull, and Sheila Buerge had seated themselves. Ellie stood nearby. The women offered weak smiles of apology, and Amy acknowledged them with a quick bob of her head. Obviously Margaret held strong opinions. But Amy had been raised by a man with strong opinions and a tendency toward stubbornness. She'd learned long ago not to respond with anger, but rather quiet reasoning.

Margaret carried the pitcher of lemonade to the refrigerator. Then she turned to the table, where every seat was already filled. Amy smiled, letting the older woman know she harbored no ill feelings. "Wait just a moment, Margaret. I'll get some of the extra chairs Mr. Hunsberger brought in."

The moment Amy returned to the table, two chairs in tow, Lorraine leaned forward. Interest sparked in her eyes. "Tell me about your quilting business, Amy." She flicked a glance toward the sewing room, where sheets shrouded the machines. "My husband says you have a machine that does the quilting for you."

Margaret lifted her chin. "I prefer hand-quilting."

Amy nodded, unaffected by the woman's mild rebuff. "I do too, when I have time for it. But since I need to complete these quilts quickly, the quilting machine is a real blessing. Would you like to see how it works? I have a small wall hanging ready to be quilted."

"Yes, please," Lorraine and Ellie chorused.

None of the others responded, but they all got up and followed when Amy headed for the sewing room. Amy showed the women how to fasten the quilt into the rollers of the long-arm machine, then programmed the stitch pattern. The women watched, interested, and even the men ambled in to observe the machine in action when Amy flipped the switch that sent the frame sideways beneath the rapidly undulating needle. A row of connected hearts appeared along the top row of the quilt's face. When the frame reached the edge of the quilt, Amy shut down the machine.

"I'll just roll it forward and continue until the entire face is done," she said. "Then I bind it and add a sleeve for hanging if the person requested it, and then it's ready to go."

Ellie traced her finger along the neat line of stitches. "Oh my, what a time-saver. And so sturdy. These stitches will hold up to hundreds of washings, I imagine."

Renae Stull looked with longing at the machine. "I suppose it was very expensive."

Amy cringed. It wasn't polite to discuss the cost of items, but she couldn't ignore Renae's comment. "A regular sewing machine is much more affordable. A long-arm machine isn't something everyone could or even should have in their home. I purchased it so I could begin my business." She didn't mention how she'd been able to afford such an expensive machine. Sometimes it still felt like blood money.

"Even so, think how much quicker quilts could be finished with a machine like this," Ellie said.

Margaret folded her arms. "I understand why Amy needs to use this—her family depends on the income she makes from the quilts. Of course she needs to make them quickly. But for everyone to own such a machine? It would encourage sloth."

Ellie hung her head.

Amy's heart went out to the younger woman. She tossed the protective sheet over the machine, adjusting it to cover the partially quilted project. "Ellie, if you'd ever like to try it yourself, just bring one of your quilts out. I've found it's a wonderful way to restore older quilts that are in danger of falling apart."

The men returned to the sitting room, but the women remained standing around the covered machine. Lorraine tipped her head, her expression thoughtful. "Amy, since you have need of providing for your family, have you ever considered advertising this machine for use? I'm sure many women who can't afford to own a machine like this would still like to see their projects finished in such a beautiful, timely manner. Or to, as you said, restore a family heirloom to make it more serviceable."

Amy blinked twice, her heart skipping a beat. "I would never have considered that. It is time-consuming for me to plan, piece, and stitch a quilt from start to finish, so there's a limit to how many projects I can reasonably commission. If others 'rented' the machine, I could generate a little extra income." Then her spirits plummeted. "But I wouldn't know how to let people know it's available. I'm afraid thus far my business has come by word of mouth. That was fine when I wasn't the sole provider, but now . . ." She didn't want to confide her worries with Margaret nearby. The older woman would probably think Amy didn't trust God to see to her financial needs.

Sheila Buerge clapped her palms together. "You know what you need, Amy? A Web site!"

Tamera looked at Sheila in surprise. "Why, what a wonderful idea. People who would otherwise never know about Amy's business could find her." The two began jabbering enthusiastically.

Amy waved her hands. "Wait, wait. I don't have an Internet connection out here, I don't own a computer, and even if I did, I wouldn't have any idea how to operate one."

"If you can program one of these things"—Ellie indicated the long-arm quilting machine—"you can learn to operate a computer."

"Why, sure you can," Tamera said. "Even if you didn't want to invest in a computer of your own right away, you could use one in the Weaverly library to get started. The librarian told me we could use the computers anytime we needed. Then, when your business has grown enough to handle an additional expense, you could buy your own and have the Internet connected to it here. I'm sure the former owners had a telephone line."

"Who knows?" Ellie held her arms wide. "Your business might grow so big you'll need someone operating the long-arm while you spend your day sewing at the other machine."

"Oh . . . oh my." Amy covered her mouth with her fingers and stared at the younger woman. If Ellie was right, she'd have a job ready and waiting for Bekah as soon as she finished school. The thought brought a feeling of security.

Lorraine joined the circle of idea makers. "I agree. A Web

site is a wonderful way to advertise. Back in Berlin, my brothers built a site to let others know about their cabinet-making business. Our fellowship approved it because with a Web site, you aren't forcing yourself on anyone, just making your services available. And all of us will pray that the people who need you can find you." She looked at Margaret, as if seeking her approval. "Won't we?"

Margaret nodded, her double chin quivering. "Of course we'll pray for God to bless Amy's business as He sees best."

Amy's mind whirled. "I . . . I don't know. . . ." She released a nervous laugh. "I've never even used a computer. I wouldn't know how to begin."

"Mom?"

Bekah stood in the doorway between the kitchen and sewing room, her hands linked at her waist. "The other day when we spent the morning at the library, the librarian helped me do some research on the computer—looking up stuff about Weaverly to kind of, well, get to know the town. I found a really neat Web site advertising a business right here in Weaverly. So if you want to learn to make your own Web site, I think I know who could help." She paused, then finished. "Mr. Roper."

10

Several car engines starting at once captured Tim's attention. He tossed aside the oiled rag he'd been using to grease the gears on the vintage apple-corer and trotted to the barn's wide opening. A cloud of dust rose in the distance. He resisted releasing a shout of elation. Apparently the meeting over at the Sanford—the *Knackstedt* place, he corrected himself—was breaking up. *Finally.*

They'd all rolled in midmorning, just as he'd finished loading the little trailer on the back of his golf cart to head out and work. Surmising they intended to worship together, he decided not to interrupt their service with the sound of his chainsaw and weed eater. But as the day wore on, he'd begun to think they'd all decided to take up residence over there.

During the morning, as he'd cleared the grassy area at the rear of the orchard with a well-sharpened scythe to prepare for the beehives, he'd been subjected to no less than a dozen hymns. When he started humming along, he sent himself to the barn where the sturdy walls blocked the sound of their combined voices. For the most part. This afternoon, a burst of laughter or a child's shrill screech still occasionally reached his ears. Aggravated with himself for hiding away, he'd come close to heading out after lunch and taking care of the tasks he'd allotted for the day—trimming weeds and cutting back a few overhanging branches that invited deer visits along the west fence line—but fear of being spotted and berated for laboring on the Lord's day had kept him in the barn.

Here it was, nearly four o'clock, closing in on suppertime, and he hadn't even fired up the chainsaw. "I can get to it now," he muttered. "And nobody'll be there to get all offended." Mrs. Knackstedt would be there, of course. But somehow he didn't picture her getting offended. He couldn't explain why, but he sensed even if she disapproved, she wouldn't utter a word of complaint, unlike the older Mennonite woman he'd encountered in the grocery store earlier in the week who'd fussed at the store owner about the price on a jar of yeast.

He plopped into the golf cart's seat. The engine played its stubborn game and delayed turning over until the third try, but then it stuttered to life. Tim rose up as high as he could and looked toward the road. The dust had all settled. The Mennonites were gone. With a satisfied expulsion of breath, he put the cart in gear and bounced out onto the road.

Tim drove the short distance to the end of the fence line, then angled the cart off the road and drove across his neighbor's pasture—the Sanfords had never minded. He stayed as close to the fence as possible without hooking a trailer tire on a post. The barbed-wire fence that ran along the west side of his orchard was closer to the old farmhouse where the Knackstedts now lived than to his own double-wide. The land gently rose midway between the house and the fence, though, hiding him from view. Unless Mrs. Knackstedt or her kids looked out an upstairs window, they wouldn't notice him out here. But they might hear him. Neither the weed eater nor the chainsaw were exactly quiet.

A smile twitched at his cheek. Parker would probably come trotting over the rise to see what Tim was up to. Then his smile faded. Mrs. Knackstedt wouldn't let Parker wander like that anymore. Since he'd done it twice already, she'd be keeping a close watch. As well she should. But even so, he couldn't deny a small prickle of regret. He didn't want the kid around all the time—he didn't need the intrusion in his ordered world—yet he'd taken a liking to the boy. Pretty hard not to like a kid who so openly liked you.

He stopped the cart and trotted to the trailer. The chainsaw had bounced to the tail, so he grabbed it out first. He clamped the hard plastic body between his knees, took a firm grip on the top handle, and gave the starting cord a solid tug. The chainsaw, much more cooperative than the testy old golf cart, fired right up.

Tim trimmed only the ends of the branches extending over the fence, careful not to carve away too many buds. Eventually he'd thin the blooms—the apples would be too small if he left them all clustered so tight—but he wasn't ready for thinning yet. The twigs fell, some landing on his head and shoulders, others bouncing on his boot toes. He had to refuel the chainsaw twice from the gas can in the trailer, but he got the entire fence line trimmed.

He glanced at the sun. Still high. Plenty of time remaining before sundown to put the weed eater to work. His shoulders ached from holding the heavy chainsaw at chest height, but the tall grass wouldn't cut itself. And nobody else would step up and take care of it, so he might as well get to it.

He tromped to the trailer, thinking back to the days when he first started working the orchard. Things sure had changed since then. One of a short crew of workers, he'd shared the duties with Julia's uncle Gator—he never could think of the man by his given name, Galen, since Charlie always referred to him as Unca Gator—and three other men who worked anywhere from two to five days a week. From his first days of employment, Tim carried the heaviest load, just because he was available. When Gator and his wife, Toka, found out he was on his own, they set him up in the renovated storage shed on the back edge of the property that had served as a makeshift guesthouse for relatives in the past. He became their 24/7 handyman, and he loved it. Working from morning to night left him no time to think, pray, or ruminate about the past. And it let him learn every aspect of running the orchard.

When he married Julia five years after arriving in Weaverly, Gator made him a full partner. Then, when Charlie was school age, Tim bought the orchard outright, and Gator and Toka packed their bags and moved to Florida to spend their retirement years chasing golf balls and relaxing on the beach. Tim kept two employees right up until the day the tractor trailer ran amok on Highway 70—a route he now steadfastly avoided—and stole Julia and Charlie from him. After that, he hadn't wanted anybody around, so he'd cut the men loose and handled the orchard on his own.

Turning the place into a pick-your-own-apples outfit made it possible for him to run it pretty much single-handedly with some part-time help at the peak picking times. And running it on his own once again kept him too busy to think, pray, or ruminate on the past. Which was exactly the way he liked it. He reached for the starter cord on the weed eater, but he froze when a glee-filled giggle carried on the late-afternoon breeze to his ears. He rose up, his gaze automatically seeking. But no child ran across the pasture toward him, face alight with joy.

A lump filled his throat. "Get busy, Rupp," he prodded himself, and gave the cord a yank. Not until he'd carved out a fair-sized patch of grass did it connect that he'd called himself Rupp instead of Roper. Sometimes, despite his best efforts, the past crept up on him after all.

Amy set aside her Bible and folded her hands for prayer. Adrianna, cuddled against her pillow, and Bekah and Parker, seated side by side at the foot of Adrianna's bed, mimicked her action. She closed her eyes and prayed aloud, giving God thanks for the time of fellowship and the opportunity to unite their hearts in worship to Him. She asked Him to keep watch over their house this night and to give the children pleasant dreams. All of her growing-up years, she'd listened to her father's nightly prayers. After she married, Gabe led nightly Bible reading and prayer, first with her and then with the children.

But after Parker's accident, Gabe—angry with God and heartsore—refused to do it. Amy couldn't bear to forego the long-held tradition, so she had assumed the practice, even though men were supposed to be the spiritual heads in a Mennonite home. Their nightly routine gave the children security and planted God's words in their hearts. She would never set it aside.

"Amen," she finished. She pulled the light sheet up to

Adrianna's chin and kissed the little girl's soft cheek. "Sleep now." Adrianna yawned, rolled to her side, and closed her eyes. Her deep breaths indicated sleep even before the others left the room.

Bekah headed for the stairs, but Amy followed Parker into his bedroom. She smiled as he flopped into his bed, his gangly arms and legs flying in all directions. He flipped the sheet to his hips and folded his arms behind his head. " 'Night, Mom."

She kissed his forehead, running her hand over his disheveled hair. He must not have combed it after his bath. "Goodnight, Parker. Pleasant dreams."

"Gonna dream about donkeys tonight."

Amy swallowed a laugh. "Donkeys?"

"Yeah. I might raise 'em someday. I think they're cute."

Where did he get these ideas? "That's quite an aspiration."

"Huh?"

"A good plan."

"Oh. Can I go to the li'bary tomorrow and find books about donkeys?"

Amy smoothed his hair again. It sprang right back up. "We'll see. Sleep now, okay?"

"Okay."

Chuckling to herself, Amy switched off the lamp beside his bed and crept into the hallway. A buzz drifted through the open window. Locusts? Amy had always loved listening to locusts sing in the trees at dusk when she was a girl. She paused beside the open window on the upstairs landing and listened for a few minutes. No, that wasn't locusts. Someone was operating a motorized . . . something. Gabe probably would have been able to identify it.

Her heart panged, loneliness creating a deep ache. At least

she still had her children. She peeked once more into each of the bedrooms, ascertaining both Parker and Adrianna were fine, then she tiptoed downstairs.

Bekah sat with her feet tucked up beside her in the corner of the sofa, a book in her hands. The book reminded Amy of Parker's request. She plopped onto the opposite end of the sofa and said, "Parker wants to go to the library sometime this week, but I need to work. Would you ride to town with your brother and sister? You could take my bicycle and put Adrianna in the child seat." Adrianna was almost too big for the plastic seat, but the little girl would never make it all the way to town on her training-wheeled bicycle.

Bekah made a face. "She wiggles so much, I'm always afraid she's going to dump the bike."

Amy had battled Adrianna's wiggles herself. "Well, then, I suppose just you and Parker could go in one afternoon, when she's napping. It'll be a lot hotter then, but if you don't mind the sun . . ."

"I'd rather be sweaty than scuffed up from falling over."

"All right, then, wait until afternoon. We'll look at the calendar together in the morning and see what day would be best."

"Thanks." Bekah shifted a bit and angled her book to the lamp.

Amy chuckled, remembering the brief exchange with Parker. "Your brother wants to check out books about donkeys. He seems to have developed an interest in them."

Bekah slapped the book into her lap and swung her bare feet to the floor. "I know why. That one boy who was here today—I think his name is Tyler—told Parker he sounded like a braying donkey when he laughed."

Amy gawked at Bekah. Joe and Lorraine Schell's oldest

son was named Tyler. Perhaps fifteen years old, tall and nice-looking, he'd been very polite when talking to Amy. "Are you sure he said that?"

Bekah huffed. "Yes, Mom. I told him he was rude—he shouldn't make fun of people. But he laughed and said Parker kind of looked like a donkey, too, with his big ears and long face. He made me so mad."

Amy's heart ached, for both Parker and Bekah. "Is that why you were over by the tree instead of with the others?"

"Yes."

"Did . . . did the others make fun of your brother, too?"

"No, only Tyler. But none of the others tried to stop him. They just let him do it, like they thought it was okay." Bekah snatched up the book again, but she didn't open it. Her eyes spat fury. "If they're going to be mean, I don't want anything to do with them."

Amy drew in a deep breath and held it, seeking wisdom. She hated that Tyler had ridiculed Parker. Apparently the teasing hadn't bothered Parker. Perhaps he'd been unaware that the older boy meant to disparage him. Right now she was more concerned about Bekah's reaction and unwillingness to associate with the other Mennonite youth. Amy needed the fellowship to draw Bekah in, not drive her away.

She reached across the center section of the sofa and tweaked Bekah's ear. "The Schells seem like good people. I'm sure they won't want their son to torment others. I'll talk to Tyler's mom about the situation, okay?"

"Okay." Bekah bounced the book in her lap and cast a sidelong look at Amy. "Are you gonna talk to Mr. Roper?"

The sudden shift in topics caught Amy off guard. "What for?"

Bekah rolled her eyes. "Remember? I told you he had a really good Web site. He could show you how he did it."

101

Amy forced a chuckle. "Honey, between Adrianna and Parker's escapades, I think Mr. Roper has seen just about enough of us since we got here."

"Well, who else can you ask?"

Amy mentally searched through her list of acquaintances. She didn't uncover anyone who had knowledge of computers or Web sites. "I don't know, but if I'm meant to have a Web site to help build my business, I'm sure God will put someone in my pathway to help me."

Bekah raised one eyebrow. "Remember what Grandpa always said? God provides food for the robin, but God doesn't throw the worm in the nest—the robin has to dig it up himself." She threw her arms wide. "Why not just talk to Mr. Roper? If he doesn't want to help you, maybe he can tell you the name of somebody else in town who could help. I don't see what it would hurt, just to ask."

Amy sighed, too weary to argue. "I'll think about it. Why don't you go up and take your bath now? Just don't be noisy. Your brother and sister are asleep."

Bekah tucked the book in the crook of her arm and scuffed around the corner. Amy sank against the sofa cushions and stared at the wallpapered ceiling overhead. The ladies had all seemed to think a Web site would be a big help in building her business. She needed a steady source of income, and she knew she could quilt. *"God doesn't throw the worm in the nest."* She chuckled. Maybe Bekah paid more attention than Amy realized.

Mr. Roper might not appreciate being called the worm to her robin, but she could use his advice. If the Lord provided an opportunity, she'd ask him about creating a Web site for Threads of Remembrance. But only if the Lord opened the door.

11

Bekah rested her fingertips on the edge of the tall counter that surrounded the librarian's desk and whispered, "Miss Bergstrom?" The group of town kids congregated in the library's Reading Corner were speaking out loud, but that didn't mean it was right. People were supposed to be quiet in a library.

The librarian lifted her gaze from the computer screen. A pleasant scent lifted with the woman's movement—floral and sweet. "Yes, Bekah? Can I help you with something?"

Bekah flicked a glance toward the Reading Corner. She hoped the kids there wouldn't overhear her request. "My brother wants to check out books about donkeys." Heat filled her cheeks. Did all brothers embarrass their sisters, or was she the only girl mortified by a younger brother's wild ideas? Bekah had hoped the chores of the first half of the week—they'd put off their trip to the library until Thursday afternoon—would chase Parker's crazy interest in donkeys out of his head, but he'd held on to it. "But the only ones I can find are too hard for him to read. Do you have any picture books about donkeys?"

Without so much as a blink, the librarian left her chair and came around the desk. The flowery scent came with her, so much more pleasant than the perspiration Bekah detected on her own skin. Miss Bergstrom looped her arm through Bekah's elbow and smiled. "Come with me. I think we can fix Parker right up." Fifteen minutes later, Parker happily hugged a stack of four children's books featuring donkeys, and Bekah trailed him out of the library.

When they reached the bicycles, Bekah held out her hands. "Here, Parker. Gimme your books." He reluctantly released them. Bekah stacked the books in the basket attached to the handlebars of her bicycle. She gave Parker a firm look. "Now, remember, stay *behind* me. We can't ride side by side on the road."

Parker poked out his lower lip and scowled. "I know, Bekah. I'm not stupid."

Bekah set her lips in a grim line. Parker wasn't stupid, no matter what some people might think, but he didn't always remember things like he should. Mom had said it was Bekah's job to look out for him, so even if it made him mad, she reminded him of important stuff. Like not riding down the middle of the road.

Without another word, they mounted their bikes and Bekah led the way out of town. The bold sun made the asphalt shimmer. Heat scorched through her clothing, until her head and shoulders felt like they were on fire. Eager to get back to the farmhouse and out of the sun, she pumped hard against the wind, her tennis shoes squeaking against the rubber pedals of her bike. Sweat trickled down her forehead and stung her eyes. The distance from town to their home wasn't long—she and Parker had ridden farther distances when they lived in Arborville—but riding in the full heat of the sun, with the wind trying to push her backward, made the two-mile trek seem more like ten.

She glanced over her shoulder to see how Parker was keeping up. To her consternation, he'd fallen several yards behind her, his red face crunched into a fierce scowl. He rode with his back hunched and his elbows high—an awkward pose she was glad no one was around to witness. She didn't like feeling embarrassed about Parker, but that dumb Tyler had made her look at her brother in a different way. It bugged her that Tyler was right. Parker's long face *did* look a little bit like a donkey. Bekah braked her bike and waited for him to catch up.

He closed the distance between them, the sound of his puffing breaths competing with the crunch of his bike tires on the roadway. Sweat glistened on his face and plastered his hair to his high forehead. Bekah braced herself, ready to push off and keep going, when Parker suddenly let out a yelp. He rose up as if the seat had shocked him, and then he tumbled sideways, landing in the grassy strip alongside the road with the bike on top of him.

Although Parker wasn't exactly coordinated, he'd mastered bike riding. She couldn't remember the last time he'd fallen off of his bicycle. Bekah hopped off her bike, pushed the kickstand into place, and raced to Parker. "Are you okay? What happened?"

Parker started to cry. "That hurt, Bekah."

"I know, Budger." As big as he was, he shouldn't be bawling over a bike spill, but sympathy still welled. "Here, let me help you up and we'll get going. We're almost home." She kind of fibbed. They were less than halfway home. But the truth wouldn't encourage him to keep going.

Parker twisted his body and threw his left leg over the handlebars, but he didn't move the one caught beneath the bicycle. "I can't."

"Yes, you can. Come on." Bekah reached to lift the bike from her brother so he could get up, but then she noticed his pant leg had gotten caught between the chain and the gear. The blue twill bore a black stain, and the gear had torn through the cloth in one place. Bekah groaned. "Oh, Parker . . ."

Parker's wails increased. "I didn't mean to!"

Bekah wiped a trickle of sweat from her temple. "I know it was an accident. But we've gotta get home." She knelt beside him, little pebbles digging painfully into her bare knees, and tugged on his pant leg. The bottom two inches were stuck fast. She huffed in aggravation and yanked harder. The fabric gave way, taking the chain right off the gear.

"Bekah!" Parker grabbed his pant leg. "Look what you did!"

Bekah grimaced at the jagged, grease-stained tear. Mom wouldn't be able to fix that.

"You ruined my pants!"

"Well, it wasn't my fault!" Bekah slapped his hands away from the ragged fabric, anger overriding guilt. "How else was I supposed to get you loose?"

Parker whimpered, "You tore my pants, Bekah. And now my bike is broke." He lifted his hands and peered at them. His eyes flew wide. "I'm bleeding!"

"Lemme see." Bekah examined his palms. He'd scuffed

them when he hit the ground, but they didn't look too bad. Probably wouldn't even need a Band-Aid. But Parker did need reassurance. She brushed bits of dried grass from his palms and spoke cheerfully. "You'll be all right. Just a little scrape. But you're right—with that chain off, you can't ride your bike. So let's scoot you off into the grass and you can wait here while I ride on home and—"

"Noooo!" His wail carried across the empty landscape. Two birds swooped out of some scraggly brush near the road and winged over their heads. He scrambled to his feet, kicking the bike across the asphalt a few inches. "Don't leave me here!"

"Just for a little bit. I'll go get Mom and—"

"Don't leave me!" His voice rose in hysteria.

There'd be no reasoning with him now. *I'm going.* Bekah gritted her teeth and stomped to her bicycle. Parker's hiccuping sobs followed her, but when she glanced over her shoulder he hadn't moved. The tears trailing down his cheeks almost made her change her mind, but it would be stupid for both of them to sit here in the sun, waiting until Mom finally missed them and came looking. He'd only be alone for ten, maybe fifteen, minutes. It wouldn't kill him.

As she straddled her bicycle, she waved one hand in the air. "Stay off the road, Parker. I'll be right back with Mom." She pumped hard on the pedals, grateful the rush of wind drowned out the sound of Parker's continuing wails. Scaredy-cat. He was eleven years old. He ought to be able to sit here by himself long enough for her to go after Mom.

She couldn't help but wonder what it would be like if Parker hadn't fallen off the back of Dad's tractor and damaged his brain. She wouldn't have to look out for him. Wouldn't have to feel embarrassed by him. Wouldn't have to be his protector and teacher. If Parker hadn't gotten hurt, they would just be brother and sister, sometimes fighting like all siblings did, but mostly being friends. And Dad would still be alive. Bekah knew that from the deepest part of herself. Dad would never have done what he did if Parker hadn't gotten hurt.

Her chest constricted, the memories stinging as badly as the sweat that dribbled into her eyes. She forced the remembrances away, squinting at the looming farmhouse ahead. The dancing ribbons from her cap tickled her neck, and she wished she could take it off and shove it in her pocket. If her dress had pockets . . . She stood on the pedals, pumping as hard and fast as she could. But no matter how fast she went she couldn't escape the confused feelings that rumbled inside her chest.

She turned in at her driveway and began yelling for Mom as she rode toward the house. When she reached the porch, Mom opened the screen door and stepped outside. She glanced at Bekah, then looked past her with her face pinching in alarm.

"Where's your brother?"

Bekah quickly explained what had happened.

"You *left* him?"

Mom's accusatory tone set Bekah's nerves on edge. She started to defend herself, but Mom turned and darted for the door.

"Stay here with Adrianna," Mom said, "and I'll go after him."

A snide question tingled at the tip of Bekah's tongue: *Are you sure you can trust me with Adri?* But she clamped her teeth together and dropped her bicycle in the grass. Parker's books on donkeys spilled from the basket. Hissing in irritation, Bekah knelt and smacked the books into a pile. As she pushed to her feet, Mom trotted out of the house, her car keys jingling in her hand. But before Mom made it halfway to the garage, a familiar pickup turned into their drive. Parker sat in the passenger's seat, his head sticking out the window.

"Hi, Mom!" Parker called as the driver drew the pickup to a stop.

Mom dashed to the passenger's side and yanked open the door. Parker tumbled from the seat directly into Mom's arms. Mom hugged him, then pulled loose and cupped Parker's face between her palms, examining him. Apparently she found him unharmed because she hugged him again. "Thank goodness you're all right."

Parker's long, gangly arms wrapped around Mom and clung. His shoulders heaved as if he'd been the one riding his bike under the hot sun instead of Bekah. Bekah battled an urge to give her brother a slug on the arm and a sharp reprimand to grow up.

Mr. Roper popped open his door and stepped out. He tipped his ball cap at Bekah, then moved to the pickup bed and lifted out Parker's bike. He set it in the grass, then ambled around the truck to Mom and Parker. "He's fine, Mrs. Knackstedt—none the worse for wear." He ruffled Parker's unruly hair, grinning. "You're okay, right, Parker?"

Bekah liked the way Mr. Roper spoke to Parker. The same way he'd talk to any kid instead of being impatient or using the nicey-nice tone some grown-ups used when they figured out Parker was a little slow. She inched around the truck's front bumper to join the little group, her shadow sneaking up on their three joined shadows. But she stopped before her shadow melded into theirs.

Parker finally tugged loose from Mom and beamed up at Mr. Roper. "I'm okay." Then he stuck his leg in the air. "But Bekah tore my pants."

Bekah huffed. "The bike chain did it, not me!"

Mr. Roper chuckled and slipped one hand in his jeans pocket. When he smiled, his eyes crinkled at the corners, the way Daddy's had. "Maybe your mom'll turn them into cut-offs for you."

Parker scrunched his face. "Cut-offs?"

"Shorts," Mr. Roper explained.

Bekah cleared her throat. "We don't wear shorts."

Mr. Roper sent her a sheepish look. "Oh. That's right. Well, then, Parker'll just have to do with one fewer pair of britches."

Bekah stared at their neighbor, biting down on her lower lip. The minister of their fellowship in Arborville had made it sound like a horrible sin to leave the church—that the person would be forever haunted with regrets. But even though Mr. Roper didn't smile a lot, he seemed comfortable driving his air-conditioned truck, wearing blue jeans and a T-shirt with the sleeves scrunched up over his shoulders. What had made him decide to not be Mennonite anymore? The curiosity burned inside Bekah. She wished she could ask him all kinds of questions, but that would be nosy. She'd wait until she got to know him better. A person could ask a friend more serious things than she could ask a new neighbor.

Mom slid her arm around Parker's shoulders. "Pants can be replaced. I appreciate you looking out for Parker. Again."

"No problem. It wasn't out of the way or anything." Mr. Roper started backing toward his truck. "He's safe and sound now, but he might want to drink some more water. I gave him a bottle because his face was plenty red—"

Bekah nearly snorted. His face was red from crying—she hadn't left him long enough to get sunburned.

"—and stay out of the sun the rest of the day just in case. Sunstroke isn't anything to sneeze at."

Mom nodded, her black ribbons bouncing. "Thank you, Mr. Roper. We'll do that."

"All right, then." He tipped the brim of his ball cap and opened his truck door. "Bye now."

Bekah darted forward. "Mr. Roper, wait!" The man paused, one foot propped inside the truck. She whisked a glance at Mom's face, then spun to look directly into Mr. Roper's eyes. "My mom could use your help with something."

"Bekah—" Mom's voice held warning.

Bekah decided to ignore it. Who else could answer her questions about becoming non-Mennonite? The only way she'd get to know Mr. Roper well enough to ask him questions was to have time with him. "Mom wants to make a Web site to help advertise her business, but she doesn't know how to do it. You have a really good one—I saw it on the computer at the library. So . . . could you maybe help my mom learn how to make her own?"

12

Amy inwardly groaned. Why couldn't her children have been born with her tendency toward reserve rather than their father's uninhibited nature? She stepped forward and curled her hands over Bekah's shoulders, turning the girl toward the house. "Take your brother inside." Bekah stiffened, but she obeyed. Amy faced Mr. Roper. "Please pardon Bekah. She's young and is sometimes too forward."

The man brushed his scuffed boot toe against the grass. "She's just looking out for you. Can't blame her for that."

Amy's heart warmed. He was a kind man. Even so, she didn't want to take advantage of his good-heartedness. She proceeded carefully. "Bekah's right that I'm considering starting a Web site for my business. But of course"—she held her hands outward in a gesture of futility—"I'm completely untrained in such processes."

He scratched his head, sending his billed cap askew. "Do you know how to work a computer at all?"

Amy released a light laugh. "I have a sewing machine with

a programmable board. I've mastered it. But an actual computer? No, I've never operated one."

"And you don't own one?"

She shook her head. "Not yet."

He chuckled. "Well, then it's gonna be pretty hard to set up a Web site."

Amy inched backward, slipping into the slant of shade cast by the house. "One of the fellowship members suggested I use a library computer to get started. Then buy one when my business has increased a bit."

He tilted his head, his brows crunching together. "What is it you do, exactly?"

"I make remembrance quilts."

His expression didn't clear.

"People give me clothing articles and other types of fabrics that remind them of someone. They fill out a questionnaire about the person's life, and I create a quilt to represent that individual from the textiles they've given me."

He stared at her as if confused.

Amy shrugged, uncertain how else to explain her business. "The quilt is meant to bring warm memories of the person it represents."

Although he didn't smile or nod, the cloudy look disappeared from his eyes. "I see. A . . . a worthwhile service, I'm sure."

"It's been well received. Since it's my only source of income, I need a little more . . ." She sought a word. "Stability. Some of the fellowship members felt a Web site would help people know how to access my service."

Mr. Roper ambled to the edge of the porch and rested his elbow on the railing. He popped his cap free and wiped his forehead with his bare forearm. Settling the hat back in place, he fixed her with a hesitant look. "I'll be honest—my Web site's the best thing I did to bring new people to the orchard. Folks drive from all over Kansas to pick apples and grapes. A lot of them make their own applesauce right there on the grounds. I keep a little meadow mowed so they can have family picnics near the trees. Since I'm kind of away from everything—" He chuckled. "How many folks know Weaverly, Kansas, even exists? I needed a way to let them know I'm here. And a Web site did that for me. Anybody doing a Google search for orchards in Kansas will find Roper's Orchard and everything they'd need to know about it."

Amy shook her head, confused. "A what search?"

He smiled, the chiseled lines of his face softening with the action. "Google. It's an Internet search engine—people use it when they're trying to locate information."

She wasn't quite certain what he meant, but she nodded.

"So I'd say setting up a Web site is a good idea for building your business."

Amy's pulse sped. "And . . . you'd be willing to show me how to set it up?"

That low-toned chuckle rumbled again. "Well, Mrs. Knackstedt, the hardest part is gonna be finding a time that suits both of us. The library closes at five every day. I work pretty much sunup to sundown during the spring and summer to get the orchard ready for visitors. And then folks start arriving in the fall, keeping me occupied. I won't have daylight hours to spare until close to winter. I imagine you'd want to get this going before then?"

Amy nodded slowly, her hopes fading. "That would be best." She thought about the money she'd deposited in the

Weaverly bank upon arrival in town. The amount would carry her and the children through the end of the year if she were very careful in how she used it, but not much beyond. "I'll need to be bringing in a more steady income by then."

He blew out a breath. "To be honest, the only way I see this working is if I can help you during the evenings—after my work is done for the day. And since you don't have a computer set up in your house, well . . ."

Amy hung her head, defeated. Mr. Roper's open response to Bekah's impulsive request had seemed as if God were opening a door for her. Now it slammed shut in her face. She'd have to find another way to market her business. She didn't have a computer and she didn't have the funds to purchase one. She forced the dark thought aside. She and the children would muddle through. God would provide. He always had.

She started to thank Mr. Roper for his time, but before she could speak, he pushed off from the railing. "I guess we'll have to use mine." A blush stole across his tanned cheeks. "That is, if it isn't breaking any fellowship law for you to come to my place in the evenings."

*

Tim leaned past Mrs. Knackstedt's shoulder and moved the mouse, using the cursor as a pointer. "See? Pictures are included in the template. You just replace the ones they've preloaded with your own." Mrs. Knackstedt had selected a template intended for a floral business, but Tim supposed its muted pastel palette would appeal to quilt lovers, too. "Do you want me to clear these out?"

"Yes, please."

Over the past half hour of tutoring her on how to use

the computer, he'd discovered she was always very polite. Not that he would have expected anything less, but learning something new had to be frustrating. Yet she remained unflustered. Her even temper and appreciative attitude made it a pleasure to work with her. With a few clicks, he cleared the preset images from the page. "There you are. Now it's ready for your pictures."

She placed her hand over the mouse. "I only have the one you took, so this shouldn't take long." For several seconds she sat without moving, her face aimed at the monitor. Then a weak chuckle sounded. "Um, how do I put my picture on here?"

"Use the drag-and-drop option. Just take it from your open file and put it on the Web page." Tim commandeered the mouse and demonstrated, depositing her single photograph directly in the middle of the page. He deleted it. "Now you try." He watched while she slowly manipulated the mouse into dragging the photograph to the lower left-hand side of the template. The woman's movements were slow, clumsy, much like her son's as he played a board game with his little sister on the floor behind them.

Tim had been more than a little embarrassed when the kids plopped down on the carpet and set up their game. Why hadn't he thought to run the vacuum sweeper before they came? He'd had plenty of notice. But Mrs. Knackstedt hadn't raised any protests to her children being on the floor, so he decided not to worry about it. He wished the older girl would join the younger ones rather than standing beside Gator's rickety old desk, observing his every move. Her unwavering gaze unnerved him—as if she was waiting for him to do something inappropriate. But he supposed it was best to have somebody keeping watch just in case any of the Mennonites of Mrs. Knackstedt's fellowship asked questions about their time together. She'd indicated she would ask their advice about visiting his house for her tutorial on Web site building, and he assumed they'd given the go-ahead or she wouldn't be here.

Mrs. Knackstedt released the mouse button, and the photograph Tim had taken two days ago of a small, colorful quilt fell into position. She let out her breath in a whoosh. "There."

The relief in her simple comment made Tim want to laugh. "That's where you want it?"

She sent an uncertain look upward. "Is it not okay there?"

Tim shrugged. "I'm not saying it isn't okay there. Just wanted to make sure it was what you intended. The mouse can be tricky if you're not used to it. I can adjust the image for you if you'd like."

Bekah stepped forward, crowding Tim. She poked her finger against the monitor's screen. "Mom, I think you should put it more up here."

Mrs. Knackstedt shook her head. The black ribbons from her cap swung gently to and fro, stirring embers of memory to life in Tim's mind. "I want it there because eventually I'll add more pictures. The photographs will make a border across the bottom that will draw the visitor's eye."

Tim hadn't thought of designing the page in that manner, but he agreed. Apparently Mrs. Knackstedt's ability to create patterns in quilts extended to making pleasing patterns elsewhere. "Good thinking," he said, then inwardly kicked himself. She was a grown woman, not a child in need of affirmation. He waved one hand toward the screen. "Finish filling in the price of each of your services in the information box, then I'll show you how to make a contact form so people can reach you from the Web page." He stuck his hands in his pockets and took a backward step, careful not to plant his heel on the board of the Candyland game or on either of its players.

Bekah spun to face Tim. "Are you gonna take pictures of all Mom's quilts as she finishes them, Mr. Roper?"

Tim bit the inside of his cheek. He hadn't considered becoming a long-term assistant in this project. He'd assumed he would get Mrs. Knackstedt set up and then let her use the library computers to visit her page and make changes there. But if she was like many of the Old Order Mennonites, she probably didn't own a camera. How would she keep adding new images without assistance from someone? Did he really want to be that someone? "I'm not sure. Maybe your mom will decide to buy herself a camera and write it off as a business expense." If she did, it would free him from future involvement in her business.

He inched around the game to the counter that separated the kitchen from the living room. Things that never bothered him when he was by himself seemed to stand out now that he had company in the house. Dirty dishes filled the sink, and crumbs from his sandwich at noon dotted the tan Formica breakfast bar. He couldn't do anything about the dishes without making a lot of noise, but he used his hand to surreptitiously sweep the crumbs onto the carpet. Some of them landed on the toes of Bekah's sneakers. Why hadn't he noticed her following him?

The girl linked her hands behind her back. "I guess working all day in the orchard, you don't have much time to clean up, huh?"

Tim almost snorted. She was nothing if not blunt.

"Bekah . . ." Mrs. Knackstedt gawked at her daughter. "Be polite."

Bekah put on an innocent face.

Tim forced a laugh. "Yeah, since I'm so busy outside, it does get a little messy around here." He raised one eyebrow and aimed a teasing look at the girl. " 'Course, just being me in the house, my dirt doesn't offend anyone."

Bekah didn't smile. "How long have you owned the orchard, Mr. Roper?"

Did she think it'd been years since he'd done any cleaning? "Owned it? Six years." But he'd lived on the property and worked the trees and land for two decades. More than half his life. So why did the years prior to coming here still haunt him?

"And you work it all by yourself?"

Mrs. Knackstedt cleared her throat. "Bekah, you're being nosy."

Bekah pushed a single crumb around on the countertop with her finger, her head low. "Sorry."

Her dejected pose stirred Tim's sympathy. Even though she had been nosy, he couldn't resist gently chucking her under the chin with his fist. "All by myself isn't so bad. It gives me lots of time to work. And I get plenty of company in the late summer and fall when the apples are ready to be picked. You wait and see how many people show up here when it's picking time."

Parker lifted his face to blink at Tim. "I picked apples one time."

Tim pretended surprise. "That right?"

He nodded, his hair bobbing. "Uh-huh. I helped my dad."

"I bet you were a big help."

Parker shrugged. "I dunno. I can't help him now. Dad died."

Tim wasn't sure how to respond to Parker's statement. Before he could form an answer, Mrs. Knackstedt called, "Mr. Roper?" Grateful for the interruption, he hurried to the desk.

She leaned back in the chair, holding both palms toward the computer. "I think I have it all set up. Besides the contact form you mentioned, that is. Is there anything else I should include?"

Tim looked the page over carefully. Rather than a full Web site with multiple pages, she'd taken his advice to start small and add to it as her business grew. A single page would be easier for her to manage, and lesser bandwidth meant less cost. Besides, one page was enough to cover everything, he noted as he examined the header, list of services, and sample photograph.

"It looks as though you're ready for—" He slapped his forehead. "Oh, wait. Weren't you going to include something about hiring out your machine to quilt other people's projects?"

She groaned. "That's right. I got so focused on the pricing of my own creations, I neglected to include that service." She started to lean forward over the keyboard, but her gaze shifted to the clock on the wall. "Nine fifteen? I didn't realize it was so late." She pushed away from the desk, the wheels on the rolling chair squeaking in protest. "We'd better head home so I can get the children to bed."

Without receiving a word of direction, Bekah crouched down and helped her brother and sister put the game pieces back in the box. Tim was amazed the children had entertained themselves for over an hour with one simple game. He didn't know of many other kids who would have been as patient.

As soon as the children finished cleaning up, Mrs. Knackstedt ushered them out the door. Floodlights mounted on the barn bathed the area in a soft yellow glow, so even though the sky was a steely gray, they had no trouble making their way to their vehicle.

Tim followed the family across the yard and stood beside their car while Mrs. Knackstedt waited for the kids to climb in. He rested his hand on the car's hood. "It shouldn't take long to get the communication form set up. But you'll probably want to list an email address. Do you have an account?" What a stupid question. She didn't have a computer or a cell phone. Why would she have an email account?

She grimaced. "Not yet. Is it complicated? Or expensive?"

"It isn't complicated, and many email accounts are free. We can get you set up when you come back to finish your page. Do you . . . do you want to get that done tomorrow night?"

She'd opened her door, but she paused in the weak glow cast by the car's interior light. "If you're sure you don't mind hosting us two evenings in a row. We can certainly wait a few days, if you'd rather."

They'd already delayed several days while she waited for the fellowship's approval. Besides, he didn't have anywhere to go, anyone else to see. The thought brought a hint of melancholy. He shrugged, tossing the fleeting feeling aside. "Tomorrow's fine. Sooner you get it up and running, the sooner you can start bringing in business." And the sooner he'd be shed of helping her. What had gotten into him lately, thinking he needed company? Especially *Mennonite* company . . .

She smiled. "That's true." The light above highlighted the

snow-white of her cap and made her sleekly combed hair seem even darker in hue than it had inside. Her widow status and position as mother of three had left Tim considering her as a middle-aged woman. Now, looking into her open, appreciative face, he suddenly realized she wasn't middle-aged at all. She was still young. Early thirties at most. Pretty too, in a clean, wholesome way not often seen.

He took a stumbling backward step. "Then come on over tomorrow around eight or so." He trotted to the porch. Her car revved to life as he stepped back inside. She and her kids would be here again tomorrow. His heart gave a funny half-skip—part anticipation, part dread. He glanced around. Where had he stashed that vacuum cleaner?

13

Bekah stood just inside the doorway of her bedroom, pulling pins from her knot of hair, and watched Mom cover Adri with the little girl's favorite orange-dotted sheet. Adri had fallen asleep on the three-minute drive home and hadn't even awakened when Mom carried her upstairs and changed her into a nightgown. How could her sister fall asleep so fast and sleep so hard? Sometimes Bekah envied Adri.

She picked up the hairbrush from the dresser. Her hair snapped and crackled with static as she brushed it. "Mr. Roper's really nice, isn't he, Mom?"

Mom paused halfway across the room. A slow smile crept up her cheek, making her lose some of her tired look. "He's a very nice man. God blessed us with a very helpful neighbor."

Bekah continued to run the brush through her hair as she ambled toward her own bed, where her nightgown waited, folded neatly beneath her pillow. "I think we should do something nice for him. To thank him."

Mom leaned against the doorjamb, her eyes twinkling. "Like what? Bake him some cookies?"

Bekah made a face. She plunked the hairbrush on the little table separating her bed from her sister's and spun to look at Mom. "He doesn't seem like the cookie type. No, I was thinking more like something he really needs." Bekah's pulse raced. She had noticed how badly Mr. Roper's house needed a good cleaning. With him working outside all day long, he didn't have time for housekeeping, and he obviously didn't have a wife to do it for him. But Bekah could do it. She'd been helping Mom with housecleaning for years already. And if she cleaned his house, she might uncover clues that would help her understand why he'd chosen to leave the Mennonite fellowship.

She licked her lips, gathering her courage. "I was thinking I could, maybe, offer to be his . . ." She searched for the word people used to describe someone who cleaned houses for a living. With a little jolt, she finished in a loud voice, "Maid!"

Adri murmured and stirred.

Mom flicked a glance at Adri, her lips sucked in. When Adri burrowed her face into her pillow and went on sleeping, Mom quirked one finger at Bekah. Bekah followed her into the hall. Mom closed the bedroom door and gave Bekah a funny look. "What do you mean, you want to be his maid?"

Bekah lifted her shoulders and held them there. "Well, not permanently." She did enough cleaning in her own house. She wouldn't want to do it for someone else forever. "But just to say thank you. For helping you with your Web site, and for being nice to Parker and Adri and me. Is it so bad to want to do something nice for him?" Bekah's conscience pricked. The deed was kind, but she wasn't being completely honest about her motivation. She hurried on. "He lives all alone. He could use some help with housework, don't you think?"

Mom folded her arms. "It's admirable that you want to return a favor, Bekah, but offering to clean his house? He could be insulted, as if you're saying his house isn't already clean."

Bekah giggled. "Well, it isn't."

An amused grin twitched at Mom's cheek for a moment, but then she set her lips in a firm line. "How Mr. Roper chooses to keep his own home isn't our concern." She sighed, raising one hand to stroke Bekah's loose hair. The gentle touch sent a tremor down Bekah's spine. "If you really want to do something nice for Mr. Roper, I suggest praying about it. God will whisper an idea that would be thoughtful without infringing on Mr. Roper's privacy."

Bekah hung her head. Infringing on Mr. Roper's privacy was the only way she'd ever find out what she wanted to know.

"I need to check on Parker. Head to bed. It's late, and tomorrow's Thursday, household lau—"

Bekah groaned. "Household laundry day."

Mom laughed. She kissed Bekah's forehead and gave her a gentle nudge toward the bedroom. "Sleep now. Pleasant dreams."

Bekah closed herself in the dark room and felt her way to the bed. Within moments, her eyes adjusted to the faint light filtering through the open window, and she dressed in her Mom-made cotton nightgown. Snug in her bed, she thought about Mom's customary good-night wish for pleasant dreams. She stared wide-eyed into the gray shadows. Maybe if Mom's wish proved true, she'd dream up a way to find out why Mr. Roper had decided to stop being Mennonite.

✣

Thursday morning, Amy sewed and the children washed sheets and towels with the wringer washer on the back porch. Usually they fussed at one another when all three were involved in a single chore, but to Amy's delight on this morning they worked cheerfully together, singing hymns and cooperating. Her machine sang, too, the third of the trio of wall hangings taking shape beneath her fingertips. The morning held a happy, relaxed feel—a settling-in that made Amy want to hum as she worked.

Adri's scale-running giggle carried through the back screen door, followed by Parker's guffaw and Bekah's distinct laughter. Amy found herself chuckling, too, even though she had no idea what was so amusing. After lunch, she'd do something special to treat them—maybe a quick run into town to purchase ice cream sandwiches at the grocer. All three children loved the dark chocolate cookies with vanilla ice cream in between, but Amy rarely purchased them. Their limited grocery budget didn't allow for extras. But she'd make the budget stretch this time. The children's good behavior deserved recognition.

At eleven thirty, Amy shut down the sewing machine and headed to the kitchen to prepare a simple lunch. During the winter she always kept a big pot of soup simmering or tucked a casserole in the oven, but during the summer months, they ate a cold lunch to avoid heating the room. Amy rummaged in the pantry and refrigerator, wincing at the nearly empty shelves. The groceries she'd brought from Arborville were nearly gone.

She removed a loaf of store-bought bread—she set baking

aside during the summer months, too—bologna, cheese, pickles, and what was left of the fruit. Perhaps when they went in for their ice cream sandwiches, they'd pick up more bananas, oranges, and apples, and some fresh vegetables. Once their garden started producing—when the men had come to till the acreage for planting soybeans a week ago, they'd taken the time to turn over the ground for a vegetable garden behind the house—she wouldn't have to purchase vegetables.

Her gaze lifted unconsciously, envisioning the rows of apple trees on Mr. Roper's property. What kind of apples did he grow? As much as the children loved fruit, she would probably be money ahead if she purchased several bushels and stored them in the cellar under the house. A smile lifted her lips as she thought about roaming the orchard, picking the fruit with the children, then using the apples for applesauce, pies, and fritters. Her stomach growled.

With a giggle, she set to work buttering the bread for sandwiches. Midway through the task, someone knocked on the front screen door. Wiping her hands on her apron, she trotted through the sewing room to the front room and peeked through the screen. Two women with white caps and arms full of bags stood on the porch. Amy broke into a smile when she recognized Ellie Hunsberger. Her smile faltered when she realized Margaret Gerber stood beside Ellie.

Margaret had taken over Amy's kitchen after their second worship service together, apparently believing her status as the eldest fellowship member granted her the freedom to be the boss even in someone else's home. Amy didn't want to dislike the older woman, but Margaret's forceful nature didn't invite camaraderie. Even so, Amy swung the door wide and warmly welcomed both women.

The pair stepped over the threshold, and Margaret charged directly for the kitchen. She called over her shoulder, "Amy, come tell us where to put these things away."

Amy stood stupidly and stared after the older woman.

Ellie nudged her with her elbow. "Better go," she whispered, her dark eyes twinkling, "or she'll put everything away where she thinks it needs to be, and you'll have to hunt for it."

Amy turned her startled gaze on Ellie. "What is she putting away?"

Ellie bounced the bags in her hands. "Groceries." She gave Amy another little nudge, and the two moved toward the kitchen. "Margaret isn't happy with the selection of groceries in the little store in town, so this morning she took Tamera and me to the Food Warehouse in Topeka. We stocked up on staples." She added her bags to those Margaret had set on the table. "Then we divided everything between the families. This is your share."

Amy began peeking into the bags. She gasped. Canned goods, bags of sugar and flour, boxed cereals, peanut butter and jelly . . . So much food!

She turned to Margaret and tried not to sound as worried as she felt. "This is very kind of you, but I don't know if I can afford to pay for it."

Margaret waved one hand, making a little *pfffft* sound with her pursed lips. "I bought everything in bulk. The cost is much less. Here's your portion." She handed Amy a little scrap of paper with an amount circled at the bottom. Amy stared at the amount, grateful it was much lower than she'd expected, considering the bulging bags. But the surprise of the unexpected bill held her in place.

Margaret began emptying bags. "We'll put everything on

the table. You put it away where you want it." Ellie joined Margaret in relieving the bags of their contents.

Amy jerked to life and bustled around, stacking items in the small pantry and cupboards. She rarely purchased more than a few days' groceries at once, but these supplies would carry her and the children for two weeks at least. Not only had Margaret purchased necessities, she'd included a few extras. Adrianna would be especially happy about the big bag of potato chips. Every time they visited the grocery store, the little girl begged for them, but Amy rarely bought them. They seemed an extravagance. But they'd be able to have chips with their sandwiches for several days, thanks to Margaret's shopping. Now that the shock was wearing off, she saw the blessing in Margaret's surprise visit.

Just as the women finished crumpling the empty bags and stashing them under the sink to use as trash bags, the children dashed in from the backyard, sweaty but smiling. Adrianna threw her arms around Amy's waist. "I'm hungry, Momma. Can we eat now?"

"You certainly may," Margaret said briskly. "Ellie and I will get out of the way so you can finish fixing the children's lunch." She caught Ellie by the elbow and propelled her toward the front room.

Amy trotted along behind them. "But I haven't paid you for my part of the groceries yet."

Margaret paused by the door, turning a gentle smile in Amy's direction. "You weren't expecting us, so you probably don't have money ready to give me. It can wait until Sunday when we come out again for worship. And if there are things your family doesn't care for, write them on a piece of paper. I'll not bring those things to you again."

Apparently Margaret intended to make this bulk grocery purchase a frequent event. Amy had always done her own shopping, and a part of her resisted giving that responsibility to someone else. She inwardly prayed for a gracious way to decline the woman's continued assistance. Words ready, she opened her mouth.

Margaret brushed Amy's arm with her fingers. "And you don't need to thank me. You're here alone with these children, without a husband's helping hands. Whatever we can do to lighten your load, we want to help. It's nothing more than I'd do for any of the members of my own fellowship. You're a part of us now, too, Amy."

Amy swallowed her protest as a lump of emotion formed at the woman's warm words of acceptance. Perhaps Margaret's brusqueness wasn't intended to be harsh. She bobbed her head in a quick nod. "I appreciate it. I'll have money ready for you on Sunday."

Margaret smiled, then turned to Ellie. "Come. We need to get out of Amy's way so she can feed her children." Ellie waved good-bye over her shoulder as Margaret steered her to the car waiting in the driveway.

Amy returned slowly to the kitchen. Parker and Adrianna sat at the table, waiting for their lunch, but Bekah stood beside the pantry with the door wide open. Her face reflected wonder. "Where'd all this food come from?"

Amy reached past her to bring out the big bag of potato chips. Adrianna squealed, clapping her hands. Amy popped the bag open and set it on the table. "The ladies from the Ohio fellowship went shopping in Topeka and shared with us."

Bekah trailed Amy to the counter. "Even without you asking them to?"

Amy returned to sandwich making. "That's right."

Bekah leaned against the counter, her eyes on the bread and bologna, her face still holding a look of amazement. "That's . . . that's really nice of them, Mom."

Bekah's positive response to the women's gesture erased Amy's misgivings. The bags of groceries became a blessing. She gave her daughter a smile. "And you know what else? Mrs. Gerber said they already think of us as being a part of their fellowship."

With an abrupt jerk of her head, Bekah's chin bounced up and she met Amy's gaze. Amy expected her daughter to smile or express pleasure at being accepted by the Ohio Mennonites. But instead, an odd look flitted across Bekah's face—panic coupled with guilt. Before Amy could address Bekah's reaction, the girl pushed away from the counter and clomped toward the refrigerator.

"I'll pour milk," she said.

No matter how many times during lunch Amy prodded Bekah to share what was troubling her, she insisted, "Nothing." Amy didn't believe her. Something had cast a storm cloud over Bekah's previously sunny mood. But what?

14

Tim propped open the solid wooden door with his foot and stood behind the smudged glass of the storm door, watching for Mrs. Knackstedt's car. The brown shag carpet still showed flattened paths where he'd pushed the vacuum last night. He'd washed most of the dirty dishes, and the ones he hadn't gotten to were stacked in a big orange Tupperware bowl and hidden in the belly of his stove. So the kitchen looked neater, too. He couldn't begin to explain why he'd felt the need to straighten up his house for the Knackstedts' next visit, but the little bit of cleaning gave him a feeling of satisfaction.

Promptly at eight fifteen, her car rolled up the lane, and children spilled out the moment it stopped. Both Adrianna and Parker ran for the porch, waving when they spotted him behind the glass door. Bekah and her mother came more slowly, the ribbons from their caps gently lifting in the evening breeze. He opened the storm door and greeted the two younger children with a hello.

Adrianna bounced past him, her little braids bobbing on her shoulders. She held a battered, duct-taped box aloft. "We brung Mousetrap. It was Momma's game when she was a little girl."

"It still has all the pieces," Parker said.

Tim swallowed a chuckle at Parker's solemn tone. "Don't know that I've ever played Mousetrap. Is it fun?"

"Yes!" Adrianna's blue eyes sparkled, and she nearly danced in place. "You gotta catch your 'ponents' mouses. Bekah doesn't like Mousetrap 'cause she says it reminds her of catchin' real mice under the kitchen sink." She grabbed Parker's wrist and tugged. "C'mon, Parker. Help me set it up." They plopped onto the carpet as if they'd visited Tim's house dozens of times.

Tim opened the door again, offering a silent invitation for Mrs. Knackstedt and Bekah to enter. Bekah carried an aluminum pie pan covered with plastic wrap. Beneath the wrap, Tim glimpsed what appeared to be cookies. He raised one eyebrow. After he'd done all that vacuuming, he wasn't keen on the kids scattering crumbs all over his floor.

Bekah held the pan to him. "These are for you." For a moment, uncertainty flitted across her face. "Um . . . do you like oatmeal raisin cookies?"

Truthfully, he'd never cared much for cooked raisins, but he wouldn't admit that to Bekah. Tim took the pan and smiled at the girl. "Home-baked goodies are a real treat around here. Thank you."

Bekah seemed to wilt with relief. She inched toward Parker and Adrianna, who'd begun to softly squabble with each other over how to set up the game board. "I'll help them with the game, Mom."

Tim and Mrs. Knackstedt were left standing just inside the door, staring at each other. He released a self-conscious chuckle. "Well, let's get busy, huh?" He pushed the wooden door closed with his hip to hold in the cool from his window air-conditioner. Moving to set the pan of cookies on his freshly wiped counter, he gestured to the desk where his computer sat. "I pulled your template up so you can add that contact form. But I think we need to get you set up with an email address first, so let me open a new window." He clicked the mouse, and a new screen appeared. He pulled out the chair and pointed to it. "Have a seat."

Mrs. Knackstedt slid gracefully into the chair, smoothing her skirt over her knees. Tim's nose filled with the essence of soap as he propped one hand on the desk and leaned close to her shoulder. Julia had always dabbed perfume behind her ears. She loved flowery fragrances, and Tim had loved tipping close and inhaling the aroma that clung to her clothes and hair. The scent of soap—clean, fresh, appealing—raised a longing inside of Tim. He swallowed hard and focused on the task at hand.

"I suggest you get a Gmail account." He kept his tone brisk and businesslike. "It doesn't cost a thing, they have a built-in spam filter so you won't have to wade through lots of junk to find your customers, and it's very easy to access."

She laughed lightly, turning her face slightly to peek at him. "Easy is best."

Up close, he was surprised by the length and fullness of her eyelashes. She didn't need makeup to enhance them. He straightened to put some distance between them. He'd been living alone too long if he was starting to see this Mennonite woman as attractive. "Yeah, I figured. So . . . have you decided what you want to use as an email address? Something that relates to your business is best."

Her brow puckered. "What is yours?"

A burst of giggles sounded from the living room. Tim flicked a glance in that direction, torn between heartache and a desire to laugh along. Of the things he missed, Charlie's carefree laughter was high on the list. He whisked his attention back to Mrs. Knackstedt. "Well, I have mine set up through my Web site for an additional fee, so mine is 'Tim at Roper Orchards dot com.' You'll use 'gmail dot com' for the latter part of your address. I suggest you use your business name for the first part."

"So . . . 'Threads of Remembrance at gmail dot com'?" She laughed softly, the tinkling sound of her laughter combining with the more raucous giggles coming from a few feet away in the living room. "That seems rather cumbersome."

"It's a little long, yes, but it's to the point." Tim shrugged. "Or you could use your name. Whichever you think would be the most relatable to potential customers."

She bit her lower lip, clearly contemplating the best option. While she thought, Tim looked again at the children. Adrianna and Parker were fully engrossed in their game, but Bekah was looking around the room as if memorizing details. She caught him looking at her. Without a word, she pushed to her feet and crossed the carpet to stand beside him. But she didn't say anything, so Tim returned his attention to Mrs. Knackstedt.

"Did you decide?"

Mrs. Knackstedt sighed. "Although it's lengthy, I believe I'll go with 'Threads of Remembrance' for the first part. You're right—it's the most relatable."

"All right, then. Let's get you set up." Tim gave directions for establishing an email address, then explained how she would access her account at the library to check for messages. She listened intently, as did Bekah. If the girl's regard were a flame, Tim felt certain he'd have a hole burned through the center of his head.

He sent a test message from his account, and when it popped into Mrs. Knackstedt's inbox, she clapped her palms together. "Oh my! It works!" Then she laughed, and Tim couldn't stop a bubble of laughter from climbing his throat. He remembered his early days in the world, learning about various technologies. She had no idea what she'd been missing, holed up in her Mennonite community. It felt good to open a small part of the world to her.

Tim drew in a satisfied breath. "It sure does. Okay, let's get that contact form up so customers can start contacting you."

Bekah stayed close, watching every move her mother made in completing the information on the Threads of Remembrance Web page. Several times she opened her mouth, as if to ask a question, but words never escaped. Tim wondered what went on behind her big brown eyes, but at the same time he was half glad he didn't know. Bekah seemed like a nice enough girl—a little forward, maybe, but not obnoxiously so. Still, he felt a little uneasy around her. As if she were examining him from the inside out.

As soon as Mrs. Knackstedt finished the form, she gave Tim a tired look. "All right. It's all set up. Now what?"

"Now we go live. Did you bring a credit card with you to start the service?"

"Credit card?" Dismay flooded her face. "I don't have one."

Once again, Tim felt like an imbecile. Of course she

wouldn't have a credit card. But if she had a debit card connected to her bank account, they could use that. "All right, then. Your debit card?"

Pink stained her cheeks, matching the dusky flowers on her caped dress. "I use checks. I haven't requested a debit card."

He wished he'd thought about mentioning the need for a credit or debit card earlier. He took so many things for granted after his years away from his simple upbringing. Tim scratched his jaw. "Well, Mrs. Knackstedt, you're going to need one or the other. There'll be a monthly fee for the Web site, and the Web site company requires electronic payment."

Her face fell. "Oh. So all this work we've done . . . all the time I've taken from you . . . is for nothing."

Her defeat pierced him. Especially since she seemed more concerned about what it had cost him in time rather than her own potential loss. Without a moment's thought, he reached into his hip pocket and removed his billfold. Flipping it open, he extracted his Visa card. "I tell you what, we can use this to get things started, and—"

She threw both hands upward as if under arrest, her eyes wide. "I can't allow you to pay for my Web page."

Tim frowned. "Not indefinitely—just to get it started. You can go to the bank tomorrow and request a debit card. When you have it in hand, come over and we'll switch the payments to your account instead."

She shook her head. "I just can't."

Bekah leaned close to her mother and whispered, "Mom . . ."

"Not now, Bekah," Mrs. Knackstedt said. She looked at Tim. "I appreciate all you've done, but using your credit card . . ." She pursed her lips for a moment. " 'The borrower is servant to the lender.' "

It took Tim a moment to realize she'd quoted from Proverbs. He couldn't recall the chapter and verse, but he'd heard the warning many times in his childhood. Did she see him as some kind of Old World feudal lord, trying to gain control of her? Resting his weight on one hip, he continued to hold the Visa out between two fingers. "I think you misinterpret my intentions." With effort, he maintained an even tone. "Around here, neighbors look out for each other. All I'm trying to do is help you get that Web page running so people looking for your kind of service can find you. I thought that's what you wanted."

She stared at the silver card caught in his fingers. "It is. But I can't be a party to creating indebtedness for you."

Suddenly he understood her hesitation. She was opposed to having *him* incur a debt. A voice—deep, harsh, critical—from his past slammed through his brain: *"Only a fool relies on credit. You might as well sell your soul."* Heat filled his face. He jammed the card back into its slot in his billfold.

"Please, it isn't that I don't appreciate—"

"I understand." He tried not to be curt, but he heard his own voice and realized he'd failed. Drawing in a deep breath, he counted to ten and brought his irritation under control. It wasn't her fault. She'd probably been given the same reprimands from her father at some point in time. He withdrew a different card. His debit card. "Would you like to use this one instead? It will come directly from my checking account, and you can give me cash to pay me back."

Bekah poked her mother's shoulder. "Mom?"

Mrs. Knackstedt turned to her daughter. "Bekah, Mr. Roper and I are talking."

"I know, but I have an idea."

The woman sighed. "What is it?"

Bekah's brown-eyed gaze flicked to Tim and then back to her mother. She clasped her hands in a prayerful position. "What if you let Mr. Roper pay to get your Web site started, and I'll pay him back?"

"Pay him back . . . how?"

The girl lifted a hopeful face in Tim's direction. "By doing housekeeping for him."

Mrs. Knackstedt's face flooded with color. She turned a flustered look on Tim. "I am so sorry. I'm sure Bekah didn't intend to infer that—"

An amused snort escaped his nose before Tim could control it. Then he doubled over, laughing harder than he could remember laughing in years. Here he'd washed up some dishes, hidden more of them away, and even tried to turn his carpet inside out with the zealous use of a vacuum, and the girl saw through it all. Yes, as he'd suspected, she didn't miss a thing. He waved one hand at the mortified mother, struggling to end his noisy bout of amusement.

"Don't apologize." His voice trembled with suppressed laughter. He gave a tug on one of Bekah's trailing ribbons, the way he used to do to tease his sisters. "Bekah knows need when she sees it. But it only costs twelve dollars to get that Web page going." He grinned at the girl. "Just how much cleaning could I get for twelve dollars?"

Bekah's face lit. "I would dust, and vacuum, and mop floors, and clean your kitchen and bathroom, and wash your sheets and towels, and—"

"And that would be way too much for one little girl." Tim softened his protest with another smile. Even though she tended to push her way in, he admired her desire to help her mom. She wasn't a bad kid at all. "Worth lots more than twelve dollars."

Bekah hung her head for a moment, then jerked her gaze to his again. "Would it be worth, maybe, a bushel of apples in the fall? We could barter—housecleaning for fruit!"

Mrs. Knackstedt shook her head, her expression flabbergasted. "Honestly, Bekah, I do not know what has gotten into you." She gave Tim another apologetic look. Rising, she took hold of Bekah's elbow. "Go help your brother and sister put their game back in the box. Then we're going to get out of Mr. Roper's way." She waited until Bekah scuffed off and then turned to Tim again. "I sincerely appreciate all you've done. But now that I know what to do to make the Web site go . . . go live, I'll wait until I have my own debit card to share with the Web site company. It won't mean much more of a delay. I can wait long enough to take care of the financial side of things myself. I'm very sorry I placed you in such an awkward position. I should have realized I'd need some way to pay for this page."

Tim chuckled again, still amused by Bekah's scheming. "This is all new. It takes time to get familiar with everything that's required."

An appreciative smile graced her face. "Thank you for understanding. And thank you for being so kind to Bekah." She frowned slightly, her gaze shifting to the children. "I don't know what's gotten into her lately. She's never been so blatantly forceful. I fear she's—" She stopped midsentence. Tim waited for her to continue, but she remained silent.

He cleared his throat. "You know, Bekah's suggestion wasn't all bad."

The woman zinged her attention back to Tim.

"About bartering, I mean." He held out his hands to indicate his surroundings. "I don't have time to keep up with cleaning like I should—especially not in the summer and fall. But I don't really have money to pay for a steady housekeeper. If Bekah's willing to come over here, say, once or twice a week during the summer and then once, maybe, on Saturdays after school starts, and give the place a going-over, we could work out a trade for apples in the fall."

"Really?" came a voice from behind him. Bekah dashed across the floor and stopped beside her mother, her hands clasped beneath her chin. "Can I do it, Mom? Huh? Please?"

Tim watched indecision play across Mrs. Knackstedt's face. He supposed having a young girl in his house—he being a single man and all—might give cause for concern. He should've thought of that before making the suggestion. He amended his request, his heart thudding as he considered what changes might come into his life if she agreed. "Parker could work, too. I bet he could cart off broken limbs or do some grass cutting."

He angled his head and cocked one hip, assuming a nonchalance he really didn't feel. "You've got a long summer ahead with three kids underfoot and a business to get off the ground. Who knows—you might get more done with them away from the house now and then. So whaddaya say, Mrs. Knackstedt? Can we barter?"

15

Early Friday morning, just as the sun peeked over the horizon and chased the pink from the sky, Tim poured a bowl of cereal, sat at the kitchen bar, and ate. In silence. His gaze roved to the living room and the smashed spot on the carpet where Adrianna, Parker, and Bekah had sat to play their game. Their voices, their laughter had brought life into the house again. No doubt that was what had compelled him to make his ridiculous agreement with Mrs. Knackstedt. He chomped down on a spoonful of Shredded Wheat, the crunch loud in his ears. Just how much help would two children be? He'd probably end up babysitting them and paying them for the privilege.

He tried to summon up indignation, but none rose. Using his spoon, he submerged a ragged square of cereal and watched it bob back to the surface of the milk. Truth was, deep down, he looked forward to the company. He just hoped the kids' presence wouldn't prove to be more hindrance than help. He had more than enough work without going behind and cleaning up mistakes. Even so, having company, somebody to talk to while he worked—that'd be nice.

And that Parker . . . A grin tugged at Tim's cheek. No doubt about it, Tim liked Parker. The boy's open heart and ever-seeking expression reminded Tim of Charlie. Not the bad memories—the painful loss—but the good ones: the hugs, the smiles, the innocence. Tim scooped the last two bites of cereal, then lifted the bowl two-handed and drank the milk. Lowering the empty bowl, he gave himself a stern warning about not transferring his feelings for his dead son to this Mennonite boy. It wouldn't be healthy for him or for Parker. But time with Parker, teaching him, watching him view the world through ingenuous eyes might ease some of the sting of missing Charlie.

A person could hope, anyway.

Tim dropped the cereal bowl and spoon in the sink with his coffee cup, then snatched his billed cap from the peg by the front door. The beehives were due to arrive midmorning—he needed to stay within shouting distance of the house until the county extension officer showed up with the colorful boxes of buzzing insects. But he had plenty of work in the barn to keep him busy until then. He strode out into the sunbathed morning.

✴

"But I wanna go to Mr. Roper's house, too!"

Bekah resisted pushing her fingers into her ears to block her little sister's whiny voice, which rose higher with every word. But then Adri would just holler louder. So she shrugged and assumed a reasonable tone. "I'm going to be working, not playing over there. It won't be any fun for you at all."

Adri's lower lip poked out. "I can work, too."

Bekah snorted. Adri might think she worked when it came time for household chores, but Bekah knew better. Somebody usually had to redo whatever she did. Five-year-olds could be such an annoyance. Bekah lifted her mesh cap and slipped it over her heavy bun, tucking stray wisps of hair beneath the cap's brim. Adri stood beside the dresser, watching, her face set in a fierce scowl. The little girl would beg until she got her way if Bekah didn't come up with a good argument.

Propping her hands on her knees, she looked directly into Adri's snapping eyes. "With Parker and me away, Mom'll be here all alone. What if she needs a cup of water or wants somebody to run out to the mailbox and get the letters? Who'll do that if all three of us are gone?"

Adri nibbled her lower lip, her brow puckered with indecision. Bekah held her breath. Would her ploy work? Suddenly Adri stomped her foot and pointed at Bekah. "You're tricking me! Momma won't let me walk to the mailbox all by myself. You're mean, Bekah!" She raced out of the room. Her bare feet pounded on the stairs, and her voice drifted back to Bekah's ears. "Momma! Bekah's being mean!"

Bekah sighed and finished securing her cap. She'd learned long ago she needed at least four pins if she was going to be out in the wind. She gave the cap a tug, then, satisfied it would hold, sank down onto the edge of the bed and wriggled her tennis shoes over her bare feet. Mom didn't like her going sockless, but as soon as she and Parker got over to Mr. Roper's she intended to take her shoes off and go barefooted. It was too hot to keep her feet locked up in the sneakers. She whisked a quick look out the window. Maybe if the sky would rain, things would cool down a bit. But all through May and the start of June, the sky had remained the same—cloudless. Just like today. As Daddy used to say, it'd be another scorcher.

With her shoes in place, she bounced up and headed for the door. Before she could leave the room, though, Mom stepped into the doorway. Bekah could tell from the look on Mom's face she was going to get a lecture. She braced herself, crossing her arms over her chest.

"Honey, would you mind letting Adrianna go with you this one time?" Mom held up her hand, staving off Bekah's argument. She lowered her voice. "You and I both know she'll quickly grow bored if all you're doing is housecleaning. After today, she'll probably never ask again. But if you leave her here, she'll pester you each time you go to Mr. Roper's."

Bekah blew out a breath. As much as she hated to admit it, Mom was probably right. She hated caving in to Adri— it seemed like her little sister always got her way—but she could put up with her one time if it meant never having to argue with her about going to Mr. Roper's again. "All right. I'll take her."

Mom smiled, her shoulders slumping in relief. "Thank you." Her gaze roved over Bekah's dress, and she nodded in approval. "Good. You chose a work dress rather than one of your nicer ones. Be sure to grab an apron or two from the clean ones in the pantry."

Bekah had already planned to take aprons, cleaning rags, a bucket, and sponges just in case Mr. Roper didn't have cleaning supplies available for her use, but she stayed silent and let Mom do her mom-thing and give directions.

"Remember, 'And whatsoever ye do in word or deed, do all in the name of the Lord Jesus—' "

Bekah knew Colossians 3:17 by heart, so she finished

reciting it with her mother. "—'giving thanks to God and the Father by him.'" She nodded rapidly, her ribbons tickling her cheeks. "I know, Mom."

Mom sighed, her expression turning tender. "It's hard to imagine you being grown up enough to take on your first job. It seems like just yesterday you were Adrianna's age. . . ."

Bekah swallowed. Sometimes she wished she could go backward in time—be little again and have a daddy who picked her up and bounced her in the air or held her on his lap when she was scared. But those days were so long ago, even the memories were fuzzy.

Mom went on. "But you're a good worker, Bekah, and I know you'll do your very best for Mr. Roper so God might be glorified through your efforts."

Guilt stung the fringes of Bekah's heart. If Mom knew why Bekah wanted to hang around Mr. Roper's house, she'd be so disappointed. Before Mom could read the guilt in Bekah's eyes, she lurched forward and captured her mother in a hug. "I'll do my best. I promise."

Mom squeezed her tight and then set her aside. "I trust you. Now hurry down and eat your breakfast. Parker has already finished his toast and is raring to go."

Bekah rushed through her breakfast, then led her brother and sister to the garage to retrieve their bicycles. She considered taking Mom's so she could put Adri in the child seat, but given the short distance to Mr. Roper's, she decided to let Adri ride her own little bike. The ride might tire her enough that she'd sit quietly and not be a pest while Bekah cleaned.

Wedging the bucket full of supplies into the basket attached to her handlebars, she gave Parker and Adri a stern look. "All right, now. Stay behind me." She hopped on the bike and took off, trusting them to do as she said. Ten minutes after climbing onto their bikes—they had to go slow for Adri's sake—they pulled into Mr. Roper's long lane. "Park by the barn," Bekah called over her shoulder, and both Parker and Adri followed her directions.

Adri let her bike drop onto its side in the dirt, but Parker painstakingly pushed down the kickstand with his hand, balanced his bicycle, then brushed his palms together. He smiled so big his whole face lit up. "Let's go knock on the door and tell Mr. Roper we're here." He and Adri started for the house at a gallop, but a voice carried from the barn—"Hey! Kids! In here!" Adri spun with hardly a pause, but Parker had to stop himself, turn, and then break into his clumsy run again.

Adri raced past Bekah, but Bekah waited for Parker, and they entered the barn together. It was a lot darker inside the barn than out in the sunshine, and it took a minute or two before she spotted Mr. Roper. Then she waved, swinging her bucket. "Hi. We're here to work."

He wiped his hands on a grimy rag and tossed it aside. His gaze dropped to Adri, who stood grinning up at him with her hands locked behind her back and her round tummy poking out. "Just what kind of work do you do, madam?"

Adri giggled. "I'm not madam. I'm Adri."

Mr. Roper snickered, then turned to Bekah. He pointed to her bucket. "I see you brought some supplies. That's good. You'll find all kinds of cleaning solutions under the sink in the kitchen. Help yourself. See how much you can get done, starting in the kitchen, then the bathroom, and then whatever you think needs doing—dusting and so forth—in the living room." His brows pinched, and his tone changed slightly, losing its lightheartedness as he finished. "But don't worry about the bedrooms. I've got those doors closed so you know you don't need to go in there."

Bekah tipped her head. "You don't want me washing bed sheets or anything?"

He chuckled, but Bekah thought it sounded forced. "I figure you'll have plenty else to do in the rest of the house. So no, don't worry about sheets. Just the main part of the house is fine." He swung his smile on Parker. "And how about you? Ready to work?"

Parker bobbed his head. "Yes, sir!"

Mr. Roper laughed—a more genuine laugh. "All right, then. Get hold of that wheelbarrow over there and we'll get busy." He flapped his hands at Bekah and Adri. "Well, go on, now—we men don't need supervision."

With a giggle, Adri grabbed Bekah's hand and dragged her toward the house. Bekah felt a little uncomfortable opening Mr. Roper's door and going in without him, but once inside she turned her attention to working. She kicked off her tennis shoes and left them by the front door. "Sit on the couch and be good," she told Adri, then she set to work in the kitchen first, as Mr. Roper had instructed. She started by washing the few dishes in the sink and putting them away. Then she scrubbed all the countertops, organizing the containers of food stores and small appliances scattered across the tan counter.

Satisfied the top half of the kitchen was clean, she turned her attention to the floor. "Blech! I wonder how long it's been since someone scrubbed this linoleum?" She hadn't intended to speak aloud, but Adri dashed into the kitchen at her sister's voice. Bekah pointed to the tall stools on the other side of the counter. "Climb up there and stay out of my way. I gotta find a broom and sweep before I can start scrubbing." She'd make good use of her bucket and sponge.

Bekah looked around for a pantry—Mom kept her broom and dustpan in the pantry at home. But the funny folding door beside the fridge hid a water heater and a box of trash bags, no broom. Bekah closed the door again and moved to the main room. A short hallway on the left of the living room invited her entrance. She stepped into the paneled hall and counted four doors—two on each side. The closest one to the living room, on the right-hand side of the hall, stood open, revealing the bathroom. But the other doors were all closed. Were they all bedrooms, or was one of them a closet?

For a moment indecision niggled. Mr. Roper had told her not to open any doors. But how else would she find a broom? "I won't go *into* the rooms," she muttered to herself. "I'll just open and peek so I can find a broom." She moved to the single door closest to the bathroom and inched it open. Although the curtains were drawn, shrouding the room in shadows, Bekah glimpsed a twin-sized bed bearing a spread spattered all over with cars and trucks in primary colors. A shelf cluttered with toys stood next to the bed. A little boy's bedroom.

Curiosity wiggled through Bekah's middle. Mr. Roper had a son?

"Bekah?"

Bekah jolted and slammed the door closed, whirling to face Adri. "Don't scare me like that!"

"But I found a broom." Adri thrust a straw-bristled broom at Bekah. "It was stuck beside the 'frigerator."

Bekah snatched the broom from her sister and gave Adri a little push toward the living room. "Go sit down, like I said.

And no more snooping!" Although she aimed the warning at Adri, she knew she needed it even more than her sister did.

She swept the floor, making sure to chase every crumb and bit of fuzz from beneath the edges of the cabinets. The accumulation shocked her. Mr. Roper must have forgotten what a broom was for. Then she filled her bucket with warm, soapy water and set to work with the sponge. Her knees ached by the time she was finished, but the old linoleum looked much better. She pushed to her feet and pointed at Adri. "You stay put. I'm gonna clean the bathroom."

Adri whined, "Can't I get down?"

"No." Bekah lifted the bucket with both hands. "You'll just get in my way." She waddled to the bathroom, careful not to splash the mucky water over the bucket's rim. After emptying the bucket in the bathtub, she gave the bathroom a thorough cleaning from top to bottom. When every surface sparkled, she rinsed her bucket and sponge and returned to the kitchen to see if the floor had dried. To her surprise, she'd spent an hour and a half in the bathroom. The clock on the stove showed eleven o'clock—the morning was almost gone. And Adri was curled on the sofa, fast asleep.

Bekah had intended to dust and vacuum, but she got another idea. Judging by the dry bread crumbs all over the kitchen floor, Mr. Roper ate a lot of sandwiches. Maybe she could make up a big casserole. Wouldn't he appreciate a hot lunch after working all morning? He had a microwave oven, so he could reheat portions and eat for several meals. Opening and closing doors carefully to avoid disturbing her sleeping sister, she explored cabinets and discovered a box of macaroni noodles, two small cans of tuna, canned peas, and a half-filled bag of rippled potato chips. A peek in the fridge revealed milk and butter, and she'd already found flour in a tall plastic canister. Mr. Roper had everything she needed to make a tuna-noodle casserole.

Humming to herself, Bekah filled a large pot with water and set it on the stove to heat. She preset the oven to three hundred fifty degrees, just as Mom had taught her, then opened all the cans, drained the contents, and set them aside. She melted butter in a skillet and stirred in some flour for thickening the sauce. The butter-flour mixture turned frothy. It was ready for the milk.

She retrieved the carton, then glanced at the big kettle of water. Steam rose, and with it an odd odor. Bekah carefully lifted the pan and checked the burner—had she neglected to clean off some food particles? But nothing seemed amiss. She set the pan back down and looked around the room, puzzled. The smell was getting stronger by the minute.

A wisp of gray crept from the edge of the oven door. Her heart pounding in alarm, Bekah cracked the door open. Smoke billowed, choking her. Fire! She slammed the door closed and raced around the counter. Grabbing Adri by the hand, she yanked the drowsing little girl from the sofa. "Wake up! We've gotta get out of here! Fire!"

Adri started to cry as Bekah dragged her out of the house. Bekah ran into the yard on her bare feet, pulling a wailing Adri beside her. She bellowed, "Mr. Roper! Mr. Roper! I set your house on fire!"

16

Tim stepped back from the row of wooden boxes he'd carefully stacked two high, three across. Bands of pastel colors—each box different—gave the illusion of a modern art sculpture. A few bees flitted in and out of the openings, and a steady low-toned hum let him know many more were inside. Not keen on hot temperatures, they'd wait until tomorrow morning when it was cooler to be active, but he smiled at the few explorers zigzagging near the safety of the hives.

He glanced down the line of trees, pleased that Parker had stayed right where Tim had directed. The last thing he wanted was for the boy to be stung. Bees wouldn't attack without provocation, but most people inadvertently provoked them by slapping at them—an honest reaction, but dangerous. He'd only been stung once in all his years at the orchard, and he'd deserved it for trying to smack loose an insect perched on his ear. Over the years, Tim had grown accustomed to bees landing on his hair or his arms, and he'd learned to just go about his business—it would fly off when it realized he wasn't a tasty blossom.

With an unhurried stride to avoid alarming the bees, he turned and walked toward Parker. The boy craned his neck, peering past Tim to the boxes. Tim reached his side, and Parker whispered, "Will they be okay now?"

Parker's concern for all creatures, great and small, had become clear to Tim over their morning together. Although startled by a spider crawling across the workbench in the barn, Parker had made no attempt to squash the creature. And he'd rescued two roly-poly bugs from frying in the sun by gently flicking them into the shady spot beneath a bush.

Tim said, "They'll be fine. They'll take an afternoon nap, get all settled in, and be ready to start visiting flowers tomorrow."

Parker hunched his shoulders and chortled. "Visiting flowers . . . That's funny."

Tim slung his arm across Parker's shoulders and aimed him for the waiting golf cart at the end of the row of Jonagold trees. While they walked, he explained the purpose of pollination. Parker listened, attentive to Tim's every word, then asked several questions that Tim answered patiently. After only a short time with the boy, Tim's fondness for him had grown tenfold. He was going to enjoy having Parker around, even if it did mean long explanations and showing him something three or four times before he grasped what to do. He found pleasure in passing on what he knew to an eager learner.

A few twists of the ignition key brought the old cart to life, and Parker braced his hands on the seat while they bounced their way along the wide pathway between the trees. Tim turned the wheel, angling the cart toward the barn. On the final turn, the yard and house came into view. Tim frowned. What were Bekah and Adri doing in the middle of the yard, hugging each other? They seemed to be staring at the house, and Tim followed their line of vision. Fingers of smoke escaped from the cracks around his front door. Fear jolted his innards.

"Hold tight, Parker!" He jammed his foot onto the gas pedal, forcing the cart to its fastest speed. He screeched to a stop a safe distance from the house, nearly sending the cart on its nose. The engine died. Tim yanked the key from the ignition and pointed at Parker. "Stay in the cart." Then he ran to the girls. "Bekah, what happened?"

Bekah clung to Adrianna, her face streaked with tears. "I . . . I don't know. I was going to f-fix you some lunch, bake a tuna casserole, but then the kitchen got a-all smoky, and—"

Tim groaned. He didn't need further explanation. "You kids stay right here." He leaped onto the rickety porch and threw open the door. A fog of whitish-gray smoke, acrid-smelling and thick, greeted him. He covered his mouth and nose with one arm as best he could and plunged forward, squinting through the murky cloud. Unable to see, he walked smack into the bar and bounced backward a few stumbling steps. With his free arm extended, he felt his way around the counter.

When he reached the stove, he waved his hand wildly, clearing a small patch in front of his face. A pot, boiled dry, sat on a red-hot burner. By squinting and continuing to wave, he managed to see well enough to locate the control knobs. He flicked both the burner and the oven dials to OFF and then yanked open the oven door. Fresh smoke, the strongest smelling yet, billowed into his face.

Coughing, Tim backed away. His eyes burning, he flung the kitchen window open and then stumbled through the main room, opening all the windows. Finally he made his way outside again. In the yard, he leaned forward, propped his hands on his knees, and breathed deeply of the hot-but-clean air.

The children dashed to him. Adrianna's wails nearly covered Bekah's blubbering prattle. "I'm so sorry, Mr. Roper. I didn't mean to set your house on fire. Honest! I don't know how it happened. I'm sorry! I'm so sorry!"

Parker started to cry, too, apparently in sympathy to his sisters' distress.

Tim's throat burned. A foul odor sat on his tongue. He really wanted to turn on the spigot and take a long drink of cool water, but the kids came first. He coughed again to clear his throat, then straightened and put his hand on Bekah's shoulder. "It's okay. You didn't start a fire. There's no fire."

"But . . . but . . ." Bekah blinked rapidly, tears swimming in her eyes. "All that smoke . . ."

"All that smoke is from plastic dishes melting in the hot oven."

The girl stared at him, her mouth agape. "I . . . I didn't put any plastic dishes in the oven."

Tim grimaced. "I know. I did." Parker quieted, but Adrianna continued to wail. Tim scooped her up, giving her little heaving back several comforting pats. "Hey there, everything's all right. You can dry up now."

Adrianna sniffled, resting her head on Tim's shoulder and holding tight to his neck. Tim swallowed hard. It'd been a long time since he'd comforted a frightened little one. The child's weight in his arms felt welcome, despite the scare they'd all been given. Clearing his throat again—the vile taste lingered—he looked at Bekah. "I stuck a bunch of dirty dishes in the oven last night before you and your mom came over so they wouldn't be sitting in the sink. I forgot about them. So don't blame yourself. I shouldn't have left them there."

Bekah hung her head and peeked at him through a heavy fringe of lashes. Even though her eyes were brown rather than blue, she looked a lot like her mom. She was a pretty girl. "I should've looked inside the oven before I turned it on."

Tim wondered what had given her the idea to fix lunch, but he decided he'd wait for another time to address the subject. His questions might be perceived as finding fault, and the girl already looked plenty guilt-ridden.

He bounced Adrianna, loosening her hold on his neck. "You okay now?"

The little girl rubbed her fist under her nose and nodded, her lower lip poking out. "I was really a-scared. I thought your house was gonna burn all up."

Tim set her down and looked at the house. A few dismal wisps of pale gray smoke still sneaked out from the open windows, but it appeared the worst of it was over. He'd probably be living with the smell for a while, but maybe the closed bedroom doors had kept the smoke from permeating his clothes and bedding. He wanted to kick himself. How could he have been so stupid?

Heaving a sigh, Tim faced Bekah. "You kids better get on home for your lunch. And don't worry about coming back afterward. The house'll take a while to air out, so you won't be doing any more cleaning today."

Fresh tears glittered in Bekah's eyes. "I really am sorry. D-do you want me to come back . . . tomorrow . . . and finish?"

Tim understood her unspoken question—did he trust her

in his house after the morning's fiasco? Sadness weighed as heavily on his chest as the smoke that had filled his lungs. How many times had he and Julia read together on the couch after putting Charlie to bed, the old Tupperware bowl full of popcorn between them? The bowl was probably one big melted lump on the bottom of his oven now. The loss saddened him. But he couldn't blame Bekah for it.

"Sure. If it's okay with your mom, you come on back tomorrow morning. The smell should be gone by then."

"My shoes are still in there," Bekah said, cringing.

Tim scratched his head. He hated to go back in right away, considering how badly his throat burned, but he couldn't send the girl home on a bicycle with bare feet. "Where'd you leave them?"

"By the front door."

"I'll get 'em." Tim held his breath and retrieved Bekah's shoes. She sat on the grass and pulled them over her feet, then stood. Her forlorn expression tore at Tim's heart. He gave her shoulder a quick pat. "Don't you worry. That smoke'll clear, and it'll be fine. Head on home now."

Heads low, the children scuffed their way to the bicycles. Minutes later, they disappeared behind the trees at the end of the lane. Tim stood for long minutes staring at the house, gathering his courage to go inside and take a look inside his oven. It was just a bowl. Just a stupid bowl. It shouldn't matter so much.

But it did.

※

On Sunday morning, Amy tucked the Mexicali corn-bread casserole into the oven, then scurried to the counter to clean the dishes. While she rinsed the items, she called over her shoulder, "Bekah? Parker? Adrianna? You need to hurry and get dressed. Mr. Hunsberger will be here soon with the chairs and will need our help setting them up."

Scuffling noises from overhead let her know the children were bustling around. She hoped Bekah had tossed aside her sour mood with her nightgown. Amy sighed, squirting dish soap into the sink. She'd hated to tell her daughter she couldn't return to Mr. Roper's on Saturday, but they had their own chores to see to in readiness for the worship time. Bekah had argued, insisting she needed to complete the cleaning, but Amy remained firm. Mr. Roper could wait until Monday.

Amy didn't say so, but she suspected their neighbor didn't mind a brief break from the children's presence, considering the mess they'd inadvertently made of his house. She'd taken over a bowl of cold chicken-macaroni salad Friday evening by way of apology and to let him know she needed the children on Saturday. The sharp tang of burnt plastic permeated his entire front room. He'd been kind about it, but the smell surely gave him a headache. Not to mention the destruction of several of his dishes and his oven's interior.

Footsteps clattered on the stairs, and Bekah wheeled around the corner. With her hair neatly tucked under a cap and wearing one of her nicest dresses and brown oxfords, she looked ready for worship. Except for her expression.

Amy quirked one eyebrow. "Did you get up on the wrong side of bed?" If she'd hoped the teasing comment might raise a smile, she was disappointed. Bekah picked up a dishtowel and began drying the clean bowls and spoons without a word. Although she preferred not to start the Lord's Day with a reprimand, Amy decided she couldn't ignore Bekah's pout. "I'll want you to lose your scowl before the others get here. Remember Ecclesiastes 7:9. 'Be not hasty in thy spirit to be angry: for anger resteth in the bosom of fools.' "

Bekah shut the cabinet door with more force than necessary. "I'm not angry."

"Your actions and attitude say otherwise."

Bekah sucked in a long breath, held it for several seconds, then let it out slowly. When she faced Amy again, some of the fire had faded from her eyes. "I'm more disappointed than anything. I told Mr. Roper I'd do a job for him, and I didn't get to do it because I . . . I messed up." Tears winked in her eyes, but she blinked and they disappeared. "I want him to think I'm responsible—like he can count on me."

Amy's irritation with her daughter melted. She tucked Bekah into an embrace. "Honey, I'm sure Mr. Roper understands you didn't deliberately melt those items in his oven. It was an accident."

"But I stunk up his whole house." With her face pressed to Amy's shoulder, her voice came out muffled.

Despite herself, Amy chuckled. "In a few days, he'll find humor in the situation and all will be well."

Bekah pulled loose. "Are you sure?"

Amy cupped Bekah's cheek. "I'm sure." Mr. Roper had been very forgiving when Amy apologized, claiming responsibility for the mess and asking about the children's welfare. Her heart warmed toward their neighbor. He really was a very kind man. "He also understood that you and Parker have responsibilities here at home, and he was perfectly willing to put off the rest of the cleaning until after Sunday."

Bekah tipped her head, crunching one ribbon against her

shoulder. "Mom, has Mr. Roper ever talked about having a child? A boy?"

Amy moved to the table and wiped the top with her damp dishrag. "No. Why?"

"There's a bedroom in his house all set up for a little boy. But he's always by himself. What do you think happened?"

Amy gave Bekah a stern look. "I don't know, but you aren't to ask. It isn't polite to pry into other people's business."

"I know." Bekah curled her hands over the back of a chair, her expression dreamy. "Maybe his boy is all grown up already and moved away, or maybe Mr. Roper and his wife got a divorce and she took the boy away."

Amy paused, frowning. "Let's not talk that way. We don't want to start rumors."

"But that man in town said Mr. Roper used to be a Mennonite. Maybe his wife wanted to stay Mennonite, and he didn't, so she—"

"Bekah!" Amy waited until her daughter met her gaze. "No more. I don't want you speculating about what you saw. If you are going to carry tales away from Mr. Roper's house, you won't be allowed to go there anymore. For any reason. Do you understand?"

Bekah lowered her gaze, scuffing her toe against the faded tile floor. "I understand. It's just . . . I like him. And it seems sad that he's there all alone if he really does have a son somewhere." Bekah's head bounced up, her eyes wide with alarm. "You don't think his son *died*, do you? Maybe he died in an accident, like Dad did."

Pain stabbed Amy's heart. They so rarely spoke of Gabe, having Bekah use the term *Dad* brought an immediate rush of memories . . . and questions. Had Gabe truly died in an accident, or had it been intentional? How she hated the dark cloud of uncertainty that surrounded Gabe's death. They'd come here to escape the cloud, but now it rolled in again.

Amy had no desire to revisit those long-ago days of searing pain. "Run up and see what's keeping Parker and Adrianna. Mr. Hunsberger will need all of our hands to bring in the chairs."

Without another word, Bekah headed up the stairs. Amy stood for a long while, thinking about what Bekah had said. Deliberately setting aside thoughts of Gabe, she focused on the comments about a little boy's bedroom, but no little boy. She shifted her head, her gaze drifting to the east. She envisioned Mr. Roper's house and the lone occupant. Questions clouded her mind—questions she had no business pondering, but she found herself unable to dismiss them. She'd wondered why the man had abandoned his faith. Now she wondered what else he might have abandoned over the years.

17

As we close in prayer today, let's take time to unite our hearts and petition our Lord for rain." Mr. Gerber's somber tone as he addressed the small group of worshipers crowded in Amy's living room brought an answering concerned murmur.

Amy glanced out the open window, her head turning in synchronization with several others. Hot wind, devoid of moisture, coursed through the aluminum screen. Dust rolled across the dry landscape, masking the tiny shoots of green poking through the soil where the men had planted soybeans. Without a permanent irrigation system in place, they relied on rain to nourish the little plants. How long could they wait for rain before the shoots withered and died?

"Shall we bow our heads?" In unison, all members from oldest to youngest followed Mr. Gerber's instruction. The man prayed aloud—simply but with deep feeling. While listening to his rumbling voice, Amy added her silent prayer to his for God to send raindrops to their crop. She also asked

Him to send mercy drops on each person gathered there as well as their neighbors. With the thought of neighbors, Mr. Roper's face immediately appeared behind her closed eyelids.

Bekah's comments about the little boy's room in Mr. Roper's house haunted Amy. If he'd lost a son, he knew heartache. If he'd suffered a broken marriage, he knew heartache. If he'd cast aside his faith, he knew heartache. No matter what had left him living in his house alone, shut away from family and fellowship, he needed prayer. *"Love thy neighbour as thyself,"* her Bible admonished. So she prayed earnestly for Mr. Roper's peace and a rekindling of faith within his soul.

"Amen," Mr. Gerber intoned, and everyone rose to sing a closing hymn together. The words from the old familiar hymn, "Great Is Thy Faithfulness," wrapped around Amy's heart and offered a mantle of peace she desperately needed.

After everyone had eaten their fill of the food the members carried in, the men gathered in the living room, the children went outdoors, and the women quickly cleaned up, then clustered around the kitchen table. In only a few weeks, they'd established a pattern that provided Amy a sense of security. Before joining the women at the table, Amy retrieved her purse and gave Margaret Gerber money for the groceries. "Thank you again for including us in your shopping. It certainly saved me a great deal of time."

Margaret tucked the bills into the pocket of her dress. "I don't mind making the trip to Topeka twice a month. Maybe you'll want to go along sometime and see what's available at the Food Warehouse."

"I'd like that." Amy set her purse on the counter, then

slipped into the remaining chair. "Have you done any other exploring in Topeka? I need to purchase fabric. Parker is growing so quickly all of his pants are getting too short."

"There's a fabric store in the mall," Sheila Buerge said, "but they are rather pricey."

"Highway robbery," Margaret proclaimed. "I can send home for an entire bolt of fabric and have it shipped to me for less money than it would cost to buy several yards in that store in the mall."

The women all murmured, voicing their thoughts.

"I do miss our shops in Berlin." Renae Stull propped her chin in her hand. "Saturday shopping was such a joy, visiting store owners and knowing exactly where all my favorite items were kept on the shelves."

Amy leaned forward. "What made you decide to leave Berlin and come here?"

The women all looked at Margaret, silently appointing her their spokeswoman. Margaret cleared her throat and straightened her shoulders. "The decision was made with much prayer and forethought. With our families growing bigger than our plots of land could support, and our young people approaching a marriageable age, we needed space to spread out and . . ." Her face mottled with pink. "We needed unrelated people of faith to consider as life partners."

Amy understood both reasons. "Yet all of you are from the same fellowship. Certainly you've gained land here in Weaverly—the acreage purchased should be sufficient to meet the financial needs of your families. But what about life partners? Did you deliberately choose families that were not related to make the move to Kansas?"

Tamera Mischler and Renae giggled. Tamera said, "Renae

and I are cousins, and Margaret is Christian Hunsberger's aunt, so we still have some blood relationships between us."

Renae added, "The elders of our fellowship shared the news with fellowships in Indiana about the land for sale in Kansas. It's very likely some other Mennonites will choose to move here in the next few years."

"We don't need to worry about it overly much yet." Margaret bobbed her head, making the black ribbons from her prayer cap quiver. "After all, the oldest of our young people is Joe and Lorraine's Tyler, and he just turned fifteen. It will be a few years before he's ready to begin courting." Her lips tipped into a teasing smile. "Who knows, Amy, he might set his sights on your Bekah. Wouldn't the two of them make a fine couple?"

Amy wasn't ready to think about Bekah being old enough to court. And she felt certain Bekah wouldn't choose Tyler after the boy had openly teased Parker. She hadn't talked to the Schells about Tyler's behavior because last Sunday he'd been kind to Parker. She hoped the teasing was finished for good. She said, "I'm already praying for God's chosen spouses for all of my children. I trust He'll bring the right mates into their lives when the time is right."

Lorraine touched Amy's hand. "We all came for land. What brought you to Weaverly?"

Amy's throat went dry. She'd assumed the question would eventually be asked, but she hadn't prepared an answer. All six women looked at her, their expressions holding interest. If she told them the truth—*I came here so I'd never have to look at the grain silo from which my husband plunged to his death and wonder if he truly fell or if he jumped*—would their faces change to reflect the same uneasy speculation carried by most citizens in her former community?

"I decided it was time for a fresh start. For myself and the children. Memories of the time before my husband's . . . death . . ." Her nose stung. She swallowed. "Memories filled every corner of the town. I needed to bury him and move forward."

Silence reigned for a few seconds, during which Amy kept her head low, uncertain of their reactions. Then a warm hand clamped over the top of hers, and she looked into Margaret's sympathetic gaze.

"How long ago were you widowed?" Margaret's normally brusque tone was absent. Instead her voice held a warmth that brought a fresh sting behind Amy's nose.

"It will be three years in August."

Tamera gasped. "But your littlest one . . . she's only five, right? So you lost him when she was hardly more than a baby?"

Amy nodded, the difficulty of that time sweeping through her in a rush of painful memories. "Yes. Adrianna has no memories of her father at all."

The women murmured, their hands reaching to pat Amy's hands, arms, and shoulders—whatever they could reach. The sympathy in the room was palpable, and Amy welcomed it. With the uncertainty surrounding the reason for Gabe's death, many in Arborville had pulled away rather than drawn near when Amy so needed empathetic support. Although the day of his death was long past, Amy finally received the kind of care and comfort she'd needed. The uninhibited, compassionate response from these women soothed Amy's heart like a sweet-scented balm.

They each offered a few more pats and gentle squeezes, and then all hands but Margaret's slipped away. The older woman clung, her grip warm and sure. "Being a widow is very difficult, especially when you have children. I lost my husband when my two were young, but a year after my first husband's death God brought Dillard into my life. He'd lost his wife, too, and was raising three children on his own. Together we had two more, creating a house full of noise and chaos." She laughed softly. "When you have that many, you learn to run the household like an army camp."

Margaret's recital gave Amy an understanding of the woman's take-charge demeanor and her determination to pinch pennies. "Where are your children now?"

Margaret sighed, her gaze drifting beyond Amy's shoulder. "Dillard's two oldest and my youngest are in Berlin with their own families. His youngest daughter agreed to marry a man in Pennsylvania and moved there almost three years ago. My oldest"—tears winked in her eyes—"died four years ago this past spring. That leaves our two, the oldest of whom married last year and settled in Van Wert, and our youngest, who is planning to join us here in Weaverly by next planting season. We needed him to stay behind and sell the remainder of our personal holdings before making the move." Suddenly a twinkle entered her gray-green eyes. "You know, Amy, our Sedgwick is yet unmarried. And he's probably very near your age. Maybe . . ."

The other women laughed, covering the end of Margaret's statement. Heat filled Amy's face, and she jumped up from the table. "Would anyone like a slice of pie? Bekah and I baked buttermilk pies yesterday." She bustled to the refrigerator, eager to leave the subject of unmarried Sedgwick behind.

She carried a pie to the counter and got out dessert plates, forks, and a knife. Listening to the women chat together, she slid the knife through the golden filling, dividing the pie into eight equal slices. After placing a slice on a plate for each of the women, one slice remained in the pan. The leftover piece of pie became representative of Amy's position of aloneness within this fellowship. Everyone else had a mate.

She delivered servings of pie to each woman seated around the table, relieved the conversation had moved on to new topics. Although loneliness often plagued her, Amy had no intention of allowing the others to play matchmaker for her. If she were to marry again, she would choose her own mate. She glanced at Margaret, recalling the woman sharing how God had brought Dillard into her life. Remarrying gave her a new love and an extended family.

Amy's chest pinched, new ponderings rising to the surface. She had come to Weaverly for a new start. Might that new start include a love God had already chosen for her?

*

Bekah leaned against the tree trunk, grateful for the shade overhead. Parker and Adri ran around in the sun with the other younger kids, their faces red and their hair plastered to their heads with sweat. How could they tolerate the heat? All Bekah wanted to do was find someplace cool and hide.

Seated under the tree in splashes of sun and shade from the swaying branches, Desiree Stull and Lissa Mischler chattered together. Bekah knew she could join them—they'd invited her—but if she sat down, she wouldn't be able to keep watch over Parker and that older boy, Tyler. Even though Tyler had been nice last week when everybody came, she couldn't forget him saying Parker looked and laughed like a donkey. She wasn't ready to trust him yet.

Tyler sat on the back porch steps with the only other boys close to his age, his brother Lucas and Donnie Stull. The three of them had spent the last hour whittling twigs down to toothpicks with their pocketknives and occasionally hollering comments to the game players in the yard.

Bekah watched Tyler toss aside what was left of his twig and shift onto one hip so he could put his knife in his pocket. As he settled back onto his bottom, his head turned in her direction and he caught her looking at him. He broke into a smile, nudged Donnie with his elbow, and unfolded himself from the step. Bekah pressed more snugly against the tree, the bark digging into her back, as Tyler ambled across the yard, dodging tag-players, and stopped right next to her.

He leaned his hand on the trunk above her shoulder and grinned. "Hey. Aren't you tired of holding up this tree?"

Both Desiree and Lissa giggled, sending flirtatious glances at Tyler, which he ignored.

She fidgeted beneath his steady gaze. "It's cool here. Cooler than in the sun, at least."

Tyler squinted upward as if examining the leaves on the tree. "Probably." He looked at her again. "But not as cool as it'd be in the barn. How 'bout we all pour ourselves some Kool-Aid and go hang out in the barn for a while?" The kids playing tag broke into a noisy argument about whether or not Austin was "it." Tyler raised his voice to be heard over them. "It'd be quieter there, too."

Lissa and Desiree bounced up and brushed grass from their skirts. Desiree said, "Sounds good. Let's go."

Bekah shook her head. "You guys go ahead. I wanna stay here and watch the game."

Tyler shrugged. "Suit yourself." He headed for the house

with Lissa and Desiree trotting along beside him. When they reached the porch, Donnie and Lucas got up and followed the others inside. Bekah stared at the back door, torn between joining the kids her age and keeping an eye on Parker. If Tyler went to the barn, he wouldn't be bothering her brother. But one of the other kids might start poking fun at the slow way he ran or the way his laugh gulped out high and then low.

Hadn't Parker become her responsibility the day they'd brought him back from the hospital after his accident? Mom had told her she'd need to keep watch over her brother, to keep him from being hurt. She still felt a little guilty about leaving him beside the road that day. As much as he aggravated her sometimes, she loved him. She didn't want him hurt.

By the time the older kids emerged from the house, each carrying a glass of red liquid, Bekah had decided to stay put. The little group of kids trailed past her, laughing together. Bekah's stomach clenched. It would be nice to be part of a circle of friends again. She missed the ones she'd left behind in Arborville. Letters back and forth couldn't make up for time together.

Tyler glanced at her, offering a grin and a wink. Instantly, the desire to join the group fled. Tyler was cute, but he wouldn't win her over so quickly. She had to be careful. She wasn't even sure yet she wanted to stay a Mennonite. If she got too friendly with the others, they'd snag her in and she wouldn't be able to leave. For now, she'd better keep some distance between herself and the Ohio Mennonite kids. When school started, she'd have the chance to make friends with the Weaverly kids.

Bekah peeked over her shoulder in time to see them all disappear into the barn. She turned back to watch the game of tag, which had started up anew with Chloe Buerge trying to tag the others. Chloe shot after Parker first. Even though Chloe was only eight or nine, she easily caught Parker and tagged him between the shoulder blades. With a good-natured guffaw, Parker stumbled in a circle and took off after Chris Stull.

Bekah sighed. For now, being Parker's keeper might be a good thing. At least until she'd decided what to be—Mennonite or not.

18

The final two weeks of June passed in a blur of searing heat, blasting wind, and seemingly endless busyness. Amy's debit card arrived in the mail, so she took the children into town to visit the library, where she finalized her Web page and, with Miss Bergstrom standing by in case Amy needed assistance, made the information available on the World Wide Web. Her stomach trembled the first time she visited her own page, and right there in the library she closed her eyes and asked God to guide customers in need of comfort to her page so she might serve them.

The same day her Web page went live, she made arrangements to reactivate the telephone line disconnected by the previous owners. She and the children drove to nearby Ottawa and visited a discount store to find a telephone so she could communicate with customers if need be. She requested a rotary dial wall-mount phone similar to the one in her father's office. The young man in the electronics department laughed until he realized she was serious. Then he did his best salesman job, insisting she needed a digital phone with caller ID and additional digital handsets so she could have telephones in several places in the house. Even though Bekah seemed to perk up at the idea, Amy remained firm and left the store with a simple, corded, push-button model that now sat on the corner of the kitchen counter, within a few yards of her sewing machine. So far it had rung three times—twice her father and once a wrong number.

While in the discount store, she visited the fabric department and purchased several yards of sturdy tan and navy twill and blue chambray to make Parker some britches and shirts. She let both Bekah and Adrianna choose fabric for new dresses, as well. Adrianna squealed in delight, dancing along the display of cotton floral prints before choosing a lavender with tiny pink flowers. To Amy's disappointment, Bekah showed no pleasure at all in the activity, turning up her nose at the limited selection and finally settling on a solid mint-green muslin. Later, as they were checking out, Amy glimpsed Bekah surreptitiously examining a teen magazine. The intrigued gleam in her daughter's eyes kept her awake and praying long into the night.

Every morning, she took time away from her sewing to work in the garden plot behind the house. How weeds could grow so abundantly in the dry, hot weather she couldn't imagine, but she faced a constant battle keeping them from stealing nutrients from her beans, peas, peppers, beets, carrots, potatoes, tomatoes, cantaloupe, and watermelon. Parker and Bekah helped with weeding, and Adrianna splashed the plants with water from the spigot. They all tired of working in the garden, but Amy reminded them they'd appreciate the fresh vegetables once the plants began to produce. Inwardly, she wondered how much they'd actually glean from the poor, wilted scrubs of green.

The men from the Ohio fellowship worked the fields around Amy's house daily, stirring up dirt that traveled on the wind and drifted through her open windows. They set up sprinklers to water the soybeans, drawing water from the hydrant behind Amy's house. Despite the sun's bold rays, the plants grew, promising at least a minimal harvest. When the fellowship members met on Sundays, they thanked God for the growing plants and continued to ask Him to bless them with rain. Yet not even a wisp of a cloud appeared in the endless blue sky.

Twice a week, on Tuesdays and Fridays, Bekah and Parker mounted their bicycles and rode to Mr. Roper's house for the afternoon. They never complained about having to work for their neighbor. After each visit, they came home sweaty and dirty but smiling, full of stories of what they'd done that day and things Mr. Roper had said. Parker, especially, seemed to blossom from the man's attention, and Amy found herself growing ever more appreciative of their neighbor. She prayed for him daily, for God to touch him with grace and healing and to draw him close again.

The last Friday in June, Mr. Schell knocked on the door just as Amy shut down her machine for the afternoon. His face glowed red from his time in the sun, and sweat circles blotched his shirt under his arms and in the middle of his chest. Amy invited him to step inside, then called, "Adrianna? Pour Mr. Schell a glass of ice water, please."

The little girl forgot the ice, but Mr. Schell didn't seem to mind. He guzzled the entire glass without pause, then smiled wearily at Amy. "I need to start carrying two big jugs of water when I come out to work. My thirst is impossible to quench in this heat."

Adrianna trotted back to the kitchen with Mr. Schell's empty glass in her hands, and Amy shook her head in worry. "It's a wonder you men all don't suffer heatstroke out there. Please feel free to come to the house anytime for more water. The back door is open during the day so you can get ice from the freezer, or you know you can always use the hydrant out back."

"That's kind of you, Mrs. Knackstedt. I'll tell the others. Now, I wanted to let you know Dillard Gerber has reached an agreement with the insurance agent in town to use the meeting room at the back of his office for worship services until we can locate a separate building. The man is very kind, only charging us a small amount to cover the cost of electricity for lights and cooling while we're there. So we won't need to trouble you any longer by taking over your sitting room."

"How nice of him." Amy tried to inject enthusiasm into her tone, but her thoughts drifted to Mr. Roper. She'd hoped the sound of their voices might reach his ears and reignite his faith. If they began worshiping in town, far from Mr. Roper's home, how would he hear them singing hymns and reading Scripture?

"We'll meet at nine thirty, just as we've been doing." Mr. Schell shared the address with Amy. "My wife still wants us to have a fellowship meal together afterward, so bring something that will keep for a few hours, and we'll trade off going to the different houses in town to eat together."

"That all sounds wonderful, Mr. Schell. Thank you." She watched him clomp across the porch and then over the withered grass to his waiting vehicle. As he pulled out of her lane,

Bekah and Parker rode in on their bicycles. Amy stayed on the porch, waiting until the children put their bikes in the garage and then ran to her.

Parker gave her a hug, and Amy wrinkled her nose. "Phew, you stink. Go take your bath before we eat, huh?"

Parker chortled and headed on in.

Bekah stepped onto the porch and paused, giving her mother a puzzled look. "Is something wrong?"

"No, not really." Amy ushered Bekah inside and to the kitchen. She told her daughter about the change in location for the worship services.

Bekah's face lit. "They won't be coming here anymore?"

"That makes you happy?"

Bekah shrugged, her expression sheepish. "We had to do twice the cleaning. We cleaned on Saturday to get ready for them all, and then we cleaned up the messes they made afterward."

"Bekah . . ." Amy clicked her tongue on her teeth and began pulling cans from the pantry to put together a simple casserole.

"Mom, you have to admit, some of those kids were really messy." While she spoke, Bekah washed her hands in the sink. She pulled out the hand-operated can opener and took one can from Amy. "They used up all our dishes, carried dirt in on their feet, and they left crumbs everywhere."

Amy stared, aghast, at her daughter. From where had this ungrateful attitude come? "We should be honored to host the worship, even if it does mean a little dirt."

"That was hardly a *little* dirt. . . ."

Only then did Amy see the teasing glint in Bekah's eye. She burst out laughing. "You scamp." She teasingly snatched the can and opener from her daughter and began opening cans.

Bekah giggled and retrieved a glass casserole dish. "Actually, the mess all those people made together is nothing compared to what I've been cleaning at Mr. Roper's house. It's sad, Mom, how he's let his house go just because he doesn't have time to clean." She leaned against the counter and watched Amy combine cans of pork 'n' beans, kidney beans, and white beans. "He really appreciates everything I'm doing to make it all neat again—he told me so. And he said his *wife,* who was an impeccable housekeeper, would be rolling over in her grave if she knew how badly he'd let the place go."

Amy didn't miss the subtle emphasis. She knew she shouldn't ask, but the question slipped out anyway. "He talked to you about his wife?"

Bekah began rinsing the empty cans. "I don't think he meant to, because he got this really surprised look right after he said it. But then when I asked about her, he told me she died five years ago in an automobile accident." Her hands paused in the task, her face clouding. "Along with their son— he was named Charlie. He showed me a picture he carries in his wallet of all of them together. They looked so happy it made me want to cry."

Amy gulped. Apparently the children had formed a tighter bond with Mr. Roper than she'd imagined. Her heart turned over in sympathy for the man, and for Bekah, who clearly cared about him. "That's awful."

"Yeah . . ." Bekah dropped the rinsed cans in the plastic bin they used for recycling. She crossed to the counter and fiddled with the little tin of chili powder. "Mom, there was something different about his son. You could see it in the picture. His face was . . . different."

Amy frowned, confused. "Different how?"

"Kind of round and almost flattish. And his eyes were shaped funny, like this." Bekah tugged the outside corners of her own eyes, lifting the lids slightly.

Amy paused midway between the counter and the oven, the casserole forgotten in her hands. "His son had Down Syndrome?"

"Is that what it is?"

"I think so." Amy stepped to the stove and placed the beans in the oven. She turned the oven on and set the timer, then took out a package of cheese from the refrigerator. Her thoughts raced back to her first conversation with Mr. Roper. He'd indicated that the school in Weaverly had a good special-education program. And from the very first moments of meeting her family, he'd reached out to Parker. His kindness toward her son—toward all of them—made sense now. He knew what it was like to raise a child with a disability.

His child had been born with a medical condition, and then he'd lost him and the child's mother. He'd suffered more deeply even than she. *Father, he needs Your healing touch more than I'd imagined.* In past prayers, Amy had asked God to move on Mr. Roper's behalf, opening his heart to the Spirit's guidance. But now, without conscious thought, her prayer changed. *Help us find ways to bring joy to him. Help us remind him he isn't alone, no matter what he's lost.*

"Mom?"

Amy opened her eyes and lifted her head to meet Bekah's gaze.

"Mr. Roper asked if we were going to the town's Fourth of July celebration next week. He said everybody in town goes, and that since we're Weaverly residents we should go, too."

Amy smiled and withdrew a knife to slice the cheese. "Well, we're definitely Weaverly residents now, so I guess that means we'll be going."

Bekah let out a cheer, the sound welcome to Amy after her daughter's days of long faces and sullen tones. "Can I go tell Parker and Adri?"

"Sure, and tell them dinner will be—"

Bekah pounded up the stairs before Amy could finish her instructions. She didn't mind, though. It was nice to see Bekah excited about something. She'd have to mention the Fourth of July celebration to the others on Sunday when they met for worship—they might all want to go together and get better acquainted with their new neighbors.

The sounds of children's happy voices drifted down the stairs, and Amy laughed softly to herself. Apparently the news of attending the town's celebration appealed to Parker and Adrianna, too. Then she sobered, thinking about the man who lived next door. How heartbreaking to have only one child, and then for that child's voice to be stilled forever.

She'd kept Bekah and Parker from visiting Mr. Roper too frequently so they wouldn't wear out their welcome, but she changed her mind. He'd opened himself to them. They must be good for him. So in the future, she'd allow them more time with the orchard owner. Perhaps God had guided them here so the children could ease Mr. Roper's loneliness.

Use us, Lord, for his good and Your glory. Amen.

19

The morning of the Fourth of July celebration, Tim rose early and saw to the necessary chores—including setting up the sprinklers so the trees would get a good drink in his absence—before fixing a pot of coffee. He skipped breakfast so he'd have plenty of room for all the goodies in town. Saliva pooled under his tongue as he thought about slow-roasted barbecued beef, baked beans, golden fresh-fried corn dogs slathered with mustard, and an unlimited selection of home-made pies. He'd learned everyone pulled out the stops when it came to these celebrations, and being a bachelor, he took advantage of the opportunity to eat his fill.

Sipping the strong black brew from a chipped ceramic mug, he ambled sock-footed to his bedroom and flicked through the shirts in his closet. He'd wear a button-up western shirt in place of his usual work T-shirts today. For a moment he paused, admiring the crisply ironed neatness of each shirt, perfectly centered on the hangers and spaced so they wouldn't crush one another. He chuckled. That Bekah would make someone a fine wife someday—she took her role as his house-keeper seriously. Her mother'd done a fine job training her.

Training her . . . He grimaced. People trained dogs, not children. Plunking the half-empty mug on his dresser, he selected a blue-and-tan plaid shirt. As he snapped it, he contemplated the *training* he'd received while living under his father's roof. He couldn't deny he'd been well instructed in caring for crops and tools, in being respectful and responsible, and in Scripture memorization. Not that he leaned too much on the Scriptures these days, even if they did try to invade his thoughts at odd moments.

He scowled at his reflection in the mirror. The older he got, the more he saw his dad's face peering back at him. Same square jaw, same thick brows, same mahogany hair with a cowlick best hidden beneath a hat. To his consternation, he looked like Timothy Rupp Senior. "But I don't *act* like him," he informed his image. When it came to parenting, he'd never barked orders, expected perfection, or quoted Bible verses at full volume to shame his son. Charlie had never been afraid of *his* father.

Turning abruptly, he moved away from the mirror and sat on the end of the bed to tug on his boots. Why think about it now? Dad'd probably forgotten he had a son named for himself. Charlie was long gone . . . and Tim needed to toss the past in the closet where it belonged and leave it there.

He rose with a cracking of knees and gave his closet door a good slam. Then he grabbed his cowboy hat from the edge of the dresser, slid it into place over his cowlick, and strode out the door. Behind the wheel of his pickup truck, he drew in a long breath and let it out slowly. By increments. Feeling the tension that had knotted his shoulders during his moments of reflection ease a little more with each deliberate expulsion of breath. By the time he reached town, he was ready to put on a smile—even if it was a forced one—and enjoy a rare day of leisure.

Wooden barricades decorated with strips of red, white, and blue crepe paper blocked Main Street from through traffic, so Tim pulled into the high-school parking lot. Most townsfolk just walked to the city park for the celebration, leaving lots of room for the rural folk to leave their vehicles. He glanced down the row of cars and trucks, identifying neighbors by their mode of transportation. His heart gave a funny lurch when he spotted Mrs. Knackstedt's blue Buick. So the kids had convinced her to come in—good. He'd give them a wave if he saw them.

He put the truck in park, killed the engine, then pocketed his keys. He didn't bother locking the truck—nobody in Weaverly would bother it, one of the perks of small-town living—then took off at a brisk pace down the sidewalk, heading for the park on the opposite side of town. His bootheels thudded against the cracked concrete, keeping time with a band playing in the distance. Based on the occasional sour note, Tim surmised the high-school band director had pulled his students together for a summer concert. Although it sounded a little rusty, the marching tune added to the day's festive attitude.

Only four blocks separated the high school from the park, nothing compared to how much ground Tim covered each day at the orchard. But the ridiculous temperature—probably close to one hundred degrees already at nine in the morning—had him feeling sticky by the time he'd walked half the distance. Maybe he should've dressed like the kids racing around, in shorts and a tank top instead of his customary Levi's.

Several buildings, those no longer in operation, were locked up tight, their windows graced with FOR SALE or FOR RENT signs. Every occupied business had its door propped open with a brick or a bucket of sand. Cool air whisked out at him as he passed by, encouraging him to slow his stride. But food waited at the park, and he was ready to find something tasty.

Tim wove between groups who lingered on the sidewalk, tipping his hat and smiling hello as he went. Down the middle of Main Street, people had set up tables to sell arts-and-crafts items. Townsfolk milled there in the sunshine, examining starched doilies, wooden cars, or handmade dolls. He didn't meander to the booths. If Julia were here, she'd be dragging him to each display, looking for ideas for her own handiwork. But he had no interest in crafty items. Besides, staying on the sidewalk put him in the shade thanks to the height of the buildings blocking the sun. He stepped off the curb at the end of the business district and crossed the street to enter the grassy park.

"Hey, Tim!" One of the town council members, Greg Eads, raised a hand in greeting, gesturing Tim over to a cloth-draped table under one of the towering elm trees. The red-checked cloth flapped in the wind, threatening to dislodge a square hand-painted sign advertising "Cold Pop: 50¢/can."

"Come grab yourself a drink," Greg called. "Looks like you could use it."

Tim rarely drank pop, and never this early in the morning, but today he'd make an exception. He dug two quarters out of his pocket and dropped them into the money jar on the corner of the table before fishing a dripping can of cola from an ice-filled cooler resting in a child's red wagon. He bobbed his chin at the wagon as he popped the top on the can. "You planning to take your business on the road?"

The man laughed heartily. "Doubt I'll need to. I've already had to restock the cherry cola—kids love it. Nah, the wagon was my son's idea. He said it put the cans up high enough that the, uh, older ladies wouldn't have to bend over to get their cans out of the cooler."

Tim laughed. "How old is that boy of yours now, Greg?"

His chest puffing with pride, Greg said, "Eight going on eighteen. Playing Little League for the first time this summer. They grow up awful fast, don't they?" Then he blanched, ducking his head. "Oh, sheesh, sorry. I wasn't thinking. . . ."

Tim took a swallow of pop, wishing he could swallow the lump of longing the man's words had innocently stirred. He forced a light chuckle. "Hey, don't worry about it. You've got a right to brag on your boy." If Charlie were still living, he'd be fourteen already. Big enough to be a help around the orchard or to participate in the Special Olympics with other challenged athletes. If Charlie were alive, Tim would take advantage of every opportunity to boast about his son's accomplishments, no matter how large or small.

Greg slapped Tim on the shoulder, blasting a laugh that held a hint of embarrassment. "If we can peel you away from your apple trees now and then, why don't you come to town some Friday evening and watch the youngsters play? I tell you, Tim, there's nothing like watching a Little League baseball game to take your mind off your troubles." He swung a look skyward, his lips pursing. "And from what I've heard so far this morning, lots of folks are troubled about our lack of rain. Can't remember the last time we made it through an entire spring without a storm or two." One brow high, he gave Tim a worried look. "How're your trees doing? They holding up under the heat?"

"So far, although I've already counted the grapes a loss." The vines were so shriveled, they might never produce again. Tim finished off his pop, then tossed the can in a barrel behind the table, where it clattered against several other cans. "I've had to water a lot more than I'd like for this early in the summer. Still, the roots've got to have moisture or the trees'll dry up on me. At least I've got well water, so I'm not paying the city to water my trees."

Tim stepped back from the table as several youngsters ran up and began tossing quarters into the jar. He lifted his hand in farewell. "See you later, Greg. Enjoy the day." He ambled toward the center of the park, taking in the activities.

The town council did a good job of organizing everything. Years ago, they'd established a contract with a carnival company out of Colorado to provide a few rides and games. Kids swarmed the booths to shoot baskets or plug a balloon with a dart for the privilege of carrying away cheap stuffed animals or straw hats that looked like they'd come unraveled at a moment's notice. Smaller kids were attached to parents' hands, but anyone age seven and up ran free, proving how safe folks felt in their little town.

Tim walked the full periphery of the park, his nose barraged by the aromas of popcorn, cotton candy, hot dogs, pizza, and tangy barbecue sauce. He stopped at a booth selling doughnuts and bought two. Then he sauntered on, munching, looking, listening. So many sounds—laughter, chatter, a few screams from kids at the top of the Ferris wheel, tinny music from the rides as well as the continued blasting of the band in the park's pavilion. His ears ached, unaccustomed to anything more than birdsong, bees humming, and wind in the trees. Yet he didn't want to go home.

He stepped from behind some metal bleachers that had been set up so people could sit and listen to the band, and he came face-to-face with the group of Mennonites. The women's dresses and caps and the men's flat-brimmed hats would have set them apart from the other townsfolk even if they weren't all clustered in one big group. On the outskirts of their circle, Tim located Mrs. Knackstedt and her children. She held Adrianna and Parker by the hands, and Bekah stood on the other side of Adrianna, her gaze aimed in the center of the park. The older girl's expression sent a zing of awareness down Tim's spine. He knew that look—he'd seen it in his own reflection at her age. He started to inch backward and cross in front of the bleachers, but Adrianna turned her head and spotted him.

Her face broke into a huge smile. She yanked free of her mother's grip and raced to him, her little braids flying. "Mr. Roper! You came, too!" She threw her arms around his legs, nearly toppling him with the enthusiastic hug.

Tim's arms itched to scoop her up, the way he had the day Bekah had filled his house with smoke, but he gave her head a pat and then gently disengaged her arms. "Hey there, Adri." He used the nickname Bekah and Parker called their sister. It fit the little girl so much better than the lengthy Adrianna. "Are you having fun?"

The child poked out her lower lip. "No. Momma won't let me do nothin'."

Parker trotted to Tim's side, his smile so wide it split his face in half. Bekah and Mrs. Knackstedt followed closely on Parker's heels. Bekah didn't offer a beaming smile like her siblings, but she greeted Tim politely, and he couldn't resist chucking her under the chin, earning a shy grin.

Mrs. Knackstedt gave Adri's shoulder a little shake. "Are you complaining to Mr. Roper?" Adri continue to pout, refusing to answer. Mrs. Knackstedt looked at Tim and lifted her shoulders in a delicate shrug. "Don't let her fool you. She's already eaten a bag of popcorn and a whole cone of cotton candy. I told her if she got on rides right now, she'd get a sick stomach." She laughed lightly. "I don't think she believes me."

Tim squatted down so he'd be eye to eye with the five-year-old. He tickled her cheek with the end of one of her braids while he spoke. "Your mom's right. You get on a ride and go whirling around with a bunch of food in your stomach, that food will whirl right out again."

Adri's blue eyes grew round. "You mean I'll throw up?"

Tim coughed to cover a laugh. "Yes, ma'am, that's exactly what I mean."

Adri's infectious giggle rang. "You're so silly." She pranced in a short circle and then took a two-handed grip on her mother's wrist, suspending herself while humming a cheerful melody.

Tim straightened, shooting Mrs. Knackstedt a sly smile. "That might hold 'er for a little while."

"Thank you." Relief colored her tone. She flicked a glance over her shoulder to the group of Mennonites. "Would you like to meet the other newcomers to Weaverly? I'd be glad to introduce you."

Tim wanted to refuse, but he noticed several of the Mennonites peeking in his direction. To walk away would be rude.

He'd been taught better than that. So he gave a brusque nod and followed her to the group. As a unit, the white-capped women and black-hatted men shifted, turning to face Tim. Although most wore kind, welcoming faces, cotton filled Tim's mouth. For a moment he wished he still had faith, because if he did he'd say a prayer for fortitude as he faced a representative piece of his past.

20

Amy introduced each adult, starting with Dillard and Margaret Gerber and moving across the circle until everyone had an opportunity to shake Mr. Roper's hand and exchange a few words of greeting. The moment Mr. Roper released Don Mischler's hand, Parker gave Amy's shoulder several inquisitive taps with his fingertip.

"Mom, can I tell him the kids' names?"

Amy smiled. "Of course."

His shoulders squared, Parker began a solemn recitation, pointing at each youngster as he rattled off their names. He only stumbled once, reversing the names of the two youngest Schell boys, but they quickly corrected him and he moved on. After completing the introductions, he put his arm around Mr. Roper's shoulders, reaching up to do so. "And this is Mr. Roper, my best friend."

Amy sent a startled look at their neighbor, and her heart turned over when tenderness sprouted across the man's face. He swallowed. Twice. Then he bobbed his head to acknowledge the children.

Parker swung a pleading look in Amy's direction, his hand still clamped over Mr. Roper's shoulder. "Mom, can Mr. Roper go on rides with us?"

Amy nearly choked. Although Parker viewed the man as a friend—something she found very sweet and touching—she couldn't allow her son to treat Mr. Roper the way he would one of his peers. She opened her mouth to deliver a gentle refusal.

Mr. Roper released a light chuckle and threw his arm across Parker's skinny shoulders. "Parker, much as I appreciate being invited, I don't *do* rides. They make me dizzy."

Adrianna blinked up at the man. "Do they make you throw up?"

Several people chortled at her question, and Mr. Roper grinned. He tapped the end of Adrianna's nose. "Yup." He stepped away from Parker, putting a few inches between himself and the group of Mennonites. "So I keep my boots planted on the ground. Usually in front of one of the food booths. Which reminds me, I need to find where Valerie—she runs the Burger Basket—has set up her pie table. I wanna buy a whole cherry pie before they're all gone."

Amy suspected he was using the pies as an excuse to escape their company. As much as she wanted the Mennonites to develop a relationship with this man so they could be an essence of Jesus to him, she knew she couldn't push. It might drive a wedge between them. Looking at her children, recognizing the fondness they held for their neighbor, she wouldn't risk alienating him.

She smiled. "I hope you'll find your pie, Mr. Roper. Have a good day."

He lifted his hand to the group. "Nice meeting you all.

Welcome to Weaverly." His voice sounded a little tight to
Amy's ears, but no one else seemed to notice. They offered
appropriate replies, and he spun on his bootheel and ambled
off toward the center of town.

The older of the Stull girls said, "May we play some games,
please? I'd like to win a blue teddy bear."

"I want a pink one!" the younger Stull girl added.

Their father laughed. "All right. Let's go see what we can
do."

The other fathers and the whole wriggling mass of children
trotted behind Mr. Stull, leaving the wives, Amy, and her
children in the stripes of sun and shade behind the bleachers.

Adrianna yanked on Amy's skirt. "Can't we go, too? I
wanna win a teddy bear."

Amy leaned down. "You have to stay with me."

Bekah looked after the group. A touch of rebellion glittered
in her dark eyes. "But everyone else is going."

Because they're with their fathers. The words quivered
on the end of Amy's tongue, but she held them in. "I'll take
you in a minute. After the ladies decide what they're going
to do." She turned to the other women. "Where are you—"

"Mr. Roper!" Adrianna's shrill voice cut off Amy's question. The little girl dashed across the grass, intercepting Mr.
Roper, who was crossing between booths several yards away.
Over the other celebratory noises, Amy clearly heard her
daughter's request. "Will you take me an' Parker an' Bekah
to play some games? Huh, Mr. Roper?"

The other women tittered. Amy's face flooded with heat.
She darted forward and captured Adrianna's hand. "That
was very naughty to run away from me. And Mr. Roper isn't
here to entertain you." She gave her daughter's hand a yank.

Adrianna fought against Amy's restraining hold. "But, Momma . . ."

"Adrianna!" Amy used her sternest tone, and Adrianna stopped fighting. She looked at Mr. Roper. His face glowed red, no doubt matching the blush she was certain still graced her cheeks. She gulped. "I'm so sorry. I don't know what gets into her sometimes."

Mr. Roper shrugged. "It's all right. She's just a little girl wanting to have the same fun as all the other youngsters." He pushed his hat back, revealing more of his face. His voice dropped to a near whisper. "You know, Mrs. Knackstedt, this is a family town—a safe town. And your Bekah's a very responsible young woman. It'd be all right to let your kids do some exploring on their own. I can't imagine anything unpleasant befalling them here in Weaverly."

Amy hesitated.

He leaned forward slightly. "You let 'em ride their bikes over to my place and into the library without you. How is visiting booths and playing some games any different?"

As much as Amy understood his reasoning, she also recognized the difference. All of the other Mennonite children were visiting the booths under the supervision of their fathers. Her children had no father to take them from booth to booth, to cheer for them, to give them another quarter or two if they didn't win the first time. If she sent them off on their own, they'd see what they were missing. But how could she explain all that to this kindhearted man without reminding him he was a father without a child?

"I appreciate your kind recognition of Bekah's maturity— she is growing up. But she assumes so much responsibility at home for her brother and sister. It doesn't seem fair to make her be in charge of them here, where she'd like to have fun instead."

He stared into her face for several seconds, as if trying to decide if her statement was the truth, the whole truth, and nothing but the truth. She resisted fidgeting beneath his intense scrutiny. Then he settled the brim of his battered brown hat lower on his forehead and gave a quick nod. "I see your point. And you're their mother, so I won't argue with you." Yet she sensed by the firm set of his jaw, he wanted to argue.

His gaze dropped to Adrianna, who stood beside Amy with one finger in her mouth, looking longingly toward the game booths. The tenderness she'd glimpsed when Parker had called him his best friend returned. He slipped one hand into his pocket and turned a bland look on Amy. "You ladies are probably wanting to do some exploring on your own, aren't you?"

Amy flicked a glance over her shoulder. The women hadn't moved on yet, but she sensed impatience in the subtle shifting of their feet and in the investigative gazes they zinged here and there. She sighed. "Yes. I'm holding them up."

"Tell you what . . ." He rubbed his jaw with his fingertips, as if coaxing out the words. "Why don't you give your kids some spending money, and I'll walk 'em around the game booths. Help 'em win a stuffed bear or a goldfish in a bowl."

Amy waved her hands. "No goldfish!"

He laughed—a genuine, rollicking laugh. The sound lifted her heart and sent it into a stuttering double-beat. "All right, then, no goldfish. But you want to be with your friends, and the kids want to explore." His shoulders lifted in a boyish, almost sheepish shrug. "I don't have anything pressing, so I'd be happy to escort them around a bit."

Amy nibbled her lip, undecided.

"That is, if you trust me."

His statement wounded her, but she didn't quite understand why. "W-why, of course I trust you, Mr. Roper. You've become a good friend to . . . to the children." Now jealousy stabbed. Equally confusing.

He reached out and plucked Adrianna's hand from Amy's grip. The little girl skittered to him without a moment's pause. He swung her hand, smiling into Amy's face. "I promise to keep 'em out of mischief, and I'll return 'em to you at lunchtime." He poked his thumb in the direction of town. "I plan to grab a barbecued beef sandwich from the Burger Basket. You can meet up with me there at noon."

Amy glanced at the women again, who all looked back at her with curious expressions. She zipped around to face Mr. Roper again. "A-are you sure you don't mind?"

"Consider it a payback for all the help Bekah and Parker have given me. They've more than earned their bushel of apples." Again, he assumed a low near-whisper that sent a prickle of awareness down Amy's spine. "I enjoy your kids' company. Will you let me borrow 'em for a while?"

Something glittered in his eyes—a hopeful pleading Amy couldn't bear to ignore. She released a sigh of surrender. "Very well. Thank you, Mr. Roper, for being so kind."

"No problem." He tipped sideways, angling his head to fix his sights on Bekah and Parker, who leaned against the bleacher's metal bracings. "Hey, want to go play some games?"

With a whoop, Parker galloped to Mr. Roper's side. "With you?"

"Yep. With me." Mr. Roper bounced his smile at Bekah, who came more slowly. "That all right with you, Bekah? Mind if I traipse around and watch you kids play games?"

Bekah sent a puzzled look in Amy's direction. "Sure. That'd be fine."

Amy unsnapped her billfold and pressed a ten-dollar bill into Bekah's hand. "Share with your brother and sister, and use the money wisely. That needs to last you all morning."

Bekah folded the bill in her fist. "Okay, Mom."

Mr. Roper lifted Adrianna into his arms, making her squeal. "All right, then. Let's go have some fun." The older two children fell into step with him as he ambled toward the center of the park.

The women watched the little group parade past, various emotions showing on each face. Lorraine Schell separated herself from the group and crossed to Amy, her eyes following Mr. Roper. "You're sending the children with him?"

"Yes. They know him well. Remember? Both Bekah and Parker work for him—Bekah does housekeeping and Parker helps in the orchard. We talked about it last Sunday."

The woman nodded slowly. "I remember. But . . ." She shifted her head to look at Amy. "He isn't Mennonite. Are you sure?"

Amy laughed softly, an attempt to cover the prickle of unease Lorraine's words stirred. "Many of our young people find employment with non-Mennonites, babysitting or doing farm work."

"But they aren't working now. They're . . . socializing."

Defensiveness niggled, and Amy bit down on her tongue for a moment to avoid speaking sharply. "They spend time with Mr. Roper every week without my presence."

Lorraine pursed her lips, the gesture thoughtful rather than derisive.

Amy touched the woman's arm. "I understand your

concerns—he isn't Mennonite anymore. But he's a good man, a caring man. And I trust him." As she said the words, the slight misgivings she'd experienced fell away. She *did* trust Mr. Roper. She knew without a doubt he would look out for her children.

Lorraine shook her head slightly, her eyes reflecting concern. "Be careful, Amy. He's a handsome man, and it's clear he is very fond of Bekah, Parker, and Adrianna. But he left his faith. While it's good to be friendly to him—we need to treat our neighbors well so they will give glory to God—we still must be cautious lest we're drawn away from our beliefs by the world's attitudes."

He's a handsome man. Amy's heart thudded in response to Lorraine's observation. "I'll be cautious, Lorraine. You needn't worry."

The woman's stiff shoulders relaxed. She patted Amy's hand, which still rested on her forearm. "Of course you're cautious. You're a very dedicated mother, and I'm sorry if I overstepped my bounds. I just don't want to see you or your children hurt. A woman alone, with three children in need of a father figure . . ."

"Don't worry," Amy repeated. "The children and I appreciate Mr. Roper's neighborliness, and we're praying for him to find his way back to his faith. But there isn't anything . . . more . . . between us."

Lorraine's smile grew bright. She gave Amy's hand a gentle tug, drawing her toward the waiting group of women. "Come, let's see what Margaret has decided we should all do."

They laughed softly as they rejoined the others. But while she browsed arts-and-crafts booths and sampled fudge and brownies with the fellowship women, Amy's thoughts kept drifting to the assurance she'd given Lorraine concerning her relationship with Mr. Roper. She'd been truthful—there was nothing more than neighborliness between them—but deep down, Amy discovered a tiny seed that sought an opportunity to grow.

Lorraine was right—Tim Roper was a handsome man. A hardworking man, strong yet tender toward her children. She found him attractive. It would be difficult not to find him attractive, given all he'd done for her, Bekah, Parker, and Adrianna. Lorraine's voice echoed in Amy's ears. *"He isn't Mennonite. Are you sure?"*

Amy swallowed. This newly recognized seed of affection must not be nurtured for growth. She sent a fervent prayer heavenward. *Dear Father, guard my heart. I can't allow myself to be pulled away from my faith. That would not honor You. Let me pray for this man, show Your love to this man, but please guard my lonely heart.*

21

Tim sat on the grass off by himself, listening to the band stumble through patriotic tunes and waiting for the fireworks display to begin. The carnival folk had shut down their rides so the lights and music wouldn't compete with the band or the explosions in the night sky. Stark white light glared in the pavilion, highlighting the band. At the far edge of the park, in the headlight beams of a fire truck, a handful of firemen from Ottawa worked to organize the fireworks show. Normally the town councilmen and Weaverly's volunteer fire department ran the show, but given this year's dry conditions, they'd invited a fire truck just in case. Tim admired their foresight.

All around him, families sat together on blankets or on folding chairs they'd dragged from home. Retired rancher Ron Elliott had invited Tim to join his family, even offering him a woven beach chair, but Tim had declined. Earlier in the day, Ron had spotted him with the Knackstedt kids and smirked, waggling his brows. Tim didn't care to listen to the man goad him about hanging out with the Mennonites. Today was special—he wouldn't make a habit of squiring those kids around town—but he didn't feel like explaining himself to Ron or anybody else. So he stayed separated from the others, a lone island in a sea of families.

The rousing rendition of "Yankee Doodle" ended with a cymbal crash. Applause broke out across the grounds and then faded away. In the ensuing silence, the director tapped his baton. The *tick-tick-tick* echoed from the pavilion's rounded shell. The man raised his hands; the band members lifted their instruments. A hush fell, interrupted by a baby's fretful cry, and the director gave the cue. "Battle Hymn of the Republic" burst across the park, raising the fine hairs on the back of Tim's neck.

Immediately, without anyone's instruction, the gathered townspeople began to sing with the band. A few voices carried over the rest, and a tingle of awareness crept across Tim's scalp. He didn't need to look. He knew who sang with such heartfelt conviction. He supposed it could be perceived as a prejudicial thought, but nobody sang like Mennonites. Generations of singing hymns in four-part harmony without the benefit of musical accompaniment had developed their abilities beyond the norm.

Tim had noted Weaverly's newest residents settling in a snug group on the bleachers, but he'd tried not to look over there for fear Parker or Adri would quirk a finger at him in invitation. Resisting Ron was one thing, resisting those kids quite another. Now their voices, sure and strong and pure, enticed him to rise, to sit among them, to open his mouth and belt out the bass line, just as he had during his growing-up years.

Clutching handfuls of dry grass, he held himself in place, but his face angled in their direction. He caught a glimpse of Parker, his face alive with joy and his mouth open wide, singing with gusto. At once, a grin tugged at Tim's cheek. What a grand morning they'd had. With his help, Parker had sunk three basketballs and won the ugliest stuffed alligator Tim had ever seen. He'd tried to convince the boy to trade it for another, since the one the booth worker handed him had crossed eyes and a crooked drawn-on smile. The poor critter looked as if it'd been on a three-day binge. But Parker insisted he liked it just the way it was. Tim figured it was Parker's natural empathy that made him keep the homely thing, and it warmed him even more toward the boy. Still, he hated to see him settle for second-best.

Both of the girls had also won new toys—Bekah a purple-and-white panda bear that sat a good two feet tall, and Adri a floppy white dog with black polka dots. The little girl named her dog Spot, and Bekah did her best to convince Adri to change it to Freckles or Speckles or something less obvious. But Adri insisted the dog wanted its name to be Spot and that was that. A chuckle rumbled in Tim's chest, remembering the child's indignation. Cute kids, all of them.

But they aren't yours.

The inner reminder jolted him. Of course they weren't his. He'd shown them some fun, enjoyed their presence, then returned them to their mother promptly at noon, just as he'd promised. He'd continue to see them—pretty hard to avoid it, considering they lived right next door and he'd hired them to help him out during the summer—but he wouldn't grow attached to them. That would be foolhardy.

The band ended their number and the band kids shuffled

off the pavilion to the sound of wild applause, hoots, and whistles. Tim pounded his palms together like everyone else. As soon as the pavilion cleared, a single boom signaled the start of the fireworks display. He crossed his ankles, leaned back on his hands, and aimed his face upward to watch the show, but his heart wasn't in it. Somehow he'd lost his desire to watch the annual splashes of color against the backdrop of stars.

Slowly, like an old man rising from a rocking chair, he pushed to his feet. He left the park, skirting past his longtime neighbors, noting not one face turned in his direction as he passed. They were watching the fireworks—he shouldn't expect them to notice his leaving—but it bothered him that nobody waved good-bye. He reached the edge of the park and paused, looking back one last time. A tiny movement caught his attention. He squinted through the deepening shadows, and then his heart caught.

Adri stared after him, using one of the paws on her little stuffed dog to wave good-bye.

The park scene disappeared, and in its stead Tim saw the rear window of a retreating vehicle, a little boy's smiling face, a teddy bear held high, and the child's hand manipulating the bear into waving. As quickly as the image appeared, it slipped away, and once again Tim was looking at Adri's pixie face.

He broke out in a cold sweat. With jerky motions, he flapped his hand at her once and then spun and strode away as fast as his feet could carry him without running. His chest ached so badly, drawing breath was torture. He missed his wife and son. Oh, how he missed them. Hard work usually kept the loneliness at bay, but now it fell on him as heavily as a wet wool blanket—stifling. Why hadn't he gotten in the car that day, too? If he had, he could be with Julia and Charlie now instead of here, all alone, spending his affection on the children of a Mennonite widow.

He slammed himself into his pickup, twisted the key in the ignition, and squealed out of the parking lot. *Escape.* The word reverberated through his middle, spurring him to action. With more recklessness than he'd ever exhibited before, he tore down the highway for home. But as he pulled into his familiar drive and killed the engine, he realized his actions had accomplished little more than senseless wear and tear on his vehicle. He'd never escape his past, or the consequences of his choices.

"I'm doomed." The words groaned from deep within. "Just like Dad told me when I ran off all those years ago, I've doomed myself to a lifetime of regret."

The Sunday following the Fourth of July celebration, Tim woke early, took a long shower, then dressed in his least-faded Levi's and one of his newer snap-up shirts. He polished his belt buckle, buffed his boots, and retrieved Julia's Bible—dust free, but only because of Bekah's attention—from the shelf in the living room.

He attended the Weaverly Community Church sporadically. When Julia was alive, he'd gone every Sunday. They'd dedicated Charlie when he was three months old, and Julia had taught fourth and fifth graders in Sunday school, which she loved. He never committed to anything more than ushering, and he'd never put his name on the church membership roll, even though Julia prodded him to do it. The minister there had performed a real nice service for Julia and Charlie, and the two of them were buried in the cemetery north of town.

He hadn't been out there to check their graves for years. A couple of granite stones couldn't take the place of flesh-and-blood people, so why bother?

Stepping onto the porch, he automatically looked upward. The morning sky was clear blue, as had become the norm, but he—hesitantly hopeful—searched from the eastern horizon to the west for a puff of white anyway. Nothing. He blew out an aggravated breath. While trotting around the park, Bekah had mentioned that their fellowship was praying for rain. Apparently God wasn't listening. Just like He hadn't listened when Tim begged for a more understanding father or for his wife and son to survive the crash.

"The effectual fervent prayer of a righteous man availeth much." The Scripture crept through Tim's memory, and he snorted aloud. "Guess I'm not a righteous man, 'cause my prayers availeth nothin'." Although he meant to sound derisive, the words exited on a tight note of hurt.

Setting his jaw, he creaked open the driver's door on his truck and climbed in. He started to fling the Bible on the passenger seat, but his fingers refused to release. Carefully, reverently—treating God's book with the respect his father had expected—he placed the Bible in the center of the vinyl seat, then started his truck.

He drove to town slowly, leaving the window down so the morning breeze, already stuffy, flowed against his face and ruffled his hair. He was early. Way early. Sunday school wouldn't even start for another hour. But the church doors were always open, and maybe Reverend Geary would be in his study. And maybe he wouldn't mind a pre-church visitor.

For the past three nights—ever since he'd left the Fourth of July doings early—he'd been haunted by a recurring dream. He'd wake up, sweating and near tears. He'd tell himself it was only a dream and drift back to sleep, only to dream the same thing again. The dark circles under his eyes proved he wasn't getting enough rest, and he didn't know anybody else who might be able to help him make sense of the dream. So he intended to lay the burden in Reverend Geary's lap and hoped, by letting it all out, it would leave him for good.

He pulled into the gravel lot behind the church. No other cars were there, but he parked far from the door anyway, leaving the choicest spots for the elderly members of the church. He tucked Julia's Bible under his arm and headed for the back door. Unlocked, as he'd expected. The back door led to a hallway with doors on the right and left. The first one on the right housed the minister's little office. A sliver of light shone under the door, letting Tim know the man was there. Sucking in a breath of fortification, Tim tapped his knuckles on the door. The reverend's deep voice, cheerful in its delivery, responded at once. "Come in."

Tim turned the knob and poked his head in. "I don't want to disturb you, but I wondered if we could talk."

"You're not disturbing me at all, Tim. Come right on in." The gray-haired minister set aside the sheet of paper he'd been reading and gestured for Tim to sit in one of the plastic chairs on the opposite side of his large, scarred desk. He extended his hand across the wooden top as Tim sank into the closest chair, and Tim gave it a firm shake. Reverend Geary settled back in his squeaky upholstered chair and offered a warm smile. "What can I do for you this morning?"

Tim winced. He missed more services than he attended, and he felt more than a little guilty taking up the minister's time. But desperation held him in the chair. "I hoped you might be able to help me to . . . well, to get rid of something."

Reverend Geary chuckled, rocking slightly with his hands folded over the unbuttoned front of his suit coat. "That's rather ambiguous."

Despite himself, Tim laughed. "Yeah, I suppose so. I just . . ." He held out his hands in a helpless gesture. "I don't know where to start."

"Start at the beginning."

"That's just it. Not sure where the beginning is."

The reverend gently rocked in his chair, examining Tim with thoughtful, narrowed eyes. "What is it you want to get rid of?"

"The dream." Tim blasted the words. They bounced off the wood-paneled walls and echoed back. His shoulders hunched in a reflexive cringe. He knew better than to raise his voice in the Lord's house.

But Reverend Geary didn't bat an eye. "What dream is that, Tim?"

Relieved by the man's calm response, Tim rested his elbows on his knees and looked directly into the minister's kind gray eyes. "The dream where I'm watching Julia drive away, and Charlie's waving at me from the backseat. Smiling. Happy. Unaware of what's coming. I watch them go, and I want to run after them—to stop them, bring them back because I *know*—" His throat tightened as the desire to save his wife and son from disaster rolled over him with the force of a steamroller. "But my feet won't move. It's like I'm stuck in concrete. So I stand there and watch them go, knowing I'll never see them again." Tears pricked his eyes, and he sniffed. "It's a stupid dream, but I've had it three nights running now, and I can't seem to get rid of it. I'm . . ." He clamped his trembling hands over his knees. "I'm afraid to go to sleep."

Reverend Geary nodded, sympathy etched into the lines of his aging face. "That's a hard thing to relive." He paused, tapping the edge of his desk with his fingertips. "Julia and Charlie have been gone how long now—three years? Four?"

Tim gulped. "Five and a half." Five and a half long, lonely years.

"And you're just now having this dream? Of seeing them leave, and knowing they won't come back?"

Tim flopped back in the chair. "Yeah. That's what's weird. Why now?"

"Excellent question." The minister pressed his palms together. "Has something happened recently—something to remind you of the day they left?"

Very slowly, stiff as a tin man in need of an oil can, he offered a nod. "Yeah." He described Adri's innocent action as he'd left the park on the Fourth. "I watched her wave, and all of a sudden I wasn't seeing the little Mennonite girl, I was seeing Charlie instead. And now I can't get rid of it."

"Losing your family was a trauma. As the husband, the father, you were the protector. You weren't able to protect Julia and Charlie from that out-of-control truck."

Tim gritted his teeth. "If Old Man Thompson hadn't had that flat tire right in front of the orchard, if I hadn't stayed behind to help him change it, I'd've been the one taking Charlie to his therapy instead of Julia. I'd've been the one driving. I could've avoided that truck."

"You don't know that for sure." Reverend Geary spoke softly, reasonably, but Tim didn't buy it.

"I was a better driver than Julia. I would've known not to swerve so sharp. I wouldn't have rolled the car." Tim's voice rose with each word, anger billowing in his chest. He clenched his fists. "And if I hadn't been able to avoid it, then at least I would've gone with them. I wouldn't be here, left behind, spending my time with a mentally handicapped Mennonite boy in place of my own son."

Silence fell, a cloying silence in which Tim could hear the rapid beat of his own heart pounding in his ears. His breath came in little spurts, and he'd clenched his hands so tightly his knuckles ached. With effort he relaxed his fists, placing his damp palms against the smooth denim covering his tense thighs. His mouth felt dry, and he licked his lips. "I don't want that dream anymore, Reverend. What do I do?"

Reverend Geary took up his rocking again, his eyebrows high. "I'm not a psychologist, and I sure can't claim to be like Joseph—able to interpret dreams—but I think I might know part of why this has come up now."

Tim leaned forward, eager to hear the minister's thoughts.

"Twice, when talking about the children with whom you've spent some time lately, you've identified them as Mennonite children. Not just children, but specifically Mennonite." He tipped his head. "You come from a Mennonite background, am I right?"

"I left it a long time ago."

"An amicable parting?"

"If you walk down that road, remember it doesn't go both ways!" The angry voice reverberated through Tim's memory. His stomach tightened. "I wouldn't say that."

"Mm-hmm." The reverend rocked some more, the chair's squeaking springs keeping beat with the passing seconds.

"And in the dream, you feel helpless, yes? As if you need to act but you can't do it?"

Tim nodded rapidly, sweat beading on his upper lip despite the cool draft from the office's window unit. "That's right."

"If you'd started having this dream just days after Julia and Charlie died, I'd say it was a response to their deaths. But too much time's passed for that. Sure, you're still grieving—a part of you always will—but I think this dream has more to do with something else you need to do and can't. Or, maybe more accurately, something else you've needed to do and haven't." The minister bolted forward, the chair springs releasing a high twang with the sudden movement. He stacked his forearms on the desk and gave Tim a serious look. "Tim, why have you never joined our membership here?"

Tim jerked, crunching his brows together. "What?"

"Your wife joined our church. Your Charlie came forward when he was six years old and asked Jesus to be his personal Lord and Savior. We baptized him the following Sunday and accepted him into membership. But you never joined. Why?"

Tim hung his head, unwilling to answer.

"Is it because this isn't a Mennonite church?"

Tim looked up quickly and gave Reverend Geary a fierce look. "No."

"Are you sure?"

No.

Reverend Geary waited several seconds, but when Tim sat in stubborn silence, he released a sigh. "You might not like what I have to say, but I'm going to say it anyway. I think that dream is tangled up in who you were before you came to Weaverly. I think your feet stuck in concrete goes deeper than wanting to save your wife and son. I think it hails back to the day you decided to leave your home and your family and your heritage. I think . . ." His voice dropped so low Tim had to strain to hear him. "You need to make peace with the part of you that is still Mennonite before you can pull your feet from that block of cement and move forward."

Tim bolted from the chair. His entire body shook with compressed fury. "Then I guess I'm gonna be stuck forever, because making peace with my father is something I will *never* do."

22

Amy pulled her car onto the highway and headed for town. She and the children had enjoyed a less-busy Sunday morning than in past weeks, not having to rise early to prepare their house for services. They'd stayed up late Saturday night, eating popcorn and playing board games, so she'd allowed the children the luxury of sleeping until seven thirty. Then she fixed pancakes, bacon, and eggs for breakfast instead of their usual Sunday-morning cold cereal and fruit. While they ate, she read the story about Daniel in the lions' den from the Bible storybook she'd received for her fifth birthday. Although the book was tattered and worn, the stories never grew old, and she delighted in sharing them with her children, just as her mother had read to her during her growing-up years. She hoped to pass on the book to her grandchildren one day.

In the backseat, between Adrianna and Parker, a wicker basket held two dozen wax-paper-wrapped peanut-butter- and-jelly sandwiches. She'd never brought something so simple to a fellowship dinner, but Mr. Schell had told her to bring food that would keep without refrigeration or the warmth of a stove, so her options were limited. Today they'd lunch at the Gerbers' home, so Margaret would surely prepare something more substantial than cold sandwiches.

She glanced in the rearview mirror and caught Parker sticking his nose over the basket and inhaling. She smiled to herself. The sandwiches might be simple fare, but at least one person was pleased with the choice. Parker would eat peanut butter and jelly every day if she let him.

Bekah cradled Amy's and all three of the children's Bibles in her lap, holding them as securely as a mother held a newborn. Despite the girl's up-and-down emotions, she remembered to be respectful of God's holy Word. The sight of her daughter's slender fingers clinging tightly to the books created a sting in the back of Amy's nose. *Train up a child in the way he should go* . . . She'd done her part; she had to trust that God's hold on Bekah would remain strong through these turbulent teen years.

She crested the gentle rise that let them know the town was just ahead, and on the other side of the rise she spotted Mr. Roper's truck, back half on the road, front half in the ditch. Wisps of smoke curled from beneath the hood.

Bekah pointed. "What's wrong with Mr. Roper's truck?"

Amy slowed her vehicle. "I'm not sure. But it doesn't look good."

Both Parker and Adrianna draped their arms over the seat and stared ahead. Amy pulled onto the shoulder and put the car in park. Although she didn't expect traffic, she pushed the button for her emergency lights before turning to the children. "You stay in the car. We don't need you on the road."

Then she hopped out and trotted across the highway to Mr. Roper, who sat on the truck's back fender with a disgruntled look on his face.

"Are you all right?"

His breath escaped in a mighty huff. "I'm fine. But my truck isn't."

White smoke continued to snake from the edges of the hood before being erased by the breeze. "What happened?"

He jammed his thumb toward the front fender. "A dog ran out in front of me. I swerved to avoid it and bounced into the ditch. Wouldn't you know I'd bounce right into a drop-off. Broke a tie rod, and I'm pretty sure I've got a leak in my radiator."

"So you can't drive it?"

He shook his head, scuffing the toe of his boot on the ground. Dust dimmed the black leather. With a jolt, she realized she'd never seen him so dressed up. Although informal in a crisp-ironed shirt, unfaded jeans, and uncovered head, he looked nice—especially when compared to his usual T-shirts, well-worn blue jeans, and scuffed brown boots. Had he been heading to church, too? None of the men in her fellowship either in Arborville or here in Weaverly would attend a service in something other than a white shirt, black pants, and a lapel-less jacket, but the pearl-buttoned western shirt and dark blue denim suited Mr. Roper. And he probably fit right in with the ranchers in Weaverly.

Realizing where her thoughts had taken her, Amy abruptly turned her attention elsewhere. She glanced up and down the road. How had he managed to end up in the opposite ditch simply from trying to avoid hitting a dog? "The children and I are going in for our morning fellowship. We're meeting in the insurance office in town. I can give you a ride, take you to your own church, and maybe afterward one of the men in your congregation will help you tow your truck to a service station."

Scritch, scritch, scritch. He continued brushing his toe on the ground. Dirt stirred, further marring the once-shiny toe of his boot. "Not attending church today."

"Oh. I thought by the way you were dressed . . ."

He shot her a startled look.

Heat seared her cheeks. She shifted her gaze to the road. "Well, I can't just leave you here. Who knows when someone else might come along? Let me take you into town, at least. If nothing else, one of the Mennonite men will certainly be willing to come tow your truck where a mechanic can look at it."

"The closest car repair shop that would be open today is in Topeka." He spoke flatly, with a tiny hint of resentment, reminding her of the first day they'd met, when he'd hauled Parker and Adrianna home. Over the weeks, he'd lost the gruff, impersonal manner of speaking to her, and she felt rebuffed by the change now, even though his tone was still mild. "One of the Mennonite men would take me all the way to Topeka . . . on worship day?"

Her fluttering ribbons tickled her cheeks. She turned her face to the wind, meeting his gaze. "If it's necessary, of course they would, Mr. Roper. 'Love thy neighbour as thyself. . . . ' That includes meeting needs where they exist."

He crunched his forehead into a series of lines. "I don't know . . ."

"Mr. Roper?" Adrianna's voice carried across the road. She'd rolled down the window and hung her head out, her fingers curled over the windowsill. "Did your truck get broke?"

His face relaxed into a weary smile. "I'm afraid so, Adri."

Parker crowded next to Adri. "What happened?"

The man pushed to his feet, slipping his hands into the pockets of his jeans. "Oh, nothing much. A silly ol' dog ran me right off the road."

"What a bad dog! My dog Spot wouldn't do that," Adri-anna proclaimed, and Mr. Roper chuckled. Then the child chirped in a cheery voice, "Why don'tcha get in our car? You can come to service an' eat lunch with us. It'll make you feel better."

Mr. Roper's terse expression returned, and he spun to face his truck. Amy glanced at the simple watch on her wrist. If they didn't hurry, they'd be late for their service. They were only a mile from their homes—he could walk to his house easily. Yet she felt guilty leaving the man sitting here in the sun beside the road.

Suddenly he pushed off from the truck's bed with a vicious thrust of his hand. "I'm holding you up. You've got places to be."

"But—"

"Go." His tone, although not unkind, was so final it forced her backward a step.

"A-all right, Mr. Roper." She trotted to her car and slowly pulled onto the road. The children chattered, questioning why she was leaving their friend behind, but she ignored them. She drove to the insurance office and parked. Only one other car sat in the street in front of the office, but through the large plate-glass windows she glimpsed several people inside. Most of the fellowship members must have walked to the building for service.

"Bekah, carry in our Bibles, please. Parker, take the basket with you. Adrianna, careful now—don't step out into the street. Go right up on the curb." She offered automatic directions, her mind a mile outside of town where Mr. Roper sat on the side of the road alone, dejected. No matter how abrasive he'd been with her, he needed help. If one of the Mennonite men wasn't willing to offer his assistance, she'd find someone else who would.

⁂

The moment Mrs. Knackstedt's car pulled away, Tim removed his keys from the ignition of his truck, locked it up—sitting on the highway here, someone might come by and bother it—and then turned his feet toward Weaverly. He needed to call for help, but he'd left his cell phone sitting on his dresser. Although pay phones were fast becoming a thing of the past, the bank still kept one in operation on the outside of the building. He'd make use of it today.

The sun tried to cook his uncovered head and forced him to squint. Why hadn't he thought to grab a hat? Wind whistled across the fields on either side of the road, raising dust devils that skipped along in their zigzagging manner. Julia had always loved to watch dust devils flit across empty fields, claiming they reminded her of ballet dancers. His feet had never felt less like dancing.

His conversation with Reverend Geary still weighed heavily on him. Make peace with his Mennonite past? How would that eliminate the burden of guilt he carried for letting his wife and son drive away on their own that day? It didn't make sense. The two halves of his lives were disconnected. One had nothing to do with the other. Yet he couldn't deny he'd thought more about Julia and Charlie in the past weeks—since the Mennonites had arrived in town—than he had in the previous two years combined.

Probably because of Parker. His similarities to Charlie. Not in appearance. Parker was tall and gangly where Charlie had been short and always a little plump. But in tenderness. In eagerness to please. In neediness. And Parker had stirred the old protectiveness to life within Tim's father-heart.

He needed to cut his ties with the boy. If spending time with Parker was what had brought back all the regrets and started the unsettling dream, then it wasn't worth it to show him how to use a hammer or run a mower or prune trees. No matter how much satisfaction it brought Tim to share his knowledge with an eager, willing learner, it couldn't make up for the unsettling dreams, lack of sleep, and haunting memories.

Tim clomped along, mopping his sweaty forehead with the sleeve of his shirt, his mind whirling. School would start in another month and a half. Seven weeks. Over the next couple weeks, he'd start backing off. Maybe have the kids come one day a week instead of two. Then, when school started and they made new friends, he'd ask them to stop visiting the orchard.

"This is Mr. Roper, my best friend." Parker's words echoed through Tim's mind. He felt the pressure of the boy's skinny arm across his back, the proud hand clamped on his shoulder. He grimaced. It'd be hard to sever ties with the boy. But for the sake of his sanity, he had to.

The sound of an engine caught his attention, and he cupped his hand over his eyes to peer ahead. An older-model pickup truck chugged toward him. Sun glinted on the windshield, turning the glass into one bright glare. Not until the truck slowed to a stop beside him did he see the driver—one of the Mennonite men he'd met at the Fourth of July doings.

The man rested his elbow on the windowsill and smiled at Tim. "Hello. Tim, right? I'm Christian Hunsberger. Mrs. Knackstedt sent me out—said you needed a tow."

Mrs. Knackstedt . . . Paying him back, no doubt, for the help he'd given her in the past. If he accepted this kind deed, would he then owe her another? Tim squinted up and down the road, hoping someone else might magically appear. No one. He sighed. "Yeah. My truck's broken down. I was heading to town to call for a tow truck to take me to Topeka."

Hunsberger smiled, flashing white teeth in a tan, clean-shaven face. "No need for that. I got a hitchball and chain, and a full tank of gas." He laughed. "Filled up yesterday, even though I wasn't even near empty. Guess the Lord knew I'd need that gasoline today."

Despite the shimmering sun overhead, a shiver climbed Tim's spine. He shuffled his feet, uncertain. "Hate to make a perfect stranger drive all the way to Topeka." He flicked a glance at the man's black flat-brimmed hat. " 'Specially on worship day."

Again, Hunsberger laughed. "Seems to me Jesus told the synagogue leader that a responsible man waters his oxen on the Sabbath, so what is wrong with necessary work? I figure making sure you aren't stranded is just as important as watering the oxen." He bobbed his chin toward the passenger's side. "Climb in—we'll go get your truck."

Tim hesitated. He needed assistance. But did he want to accept it from this affable Mennonite man?

23

"Remember to be home by four today," Mom called as Bekah herded Parker toward the back door on Tuesday. "I want all of us to go in to the library so I can check my email."

"I know, I know," Bekah muttered under her breath. She let the screen door slam shut behind her, then gave Parker a little push that sped his feet.

"Stop pushin', Bekah." Parker sounded grumpy—he'd been out of sorts all morning for some reason. Mom had to call him three times before he got out of bed. Then he'd picked at his breakfast and dragged himself around. He needed to straighten up. Mr. Roper wouldn't want a grouchy worker on his property. He had enough worries with his truck in the shop and his grape harvest for the year ruined. Why couldn't it rain, anyway?

At least the apple trees were showing signs of a decent harvest. Mr. Roper had taken them on a walk through the trees last week, showing them the hard little balls that would develop into full-grown apples by mid-September. He'd shown them how to count the number of apple buds in a cluster and pick all but three so the apples would grow to a decent size. Too close together, he'd said, and they didn't develop like they should. Sometimes Bekah wondered if she was like an apple bud, all cramped up with too many others. She needed space to grow into who she was supposed to be, too.

She wheeled Parker's bicycle to him, waited until he took hold, then hurried back into the garage for her own. "C'mon. Let's get going."

Hot wind smacked her in the face, threatening to dislodge her prayer cap. She lowered her head and pumped hard. Parker lagged behind. She called over her shoulder, "Hurry up! You're slower'n a snail today!" Parker grunted, but he rose up from the seat and put his weight behind the pumps on the pedals, and he caught up to her.

They turned into Mr. Roper's lane. They hopped off their bikes and leaned them against the barn. Then Parker scuffed inside the barn while Bekah skipped to the house. Mr. Roper always left the little box air-conditioner going, and stepping from the hot, dry wind into the cool trailer home raised a sigh of relief.

As she'd come to expect, Mr. Roper had left a note on the counter, listing things to do that day. Every task looked familiar, except one. *Clear everything from hall closet,* he'd written. Bekah frowned at the instruction. Did he mean for her to throw away everything in the closet, or merely remove the items and put them somewhere else?

Nibbling the inside of her lower lip, she crossed to the hallway and opened the closet door. She examined the contents carefully. Three coats hung on hangers—two of them obviously for a woman and a third for a little boy. Bekah fingered the sailboat design embroidered on the corduroy front of the child's coat. A few threads were loose on the sail, but Mom could fix that easily. Overall, the coat was in good shape. Why would Mr. Roper want this thrown away? She'd been taught it was irresponsible to dispose of something that could still be used.

Then realization struck. Bekah recoiled from the coat, plastering herself against the paneled wall behind her, her heart pounding. These things had belonged to his wife and son. His *dead* wife and son. She stared at the coats, the faces from the picture Mr. Roper had shown her springing to life in her imagination. She pinched her eyes tight, willing the image away. When she slowly opened her eyes again, right eye first, then left, all she saw was three coats—one little and two big.

Tears stung behind Bekah's nose, and she sniffed hard. Mr. Roper wanted these things gone because the memories hurt him. She understood. Mom had given away almost all of Dad's things shortly after his funeral. She'd said it was because they were moving in with Grandpa and there wasn't room for Dad's stuff at Grandpa's house, but even then Bekah had known it was too hard for Mom to look at those things and remember Dad would never use them again.

Mr. Roper had held on to his wife's and son's things for a long time. Why would he choose now to let them go? She didn't know, but she'd do as he asked. He kept empty grocery sacks under his sink to use as garbage bags. Bekah pulled all of them out and began filling them with the items in the closet. The coats went first, wadded into balls. Then she reached for the shoe boxes that lined the closet floor.

She started to jam them into a sack, but curiosity got the best of her. With a surreptitious peek at the windows to be certain no one peered in at her, she lifted the lid on the first box and looked inside. Letters, all addressed to Julia Roper from someone named Grace Armstrong. Bekah came close to opening one of the envelopes, but she and her friends from Arborville wrote letters back and forth, and she wouldn't want a stranger reading them. So she put them back in the box and closed the lid. She slipped the box into a sack.

In the second shoe box she found photographs. For several minutes she sat cross-legged on the floor and examined each photo by turn. In her religious sect, photographs weren't allowed, so she didn't have pictures she could hold to remind her of her past. Not of the house where she'd lived with Mom and Daddy, not of Daddy, not even of herself. But in her hands, right now, she held captured moments from Mr. Roper's years with his wife and with his son. Her chest felt as tight as an overfilled balloon as she flicked slowly through the images. So many smiling faces. So much pride and joy captured on the shiny paper.

All of a sudden it hurt too much to look at the pictures. She dropped them back in the box, slammed the lid in place, and shoved the container into the nearest sack. She started to simply push the third box into the sack without looking inside, but something inside of it rattled, and she couldn't resist taking a peek.

Only four items rested in the bottom of the box, and Bekah knew they'd been Charlie's. She stared down at a blue, baby-sized hairbrush with a duck decal on the handle. Nestled next to it was a green-and-yellow-striped rattle. A little plastic case, no bigger than a matchbox, lay snug in the shoe box's corner. Written on the top was "My First Lost Tooth." Bekah didn't unsnap the lid to see if a tooth still sat inside. The final item—a tiny beaded bracelet with the letters on the beads spelling the name CHARLIE—brought a rush of tears.

She slid the last box into the trash sack, her heart aching. How could Mr. Roper ask her to get rid of these things? Maybe he'd asked her because he knew he couldn't do it himself. Looking at the lumpy sack, envisioning what filled it, Bekah didn't know if she could do it, either.

A big box was pushed clear back in the corner of the closet. Bekah dragged it out and peeled open the folded-over flaps. The box contained women's clothing—jeans, shirts, a few skirts and frilly blouses. The kind of clothes Bekah wasn't allowed to wear. She rummaged through the neat stacks, seeing hints of Julia Roper's personality in the flowered tops, embroidered blue jeans, and ruffles and flounces. These were the clothes of a pretty woman who was sure of herself. Bekah had never met her, but suddenly she envied Mrs. Roper.

She shoved the box next to the line of sacks and stood. The closet rod and floor were all cleared, but the shelf above the rod still held two boxes—the kind you bought in the store and folded to make a bottom and fitted top. She stuck her fingers through the slotted handle on the closest one and pulled. The weight took her by surprise, and she dropped it. The top popped off, and little boy's clothing spilled across the floor. With a grunt, Bekah knelt and started to stuff the clothes back into the box, but even if they were just going to the burn pile, she found she couldn't jam them in any old way. She took the time to fold each item, from plaid shorts and gray-striped overalls to button-up shirts and footed pajamas. By the time she finished, she felt like crying again.

Exercising care, she removed the final box from the shelf. It contained more boy's clothes as well as a stuffed bear and a soft blanket with one shredded corner. Bekah imagined the round-faced little boy from the pictures holding that corner to drag the blanket around, wearing it out with his grubby fist. A lump filled her throat. She stared into the box. The teddy bear seemed to stare back at her. She slapped the lid in place, hiding the bear from view. Her chest ached. She wished Mr. Roper hadn't given her this job!

She put the boxes, one on top of the other, by the front door and then piled the sacks around the stack of boxes. Although she knew she should carry it all out to the burn pile now, she couldn't do it right after seeing what all was inside. It could wait until she'd finished her other cleaning.

Her chin set in a determined angle, she returned to the kitchen. *Wash dishes,* Mr. Roper had written. The task would get her focus elsewhere. As she ran a sink of sudsy water, the front door creaked open. Mr. Roper and Parker stepped inside.

"Bekah, I think Parker needs to go home." Mr. Roper held his arm around Parker's shoulders. Worry lines marched across his forehead.

Parker's face had gotten tan this summer working outside with Mr. Roper, but now he looked sunburnt. Bekah shut off the water and hurried to Mr. Roper's side. She touched Parker's forehead. So hot! "Oh, you're sick." Regret rose up to choke her when she thought about how impatient she'd been with him. She used her kindest voice. "I'm sorry you're not feeling good."

Parker took a step away from Mr. Roper and rested his head on Bekah's shoulder. He'd grown a lot this summer. She and her brother were now nose to nose in height. She felt awkward patting his back, but she comforted him anyway.

"I think he should go home, but I don't want him riding his bike." Mr. Roper grabbed the bill of his cap and shifted the cap back and forth. "I don't have my truck, so I can't take you. Do you think your mom would be able to put your bicycles in her trunk?"

Bekah nodded. "She's put the bikes in the trunk before. Can I use your phone? I'll call her and have her come get him."

Mr. Roper led Parker to the sofa. "Parker, you stretch out on the sofa there and wait for your mom, okay?" He stood near while Parker flopped onto the thick cushions. Then he sent an apologetic look in Bekah's direction. "I'd stay with him until your mom comes, but I agreed to meet the pesticide people at ten thirty so we can spray the trees. They'll be here any minute."

Bekah looked at Parker. He curled on his side, his eyes closed. She turned to Mr. Roper. The man seemed to need as much assurance as Parker did. "He'll be okay—he'll probably sleep. He always does when he has a fever. Besides, Mom'll be here in just a few minutes. Go ahead and do what you need to."

Mr. Roper gave Bekah's shoulder a quick squeeze. "Thanks, Bekah. You're a good kid."

Bekah's cheeks warmed at his praise. She offered an embarrassed smile as a thank-you, and he strode out the door. Bekah poked the numbered buttons on Mr. Roper's phone. Mom answered on the second ring, and Bekah told her about Parker's fever. A few minutes later, Mom and Adri pulled up Mr. Roper's lane. Adri stayed in the car, but Mom ran to the house and went straight to Parker, cooing over him as if he were two years old rather than eleven.

Bekah, watching, didn't mind. When she was sick, she liked having Mom fuss over her. Besides, he deserved it after the way they'd all scolded him that morning, the poor guy. Mom helped Parker to his feet and aimed him for the door. As they headed outside, Bekah's gaze fell on the tumble of sacks and the boxes.

Clear everything from hall closet. She knew she should follow Mr. Roper's instruction, but she couldn't bear the thought of throwing away the clothes and coats and photographs. Bekah would give anything to have pictures of her dad. Someday Mr. Roper would want those photographs back. And somebody could wear the clothes.

Bekah grabbed Mom's arm. "Mr. Roper doesn't want this stuff anymore. Can we put it in the trunk with Parker's bike?"

Mom glanced across the pile. "It would all fit in the backseat of the car, I think. But are you sure he doesn't intend to keep it?"

"I'm sure."

"What are you going to do with all of this?"

Bekah sucked in her lower lip for a moment. "I don't know . . ." She didn't know for sure what she'd do with the clothes, but she'd hide the photographs and other little things in her closet so they'd be ready when Mr. Roper wanted them again.

Mom moved forward. "Well, I don't have time to worry about it right now. I need to get Parker home and to bed. If you want the things, load them quickly so I can go."

"Thanks, Mom!" Bekah grabbed a handful of sacks. It took three trips, but she crammed everything in beside Adri or around Parker's bicycle. She felt a little bit like a thief as Mom drove off with Mr. Roper's things in the car, but she also felt relieved. She turned back toward the house to finish her work for the day, satisfied.

Someday, surely, Mr. Roper would be glad she hadn't thrown his wife's and son's clothing and all those photographs on the burn pile.

24

Parker's fever continued for three days. On the second day, Amy called the clinic in Weaverly and talked with a nurse, who asked several questions. After their conversation, Amy decided not to take him in. He had no rash, no swollen tonsils or glands, no other symptoms that would indicate a serious illness. The nurse surmised he'd contracted a summer cold and advised making sure he drank plenty of fluids and got a sufficient amount of rest; if the fever hadn't abated by Friday, Amy should bring him in.

Amy found following the nurse's advice concerning rest easy—all Parker wanted to do was sleep. But she woke him frequently to offer water, juice, or clear broth. He fussed at each interruption but obediently drained cup after cup.

Because he slept so soundly, requiring little attention, Amy was able to continue working. With Bekah entertaining Adrianna, she managed to complete the face on a twin-sized bed quilt. She'd finished the trio of wall hangings previously but still needed to ship them. That required a trip into town to the post office, and she didn't want to leave Parker while he was ill. Bekah offered to watch him, but Amy didn't feel comfortable leaving the children alone, even for a little while, until Parker was well again. So Amy's plans to mail the projects and to check her email at the library were postponed for several days.

Finally, on Friday morning, Parker awakened with a fever-free smile. And a raging appetite. To Amy's delight, he consumed four pieces of toast and a pile of scrambled eggs, then asked for more toast.

Laughing, Amy ruffled his sleep-flattened hair. "I think you've had enough for now. You don't want to make your tummy sick from too much food all at once."

Parker sighed, dropping his chin. "Okay, Mom." He lifted a hopeful face to her. "Can I have peanut-butter sandwiches for lunch, though?" He thrust two fingers upward. "Just two, not three. And a banana."

Amy laughed again. She pushed out of her chair and planted a kiss on the top of his head. "You sure can." Picking up her plate and silverware, she looked at Adrianna, who was using her toast as a scoop to push fluffy bits of egg around her plate. "Eat your food instead of playing."

Adrianna rested her cheek on her fist and carried the toast to her mouth.

Bekah rose from the opposite side of the table. "Yes, Adri, hurry up. I need your plate." She grabbed Parker's empty plate and stacked it on top of her own. "As soon as I'm done with the dishes, I'm going over to Mr. Roper's. It's his laundry day."

Parker shot out of his seat, knocking the chair up on two legs with the jerky movement. "I'm going, too." He started for the stairs.

"Oh no, not you." Amy caught Parker's arm and drew him to a stop. "You're resting today. I'm glad you feel better, but fever wears a body down. Too much activity today could make you sick again. So this is going to be a lazy day for you, young man. You'll spend it reading or working on a puzzle, not following Mr. Roper around the orchard."

Parker stuck out his lower lip. "But it's Friday. It's a work-day. And I didn't get to work on Tuesday 'cause Mr. Roper made me go home. He *needs* me, Mom."

Her son's abject disappointment pierced Amy, but she remained firm. "You can go back next week. But not today."

Adrianna stuffed the last bite of toast in her mouth and spoke around it. "I'w go to Mr. Woper's an' work for Pawkuh today."

Amy frowned at her youngest. "Mind your manners. And you'll stay here. You can entertain Parker." She turned to Bekah, ignoring Parker's and Adrianna's hangdog expressions. "What time do you think you'll finish today?"

Bekah placed the dishes on the counter, lifting her shoulders in a shrug. "I don't know. Laundry doesn't take as long over there because he has the automatic dryer." A dreamy look crossed Bekah's face. "Sure is nice not to have to fight the wind to hang his sheets and towels on the line."

Amy's heart caught. Was she making a mistake, allowing the children to sample so many conveniences at Mr. Roper's house? He'd said they'd already more than earned their bushel of apples. Maybe she should consider bringing to an end their time with the man. They could continue to pray for him without spending time with him. "Then what time will you be done?"

"If all I do is laundry and clean his bathroom, I'll be done before noon. Why?"

Amy peeked at her two youngest, waiting to see if their pouts would disappear with her next statement. "I want to go to the library, and I thought all of you would want to go, too."

Adrianna sat upright, her face lighting. "Yay! I like Miss Bergstrom. She lets me play with the puppets."

A smile curved Parker's lips. "I like the puppets, too."

"Good." Amy nearly sighed in relief at their change in attitude. "Adrianna, if you're finished there, you and Parker can go up and get dressed. Then come down and dry dishes for Bekah."

The two youngest headed upstairs. Bekah was already running water for dishes, so Amy turned toward the sewing room to get started on her work for the day. As she passed the telephone on the corner of the counter, it rang, nearly startling her out of her skin. She yanked up the receiver and said breathlessly, "Hello?"

A familiar throaty chuckle rumbled through the line. "You sound frazzled. Did I call at a bad time?"

Amy laughed, pressing the phone to her ear. "No. The ring just scared the wind out of me. Good morning, Dad."

Bekah flicked a grin in Amy's direction and waggled her fingers.

"Bekah says hello," Amy said into the phone.

"Hello to Bekah, too."

Amy waved at Bekah, then leaned her hip against the counter. "How are things in Arborville?"

Dad chuckled again, but with restraint this time. "Hmm, that's the first time you haven't asked, 'How are things at home?' Does that mean Weaverly is home to you now?"

Amy considered Dad's question. She'd lived her entire lifetime prior to this move in the little community of Arborville,

Kansas, surrounded by people she knew as well as her own family. She'd only resided in Weaverly two months, and she knew only a handful of people, yet she felt settled here. She drew in a satisfied breath. "Yes. It is home."

A short silence reigned, and then Dad's voice came again, laden with both relief and remorse. "That's good, Amy. I'm happy for you."

Amy was happy for herself. "The children and I would sure enjoy a visit from you. We have a sleeping porch upstairs, and Parker and Adrianna love to use it, so we'd put you in Parker's room if you wanted to spend the night. You could meet the fellowship members from Ohio, and maybe even worship with us if you stayed a whole weekend. What do you say?" Talking to her father, hearing his voice, made her miss him. She hoped he'd agree to a weekend visit.

"Actually, that's why I called. I need to come see you and bring someone with me."

Something in Dad's tone—a forced lightness—offered a warning. A prickle of trepidation crept up Amy's spine. "Who's that?"

"James Corey. Do you remember him? He's the representative from Farmers Aid Agency who . . ."

The prickle increased in intensity. James Corey had paid the accident claim after Gabe's death. "Is something wrong?"

"I think it would be better for us to talk in person. What if we drove over Monday? Would that be all right?"

"M-Monday?"

"The sooner we get this settled, the better." Now Dad sounded grim.

Amy clutched the receiver with both hands. Her fingers trembled. During her conversation with Dad, Adrianna and

Parker had come downstairs and joined Bekah at the sink. They chattered softly together, clinking dishes and rattling silverware into the drawer. She prayed they wouldn't overhear her next words. "It's about Gabe, isn't it? The way he died . . ."

A sigh whisked through the line. "Now, I don't want you to worry."

"How can I not worry, Dad?"

"By trusting instead."

"But—"

"'The Lord is my rock, and my fortress, and my deliverer; my God, my strength, in whom I will trust. . . .'" Dad's no-nonsense recital of the verse from Psalm 18 offered a gentle reprimand.

Amy drew in a slow breath. "Yes, Dad."

Dad spoke again. "Mr. Corey has some questions, but I don't want you to spend the weekend fretting about this. You know you've done nothing wrong."

No, she hadn't done anything wrong. But had Gabe?

"I'll let you go now. Give the children a hug and a kiss from Grandpa. I'll see you Monday."

"All right. Good-bye." Amy placed the receiver in its cradle, then clutched her trembling hands to her ribs. Her stomach whirled, and cotton filled her mouth. She'd come here to escape the speculation. But apparently the speculation was going to follow her all the way to Weaverly.

✳

Bekah poked her head inside the musty barn and called, "Mr. Roper? You in here?"

"Sure am." The reply came from the far corner of the

barn, where a workbench stretched halfway across the wall. "Whatcha need?"

Although morning sunshine painted the yard in bold yellow, the dusty windows blocked light from entering the barn. Bekah hated going inside the wood-framed, creaky building. Even though it was big, it reminded her of an underground cellar with its funny odors and lack of light. Maybe she should ask Mr. Roper about giving the windows a good wash one of these days. It wouldn't fix the smell, but at least the sun could get in there. "I need to tell you something."

Mr. Roper stepped toward the middle of the barn. He carried an odd-shaped tool in one hand and a greasy-looking rag in the other. The smell of turpentine drifted to Bekah's nose. She crinkled her face in distaste and remained rooted in the wide doorway.

"Parker's over his fever, but he didn't come with me. Mom wanted him to stay home today and rest. I'm gonna do your laundry, okay?"

"No Parker today, huh?" Did regret or relief tinge his tone? Bekah couldn't be sure. Before she could reply, he added, "I got bored last night and did a few loads of wash myself. All that's left is sheets and towels, so you won't have to hang around long today."

"Oh." Bekah inched backward, puzzled by his aloofness. He usually teased with her a little bit. "So . . . there isn't anything else you want me to do?"

"Nope. Not a thing. Thanks, Bekah." He turned on his heel and disappeared into the shadowy corner.

Chewing her chapped lower lip, Bekah crossed to the house and let herself inside. After her weeks of working for Mr. Roper, she no longer felt like a trespasser when she entered his house. Without a moment's pause, she gathered the towels from the bathroom—off the rack, from a hook beside the shower, and off the floor—and threw them into the washing machine. She set the machine, measured in detergent, then went to his bedroom to strip the bed.

Apparently Mr. Roper never made his bed. Every time she'd come in, the spread was all rumpled and the sheets tangled. It looked like he wrestled all night instead of sleeping. She flopped the spread—a tattered blue-and-green plaid with a coffee stain in the middle that wouldn't wash out—to the floor and then tugged all the sheets free. After dumping the pillows from their cases, she carried the wad to the little utility area off the kitchen and dropped it all on the floor next to the washer.

No note waited on the counter for her, but she always cleaned the bathroom on Friday, so she grabbed the cleaning supplies from the plastic basket under the sink and went to work. She finished just as the washing machine buzzed. She transferred the towels to the dryer, smiling because she didn't have to send them through a wringer to remove excess water—modern washing machines were wonderful! Then she carefully layered the sheets and pillowcases into the belly of the washer. She'd learned to balance everything so the machine didn't jiggle back and forth and threaten to walk right out of the utility closet. After programming both machines, she had nothing to do except wait for the humming machines to finish their jobs.

So she went to the living room and looked around. Mr. Roper had magazines on the table in front of the sofa, but she wasn't interested in tools or woodworking. A television set lurked in the corner. For a moment, Bekah considered turning it on. She'd watched a little TV before, in stores and in some of her schoolmates' homes back in Arborville, but she knew Mom wouldn't want her watching it. Mom wouldn't know if she did it or not, but her conscience wouldn't let her turn it on.

She wandered the periphery of the room, looking for something to clean, but she'd dusted and vacuumed on Tuesday. The house still looked clean. She couldn't find anything out of place. With a sigh, she plopped onto the sofa. The moment her bottom hit the cushion, an idea struck. She'd wanted to ask Mr. Roper questions about why he decided not to be Mennonite anymore. With Parker always around, she hadn't been given a chance, but Parker was gone today. She didn't have any pressing tasks waiting. Mr. Roper was still in the barn—she knew because the golf cart he drove around the orchard sat between the barn and the house.

She hopped up, then paused. Mr. Roper had been kind of funny this morning. Standoffish instead of friendly. Maybe she shouldn't bother him. Slowly, she sank back onto the sofa, but then she stood again. She might never have another chance to question him alone. She had to do it today.

Anticipation quickening her pulse, she checked the dials on the washer and dryer. Still plenty of time before the towels needed to come out. With a skip in her step, she hurried out the door and across the yard. Wrinkling her nose, she entered the barn. "Mr. Roper? Can I talk to you?"

He turned from the rough workbench in the far corner of the barn. Iron parts lay scattered across its top. He dropped a hunk of iron next to the others with a *clank*. "Okay."

Although he didn't sound overly friendly, he didn't seem perturbed, either. Bekah skittered forward. The smell of turpentine threatened to singe her nose, but she stepped up next to the bench, resisting the urge to pinch her nose shut with her fingers. "What're you doing?"

"I took apart the apple grinder to clean the parts. It gets a little gunky when it's not in use. I guess I need to find something other than gunnysacks to cover it during the off-season."

Bekah glanced across the collection of odd parts to be polite, but she hadn't come to talk about grinding apples. Shifting to face him, she blurted out the question that had burned in the back of her mind for weeks. "How come you're not Mennonite anymore?"

The man's eyebrows dropped low. "What?"

Bekah hunched her shoulders, intimidated by his scowl. But she couldn't seem to stop the torrent that poured from her lips. "Did you quit being Mennonite because you wanted . . . more? Sometimes when I look at other kids and the clothes they wear and the things they get to do, I wish I could be like them instead of like me. Sometimes I wish I had a cell phone"—she flicked a glance at the little silver phone tucked in a pouch on his belt—"and a radio or a television. I wish I could get my hair cut in a really cute style instead of wearing it under my cap like the old ladies, and paint my fingernails, and maybe put on makeup. Sometimes I don't want to learn to sew and cook and clean. I just want to have fun and go swimming in the public pool like other kids. Sometimes I wonder what it's like to be like . . . like you."

She paused, her chest heaving. Mr. Roper stared at her. Even in the muted light, she recognized surprise in his eyes. He didn't say anything, so she licked her lips and said, "You used to be Mennonite, but now you're not. And you're happy about it, right? So why'd you change, Mr. Roper? Why aren't you Mennonite anymore?"

25

Tim dropped the oily rag on the workbench and wiped his palms down the front of his filthy jeans. He should never have asked these kids to come to work for him. He'd planted ideas in Bekah's head. Ideas that had no place in her youthful Mennonite mind.

He wanted to disregard her questions—pretend he hadn't heard them—but looking into her pleading face, he didn't have the heart to turn away. With a sigh, he plopped onto an upturned apple crate and clamped his hands over his wide-spread knees. "Have you ever heard the expression, 'The grass is always greener on the other side of the fence'?"

The girl's face puckered. "Sure."

"What do you think it means?"

"It means some people think what they have is never as good as what other people have."

Tim nodded. "That's a good way to put it. And it's something you should remember."

She folded her arms over her chest, crushing the modesty cape of her pale yellow dress. "But why?"

Tim worked his thumbs back and forth. His calluses caught on the worn denim, creating a soft *skritch-skritch*. " 'Cause otherwise you'll always be discontent. And that's no way to live your life." To his surprise a Bible verse, long buried, found its way out of his mouth. " '. . . godliness with contentment is great gain.' " What was the reference? He couldn't remember, but it came from First Timothy.

Bekah scowled. "You sound like my mom. She always quotes the Bible at me instead of just telling me what she thinks."

"Parents do that," Tim said. "My dad did it, too." Over and over and over . . . until Tim had had enough and walked away in search of that greener grass.

"But didn't it make you mad?" The girl tipped her head, scrunching a white ribbon against her shoulder. "Didn't you ever wish you could do what you wanted to without someone saying, 'No, the Bible says you shouldn't,' or 'No, that doesn't honor God.' " She released a mighty huff and threw her hands wide. "Well, you're not Mennonite anymore, so you don't have to worry about it. Aren't you happy now?"

Happy? Tim examined his life. He'd found a level of happiness with Julia and Charlie. He'd found satisfaction in working the orchard, in watching the trees blossom. But if he were honest, somewhere in the back of his heart, something was missing. It had been missing for years. What would Bekah say if he confided how much it hurt that he'd never been able to share his lovely wife and precious son with his own parents?

His chest constricted, imagining his parents together with Charlie. How Mom would've adored the cheerful little boy with the heart as big as the endless Kansas sky—and Charlie would have adored her in return. Tim's choice had robbed

Charlie of a loving grandmother. Because of Tim, Charlie had never enjoyed a huge family gathering at Christmas or Thanksgiving. He'd never played in the haymow with a half dozen cousins. Tim assumed Charlie had cousins. By now most of his younger siblings were probably married and had kids. It was the Mennonite way to marry and raise a family.

Tim's chest ached as his thoughts tumbled onward. He couldn't call his dad and ask for advice or tell him about the promising abundance of Gala apples in this year's crop. He couldn't go ice fishing with his brothers or tease his sisters about being courted. If he had nieces and nephews, did they even know he existed? Or had his family buried him, the way he'd tried to bury them?

So he had a cell phone. He wore blue jeans instead of home-made twill pants. He watched television on Saturday nights and had even gone to the movie theater on a regular basis with Julia. He lived a regular, normal, everyday existence similar to every other citizen of Weaverly. He had more than he'd owned as a boy in possessions and conveniences. But was all that enough to replace what he'd given up the day he threw his hat at his father's feet and proclaimed he was fed up with the rules and regulations and he wanted out? Tim couldn't honestly say yes.

And he wouldn't have come face-to-face with any of these painful questions—he wouldn't know for sure that he wasn't happy—if those Mennonites hadn't chosen to buy the land next door and settle in Weaverly.

He jerked upright, his knees cracking. "Bekah, I think you'd better head home now. And maybe"—his throat tightened down, making it hard to speak—"it'd be best if you and Parker didn't come back here anymore."

Bekah gaped at him in dismay. "B-but, I haven't finished—"

"No more questions!" He didn't mean to bark, but his tone reflected his inner turmoil.

Tears flooded Bekah's eyes. "I . . . I meant I haven't finished your laundry."

Tim's shoulders slumped, the burden of regret bending him toward the ground. Regret for choices in the past. Regret for the present. He shook his head, flicking his hand toward the barn's wide opening. "Go then. Finish up. And then . . . we're done. You've earned your apples. When they're ready to pick, I'll let you know."

The girl stood staring at him, wide brown eyes swimming with unshed tears. Her chin quivered. "I . . . I didn't mean to make you mad."

A bitter taste flooded his mouth. "I'm not mad, Bekah, I'm—" *Sad. Weary. Lonely. Riddled with regrets.* There were so many things he could say. But he wouldn't share those deepest emotions with a thirteen-year-old Mennonite girl. He swallowed, then spoke very kindly. "Just go. Please?"

Bekah spun and dashed out of the barn. But not before she burst into tears.

Tim turned to his workbench and braced his palms on the warm, worn wood, letting his head hang low. Why had he opened himself to these kids? It hadn't done them—or him—any good. With a growl of frustration, he swept his hand across the row of cleaned parts, flinging them across the bench and onto the floor. The discordant clatter rang in his ears, but he welcomed the painful ring. It covered the sound of Bekah's heartbroken sobs.

Tim skipped lunch. He wasn't hungry, and he didn't want to risk crossing paths with Bekah. He spent the rest of the morning and the early afternoon in the orchard, checking the trees for signs of insect infestation. He'd had the trees sprayed, but he'd learned that sometimes, even with insecticide, troublesome bugs invaded his trees. To his relief, he found nothing alarming. Pinching a few smooth green leaves between his fingers, he acknowledged the one positive in the long days of record highs and no rain—apparently even the bugs thought it was too hot and dry to bother coming around.

Walking the length of the rows, he examined each sprinkler head, adjusting several. His back ached from bending down and straightening again and again. But he had to make sure the water would go to the roots of the trees rather than shoot in the air where the droplets could evaporate before they did any real good. It was a mindless task, leaving him open to meandering thoughts, but he managed to hold introspection at bay by humming country-western tunes he'd heard on the radio.

As he bent down to adjust the angle of the last sprinkler beneath the Gala trees, his cell phone vibrated. He straightened with a groan, pressing one hand to his lower back while yanking the phone free of its holster with the other. A fleeting thought trailed through his brain—*Probably Mrs. Knackstedt, calling to read me the riot act for upsetting her daughter.* But a glance showed a Topeka number glowing on the little screen.

Blowing out a breath of relief, Tim put the phone to his ear. "Tim Roper here."

"Tim, hey, this is Eric at Cecil's Auto Repair." A nasally twang blasted Tim's ear. "Good news. We got your truck finished. Took forever to get the right tie rod in. Kansas City sent the wrong one, so we had to send it back and reorder. Sorry for the delay. Boss says we'll give you a ten-percent discount on parts and labor since you had to wait more'n four days."

Suddenly the wait held a silver lining. Tim didn't have money to spare, and he wouldn't turn down the discount. "I appreciate that. When should I come get it?"

"We're open 'til seven tonight—"

Tim checked his wristwatch. If he left within the next two hours, he could make it with time to spare.

"—or you can come in anytime between eight and six tomorrow. Just come to the east shop and ask for Mark. He'll be the one to make sure they discounted your invoice."

"Okay. Thanks a lot." Tim disconnected the call, then stood in the dappled shade of the trees, tapping the telephone's slick edge on his open palm. Christian Hunsberger had said he'd be glad to take Tim to Topeka to retrieve his truck when the repairs were finished. Tim appreciated the man's willingness but preferred not to rely on one of the Mennonites. Who else could he call? In his mind's eye, he flicked through people from town. Not one name stood out as a person he felt comfortable calling to ask a favor. With a jolt, he realized he really didn't have anyone he considered a friend in Weaverly. Acquaintances, sure. Lots of them. But he couldn't think of one person who would willingly drop what he was doing to drive Tim to Topeka. The thought didn't sit well.

Pressing his lips in a grim line, he popped open his phone and scrolled to his contacts. There were so few, he easily located Christian Hunsberger. The row of numbers glared up at him, as if daring him to use them. Tim gave the button a sharp poke with his finger. One ring, two, then three. He started to punch the disconnect button, but then a cheerful female voice greeted, "Hello! Hunsberger residence."

Tim cleared his throat. "Hello. May I speak to Christian, please?"

"Christian is in the fields. This is his wife. May I take a message?"

Tim groaned inwardly. Of course the men would still be out working. And by the time they finished, it would be too late to make the trip to Topeka this evening. He quickly revised the request he'd been prepared to make. "This is Tim Roper. Your husband towed my truck to Topeka last Sunday."

"Oh! Yes, Mr. Roper. He said you might be calling. Is your truck ready to be picked up?"

"Yes, ma'am."

"I'm sure you're happy about that. We do rely on our vehicles, don't we?"

He wished she'd be a little less congenial. He caught himself wanting to smile at her perky tone and welcoming demeanor. Kindness seemed to ooze right through the telephone. Tim swallowed. "Yes, I guess we do. Could you ask your husband if he's available to take me tomorrow? Anytime between eight in the morning and five in the afternoon would be fine. The shop's open until six."

"I'll tell him just as soon as he gets home." The woman's sweet voice eased some of the tension in Tim's shoulders. "You can expect a call by suppertime."

"Thank you." Tim slipped the phone back in its holster. His stomach growled. By now Bekah was long gone—he could safely return to the house and have an early supper. Just as he reached his yard, the phone vibrated. Tim snapped it open. The Hunsbergers' number showed on the screen. The men must have come in early.

He jammed the phone to his ear. "Mr. Hunsberger?"

"No, this is Ellie Hunsberger again. I know I said I'd have Christian call you, but I just remembered something."

In the background, Tim heard homey sounds—a child's singsong voice, spoons clanking against pots, and cabinet doors opening and closing. Family sounds of supper preparation. They made his heart pang. "What's that?"

"Christian's aunt plans to go to Topeka tomorrow to do some shopping. She owns a Chevy van, so there's plenty of room for passengers. Since she's going in anyway, she said she'd be glad to take you to the auto repair shop before she does her own errands." A self-conscious laugh carried through the line. "If you'd rather have Christian take you, it's fine. I just thought, well, rather than sending *two* cars . . ." Her voice drifted off, but Tim didn't need to hear the rest of her thought to follow her reasoning.

It might be a little strange, riding with a Mennonite woman instead of a man, but a ride was a ride. And once he had his truck back, he wouldn't need to bother these people again. "There's no sense in wasting gasoline. Please let her know I appreciate her thoughtfulness."

"I will. She intends to leave early—eight o'clock, she said, so she'll pick you up around eight fifteen. Maybe eight twenty at the latest. She's taking one of our other fellowship families with her, and she'll pick them up first." A bang sounded in the background, followed by a child's shrill cry. Ellie Hunsberger raised her voice over the din. "But as I said, her van has plenty of seats, so there will be room for you and Amy Knackstedt and her children."

"Oh, but—"

"Good-bye now, Mr. Roper."

The phone went dead. Tim slapped it shut and curled his

fist around it, battling frustration. Trapped in a van with Mrs. Knackstedt, Bekah, Parker, and Adri? Tim released an audible groan. Raising his face to the blue sky overhead, he uttered his first prayer in years. "God, what are You trying to do to me?"

26

Amy herded the children to Margaret's van the moment it pulled into the driveway. Although she was beginning to feel at ease with the older woman and realized her brusqueness wasn't intended to be unkind, she still didn't want to create an unnecessary delay. Margaret liked to keep to a schedule.

She opened the sliding door behind the driver's door and gestured for the children to climb in. Parker gave Adrianna a boost and then clambered in behind her. They flopped into the middle seat.

Margaret leaned sideways and advised over her shoulder, "We'll have another passenger, too—your neighbor, Mr. Roper—so let's leave room for him. Children, climb into the rear seat, please."

Adrianna and Parker moved to obey, but Bekah shot Amy a panicked look. Amy gave her daughter an assuring pat on the shoulder. Bekah had come home yesterday with very sore feelings. Although Amy regretted the hurt her daughter had experienced, she couldn't deny relief that the decision to sever the children's time with Mr. Roper had been taken out of her hands. She disliked being the bad guy. She whispered, "It'll be fine. Just a short ride—thirty minutes."

Tears shimmered in Bekah's eyes. "Can't I stay here, Mom? Please?"

Amy hesitated. At thirteen, Bekah was old enough and responsible enough to be left alone, but motherly protectiveness rose up anyway. "Are you sure, honey? We'll be gone most of the day. You won't get lonely?"

"I can work on my dress, and I have a book to read. I'll be fine. Please?" Bekah's voice dropped to a raspy whisper. "I don't want to see him. Not yet."

Amy sighed and gave Bekah a quick hug. "All right. But stay in the house and keep the doors locked. I'll call from a pay phone in town to check on you. You have the numbers for the fellowship members by the telephone if you need something."

Bekah's arms tightened around Amy's neck, almost a stranglehold. "Thanks, Mom." She darted back to the house.

Amy peeked to make sure both Parker and Adrianna were settled in the rear seat, then gave the sliding door a pull. She trotted around the hood and opened the front passenger door. As she started to climb in, she glanced at the middle seat. "Should I take the back and let Mr. Roper sit up here, do you think?"

Margaret laughed, her double chin wobbling slightly. "I think I'd rather have you to talk to. Besides, there's plenty of leg room in that middle seat. He'll be fine. Fasten your seatbelt and let's go." She pulled out of Amy's lane onto the highway.

A gaping hole in the van's dash showed where the radio

used to be. The van had air-conditioning, but Margaret left it off. The front windows were lowered several inches, allowing in the morning breeze which, thankfully, hadn't turned hot yet. Way in the north, a few puffs of white interrupted the pale blue expanse of sky. Amy pointed. "Do you think we might get some rain?"

Margaret squinted toward the clouds. "They don't look very promising yet, do they? But we can pray they build during the day. I don't think anyone would complain about a rainshower."

Amy nodded in agreement, then turned her attention to Mr. Roper's trees as they drove past the orchard. Parker had mentioned that the man's grapevines had withered too much to produce this year, but the trees looked full and green. Apparently his every-day sprinkling was keeping the trees adequately nourished. Dots of yellow, red, and pale green peeking from the leaves offered the assurance of a good apple crop. Amy winged a quick, silent prayer heavenward that the apple crop would be abundant enough to cover the loss of the grapes.

Margaret turned into Mr. Roper's lane. He sat on his porch, his long legs stretched over the single riser and feet planted wide on the ground. He pressed his palms to his knees and rose as the van approached and ambled to meet them. Amy's chest pinched a bit when he peered through the front window at her and seemed to flinch, his steps slowing. But then he trotted the remaining distance and opened the sliding door.

"Thank you for the ride," he said the moment he closed the door behind him. He shoved a ten-dollar bill through the gap between the front seats. "This is to help pay for gasoline."

Margaret sniffed, lifting her chin. "You put that right back in your pocket, Mr. Roper. I was going to Topeka anyway. Having an extra person in the van doesn't cost a bit more than going by myself."

His hand remained between the seat, the bill rippling a bit in the breeze whisking through the open windows. "Are you sure?"

"I'm sure."

"Well . . . thank you, then."

Margaret put the van in reverse and backed up. Amy watched Mr. Roper's hand slowly withdraw. She sensed it bothered him to accept the ride without paying for it. Male pride—never wanting to take without giving in return. But Mr. Roper had to know fellowship members looked out for one another and for their neighbors. He might not be Mennonite any longer, but he still followed the Mennonite practice of helping his neighbors. She'd been the recipient of his assistance many times.

They headed up the lightly traveled Highway 31, their ears filled with the howl of the wind coursing through the windows. Oddly, the children didn't jabber at Mr. Roper. They'd witnessed Bekah's upset, and they were probably feeling unsure of him now. The thought saddened Amy when she remembered Parker calling the man his best friend. How quickly things had changed.

Margaret eased onto Highway 50. The four-lane road, although far from crowded, seemed very busy when compared to the typical traffic that went past Amy's house. But the main thoroughfare would bring customers to Mr. Roper's orchard, and hopefully to her business, as well. When she'd checked her email at the library, she'd been thrilled to find three inquiries about her services.

Turning in the seat, she sent a shy smile to the silent man

in the middle. "Mr. Roper, I want to thank you again for helping me get my Web site and email set up. It is already bringing customers to me."

The wind ruffled the short-cropped hair on his forehead, showing the line of white where the sun hadn't touched. He sat with his legs spread wide, his open palms resting on his thighs. Although he didn't smile, he offered a nod. "I'm glad it's helping." He turned to look out the window.

Feeling rebuffed, Amy started to turn forward, but Parker called out, capturing her attention.

"Mom, what time will Grandpa get here Monday?"

Margaret sent Amy an interested look. "Your father is coming for a visit?"

Amy nodded. She answered Parker. "He thought around ten thirty." Her pulse immediately increased its tempo as she thought about the visit and the conflict it might bring to her door.

"Will he eat lunch with us?" Parker's voice rose, holding a hint of excitement.

"I'm not sure, honey. Remember, he isn't coming by himself. But if he stays, we'll have to fix something special, won't we?" Amy settled into the seat and looked at Margaret. "It will be a short visit—maybe only an hour or so. And it's . . . it's really more for business than pleasure." She didn't know how much to say. The fellowship members didn't know the whole truth of Amy's change of communities, and she wasn't sure she wanted them to know. Yet she desired to have someone praying for God's favor. *Lord, should I trust these people? Will they support me, or turn away in revulsion?*

Margaret kept her eyes on the road. "Concerning your quilting business?"

Amy nearly chuckled. She should have known Margaret would ask questions. "No, not really." Although the outcome might very well affect her quilting business. If the insurance agent determined Gabe's death hadn't been an accident, would they demand back the money the elevator owners had given her to compensate for her loss? If so, she wouldn't be able to keep her quilting machine. Or her new house. Her heart pounded hard and painfully beneath the modesty cape of her dress. "It has to do with my husband. And how he died."

Margaret's lips pursed into a sympathetic pout. "You said he died in an accident?"

Before answering, Amy whisked a quick glance into the rear seats. Parker and Adrianna had their heads together, talking quietly. Mr. Roper's eyes were closed, his head back. His Adam's apple bounced in a swallow, but he appeared to be asleep. With a soft sigh, Amy turned to Margaret.

"Yes. He was on top of a grain elevator, checking a clogged grain spout, and he"—she gulped, heat rising from her middle to sear her chest—"fell. He was killed instantly."

"Oh, Amy . . ." Margaret released the steering wheel long enough to give Amy's hand a quick squeeze. "What a shock for you."

Despite the passage of years, the shock hadn't left. It would never leave until she knew the truth about his tumble from the top of that elevator. Was it really a fall that stole him from her, or had he jumped to his death? Pain writhed through Amy's belly.

"Leaving you with three children, and one of them handicapped. Such a burden . . ." Margaret clicked her tongue on her teeth.

Amy swallowed. She didn't see her children—not even

Parker, with his challenges—as a burden, but she chose not to refute Margaret's comment. Being widowed was a burden. Carrying this horrible uncertainty was a greater burden.

Suddenly Margaret sent a low-browed look at Amy. "Was Parker born disabled?"

Although the woman had broached another painful subject, Amy decided it wouldn't hurt for the fellowship members to know Parker's history. "He was as normal as any other little boy until he was four years old. One day, he was riding on a tractor with his father, and a tire blew. The tractor jerked, and Parker was bounced off. He hit his head."

Memories from that awful day crashed over Amy. In the back of her tongue, she could still taste the strong antiseptic that permeated the hospital's halls. "For three days, he lay in a coma, and we didn't know if he'd live. But we prayed unceasingly, and the swelling went down in his brain. God roused him from the coma, so we were able to bring him home again. But, of course, he wasn't the same little boy anymore." And Gabe, riddled with guilt, was never the same man.

Margaret shook her head. "My, Amy, you have suffered many trials. Yet you've maintained your faith and you stand strong, a testimony to God's hand on your life. You must make your heavenly Father very proud."

Tears stung behind Amy's nose. She offered Margaret a wobbly smile of thanks.

They fell silent then, Amy unwilling to continue to speak over the wind noise. A sign indicating the Topeka turnoff appeared on the right, and Margaret angled the wheel to follow the exit ramp. She called, "Mr. Roper, would you please tell me how to find the auto repair shop?"

The man roused, tipping forward to rest his elbows on

his knees. He gave instructions, and minutes later Margaret pulled into the parking lot of Cecil's Auto Repair Shop. Mr. Roper's familiar pickup truck sat at the edge of the lot. Mr. Roper thanked Margaret for the ride, then climbed out without offering a good-bye to the children or to Amy. She watched him amble toward the cement-block building, an ache in her throat. But she couldn't define its cause.

⚜

Tim paused with his hand on the doorknob and watched the white van pull out of the parking lot. His chest felt tight—as if his lungs had grown too stiff to draw a breath. Bits and snatches of the women's conversation rolled around in his brain, one comment rising above the others. *"My, Amy, you have suffered many trials. Yet you've maintained your faith and stand strong, a testimony to God's hand on your life. You must make your heavenly Father very proud."*

Why did the older woman's statement bother him so much? Maybe because Tim had spent the last two decades disappointing the heavenly Father to whom he'd entrusted his life when he was not quite twelve years old. He'd probably never hear the words for which every good Mennonite longed— *"Well done, thou good and faithful servant. . . ."* The realization stung a lot more than he wanted to admit.

Giving the doorknob a twist, he pushed open the heavy metal door and stepped into the shop's cool, messy office. Sniffing against the onslaught of grease and gasoline, he paid his bill, listening as the mechanic explained everything they'd done to get his truck in working order.

"Still got some dents in the fender, but it'll take a body repairman to fix that," the man finished.

Tim shrugged. "Not a problem. Dents in the fender won't keep it from running."

"S'pose that's true," the mechanic said with a smile, "but I betcha that was one pretty truck in its day. Like everything, though, time takes its toll."

Tim nodded absently. He took his truck keys from the man's hand and clomped across the lot to his waiting vehicle. He paused for a moment, his gaze roving across the old truck, recalling the day he drove it off the showroom lot. Such pride had filled him then at the sleek blue paint and abundance of silver chrome. Years of sitting in the sun had faded the once bright blue to a dingy gray. Some of the chrome strips had fallen off. Other pieces were bent or tarnished. Another Scripture tiptoed through his mind, offering gentle admonishment. *"Lay not up for yourselves treasures upon earth, where moth and rust doth corrupt . . ."* He climbed into the truck and slammed the door.

Although work waited at home, he took advantage of his visit to the larger city to shop at the grocery store. He stocked up on paper products, including the biggest bag of paper plates he could find. Since Bekah wouldn't be doing the dishes anymore, he might as well simplify his life a bit. He roved the aisles, aware of the muffled thump of his bootheels against the tiled floor, the sound out of place with the squeak of tennis shoes and *flap-flap* of rubber-soled flip-flops worn by most of the other shoppers.

Funny . . . As a boy he'd always felt like he stuck out in his homemade clothes, trailing his white-capped mother. Now here he was dressed in store-bought Levi's and a pocketed T-shirt—typical farmer's attire—feeling the same way. Like a misfit. What would it take for him to feel as though he belonged somewhere?

His cart stacked high with flat cases of canned soup, boxed mac-and-cheese, cereal, and frozen pizzas, he squeaked to the checkout and loaded everything on the conveyor belt. The cashier—maybe twenty-five years old with streaked blond hair lying in flattened locks across her shoulders and an abundance of makeup accentuating her dark eyes and high cheekbones—flirted with him while she scanned the items, calling him "Cowboy" and hinting that he could benefit from a good home-cooked meal. Tim imagined most men would be flattered by that kind of attention, but it left him feeling as though bugs crawled under his skin.

He flicked his debit card through the scanner, wincing at the amount owed, and scooted out of the store as quickly as possible. Out in the parking lot, a gust of wind roared around the building and tried to lift the bag of paper plates from the cart's belly. Tim clamped his hand over the bag and looked skyward. His heart gave a leap of hope. Clouds—thick and billowing, with gray underbellies—formed a wall in the north. Rain?

Another blast of wind, hot yet heavy with moisture, propelled him forward. He thumped the cases of canned goods into the truck's bed and piled everything else on the passenger side of the cab. That wind was liable to lift anything lighter than ten pounds and send it sailing. Eager to be back in Weaverly before the storm hit, he pushed the empty cart into a nearby corral, then climbed behind the steering wheel and set off for home.

When he reached the highway, he snapped on his radio, hoping for a weather report. Static crackled, making his ears hurt, but he kept it on. He sat through two country tunes and a few lame jokes offered by an announcer before he heard, "And now, let's get our latest weather news. . . ."

Tim cranked up the volume and tipped his head, straining to hear over the whine of the wind through a crack in the windshield. "Folks, what we're looking at is a hot, extremely humid and highly unstable air mass with dew points exceeding eighty degrees, joining up with a cold front traveling from the Midwest." The announcer's voice held a bright tone that contradicted the grim report. "Strange as we might find it, considering it's summertime rather than spring, this kind of activity can develop tornadoes. That's right, tornadoes in July! Right now we're saying we're at moderate risk for severe weather, but stay posted. We'll update you as things change. And now, let's go to sports . . ."

Tim snapped off the radio. Rain they needed. But tornadoes? No thanks! He looked at the sky again. The clouds that had given him such a lift a few minutes ago now appeared ominous. He gritted his teeth, battling the urge to petition the heavens for protection. But why bother? The Father he'd ignored for the past umpteen years had no reason to listen to anything he'd say now.

Besides, surely the Mennonites were already praying the tornadoes away. For one brief second, he experienced a strong desire to join them.

27

Bekah hunched over Mom's machine, guiding fabric beneath the rapidly undulating needle. A neat seam emerged, binding the skirt to the bodice. Amazing how much she could get done with no one around to bother her. She'd only cut out the pieces for her new dress last night, and already she was more than halfway finished sewing the pieces together. By the time Mom and the kids got back from Topeka, she might be ready to try it on so Mom could pin the hem.

She finished sewing the seam and snipped the threads with the scissors. Laying the pieces aside, she reached for a sleeve, and the telephone rang. She rolled her eyes. Probably Mom, checking in. As if Bekah was a baby who couldn't take care of herself.

Bekah trotted to the telephone and lifted the receiver. "Hello?"

"Hi, honey. It's Mom. How are you?"

Bekah fiddled with the phone's cord, itching to return to her project. "Fine. I've been sewing."

"What's the weather like there?"

Bekah'd been inside all morning, just as Mom had instructed. How should she know what was going on outside? "Fine, I guess. I haven't been out."

The line crackled a little bit, but Mom's voice came through. "The sky's pretty dark in the north. Mrs. Gerber thinks a storm might be coming. Just to be safe, why don't you go out and open the cellar doors so it's ready for us in case we need it."

Bekah's heart started to pound. You didn't go into the cellar just for a rainstorm. She clutched the telephone receiver two-handed. "She thinks there might be a tornado?" She looked out the window, noticing for the first time a murky gray tinged with an ugly shade of green in place of the usual blue sky. Her hands shook, and she gripped the phone tighter.

A light chuckle came through the line. "Well, honey, it would be a rare thing to have a tornado in July, but it doesn't hurt to take precautions." Mom's sure, unruffled voice helped take the edge off Bekah's fear. "So prop open the cellar doors and be ready, but don't worry, all right?"

"All right." Bekah hugged the phone to her cheek. "When will you be home?"

"We've finished at Farm Supply and the bookstore, but we still need to go to the grocery store. I would imagine we'll be home within another two hours. Will you be all right that much longer?"

Bekah looked at the clock above the stove. Mom and the kids would be back around one thirty. "Yeah, I should be okay."

"Remember, if you need anything, you can call the Mischlers or the Schells."

"I know."

"All right, then. We'll see you soon, Bekah. I love you."

"I love you, too. Good-bye." Bekah placed the receiver in its cradle very carefully, then stood for a few moments, staring at the phone. She hadn't felt lonely at all until she'd heard her mother's voice. But now the house felt too empty and quiet. Except for the wind.

With a start, she realized she'd been so busy listening to the hum of the sewing machine, she hadn't even noticed the wind was blowing harder than usual. She scurried to the kitchen sink and leaned against the cabinet to peek outside. Dust rolled across the ground, carrying bits of dried grass. She crossed to the back door, watching the soybean plants, which had grown to the size of small bushes, sway and dance in the gusting breeze, nearly flattening to the ground with especially strong blasts.

She gave a start. Where were the men? There was always somebody working out there, Monday through Saturday. Why weren't they working now? Were they fearful of the weather, too? Even though it was hot, Bekah shivered.

Mom had told her to get the cellar doors open, so she retrieved the key for the padlock that secured the planked wooden doors and stepped outside. The wind whipped the screen door from her hand and slammed it against the house. Her skirt plastered to her legs in the back and sent it billowing out front as she walked the short distance to the storm shelter's doors. She crouched down, pinching her skirt between her knees to hold it out of her way, and unlatched the padlock.

Slipping the heavy lock into her apron pocket with the key, she grabbed one door and flung it open. It landed against the sloped ground with a thud. She opened the second door, then stood for a moment with the wind strong on her back, the ribbons from her cap dancing wildly against her cheeks, and peered into the dank depth of the cellar. She hugged herself. She hated going into the cellar.

Whisking a quick look at the boiling sky, she offered a quick prayer. "God, please don't make me go in that hole under the ground." Especially not all alone.

⁕

Tim unloaded his truck, keeping an eye on the sky during trips back and forth from the house and his pickup. When he finished, he drove the truck into the barn. The opening was barely wide enough to accommodate the truck's body, and he brushed the passenger's side mirror on the warped frame. He'd have to be extra careful backing out again, but the truck would be safer inside in case those clouds let loose with hail.

He cringed, considering the damage hail would do to his trees. The urge to pray, to ask God to hold the storm at bay, tugged at him as strongly as the wind tugged his clothes and hair as he walked to the house. But he gritted his teeth together and held the petition inside.

In the house, he put away everything he'd purchased, taking note of the neatly organized shelves, the clean-swept floors, and scrubbed countertops. Thanks to Bekah's efforts, the house was as clean as it had been when Julia lived there. *Julia* . . . His mind flooded with memories of his last moments with her. The kiss good-bye. The wave. The car disappearing over the rise in the road with Charlie in the backseat holding up his favorite tattered teddy in a gesture of farewell.

He clenched his fists to his temples, willing the persistent images away. He needed to replace them, but with what?

Photographs—he'd look at photos. Snapshots of happier moments, together moments. Maybe imprinting those on his brain would send the final, heartrending remembrance far away so it would stop haunting him.

His feet clumsy in his eagerness, he stumbled to the hallway and threw open the closet. An empty space greeted him. For a moment he stared, stunned, certain his eyes deceived him. But then he recalled giving Bekah the task of clearing out the closet. At the height of his nightmares, he'd chosen to dispose of Julia's and Charlie's things, hoping the distressing dream would disappear with them. It hadn't worked—the dream still awakened him at least once a night.

He snapped the closet door closed and aimed his steps for the back door, resolve setting his jaw in a firm line. So getting rid of the stuff hadn't achieved the purpose. He'd just bring everything back in. He hadn't lit the burn pile in more than two weeks. The boxes should still be out there, battered and dusty no doubt, but available. He swung the back door open. The wind tried to snatch it from his hand, but he held tight and latched it behind him. He glanced at the sky, noting the sickly grayish-green. His stomach churned. He'd better hurry.

Bending forward into the wind, Tim broke into a jog. He rounded the corner of the barn, heading to the cleared area where he burned his trash. But halfway across the grounds a sudden change in the atmosphere brought him to an abrupt halt. Chills broke out over his body, a prickling awareness of impending doom.

He turned a slow circle, tasting the air, which had fallen heavy and eerily still. His eyes scanned the horizon, from the clear blue in the south to almost lavender in the west and ending at the brackish ugliness that shrouded the north. He lifted his gaze from the wall of gray to the swirling green and black clouds above, and a strange movement caught his attention. A writhing tail, wide at the top, narrowing as it reached toward the earth, emerged from the angry gathering of clouds.

Fear exploded through Tim's middle. A tornado. Miles away, but traveling in his direction. Panic spurred him to action. He took off at a run for his house to seek protection. But as he reached his back door he suddenly remembered that Mrs. Knackstedt, Parker, and Adri had been in the van, but he hadn't seen Bekah. Which meant she must have stayed behind. She'd be terrified, there alone. Or maybe she didn't even know the storm was coming. There'd be no television or radio to warn her.

Tim's pulse raced so quickly his entire body quivered. Would Mrs. Knackstedt be home by now? There was no way of knowing. But he couldn't risk leaving the girl to face a tornado alone. With another quick glance at the approaching storm, he changed direction and raced for the barn. Moments later, unmindful of the sideview mirror he'd stripped from the passenger door when backing out of the barn or the dust-laden wind stealing his visibility, he tore down the road toward the Knackstedt place.

⁕

Amy resisted tapping her toe in impatience as Margaret checked off the lengthy list of items in her hand. Both women and Parker pushed carts, all of which were well filled. Even if something else were listed, there wasn't room for one more thing in any of the carts.

Adrianna leaned against Amy's leg. "Aren't we done yet,

Momma?" The little girl yawned widely. "I'm tired. And hungry."

"I know." Amy gave Adrianna a one-armed hug, then lifted her into the basket. She was really too big for the child seat in the cart, but the hours of shopping had worn her out. "As soon as Mrs. Gerber finishes, we'll go to a drive-through and get you something to eat, all right?"

It seemed silly to purchase fast food when they had full carts, but if they waited until they got home, lunch would be delayed at least another hour. Amy's stomach growled, too. A hamburger would taste good right now.

"I guess that's it," Margaret said, triumph in her voice.

"Then we can go?" Parker grabbed the handle of his cart, his slumped shoulders squaring.

"We can go." With a grunt, Margaret pushed her cart into motion.

Amy fell in behind Margaret with Parker huffing along behind her. They reached the checkout lines and passed the row of 20-Items-and-Under lanes. Amy had lost count, but she felt certain between the three carts, there were well over one hundred items. She found the shopping exhausting, but somehow Margaret seemed refreshed by the prospect of finding the best bargains so the fellowship's food dollars stretched the farthest.

Margaret settled on a lane, and Amy moved forward to help her unload the contents of her cart onto the conveyor belt. As the cashier scanned items, the store's announcement system clicked on. A male voice boomed over the speakers. "Hello, Food Warehouse shoppers. I have just received notice of the possibility of a tornado near Weaverly, Kansas, and moving toward Topeka."

Amy grabbed for Margaret, who grabbed for Amy at the same time. The women clung, their gazes locked. Amy wondered if her own face was as white as Margaret's.

"We've been advised to remain in the store until the threat passes. If necessary, we will take all customers to the storage room beneath the store. A buzzer will sound, like this—" A blaring *bzzzzzzt* sounded, and then the man's voice returned. "If you hear the buzzer, please make your way in an orderly fashion to the northwest corner of the store, where employees will guide you to the storage room. Again, all customers are advised to remain in the store until the storm has passed." A click signaled the end of the announcement.

A hum of voices—some concerned, others laughing—filled the air. Stuck in the cart's seat, Adrianna wriggled, stretching her hands toward Amy. "Momma? Momma?"

Parker stumbled toward his mother. "Mom, I'm scared."

Amy still held tight to Margaret's hands. "I have to get home. They said the tornado was near Weaverly. Bekah . . ." Panic cut off her air, and she gasped for breath.

Pulling away from Margaret's grip, Amy grabbed Adrianna under the arms and tried to lift her from the cart. But her shaking limbs didn't possess enough strength. She let go, and Adrianna flopped back into the seat. She began to cry.

Parker grabbed hold of Amy's arm, his cold fingers digging into her flesh. "Mom? Mom?"

Amy shook loose of Parker's grasp and glared at Margaret. "Help me! We've got to get out of here!"

Margaret worked her way between the carts and the display rack of candy, her expression grim. She took hold of Amy's shoulders and gave her a firm shake. "Stop this right now." She spoke in a low, even tone. "You're frightening your children."

Amy flicked a glance into Adrianna's and Parker's faces. The terror reflected in their eyes raised a wave of protectiveness. Wrapping one arm around Adrianna and the other around Parker, she held them close and whispered assurances into their ears. Adrianna continued to cry softly, her face pressed to Amy's neck. Parker sniffled against her shoulder. Amy wanted to cry, too, but she held her own worries at bay and comforted her children.

Between their carts, Margaret knelt on the floor and folded her hands. Her lips moved in silent prayer. Guilt flooded Amy's frame. How could she have been so short-sighted? Margaret had a husband and several friends in Weaverly who were also in the tornado's path. Amy wasn't the only one fearing for a loved one.

Letting her eyes slip closed, she clung hard to her children and silently petitioned her heavenly Father. *Protect them, Lord. Oh, please, please, keep Your hand of protection over Bekah and all of the residents of Weaverly.*

28

"Bekah! Bekah!" Tim pounded on the ancient wooden door, rattling the oval glass pane. Wind howled, angry as a chorus of wolves. Particles of dirt blasted the back of Tim's bare neck, stinging his flesh. He hunched his shoulders and pounded again. "Bekah! Are you in there?"

He squinted across the grounds. Where was that girl? Had she gone into town? Just as he'd decided to climb back in his truck and leave, the curtain behind the window whisked to the side and Bekah's fear-filled face peered at him.

Relief nearly collapsed Tim's legs. "Open up!"

The curtain dropped into place, and the latch clicked. Tim pushed the door open and crossed the threshold. His chest heaved with wild breathing as he searched her white face. "Are you all right?"

"I'm scared. There's a bad storm, and Mom isn't here."

The usually reserved, mature young woman seemed to dissolve into a frightened little girl. Automatically, Tim captured her in a quick embrace. "I'm here, and I won't let anything happen to you." His statement of assurance, as well as the determination that filled him, surprised him. He cared about this girl. Cared deeply.

Slipping his arm around her waist, he herded her toward the kitchen. He'd spent storms in the Sanford cellar in past years, so he knew where to go. "We'll be safer underground. Get me the key for the cellar and—"

"It's open." Bekah's voice quavered. "I got it ready, but I didn't want to go down. It's dark and smelly in there."

Despite his worries, Tim flashed a grin. "That's 'cause it's a cellar. If it isn't dark and smelly, it isn't doing its job."

A wobbly smile formed on Bekah's pale face, giving Tim a lift.

"C'mon—let's hurry." He hustled her out the back door, keeping a firm grip on her waist as they battled the wind. Just a few yards to the cellar opening. One of the doors had flapped shut in the wind, so Tim held it upright while Bekah made her way down the earthen steps. He waited until she reached the bottom before he followed, pausing to pull the doors closed behind them.

Complete darkness surrounded him, making his head spin. He focused on the sliver of muted light creeping through the crack between the rattling doors. Squinting, his hands gliding along the damp earth walls, he inched his way downward until he bumped into something warm—Bekah.

"I wish I had a flashlight." Bekah's voice sounded unusually high. Panic, no doubt.

Tim couldn't see well enough to reach for her, so he injected as much confidence into his tone as possible. "Give it a few minutes—our eyes will adjust."

Bekah fell silent, but he could hear her rapid breathing.

Tim's nose wanted to pinch shut against the musty odor filling the underground space. The doors bounced in their frame, the off-beat thuds providing percussion to the gale's mournful woodwinds. Then a loud spatter—like gunfire—erupted. Bekah let out a squeak of alarm, and Tim reached without thinking. His knuckles brushed her arm, and she grabbed his hand. Her icy fingers clung, and Tim was able to follow the line of her arm to her shoulders and draw her snug to his side.

He felt her face pressed to his collarbone, felt her shoulders heaving in silent sobs. His heart ached in response to her terror. He murmured, offering comfort. "Rain, Bekah. It's just rain. We need it, right?" But such hammering rain, drops falling as hard as ball bearings from the sky.

It seemed hours crept by while they stood in the small space, hearts pounding, but in reality it couldn't have been more than fifteen minutes before Tim's ears recognized a change. The piercing whistle became a distant flute. The fierce pounding softened to fingertips tapping on a table's edge.

"Stay here." He set her aside and groped his way to the doors. Slowly, apprehension holding him in its uncomfortable grip, he pushed one heavy door upward. Rain, soft and cold, landed on his face. The sky was gray overhead, glorious blue in the north. The storm had passed. He reached his hand toward Bekah. "Come on up. We can go to the house now."

Hugging herself, she scurried up the stairs. They hunched forward against the steady rainfall and dashed across the slippery, leaf- and twig-strewn ground to the back porch. Tim sent her in first, then stepped in behind her, shaking his head to rid his hair of water. He glanced at her shivering frame.

"Why don't you go change into a dry dress? I want to look around the house, make sure everything's all right."

She gave a quick nod, then darted for the stairs. Tim searched each of the downstairs rooms. Apparently Bekah had closed everything up against the wild wind earlier, because the windows were all snug in their frames. The house felt stuffy, so he inched each window upward just enough to allow in the breeze without inviting rain to enter. One of the living room windows had a crack running from the bottom edge nearly to the top. Bekah entered the room on bare feet, her cap askew, but with a clean, unrumpled dress in place.

He pointed to the crack. "Looks like the storm broke one of your windows."

Bekah stood with her arms wrapped across her middle, as if she were holding herself together. "Parker did that goofing around in here the other day. Mom just hasn't had time to replace it yet." Bekah's chin quivered. "Mr. Roper, do you think Mom got caught out in that—"

Tim shook his head. The thought of Amy, Parker, and Adri in a van during a tornado sent a spike of fear through his chest. He didn't want to think what might happen. "Don't borrow trouble." His father's standard response to moments of fear or worry slipped from his mouth. "Just trust."

"I'm trying." A funny, bashful smile toyed on the corners of her lips. She kept her head low rather than meeting his gaze. "Before you got here, I was praying like crazy that somebody would come because I didn't want to go into the cellar by myself. And God answered." She flicked a shy glance at him through her eyelashes. "He sent you."

Tim's heart skipped a beat. He wouldn't have considered himself the answer to anybody's prayer.

Bekah ducked her head again, sighing. "Just wish Mom'd

hurry and get home. I don't like being here by myself in the rain."

"Tell you what . . ." Tim strode forward slowly, his legs weak and trembly. "I'll stay here with you until your mom gets back."

The girl's shoulders rose and fell. "Thank you, Mr. Roper."

Tim gestured toward the kitchen. "Do you have bread, and maybe some bologna or cheese? I could use a sandwich."

Bekah's chin shot up. She grinned, then giggled. "Okay." She turned and skittered to the kitchen.

Tim followed. He wasn't really hungry, but Bekah needed something to keep herself occupied. He needed to be busy, too, but rather than helping her, he slipped into a kitchen chair and watched her buzz between the pantry, refrigerator, and cabinets. Within minutes, she'd cluttered the tabletop with sandwich fixings—bread, sliced tomatoes, lettuce, three different kinds of cheese, pink ham, pickles, mayonnaise, and mustard.

She slathered mustard on a slice of bread, then layered meat and cheese over the golden smear. "I'll make a whole bunch. That way, when Mom and the kids are back, lunch'll be waiting for them."

Tim smiled to himself. Now she was thinking positively—a good sign. He helped arrange the sandwiches on the plate, stacking them into a pyramid. When she'd completed six sandwiches, she retrieved a carton of milk from the refrigerator. "Do you want—"

A bang intruded, followed by a frantic voice. "Bekah! Bekah!"

Bekah plopped the carton on the table and dashed around the corner. Tim trailed behind her, his heart catching at the sight of Mrs. Knackstedt clinging to Bekah. Parker and Adri surrounded them, their arms wound together. Their unity—their obvious relief to be together again—put a lump in Tim's throat. How long had it been since he'd been wrapped in the embrace of people who loved him?

Mrs. Knackstedt pulled back, cupping Bekah's face between her palms. "Oh, sweetheart, I'm sorry you had to face that storm alone. Are you all right?"

"I'm fine." Bekah flashed a smile at Tim. "Mr. Roper came over. He went into the cellar with me, and he told me to trust you'd be home soon." The girl's image blurred, and Tim realized his eyes had misted over. He blinked rapidly, clearing the moisture. Bekah finished, "We were just gonna eat a sandwich. I made plenty."

Mrs. Knackstedt stepped free of her children, leaving them in a huddling group in the doorway between the living and dining rooms. She crossed the floor and then stopped mere inches from Tim. Her eyes locked on his. His stomach trembled as he read a jumble of feelings in the steadfast gaze of her blue eyes. Gratitude. Admiration. And sympathy.

"Thank you for being here with Bekah when I couldn't. I prayed fervently she wouldn't be alone. I knew God was with her—He is always with her—but I'm so grateful He sent a human form to be His hands on earth."

Her kind words wrapped him in warmth. Looking into this woman's sincere, tender, open face, something inside him seemed to bloom to life. He cared about the children, yes, but he also cared about their mother. Seeing her safe and home again raised a desire to draw her close, to thank someone for delivering her from the storm, to shelter her within his arms and hold her in his heart. When had resentment for her intrusion in his life changed to devotion?

He shoved his hands into his pockets and cleared his throat. "Y-you're welcome." He bobbed his head toward the kitchen doorway. "Bekah's sandwiches are drying out. You probably ought to eat."

But she didn't move. Her hand stretched toward him, and her fingers descended lightly on his forearm. A sweet tenderness softened the gentle lines around her eyes. "Mr. Roper, I must tell you . . ."

Tim held his breath, his heart pounding so hard his ears rang. Did she sense how he felt? Did she feel the same way toward him?

"Your orchard. The tornado . . ."

Tim didn't wait to hear more. He shot past her, nearly knocking her aside in his frantic bid to escape, and ran out the door.

29

Tim stood in the drizzle, fingers in the back pockets of his Levi's, boots planted wide, and stared at what was left of his house and barn. Thunder rolled gently in the distance, its growl an appropriate accompaniment to the emotions swirling through Tim's chest.

The destruction to his house didn't surprise him. Not too many mobile homes could stand up to the force of a tornado, even an F2, which, according to the radio announcer, was what they'd had. Seeing it twisted off its concrete-block foundation, a section of roof crinkled up like a huge wad of tinfoil and a gaping hole where his bedroom used to be was painful, but not unexpected. But the barn . . .

Julia's uncle had told him the barn was built in the late-1860s by German immigrants, back when they did things right. He'd given the barn a coat of paint every other year, always kept the roof in good repair, and never lit a lantern inside it. The oak timbers—a good six inches square—that served as support beams had always seemed indestructible.

Solid. *Permanent.* Now he realized how foolish he'd been to think that nothing could destroy the huge wooden building.

A churned strip of bare ground, no longer holding so much as a blade of grass or a scrap of weed, showed the path the tornado had taken between his house and barn. And then it must have gone back up into the clouds, because the clean path ended at the road. Tim wanted to be happy the neighbors' fields and homes were safe. But happiness for his fellow Weaverly residents would have to come later. Right now, he needed to be selfish and mourn his own loss.

The sound of car tires crunching on rain-soaked ground met his ears. Company. He craned his head to look, too weary to move his body. Mrs. Knackstedt's Buick inched up the lane. Her windshield wipers squeaked on the wet glass, tossing raindrops aside. He remained in place, waiting and watching until she stopped the car, climbed out, and tiptoed her way through the leaf-strewn mud to stand beside him. Her cap and the shoulders of her dress gathered wet polka dots.

Tim shifted his focus to the hole in the side of his house. His bedspread gently flapped in the light breeze, and a picture of flowers—one of Julia's oil paintings—still hung on the wall. Tornadoes were mighty strange storms. "I'd say let's get in out of the rain, but I'm not sure where to take you." He supposed his voice should hold bitterness or sarcasm, but instead he just sounded tired.

"Mr. Roper . . ." Her words caught. She didn't touch him, but her hand hovered near his arm. The fingers trembled. "I'm so sorry."

"Yeah. Me too."

She folded her arms across her chest, her head bobbing

here and there as she examined the area. "Have you checked your trees? Did you suffer much . . . loss?"

He swallowed a derisive snort. "The tornado steered clear of the orchard. I haven't gone clear through, but from what I've seen, the trees are mostly wind-damaged but nothing more. Some broken branches. Leaves and apple buds blown to kingdom come." When he'd driven home, he'd thought it looked like a parade had passed by, leaving a trail of confetti behind. "Won't have much of a crop this year—not as much as I'd hoped for—but there'll be some."

Blowing out a big breath, he flipped one hand toward the barn. " 'Course, I can forget folks being able to make their own applesauce or squeeze their own juice. My equipment . . . it's all buried underneath that tumble of beams and shattered lumber. Can't imagine finding anything of use in there now."

Her hand descended on his arm. A light touch—yet delivering heartfelt sympathy. "Do you have insurance?"

"Some." Tim ground his teeth together. He'd skimped on insurance and he knew it, trying to save money with a smaller policy. No way he'd get what he needed to rebuild his business to where it had been before the storm struck. "Guess it'll have to do."

"I suppose . . ." She sounded sad. "I'm so grateful you came to the house and went to the cellar with Bekah. She needed someone with her, but more than that, it kept you safe, too. If you'd been in either the house or the barn when the storm hit, you could have been seriously injured."

Tim hadn't considered how running next door had saved his own skin.

"I'm thankful God spared you."

Her innocent comment, so sweetly uttered, stirred an unexpected flame of fury in Tim's gut. Sure, God had spared him, but for what? He had trees but no equipment to harvest the fruit. He had land but no shelter. He'd clung to this orchard in lieu of clinging to his wife and son, and now it seemed as though everything had gone up in a gust of wind. All of the hurt and frustration of the past lonely years roared through Tim's chest and exploded in an angry deluge of words.

"Our great and powerful God could've spared a whole lot more, don't you think? After all, He put the stars in the sky. So why couldn't He keep that tornado in the clouds where it wouldn't do any harm? Why'd it have to land on my barn? My house?"

Mrs. Knackstedt stared at him in dismay, but once the words started, he couldn't seem to stop them. He'd held them inside far too long. Every element of resentment poured from the center of Tim's soul.

"Wasn't it enough He gave me a son with needs I couldn't meet without help? A son I had to send to therapists in an-other town, requiring a trip on the highway where an idiotic driver fiddling around with his radio dial crossed the center line and took my wife and son from me? Why didn't God spare Julia and Charlie? I wasn't ready to tell them good-bye!"

His voice boomed out louder than the thunder that contin-ued to roll. "And why'd He bring you and—and those other Mennonites to Weaverly? He knew a boy like Parker would remind me of Charlie. He knew a loving, warm, giving mother like you would remind me of Julia. He knew having all of you here would remind me of the life I threw away. Couldn't He have spared me from coming face-to-face with every one of my past regrets?"

Tim ran out of steam. His shoulders wilted, his stiff knees

relaxed. Right there in the mud, with rain still saturating his hair and clothing, he went down on one knee. "He spared me, Amy Knackstedt, but for what purpose?"

She stared at him, silent, her hands clasped in a prayerful position against the bodice of her dress. The top of her cap was soaked, and little rivulets of water ran down her face. Or were some of those trails of moisture tears?

Tim hung his head, heaving a sigh. "Go home. There's nothing you can do here."

"What are you going to do?" She wrapped her arms around herself like Bekah had after the storm, sending a lengthy gaze across his house. "You can't stay out here. There isn't a safe shelter."

Tim jolted to his feet. "I'll drive into town. Talk to my minister. Reverend Geary and his wife'll put me up for a night or two. I'll be fine." He tipped his head in the direction of her car. "Thanks for coming by, but you should be with your children. They've had a scare today, too."

"They sent me over—insisted I check on you." A soft smile curled her lips. "They were worried about you."

Droplets of water clung to her eyelashes. Bedraggled ribbons hung alongside her cheeks, plastered against the damp wisps of hair at her temples. Rain-soaked, weary . . . and somehow still beautiful. Her faith shone through. Tim's throat tightened. He blinked. "Tell 'em thanks. Tell 'em I'll make sure they get their apples before I do any other selling." He steeled his heart. "But tell 'em not to come over." He sent a sorrowful look across his property. "There's nothing here for them anymore."

Tim drove into Weaverly after covering the gaping hole in his trailer with a tarp he found in the old storage shed on the back corner of the property. Strange how the ramshackle shed still stood, but the mighty barn had been toppled. Tim tried not to think about it too much, but he couldn't deny a sense of unfairness at the whole ordeal.

As he'd expected, Reverend Geary and his wife, Marjorie, told Tim he could stay in their guest room for as long he needed. Marjorie got busy on the telephone, and by seven o'clock that evening, the whole town had heard about the tornado tearing up Tim's place. In typical small-town fashion, they rallied to help.

Dean Bradley, one of Charlie's teachers from the grade school, brought over a sackful of jeans and T-shirts he'd intended to take to the Goodwill in Ottawa. Although the clothes were used, they were in as good a shape as any Tim generally wore for working in the orchard. The general store owner, Ralph Miller, opened his store after-hours and let Tim help himself to packages of socks and underwear and whatever toiletries he needed, free of charge. Tim had noticed his dresser still stood along the wall, seemingly untouched, but the sagging roof above the piece of furniture made him hesitant to retrieve anything from it. So he appreciated putting his hands on articles of clothing.

By bedtime Saturday, the civic club had already decided to do a pancake feed to raise money to help pay for a new barn and equipment, church ladies had delivered more covered dishes than Tim could eat in a month, and Jeff Allen, a local rancher, promised to haul his fishing trailer to Tim's land so he'd have someplace to sleep until insurance paid out and he could buy himself another mobile home.

Tim fell into bed Saturday, thankful for the support of his townsfolk but still worried. All of the paper work for his insurance policy was in his desk drawer, so he couldn't double-check it, but he was relatively certain the policy he'd purchased—the one that fit his limited budget—included a sizable deductible. Even with the pancake feed proceeds, how in the world would he be able to replace the barn?

On Sunday morning, Tim dressed in a pair of Dean's hand-me-over jeans and one of Reverend Geary's dress shirts, which Mrs. Geary offered him after seeing the T-shirt he'd pulled on before coming to breakfast. As he brushed his teeth, he grimaced at his reflection. Despite the night in the comfortable bed, he looked haggard. And he wasn't much in the mood to attend a *worship* service.

A person shouldn't get sore at God. His father would probably quote Proverbs 19:21 if he knew what Tim was thinking. *"There are many devices in a man's heart; nevertheless the counsel of the Lord, that shall stand."* Timothy Rupp Sr. was particularly fond of the verse, but at the moment, Tim wasn't terribly interested in the Lord's counsel. In his opinion, the Lord had allowed one too many calamities to befall him.

Still, he wouldn't disappoint the ones who'd given him shelter last night. The Gearys expected him to attend service, so he'd go. But he couldn't guarantee he'd listen to any sermon. Especially if it involved goading people into believing God had a good plan in the hard situations. Some people might still buy into it, but any shred of belief Tim might have possessed was crushed along with his sturdy, seemingly indestructible barn.

The sanctuary filled quickly, people slipping into pews at the back first and forcing latecomers to take the seats in the front. Tim had arrived early, so he sat on the second-to-last pew. He used a bulletin to stir the air. The church possessed a fairly new central air unit, but Mrs. Geary had come over and opened windows to let in the breeze. She said they could all benefit from the leftover scent of rain after the long, dry weeks. Tim admitted the breeze carried a nice scent, but the sun was already high, as was the humidity, and even before the song leader stepped behind the pulpit to direct the congregation in the opening hymn, Tim felt sticky.

He rose for hymn singing, remained standing for prayer, sat for the Bible reading and children's feature, stood again for another song, and then settled into the pew for the sermon. None of the sounds of a church service—a minister's deep voice, the flutter of Bibles' pages being turned, a child's occasional whining complaint followed by a mother's stern *shh!*—were new. He'd sat through countless services as a boy. Back then he'd held his head erect, his spine straight, doing his best to at least appear attentive lest he earn a stern glare or a reprimand from his father for woolgathering. Today, at the back of the church, hidden from the majority of worshipers and free of his father's watchful gaze, he could let his mind wander. He had plenty to think about.

After the wind's force, his trees needed pruning. The grounds would require a good raking to dispose of all the fallen branches and leaves. He hadn't checked to see if the beehives were toppled—if the bees had scattered, he'd probably have to pay to replace them. Another expense he couldn't afford. Somehow he'd have to dig through his house and salvage anything still usable. What remained of the barn would need to be hauled away—or burned—and another structure erected in its stead.

The list grew lengthy, and as Tim considered the amount of work awaiting him, a tension headache built in the back of his skull. He'd never get it all done by himself, but how would he hire workers without money to pay them? Caught up in his thoughts, it took a few moments for him to realize everyone was shifting to stand for the closing hymn. He shot to his feet, holding the back of the pew in front of him to keep himself steady—how his head ached—and focused on the music leader. The piano played the opening chords, but before the director began the first verse, a shuffling sound filled the rear of the sanctuary.

People turned to look over their shoulders. Surprise registered on faces. Whispers broke out across the room, and children pointed. Tim squinted his eyes against the pain stabbing in his head and turned slowly to look at what had caused the uproar. There, in one big cluster, the Mennonites from Ohio stood just inside the double doors at the back of the worship room.

The director waved his hand, and the pianist came to an abrupt stop. Reverend Geary hurried down the center aisle and greeted the guests as if the community church welcomed a group of visitors at the close of every service. More whispers floated across the room as Reverend Geary and the oldest of the Mennonite men spoke quietly together. Then Reverend Geary threw his arm around the man's shoulders and herded him to the pulpit. He said, "Folks, sit down, please, and give this man your kind attention."

More whispers rippled, but everyone settled into their seats. Reverend Geary held his hand toward the Mennonite man, granting him permission to speak. The man pressed his hat against the front of his buttoned black coat and leaned toward the microphone on the pulpit.

"I thank you for letting us come in and interrupt your

worship. I am Dillard Gerber. My wife and me and several people from our town in Ohio moved here to Weaverly a couple months ago. We haven't got to meet most of you yet, but we hope to make good friends with all of you."

The lingering German inflection in the man's voice brought back childhood memories for Tim. His father had spoken with the same thick accent. Tim fidgeted, the pounding in his head growing more intense by the moment. Would the man hurry? He wanted an aspirin and to get out to his land. To begin to make order out of chaos.

"As you all know, the storm that come through yesterday did a lot of damage to one person's home. Timothy Roper, who lives next door to the land we farm. It burdens us to see our neighbor's house and barn destroyed. Especially since he's been so kind to one of our members. Mrs. Knackstedt, would you come up here, please?"

Amy Knackstedt separated herself from the group and moved to the front of the church with a graceful ease. Rather than joining Mr. Gerber on the raised dais, she stood on the floor and bounced a shy smile across the sea of faces. But she didn't catch Tim's eye. Disappointment slouched him into the pew.

"Mrs. Knackstedt told us this morning about all that got damaged, and she wanted us to be able to help Mr. Roper the same way he's helped her and her children. So she brought us the idea of a barn raising." A murmur swept through the room. Mr. Gerber nodded, his smile growing. "You see, back in Ohio, when someone needs a barn, we all get together and put it up. It don't take long when you have many hands. Between us who just moved here, we have half a dozen pairs of hands." He held his leathery palms aloft, earning a few chuckles. "But we can always use more. So we thought, since this is Mr. Roper's church family, maybe some of you would want to join us and get Mr. Roper another barn built."

The man paused, his gaze searching the congregation until he found Tim. A gentle pleading entered his eyes. "That is, if Mr. Roper will allow us to serve him in this way."

30

I realize this is difficult for you, and it gives me no pleasure to upset you, but the issue really needs to be settled."

Amy faced the insurance agent and squirmed. Dad, seated beside her on the sofa, placed his hand on her knee and squeezed. His presence provided comfort as past memories took their ugly grip. "I don't understand why the question has been raised again, Mr. Corey. Gabe has been gone almost three years now. Farmers Aid Agency wouldn't have paid the claim if they hadn't deemed Gabe's death an accident, would they have?" Amy remembered the day the sizable check arrived in her mailbox. She'd held it, tears raining down her face, praying the payout was proof Gabe hadn't chosen to leave her.

"I'm afraid that some information, which we consider pertinent, has come to light." The man pinched his lips tight. "We've received a sworn affidavit claiming your husband was deeply depressed at the time of his death."

Amy looked at her father, who looked back at her. Confusion marred his brow. She knew the same question that hovered in her mind tormented him, as well. Who in Arborville would have done such a thing? Amy knew townspeople had talked—the passage of years hadn't erased the speculative whispers. But to contact the insurance company and make such an accusation . . . What had that person hoped to gain?

The agent removed a handkerchief from his pocket and swiped it across his forehead. He glanced toward the open window, where a soft breeze fluttered the curtains. Muffled clanks, the *rat-a-tat-tat* of power tools, and a cacophony of voices—evidence that Mr. Roper's barn raising was already in full swing—carried through the window. Amy wished she could be with Mr. Roper, the Mennonite builders and their wives, and the gathered Weaverly residents rather than sitting under the insurance agent's scrutiny.

Mr. Corey turned to Amy again. "We must investigate the possibility that your husband committed suicide. In which case, an accidental death claim is null and void."

Dad straightened in the seat, his shoulders squaring. "Do you mean to say your company would take money from a widow and her children?" Dad's tone was respectful, but Amy heard the undercurrent of disbelief.

Mr. Corey's expression turned grim. "I am saying, Mr. Ohr, that if your daughter accepted money under false pretenses, not only will she need to return the money, but she may face criminal charges."

Amy gasped. "But I did nothing wrong!"

The agent fixed Amy with a penetrating look. "Then you're denouncing the witness's signed statement that your husband was depressed?"

Tears threatened, but Amy held them at bay. As painful as it would be, and even if it meant losing her home, losing the machine that allowed her to provide for her children, losing her security and dignity, she had to speak the truth. "Gabe suffered great remorse. What loving father wouldn't suffer remorse and depression if he felt accountable for permanently disabling his son? But did he elect to end his suffering by leaping to his death?" She shook her head, willing away the niggling doubt that lingered in the back of her mind. "Only Gabe can answer that question."

Dad gave her knee several brisk pats. "Mr. Corey, how do we prove these accusations wrong? What do you need from us?"

The man held his hands outward. "I'm here as a courtesy. We intend to fully investigate Gabriel Knackstedt's state of mind. Thus far, our company has received signed statements indicating he might very well have deliberately jumped from the elevator. Mrs. Knackstedt's comments today seem to substantiate those claims. Of course, if you have evidentiary statements to the contrary, they should be notarized and submitted to our main branch."

He handed Amy a business card. "The accidental death case was reopened two weeks ago. It will remain open for three months. If, by the end of that time, we haven't received convincing arguments to support an accident claim, then we will expect a check for the full amount you were paid. It can be mailed to the address on the card."

Amy held tight to the crisp white rectangle, fear creating a lump in her belly. How would she return the money? After paying for Gabe's simple funeral, she'd given the remaining balance to the fellowship's benevolence fund. Some of those funds were used to purchase her long-arm machine and the house in which she now lived, but some had been used to assist other members of her former fellowship. She could sell the house and her belongings, but she'd never be able to recover all of the money.

Mr. Corey flicked an unsmiling glance across both Amy and her father. "Any other questions?"

"What if I can't pay it back?" Amy blurted.

Mr. Corey cleared his throat. "I'm afraid that isn't an option, Mrs. Knackstedt. It must be paid back if it was received erroneously." The man rose, and for the first time a hint of sympathy appeared in his eyes. "I know this has come as a shock to you, and I apologize for the necessity of opening old wounds. But surely you understand we can't pay an accident claim if it truly wasn't an accident."

Amy pushed to her feet and stood on quivering legs. "I do understand, sir. I just . . ." How would she prove Gabe hadn't jumped? As much as it pained her to admit, she wasn't one hundred percent certain herself. She drew in a deep breath. "I'll be in touch."

Mr. Corey held out his hand, and Amy's father shook it. Amy followed him to the door and opened it for him. All three children sat on the edge of the porch, their bare feet dangling. They looked up as Mr. Corey stepped outside. Bekah scowled at the man, but Parker and Adrianna offered shy smiles.

He ignored the children and looked toward the east, where a near-steady hum of bangs, bumps, and voices continued. "It sounds as if a construction crew is hard at work."

Parker lumbered to his feet. "The Mennonites are building Mr. Roper a barn 'cause a tornado blowed it down. He needs a new one for his apples."

Mr. Corey stared at Parker, an unreadable expression on his face. Then his shoulders jerked, as if he were awakening.

"I see." But it was clear he didn't follow Parker's explanation. He nodded at Amy. "Good day, Mrs. Knackstedt. I hope to hear from you soon." He crossed the mushy ground and climbed into his car.

Dad gave Amy a hug, whispering a promise to pray for God to make known the truth. He hugged and kissed the children by turn, then joined Mr. Corey. The two drove away. The moment they turned the corner at the end of the lane, Parker grabbed Amy's hands.

"Can we go to the barn raising now? Please? I wanna see what Mr. Roper's new barn looks like."

Adrianna bounced up and added her begging to Parker's. Only Bekah remained silent, her narrowed gaze seeming to bore a hole through Amy.

Amy gently freed herself from Parker's grip. Mr. Roper had specifically asked her to keep the children away from his property. Although she, too, was curious about the progress being made, she would honor the man's request. "No. We need to stay home."

"But, Mom!" Parker and Adrianna chorused.

Amy gave the pair a firm look. "Barn raising is a workplace for men, not a play area for children. It can be dangerous. We're going to stay here." She aimed her finger at their crestfallen faces. "Stay in our yard. I'm going to go prepare our lunch." Ignoring their groans, she went inside.

In the quiet of the kitchen, she sank into a chair and lowered her head to her hands. *God, I want to know the truth. There's no new beginning here for the children and me with the uncertainty still hanging over our heads. Even if it's painful, knowing is better than forever wondering. Even if it means returning the money, even if it means facing criminal charges . . .* Tears pressed behind her closed lids. She sniffed and finished her prayer. *Reveal the truth, Lord, so we can put this part of our lives to rest. Oh, Father, reveal the truth so I can be free.*

⁂

"It's kind of like a miracle, isn't it?" Dean Bradley threw his arm around Tim's shoulders, his face tipped toward the very top of the barn, where plain-dressed men swarmed, securing large panels of bright green tin to the preformed rafters.

Tim had witnessed barn raisings before—at least three in his former town—but he agreed it was an amazing process to see a large structure go up in such a short amount of time. Familiar with the Mennonite way of working together, Tim saw the greater miracle in how quickly they'd secured materials. Mr. Gerber and two others had driven to Kansas City Sunday afternoon, and Monday bright and early trucks had rolled in with everything necessary to replace the old wood barn with a new metal one. They'd even chosen red metal siding so it would emulate the look of the former dwelling. Tim didn't know who'd paid for the materials, but he intended to find out before the Mennonites left that evening.

Dean whistled through his teeth. "And nobody even in charge! They just all seem to know what needs to be done, and they do it. I've never seen a project go so smoothly without a foreman shouting out directions. And I've never seen such a group of hard workers in my life."

Tim remained silent, but inwardly he acknowledged how much the Mennonites had accomplished. Thanks to the children's efforts, the entire orchard was raked clean of debris. The two oldest youth spent the day at the burn pile, turning branches and scraps of wood into ashes. Nobody'd gone hungry with all the food the women had carted in. Between meals the women—after Mr. Gerber did a walk-through and gave the okay—entered Tim's damaged house and retrieved everything that hadn't been ruined by rain coming through the roof. A handful of Weaverly men helped carry heavier items to the storage shed. Tim planned to sort through it all later, but the women had excitedly reported just how much was salvageable. They seemed as happy as if the things belonged to them rather than to a stranger.

In one day, the group of workers had accomplished what would have taken Tim weeks to accomplish on his own. He couldn't deny being grateful for their unselfish giving, but a part of him resented their intrusion. It seemed, once again, the past had sneaked into his present, giving him reason to lament long-ago choices.

Dean gave Tim's shoulder a whack and dropped his arm. "You know, Tim, it must feel good to know you come from such a strong heritage. Me? I didn't grow up in the church. Started attending when I was in college at the invitation of my roommate. I'm grateful to have a relationship with Jesus now. But if I'd grown up witnessing this . . ." He swept his arm outward, indicating the bustle of activity of women cleaning up, men gathering tools, and children hauling trash bags of debris to the end of the lane. "I'd be a better man, I think." Tipping his head, he gave Tim a serious look. "From the first time we met, when you enrolled Charlie in school, I've admired your dedication to doing everything you could to help in your son's education while running this business pretty much on your own. I think I'm seeing where you in- herited your work and family ethic. It was passed down from generations of family-oriented, good-hearted, hardworking people. I envy you, Tim."

Dean strode away, joining the men who piled scraps of left-overs in the bed of Christian Hunsberger's pickup truck. Tim stood rooted in place, Dean's words reverberating in his head. Dean *envied* him his Mennonite heritage? But Dean didn't know the other side—the critical-of-mistakes, unrealistic-expectations, work-from-dawn-to-dusk side that Tim had despised as a teenager. If Dean witnessed that part of the hardworking, family-oriented lifestyle, would he still be en-vious, or would he be relieved that he'd been spared such an upbringing?

Dillard Gerber marched toward Tim, a wide smile on his sun-reddened face. "Well, Mr. Roper, it's all up except for the finishing. Since it's past suppertime, we're all gonna go to our homes now. But tomorrow some us will come back and put in your windows and get the door in place."

"You don't need to bother." Tim heard the abrasiveness of his tone, and he tempered his voice. "Not that I don't ap-preciate it. What you've all done here today . . ." He hadn't deserved their help. Not after abandoning the people of his faith. "Thank you. Thank you very much. But it's enough. I can finish on my own."

Gerber frowned. "The windows you can sure do on your own. But the door? It's a sliding door. A big one." He stretched his arms from side to side and then up and down. "It'll take a couple of strong men to lift it. You can't do that all by yourself."

Tim sighed. "All right. I appreciate the help."

Rubbing his whisker-dotted chin, the man frowned. "I think maybe I'll bring Mischler and Schell, and Schell's two oldest boys. The boys can keep working at the burn pile while we men finish up." He clomped off, leaving Tim alone.

Tim stared after him, realization making him break out in a cold sweat. The burn pile. He'd never made it to the burn pile. The box of photographs he'd intended to retrieve, if they hadn't been blown away by the tornado or ruined by the steady rain that had fallen all through the night, were now certainly burnt to cinders.

He groaned, closing his eyes in silent self-recrimination. Why hadn't he remembered to go out there before the workers arrived? Thanks to the Mennonites, he had a barn in place. But Julia and Charlie were gone, and so were his reminders of them.

31

Bekah spent the afternoon in her bedroom. It was stuffy upstairs even with the windows open, which made it the least comfortable place to be in the house. Parker and Adrianna thought so, too, which meant they weren't interested in hanging around her. That suited her fine. She had a lot to think about, and she wanted to be alone.

She sat on the edge of the bed, the box of women's clothing she'd taken from Mr. Roper's closet on the floor between her feet, and sorted through the items while her mind tripped over the conversation she'd overheard that morning. She supposed she should feel shameful for listening at the window when the insurance agent talked to Mom. But how else would she know what was going on? Mom didn't talk about important stuff with her.

A part of her wished she didn't know what the insurance people thought. She didn't want to consider the possibility that Dad might have jumped. She'd heard people whisper about it in Arborville, but she'd convinced herself it couldn't be true. Sure, Daddy'd been sad. They'd all been sad about how the accident changed Parker. She winced, remembering how it had hurt to see her smiling, teasing, always-busy dad shrink into a slow-moving, quiet, sad-eyed stranger. Before the accident, he'd had time for all of them. After the accident, he only had time for Parker. As if he felt guilty about damaging him and had to give him lots of attention to make up for it. Bekah had missed her dad even before he died.

With a sigh, she laid items out side by side on the bed and examined them. Temptation to try on the things and peek in a mirror—to see what she looked like in something other than her homemade Mennonite-approved dress—tugged hard. But fear Mom would come upstairs and catch her prevented her from following through. Some of the things sure were pretty, though, with ruffles and lace and soft, flowing fabrics. Bekah took a few minutes to sort them by color, noting Mrs. Roper's preference for pastels, before stacking them neatly back in the box.

Then she retrieved the box of little boy's clothing and went through those piece by piece. Charlie Roper must've been an active boy, because the knees of his overalls were worn through. Unlike his mom, he liked bold colors judging by the bright reds, blues, greens, and yellows of his T-shirts.

Fingering the clothing made Bekah sad, and she quickly folded everything and tucked it all back in the box. She slid both clothing boxes into the far corner of her closet and pulled out the shoe box that held photographs. She couldn't believe Mr. Roper wanted to throw these away. If she had pictures of her dad, she would treasure them. She would put them in frames to hang on the wall. Or organize them in a pretty book.

"He made a mistake," Bekah murmured. "He's sad, and when you're sad you make mistakes." A lump filled her throat as she applied her thought to Dad. Had he been so sad he made a mistake that day on top of the elevator? Had sadness made him think he didn't want to live anymore?

Bekah leapt up, scattering photographs across the floor. She knelt and scrambled to retrieve them, her hands shaking. She couldn't bring Dad back—he was gone forever. But Mr. Roper didn't have to live forever without the pictures of his wife and son. She could return them to him and maybe give him a little piece of his happiness back again. An idea formed in her mind, bringing a rush of eagerness. Why give them to him stuffed in the shoe box? Instead, she'd put them in a book. A book he could open again and again and remember his family's smiles.

The this-and-that store in Weaverly had albums for photographs—she'd seen them when she'd shopped there. A man wouldn't want a fancy book with flowers and frilly stuff on the cover. Just a plain one. Maybe blue or green. And a plain one probably wouldn't cost very much. Bekah placed the photos back in the box and dug out her money jar from beneath her socks in the dresser drawer. She dumped the contents on the bed and quickly counted the few dollar bills and assorted change.

She nibbled her lip. Almost eight dollars. Would it be enough? Even though the pictures didn't hold her own memories, it was very important that they be retained for Mr. Roper. She couldn't understand why it meant so much to her, only that it did.

Oh, please let seven dollars and eighty-six cents be enough to buy an album.

With the prayer lingering in the back of her heart, she stuffed the money in her little pocketbook and raced downstairs to ask Mom for permission to ride her bicycle into town.

※

Tim heated a can of soup on the little propane stove in the fishing trailer. He bent forward slightly to avoid bumping the top of his head on the padded ceiling. He appreciated the shelter, but if he had to stay in this little camper very long he would end up with a permanent crick in his neck from constantly ducking. Didn't camper makers realize some men were more than six feet tall?

He crushed half a package of saltine crackers into the broth, then sat on the little bench that folded out into a bed and ate his feeble supper directly from the pan. For a moment, he wished he'd accepted Luke Mischler's invitation to eat supper with his family. He'd be dining on something more substantial than watery vegetable beef soup. His stomach growled as he swallowed the last spoonful, reminding him how inadequate the meal had been. But sitting down to a meal with the Mennonite family would have drawn him even closer to the newcomers from Ohio. Now that the work was done, he needed to resume his solitary existence. Forget—again—his joint heritage with these people.

He clanked the empty pan and spoon into the shallow sink and stood, slope-shouldered, staring out the tiny square window above the minuscule counter. The completed barn loomed where only yesterday a twisted pile of timbers had rested. Even though he'd witnessed the Mennonite practice of goodwill before, he still found it hard to believe they'd pooled their own funds to purchase the supplies needed for the new barn and spent time away from their families and fields to help him. Tim Roper, a man who had abandoned the Mennonite faith.

With a soft whistle of amazement, he examined the barn by increments, from the sleek green roof panels to the red siding all the way to the rock foundation. Although the metal structure wasn't as proud looking as the age-worn wood-planked barn the tornado had destroyed, it would suit his purpose. And the colors emulated a ripe Red Delicious. What a gift, that big, metal, barn-shaped building. As soon as his insurance check arrived, he'd pay them back. That should end his contact with the affable Mennonites.

Until picking time.

The men had indicated they'd bring their families out when the apples were ready for harvesting. He scratched his chin, thinking ahead. Maybe he'd offer the families a discount to say thanks for all their help. Then he wouldn't have to feel beholden to them. Yeah, a discount. That'd even the score.

He turned from the window and unfolded the bench into a cot. He couldn't recall the last time he'd gone to bed before nine o'clock, but what else did he have to do but sleep? No television, no books to read, no one to talk to . . . Besides, he was worn to a frazzle by the long day of nonstop activity.

As he unrolled his sleeping bag across the thin foam pad that masqueraded as a mattress, his mind drifted back several years. He'd offered a discounted price to a group of Mennonites one other time. Four adult men and a handful of kids had driven over from someplace else in Kansas, arriving in two rented vans with cargo space in the back to cart the apples home again. They'd picked for themselves, and then they'd picked extra bushels to have ready for customers who weren't

interested in pick-your-own, so Tim knocked ten percent off
their cost for their trouble.

A sad smile twitched at his cheek as he flopped onto the
lumpy cot. That'd been the last harvest before Julia and Charlie's accident. Charlie had made friends with one of the Mennonite boys—a kid maybe a year or two younger than Charlie
who'd been a little slow. Not Down Syndrome or anything
Tim could identify—just slow. The boy and Charlie'd had
a good time that day, playing in the barn and chasing each
other between the trees. Tim and the boy's father'd had a
good talk, too. Even though Tim had wanted to hold his
distance from the Mennonite men, he'd felt a kinship with
this father who understood what it was like to raise a boy
with special needs.

He crunched his forehead, trying to recall the Mennonite
boy's name. It was different—Bumper? Bunker? The name
had long escaped Tim's memory. But he did recall his conversation with the dad. They'd agreed when you had a child
who needed extra attention, you stuck close. You gave more
of yourself. What had the man said? Tim pressed his memory,
determined to recall the exact words. *"When you have a child
who will always be a child, you make plans to be there for
them. Not just 'til they're old enough to be out on their own
the way you do for most children, but* forever." Tim had
nodded at the man's emphasis, understanding completely.

But then Tim had been freed of his lifelong commitment
to Charlie long before "forever" came. He rolled to his side
and closed his eyes against the memories, but they continued
to play out behind his closed lids. He'd give most anything to
have his son and every aspect of responsibility back again. But
then his eyes popped open, realization dawning. All these years

of working the orchard on his own, he'd convinced himself he was fine alone. He was better alone. No risk of being hurt or abandoned or even betrayed if he was alone. But now, after being accepted by the Knackstedt children, by their mother, and by their fellowship, alone just didn't sit as well as it once had.

Tim heaved a mighty sigh. He'd handled alone before. He could do it again. *"I can do all things—"* Before the verse could complete itself in his mind, he threw his arm across his eyes and forced himself to shut out the world.

⁜

Amy set aside her Bible and gave Parker a kiss on the cheek. "Sleep well," she said, receiving his sleepy smile in reply. Adrianna and Bekah rose from the foot of the bed, and Amy followed them down the short hallway to their bedroom. She tucked Adrianna beneath the sheet, making her giggle by giving her a flurry of kisses on her sweet-smelling neck. With a soft laugh, Amy smoothed her hand over the little girl's hair. "Sleep well."

"I will, Momma. 'Night." Adrianna rolled to her side and scrunched her eyes closed.

Amy turned to Bekah, who stood in the dim glow of the bedside lamp removing the pins from her hair. "Are you going to stay up and work on Mr. Roper's book?" She kept her voice low to avoid disturbing Adrianna.

Bekah nodded. Hair tumbled down her back in a wave. The sight of her daughter, standing tall with squared shoulders, her dark hair shimmering in the soft light, put a lump in Amy's throat. What a pretty young woman Bekah was becoming. Bekah lifted the denim-covered album and held it out, her expression bashful. "Want to see what I have so far?"

"Sure." Amy sat next to Bekah on her bed and laid the album in her lap. She opened the album and admired her daughter's efforts. Bekah had done a commendable job of sorting the photographs into groupings that complemented one another. A chill tiptoed up her spine as she received a glimpse into Mr. Roper's family life. Amy turned the pages slowly, examining each photograph by turn. Admittedly, jealousy pricked. How she'd love to have images frozen in time of her children and of Gabe to look at again and again. When she reached the last filled page, she gave Bekah a one-armed hug. "It looks so nice, honey. I'm sure Mr. Roper will be pleased you took the time to do this for him."

"I hope so." Bekah pulled the album into her own lap. She turned a few pages, then used her finger to outline the figure of the little boy, perhaps five years old, standing in front of the old barn. "This is my favorite. He looks so cute in those striped overalls and bare feet. And his whole face is smiling, not just his mouth, do you see?"

Amy chuckled softly at the boy's grin, so huge it squinted his eyes to slits. "I do see. He looks very happy there."

Bekah nodded, her chin low. "He must've really liked those overalls. He wears them in lots of pictures, and Mr. Roper even kept them." Bekah angled a quick glance at Amy. "Wanna see?"

Amy nodded, and Bekah slipped from the bed. She opened the closet door slowly, cringing at its creak. But Adrianna, sound asleep, didn't even stir. Bekah pulled a box from the closet and tugged the flaps open. She lifted out the overalls shown in the picture and held them up. "The knees are worn through, but Mrs. Roper must've sewn in some fabric behind the holes."

"May I see them?" Amy took the overalls, examining the frayed hems, the ragged holes with patches of green-and-red-plaid flannel sewn inside the legs. "My, these were well loved." She shot Bekah a startled look. "How did you happen to come by these?"

Bekah shrugged slowly, crunching her lips to the side. "Mr. Roper told me to throw them away. These, and his wife's things." She gestured to another box in the closet. "But it seemed like a waste. I thought maybe somebody could use them. So I brought them home."

An idea whisked through the far corner of Amy's brain. "Do you have plans for them already?"

Bekah sent a wistful look toward the box in the closet. "Not really."

Amy patted the mattress. "Well, come here, then, and tell me what you think of this. . . ."

32

The last half of July and early August disappeared quickly. After the tornado, humidity descended on Weaverly, making Amy long for the dry days preceding it. Yet she gloried in the occasional rain shower that nourished the soybeans and her garden. She and the children worked in the garden early each morning before the day grew too hot while the fellowship men harvested the soybeans and readied the soil for a winter wheat crop.

The first few weeks after the tornado, the children begged daily to visit Mr. Roper. Although a part of Amy desired to see him, too—to ascertain he was recovering from his losses—she refused the children's requests and steadfastly turned her thoughts elsewhere. She continued to keep him in her prayers and encouraged the children to pray for him, as well, but he'd asked them to stay away. As much as it hurt her to deny the children, she knew it would hurt them more to suffer cold rejection from the man who'd been so open and caring in the past. Parker, especially, wouldn't understand Mr.

Roper's change in demeanor. So she consistently refused, and over time, they stopped asking.

On Saturdays, the fellowship women met to can the bounty from their gardens, exchanging tomatoes for beets or peas for cucumbers so everyone would have a variety of vegetables for the winter. Amy's cellar shelves bowed beneath the weight of full quart jars, and her heart rejoiced at the security the food stores offered her and the children. Each Sunday, the Mennonites gathered and praised God for the fruitful land and opportunity to serve Him together. Weekly, Amy felt herself drawing closer to these men and women from Ohio who'd accepted her and her children into their fellowship. But although she prayed daily for God to expose the truth concerning Gabe's death, she never mentioned the need to her new friends.

She and the children developed a routine of visiting the Weaverly library Friday mornings after finishing in the garden. To her delight, each week she discovered several new contacts in her email box. Over the weeks, she accepted jobs from four new clients. Even as she confirmed her intention to complete the projects, she wondered if she'd be forced to sell her house and expensive quilting machine to repay the insurance agency. She and her father spoke on the telephone several times after the children had gone to bed, but thus far God hadn't answered their prayer to provide evidence that Gabe hadn't taken his own life. The worry ate at her, stealing her sleep at night and giving her stomach pangs during the day. But she took the jobs as a statement of faith that somehow she'd be able to fill the orders.

While Amy sewed on her projects, Bekah worked on the other side of the room. Margaret Gerber had loaned them her older-model Singer, claiming she only sewed during the winter months. Using pieces cut from the clothing that had once belonged to Julia and Charlie Roper, Bekah stitched the pieces into colorful Tree of Life blocks. When perusing Amy's book of quilt patterns, they'd both agreed the tree formed of triangles and squares was the perfect choice for a man who operated an orchard. The appeal of the pattern lay not only in its simple beauty, but in its reminder of faith and the truth of eternal life.

For the quilt's center block, Bekah had chosen a square of sturdy muslin and hand-embroidered a Scripture from Job, chapter fourteen, which spoke of a tree's roots sending forth new growth. While meticulously stitching the letters onto the stretched muslin, Bekah had mused, "You know, Mom, this verse works for the apple trees that're still blooming even after all the damage from the tornado, but it also kinda talks about people, doesn't it? We might get knocked down by life, but God gives us strength to get up again. And even when our bodies on earth die, we get a whole new life in Heaven with Him—a life that goes on forever."

Tears had burned in Amy's eyes for hours after Bekah's thoughtful expression. Her daughter's insights offered a peek at the spiritual growth taking place within Bekah's heart, giving Amy's mother-heart a reason to sing.

The last Friday before school started, Amy took the children to the library and then to the Burger Basket for an end-of-summer-vacation lunch. Parker and Adrianna played tic-tac-toe on a napkin while Amy and Bekah visited. With school around the corner, Bekah seemed nervous. Amy surmised going to a new school with new teachers and many unfamiliar faces created her daughter's uncertainties, but her heart turned over when Bekah confessed the true reason for her apprehension.

"It'll be the first time Parker and me aren't in the same building. What if he needs me? I won't be close by like I've always been before."

Amy took Bekah's hand and gave it a squeeze. "If you aren't there, Parker will learn to handle his problems on his own. That would be good for him, wouldn't it?"

Bekah cast a tender look at her brother. "I guess so. He is getting bigger." She sighed, facing Amy again. "But it's hard for me. I feel like I'm letting him down by not being there."

Amy hadn't realized how deeply Bekah's long-held position as older sister and protector had become ingrained in her being. She sought words of encouragement, but before she could speak again, Bekah suddenly blurted out a statement that stilled Amy's voice.

"But maybe we'll end up back in Arborville and in the same building after all."

Amy stared at Bekah, her jaw slack.

Bekah shrugged. "If you have to pay back the money you got from the grain-elevator owner, you'll have to sell the house we're in, right? And we'll move back to Grandpa's house?"

How had Bekah known about the threat? She hadn't mentioned it to the children, fearful of creating a sense of panic. Yet apparently Bekah had kept the secret for weeks. Amy shook her head. "I—"

"Here you go!" The cheerful server plopped plastic baskets of hamburgers and french fries on the table.

Amy led them in a prayer of thanks for the food. The conversation steered to other topics, but Amy couldn't stop thinking about Bekah's questions. She'd put off planning what would happen if she was forced to pay back the money, but she knew she didn't want to return to Arborville. Not after someone there had made such hurtful accusations not only about Gabe, but about her. The insinuation that she would be deceitful enough to accept money that didn't rightfully belong to her stung.

While the children jabbered, enjoying their meal, Amy fell silent, lowered her head, and let her thoughts dissolve into prayer. *God, help me forgive those in Arborville who wronged me. I want to believe Gabe wouldn't choose to leave us—I want to assure my children their father would rather be here to watch them grow into God-honoring adults. But time is quickly running out for me to offer proof that Gabe didn't take his own life. If I'm unable to keep the money, the children and I will have to move. Are we meant to return to Arborville, that place of painful memory? Or do You have another place of beginning for us?*

Her heart stabbed as she considered leaving Weaverly. In only three short months, she'd grown to love the town, her new fellowship members, and—a tiny gasp escaped her lips as realization rolled through her—her neighbor. Her eyes closed tightly, she offered a deeply felt entreaty. *Reveal Your plan, Father, so the children and I might be at peace.*

"Mom?"

Amy startled at Bekah's hesitant voice. She lifted her gaze. "Yes?"

Her hand next to her cheek, Bekah pointed toward the door. Her face reflected apprehension. Adrianna and Parker turned backward in their chairs to peek. Adrianna squealed, "Mr. Roper!" Before Amy could stop them, the two youngest bounded out of their chairs and raced across the tile floor to the man who'd somehow, inexplicably, stolen a piece of their mother's heart.

Tim's heart fired into his throat as Adri and Parker flew toward him, arms outstretched. Unmindful of the other diners, he went down on one knee and captured Adri in a hug. Parker bent forward, wrapping his skinny arms around Tim's neck. Tim's baseball hat bounced off his head and hit the scuffed floor, but he didn't care. Not until that moment did he realize how much he'd missed them. But their exuberant greeting brought back every lonely minute he'd held them at bay. What joy he'd denied himself by remaining aloof from these open, smiling, accepting children.

Chuckles rumbled from those seated at the closest table, reminding Tim they were being observed. Gently, he disentangled himself from their grips and rose, scooping up his hat and settling it back over his hair as he pushed to his feet. Adri danced in front of him, her little braids bouncing.

"Mr. Roper, guess what? School starts next week, an' I getta go. Parker an' Bekah, too! We all getta go. Momma bought us backpacks an' pencils an' paper an' scissors an' *everything*. An' Bekah got a cackulooter that does numbers."

Several people at the table laughed loudly, but Tim ignored the amused snorts and put his hand on Adri's head. He smiled down at the little girl. "Sounds as if you all had a fine time shopping." He hoped the shopping spree meant their mother's business was flourishing.

"Uh-huh." She whirled and skipped back to the table in the far corner of the crowded little dining room. Tim's eyes followed her, and his gaze collided with the children's mother, who stared at him unblinking. Something lit a fire beneath his skin, heating him from the inside out. If it hadn't been for the AC blowing cold air directly on the back of his neck, he might've melted right there on the spot.

A hand tapped Tim's arm. "Mr. Roper?"

With effort, Tim dragged his attention away from Amy Knackstedt's sky-blue eyes and focused on the gangly youth standing beside him.

"Wanna sit with us?" Parker's eyes—wide, innocent, so like Charlie's—begged.

Tim knew he should say no. He had nothing to offer these children. Or their mother. He shook his head slowly, but when he opened his mouth, he heard himself say, "I sure do." Parker broke into a wide smile. He captured Tim's hand and escorted him to the table. Tim borrowed a chair from another table and scooted in between Parker and Adri, who both giggled as if he'd done something spectacular.

Tara, the café's server, bustled to the table. Tim ordered a double cheeseburger, onion rings, and a chocolate milkshake, adding, "Make it to go. I'm just passing through—lots of errands to run today." He wasn't sure, but he thought Mrs. Knackstedt released a little breath of relief.

"Be right up." Tara scurried away. With her departure, Tim turned his attention to his tablemates. Adri and Parker both grinned at him, clearly delighted to have him there, but Mrs. Knackstedt stared at her half-eaten burger, her cap's ribbons trailing past her bright red cheeks. Bekah nibbled her burger, her gaze zinging around as if she didn't know where to look.

Tim's deliberate separation had obviously created a great deal of angst, and once again regret smote him. How he wished they could all relax. Talk. Maybe laugh together, the way friends did. He cleared his throat—loudly—and both Mrs. Knackstedt and Bekah shot him a startled look. He poked his thumb over his shoulder. "Would you rather I wait for my food elsewhere? There're other empty seats. I can sure move."

"Nooo!" Adri crooned, and Parker immediately curled his hand over Tim's wrist.

Mrs. Knackstedt licked her lips. "Of course not."

Adri clapped her hands and then snatched up her burger. Parker reached for a french fry, and the two began munching cheerfully.

"In fact . . ." Mrs. Knackstedt flicked a questioning glance at Bekah, who sat as wide-eyed as an owl. "We've been meaning to give you a call. Bekah has something for you at the house."

Tim looked at Bekah. The girl's face flooded with pink. He offered a smile, desperate to put her at ease. "Oh yeah? What's that?"

Bekah toyed with a french fry, repeatedly dipping it in a pool of ketchup. But she didn't answer.

Adri piped up. "A pitcher book. It's blue. Do you like blue, Mr. Roper?"

Tim looked into Adri's clear blue eyes. The same color as her mother's. The same color as Julia's and Charlie's, although theirs had been grayish blue. His lips twitched into a sad smile. "Blue is the best color ever."

Adri hunched her shoulders and giggled.

Mrs. Knackstedt touched Adri's arm. "You need to eat."

The little girl obediently bit into her cheeseburger.

Tim wanted to question Bekah, but the girl's bashful

countenance held him at a distance. Was she thinking about their last conversation, and how he'd sent her away? She hadn't deserved his anger that day. She'd come to him legitimately seeking, and he'd let past hurts color his reaction. He needed to apologize, but he wanted to do so when he didn't have an audience.

He said, "Should I come by this afternoon . . . after I've run my errands? I could stop on my way home." As of a week ago, he had a home. A mobile home dealer from Topeka had delivered a single-wide trailer, compliments of his insurance payout. It was half the size of his old trailer house, but why did he need lots of space? Nobody else occupied it. Sadness took hold of him again.

Bekah looked at her mother, and Mrs. Knackstedt gave a brief nod. Without meeting his gaze, Bekah bobbed her head up and down. "That'll be fine."

Tim visited with Parker and Adrianna, occasionally earning a one-syllable response from Bekah or a brief comment from their mother. He enjoyed chatting with the children—their happy voices filled an empty place inside—but he caught himself longing for the woman across the table to open up and share as candidly as she once had. It was true a person didn't appreciate what he had until it was no longer his. How could they regain the ease they'd once felt in one another's presence? The question hovered on the tip of his tongue, and he leaned forward with his elbows on the table, ready to let it spill from his mouth.

"Here ya go, Mr. Roper!" Tara plunked a greasy sack and tall Styrofoam cup beside him. "Those onion rings just came out of the fryer and they're really hot, so be careful. I tossed in a few ketchup packets, but if you want mustard you'll have to ask at the counter. Can I get you anything else?" The girl stood waiting with an expectant smile, her eyebrows high.

What would she say if he answered, "Yes, I'd like you to find me a gallon of friendship restorer and dish it up to everybody at this table so we don't have to be at odds anymore"? They'd all think he'd lost his mind.

"This'll do, Tara. Thanks." He stretched to his feet, grabbing his bag and cup, and gave a weak smile to everyone at the table. "Thanks for letting me join you." He focused in on Bekah. "I'll stop by later and pick up that best-color-ever book." Although he injected a teasing note, Bekah didn't smile in reply.

He nodded good-bye and headed for the counter to pay for his lunch. A mix of curiosity and dread twined through his middle. What waited for him at the Knackstedt place?

33

Amy watched her neighbor's face as he paged through the album of photographs Bekah had organized. In typical masculine fashion, he held his emotions inside, but the slight shimmer in his eyes, tremble in his hand, and tightly set jaw spoke very clearly. He was touched. And seeing his response put a lump in her throat.

Although she'd invited him to sit on the sofa and look at the album, he'd elected to stand in the doorway. Parker and Adrianna had gone upstairs to nap when they'd returned home, but Bekah stood beside Amy, her hands clasped at her rib cage and her gaze fixed on Mr. Roper's face. The moment he closed the back cover, Bekah lifted one hand to gesture to the book. "The pages . . . all those little pockets? You can take the pictures out and move them around if you want to. You don't have to leave them like I put them."

"It's perfect just the way you have it." Mr. Roper didn't lift his head. His hands held tightly to the album. His Adam's apple bobbed in a swallow. "Thank you."

Bekah's breath whooshed out. "You're welcome." She backed up a few inches, waving toward the sewing room. "I'm . . . gonna go do some sewing." She flashed a secretive grin at Amy. "With school starting next Wednesday, I won't have as much time to work soon, and . . ." She zipped around the corner.

Mr. Roper looked after her, a tenderness in his eyes. Then he shifted his face slightly, meeting Amy's gaze. A warm smile slowly climbed his chiseled cheeks, making Amy's heart patter in response. He patted the album's smooth denim cover. "I thought these were gone forever. I can't believe she . . ." He shook his head, releasing a soft sigh. "She's a good kid—a thoughtful kid. You've raised her right." A soft laugh rumbled from his throat. "And I'm sure grateful to have them. I never should have told her to throw them out. Don't know what I was thinking."

Amy wondered if she should tell him about the boxes of clothes and what she and Bekah had done with them. But the quilt was more Bekah's project than Amy's. Bekah should be the one to share it with him. Amy glanced at the album, longing sweeping through her. "I'm glad she brought them here, too. Of course I don't have photographs of Gabe or . . . or anyone else. Our sect—" She shrugged. He understood the Old Order Mennonite lifestyle. "I carry pictures in my head, of course, but over time . . ."

"They become fuzzy?"

"Yes. And then you aren't sure if what you're remembering is real or merely a figment of your imagination."

An odd pain creased his face. "Yes. I suppose you're right." His voice sounded tight, distant.

Eager to restore his relaxed, warm countenance, Amy said,

"But you have the photographs now, to keep your wife's and son's faces alive in your mind. I pray the photographs will be a comfort to you, Mr. Roper."

"Tim," he blurted.

Amy tipped her head, puzzled.

"Call me Tim. We're neighbors, after all, and . . . and I'd like us to be friends."

In her entire life, Amy had never addressed an adult male—other than Gabe, of course—by his first name. What would the fellowship members think? Or her father? They'd surely disapprove, considering it forward. Yet she discovered she wanted to cast off the formal address. She wanted to be friends. She wanted to be more than friends. . . .

Lord, guard my heart. The wisest thing would be to continue referring to him as Mr. Roper, but her time here might come to an end soon. What would it hurt to call him by his first name? "I'd like that, too. And please, call me Amy."

"Amy . . ."

Not since Gabe's death had any man, other than her father, called her by her given name. Hearing it in his deep, warm vocal tone brought a rush of unprecedented pleasure.

"Well, Amy, I should probably . . ." He grabbed the screen door handle and pushed, the discordant creak of the hinges a direct contrast to the smooth delivery of his voice uttering her name. Stepping out onto the porch, he gave a quick, almost bashful, nod of good-bye and then turned and tromped off the porch, holding the album tight in the bend of his elbow.

Amy watched through the mesh screen as he climbed into his pickup, his movements strong and sure. She remained watching until his truck turned off at the end of the lane, dust whirling behind it. Even then, she watched until the dust settled. Then, with a soft sigh, she turned from the door. And she found Bekah standing in the doorway between the living room and sewing room, watching her.

✣

Tim pulled into his driveway and parked in front of the barn. With the new, wider doorway, he could pull his truck clear inside, but he'd developed the habit of parking outside. His hand still rested on the cover of the photo album, and even while he'd driven the short distance between the Knackstedt place and his own, his mind's eye had skipped through the images carefully saved behind layers of clear plastic.

Flashes of Julia and Charlie played through his memory, followed by other images not captured on photo paper but preserved in the back recesses of his mind. Yet he couldn't be sure if the remembrances were actual events. *"You aren't sure if what you're remembering is real or merely a figment of your imagination."* He completely understood Amy's comment. After all the years that had slipped by, he couldn't be certain the way he remembered his father and mother was even remotely close to fact. And it bothered him.

He picked up the album and hopped out of the truck, crossing the slanted path of shade cast by the tall barn. The whirr of the central air unit greeted him as he neared the house, and cool air whisked across him as he stepped inside. He plopped onto the sofa, laying the closed album on his lap. Work waited—he needed to finish the new slatted display boxes for apples, and he'd intended to mow the picnic meadow again before sunset—but for the first time in more years than he could count he wanted to look back. Wanted to remember.

So he tipped his head back, closed his eyes, and deliberately sought snatches of time from his years living beneath his father's roof. The first memories to surface were sour ones—angry words and fierce reprimands. The reason he'd left. But as he forced his mind backward, other pictures emerged. Mom's sweet smile, her soft hand on his forehead as he drifted off to sleep. Laughing with his brothers as they swung hand over hand from the barn rafters. His youngest sister's delighted squeals as he spun her in the tire swing Dad had hung from the old oak tree in the backyard. And Dad . . . Dad on the couch with the children gathered at his feet while he read aloud from the Psalms.

A lump filled Tim's throat. As a very young boy, he'd thought his dad's voice must be just like God's voice—rich, tender, filled with strength and wisdom. When had it all changed? He couldn't recall the moment when peaceful acceptance of their simple lifestyle turned to discontent and a feeling of being restrained. Timothy Rupp Sr. had done his best to drive the rebellion from his eldest son's soul. But it hadn't worked. Instead, he'd driven the son away.

Something tickled Tim's cheek. A loose hair or a spider's web? He reached to brush it away and encountered moisture. His eyes popped open, releasing another tear. He swiped at the trickle of wet with his fingers and sniffed hard, determined to gain control. But despite his efforts, a new trickle slid down his cheek and met his lips, salty and warm. He sat up, pushing the album onto the sofa cushion beside him. There he remained, bolt upright, staring at the album while images flashed like bolts of lightning across his memory. Julia, Charlie, Dad, Mom, his brothers and sisters . . . How he missed them. *All* of them.

He groaned, burying his face in his hands. Real or imagined? Were the reasons for staying away so long from his parents and his Mennonite heritage based on truth . . . or the mistaken remembrances of a rebellious youth? And how would he ever know for sure?

Ask.

The suggestion came with such force, he almost thought it had been given by an audible voice. Tim's head jerked upright, his eyes seeking. But the room was empty, as always. Licking his lips, he whispered a question. "Ask . . . who?"

He didn't need a thundering voice from the heavens for an answer. He knew who to ask. The person who'd witnessed Tim's leave-taking. The person who knew why Tim had marched down the road that day so long ago. His heart set up a mighty clamor in his chest, just considering talking to Dad after all this time apart. He and Dad might argue, exchange more ugly words. Dad might not want to talk at all. He'd stated clearly that if Tim left, he shouldn't ever come back. Dad'd been angry that day—angrier than Tim had ever seen him. But maybe, just as Tim often regretted words spewed in a moment of fury, Dad wished he could take the words back. He'd never know unless he asked. His heart continued to pound hard against his ribs, apprehension making his mouth like cotton. But the more he thought about it, the more he wanted to do it.

Back then, his folks had owned a telephone. They kept it in the barn rather than in the house, but they had one. Tim glanced at the clock, and a prickle inched its way across his scalp. Right about now, in Indiana, if Dad were still alive— was he still alive?—he'd be out in the barn, climbing into his work coveralls, preparing to bring in the cows for milking.

He'd hear the phone ring because the machines would still be silent.

But would they still have the same number? *Check online.* As if propelled by a stout breeze, Tim shot across the room to his desk where his computer sat, ready and waiting. A few clicks, and he sat staring at the entry for Timothy Rupp, Goshen, Indiana. His breath came in little spurts, his hand shaking so badly he had difficulty copying the number onto a scrap of paper. He took several deep breaths, releasing the air slowly, bringing himself under control, gathering courage. His breathing fairly normal, he removed his cell phone from its pouch. Put it back. Brought it out again.

"You'll never know unless you ask," he told himself in a firm tone, his voice bringing back memories of his father's firm, no-nonsense tone. Sucking in one more long, deep breath, he lifted the cover on the phone and, with deliberate pokes of his finger, entered his father's telephone number.

Ring! . . . Ring! . . . Ring! . . . Ring! Dad must be milking already. Half disappointed, half relieved, Tim pulled the phone away from his ear and started to flip it closed. But then a male voice, familiar and yet belonging to a stranger, said, "Rupp Dairy. Timothy Rupp speaking."

Dad! Tim's entire body began to quiver. He pressed the telephone receiver tight against his cheek to hold it steady and drew in a shuddering breath. "Dad? It's me . . . Tim."

Silence. Tim gulped. "Tim. Your son."

Another few seconds of silence ticked by, and then a strange gurgle came through the line. Tim held the telephone out for a moment and frowned at it, puzzled. Then he put it to his ear again. The gurgling exploded into wracking sobs interspersed with stammered speech. "Tim . . . my son . . . Oh, thank You, my God and Father. How long I've prayed . . . my son, my son . . ."

Tim's body went weak. Had he not been sitting, he would have collapsed onto the floor. As it was, he nearly dropped the telephone. Dad . . . *crying.* Tears filled his eyes, and he clutched the phone two-handed, his desire to climb through the line and embrace his father so strong it was all he could do to keep the seat of his pants planted on the chair. "Yeah, Dad. It's me. It's me." For several minutes they cried together— miles apart yet connected by the unending bond of love.

34

Two weeks after Tim's hour-long phone conversation with his father—a conversation that had to be ended before either was ready due to the cows' pitiful bawling in the background—a black sedan pulled into the lane and parked in the area Tim had cleared for customers. Caught up in telling a group of visiting homeschooled youngsters about the importance of pollination, he barely glanced at the vehicle. But when an older couple in Mennonite garb stepped from the car, Tim's recital came to an abrupt halt.

He stared as the man caught the woman's hand and led her across the ground toward Tim. Both pairs of eyes seemed fixed on his face. Even from the distance of forty feet, Tim could see their lips quivering, caught between smiles and tears. Their feet—his in sturdy work boots, hers in black-laced oxfords—moved slowly, stiltedly, determined yet hesitant.

Puzzled mutters reached Tim's ears, his guests no doubt wondering why their lecturer had lost the ability to speak.

With effort, Tim tore his gaze away from the approaching couple to offer a quick, "Excuse me."

He pried his stiff legs from their wide-set stance and took two stumbling steps toward the couple. Then, eagerness chasing away anxiety, he broke into a run, his chest full and aching. Their faces were older, the hair peeping beneath black flat-brimmed hat and white mesh cap streaked with gray, but as Tim ran toward them the years peeled back and, in their eyes, Tim saw the parents he remembered. "Mom! Dad!" Arms wide, he flew to them, feeling the weight of separation fall from his shoulders until it seemed his feet hovered inches above the ground.

They stopped in a patch of dappled sunlight and opened their arms to him. He fell into their embrace, burying his face in the crevice formed by their tightly pressed shoulders. Beneath his encircling arm, Mom's shoulders shook. Dad's hand gripped handfuls of Tim's shirt, his fingers convulsing. Tim clung in return, laughing while he battled tears. Disbelief and joy mingled in his chest. They'd come!

Pulling free, he looked into his father's square-jawed, thick-browed face. "What about the cows? Who's minding the dairy?"

"Ach, cows." Dad flicked his hand, the thick leathery palm familiar but the thick veins and age-splotched back belonging to a stranger. "Your brother and his sons took over for the week. How could your mother and me stay away? A telephone call doesn't tell us what we need to see after so many years of daily prayer that the Good Lord would return you to us—our oldest boy in flesh and bone." Tears flooded Dad's eyes, and a sob broke from Mom's throat. Mom leaned into Tim's chest, her mesh cap brushing his chin while Dad curled his hand around Tim's upper arm. "You look good, Tim. You look so good." Dad's voice was gruff from emotion.

During his teen years, Tim had often inwardly grumbled that the cows meant more than anything to Dad, but Dad had left the dairy and driven nearly seven hundred miles to see him. He mattered to his father. He truly mattered. And even though he wore faded Levi's and a snap-up western shirt instead of Mennonite-approved attire, Dad thought he looked good. The years had mellowed his father. An unfamiliar prayer, borne of gratitude, formed in the center of Tim's heart. *Thank You, Father.*

He wanted to stay there, memorizing his parents' changed faces and catching up on the lost years, but duty called. The cows were in capable hands, but no one else could finish the planned tour for the students and parents waiting near the barn. Regret twisted Tim's lips into a grimace, but there was no other choice.

He gestured behind him. "I was just starting with a tour group. I wish I could take the afternoon off and talk, but—"

His father shook his head, waving both hands. "No, no, we took you by surprise, just showing up like this. You have work. We can go back to the hotel and come see you later. When your workday is over."

"Or . . ." Did he dare make the suggestion? Part of the reason Tim had left home was feeling as though he could never meet his father's high expectations. Would Dad find reason for criticism if Tim invited him fully into his world? He licked his dry lips and finished the suggestion. "You could follow the tour. See what . . . what I do now."

Mom bobbed her head, the ribbons on her cap bouncing. "I would like that."

Dad smiled. "All right, then. Let's go."

Tim escorted his parents to the group, introduced them, and then released a nervous chuckle. "All right, then. Let's go." Not until he'd pointed the visitors toward the path between the trees did he realize he'd exactly mimicked his father's comment. And, oddly, after all the years of trying to be completely different from his father, the realization made him smile.

The tour went well, in Tim's opinion. Although his parents followed well behind, never contributing, he caught their interested, approving glances, and he might have been ten years old again, highly marked school report in hand, receiving their praise for a job well done. Each of the homeschool kids went home with a small box of apples and a sunburned nose, and the parents thanked Tim for his time. The last car turned out of the drive, and Tim found himself alone with his parents.

They stood in a silent circle, examining their own feet or the clouds or the trees. What should they do now? With younger siblings always around in his childhood home, he couldn't recall ever having his parents' full, undivided attention to himself. Here he was, thirty-eight years old and uncertain how to proceed. Talking on the phone had been easier—less intimidating, since if things went awry, he could simply hang up. But face-to-face? What if anger surfaced again? If only Julia were here. She'd know how to bridge this awkward silence.

Tim jolted, awareness dawning. "Would you like to come to the house? I have . . . I have something I'd like to show you." His parents fell in step beside him, Mom centered between Tim and his dad. Tim swallowed the bitter taste of worry that sat in the back of his throat. They might not approve of his having used a camera over the years, capturing images of God's creation in a man-made manner, but Tim was willing to risk their censure to let them see his wife and son.

Thank You, Lord, that Bekah didn't dispose of those photographs.

※

Bekah stood next to the automatic quilting machine, nibbling her nails. Amy chuckled as she rolled the layers of backing, batting, and completed quilt face into the frame. "You don't need to look so worried. I've done this before, you know."

Bekah zipped her hand from her mouth, tangling her fingers in her apron skirt. "I know. But this is *my* quilt. What if some of my stitching comes undone or something?" Her gaze roved across the blocks bearing the Tree of Life pattern. "I wish all the points were perfect. Sometimes they didn't line up just right."

Amy paused in her task to tickle Bekah's chin with one of the ribbons dangling from her cap. "Honey, the quilt is beautiful. Ti—Mr. Roper is going to be so appreciative."

"I hope so . . ."

Hiding a smile, Amy turned back to the frame. "Why don't you go get the supper dishes washed and put away? I'll get started here, and by the time you're done I'll probably have one row quilted. You'll see how nice it looks with the stitching."

Bekah sighed. "All right." She scuffed toward the kitchen, peering back over her shoulder with a look of longing.

Amy laughed quietly and completed rolling the quilt. Although not all of the triangles were perfectly on point, Bekah had done a commendable job putting together the squares. Even well-practiced quilters sometimes missed crisp points. The overlapped edges reminded Amy of the way leaves clustered, one hiding behind another, and seemed to fit the quilt's theme. She felt certain once Bekah saw the quilt all stitched, she would be satisfied with her handiwork.

With the layers in place, Amy programmed the machine. Bekah had chosen a stitch pattern called Indian Summer, which incorporated the shape of maple leaves with swirls, as if the leaves were blowing in the wind. Although Amy had never used the pattern before, she was certain it would prove to be the perfect choice for the Tree of Life quilt. Pride filled her as she considered Bekah's natural artistic abilities. She'd be an expert quilter one day.

She flipped the switch, and the long-arm machine roared to life. Amy carefully guided the frame beneath the needle, watching the pattern emerge. As always, satisfaction welled as she completed a project. How she'd miss this machine if she were forced to sell it.

The verse Bekah had chosen to stitch into the center of the quilt repeatedly played through Amy's mind, serving as a reminder that God would bring new growth to them, no matter where they might have to move. Two nights ago, she'd placed her future—and her children's futures—into God's capable hands and decided to stop worrying. As her father often encouraged her, she would trust God to meet their needs whether they were able to keep this house or not. Surrendering the worries brought the peace she'd been seeking.

She smiled to herself as the needle bounced, the thread forming a leaf. How good to have peace, fresh and green and alive, unfurl in her heart. She reached the end of the first row, stopped the machine, and rolled the quilt upward to expose the next row of blocks. As she reached to flip the On switch again, the sound of feet tromping across the porch boards sounded, followed by a firm rap on the doorjamb.

Parker and Adrianna dashed through the sewing room, a dishtowel flapping in Adrianna's hand. Both children exclaimed, "I'll get it. No, *I'll* get it!"

Amy stepped between the arguing pair. "I will get it." She stilled their complaints with a frown, then shooed them back to the kitchen. She looked through the screen door and gave a start when she saw Tim Roper and an older Mennonite couple looking in at her. She gave the door a push, offering a hesitant smile. "Good evening."

Tim popped his billed cap from his head at the same time the gray-haired man removed his black church hat. Tim ushered in the woman first. She gave Amy a bashful smile. The men stepped inside next, and Amy let the door bounce into its frame. Tim met her gaze, seeming embarrassed yet glowing with a happiness she'd never witnessed in his green eyes before. "Forgive us for dropping in unannounced, but—" He swallowed, his gaze flitting to the couple. "This is Timothy and Marianne Rupp."

Amy held out her hand to the man, who shook it somberly. "It's very nice to meet you, Mr. Rupp," she said. She shifted to bestow a smile on the woman. "Mrs. Rupp."

Tim cleared his throat, twisting his hat in his hands. "My parents came for a visit, and when I told them about you and your children, they wanted to meet you."

His parents? Amy blinked in surprise. She'd known Tim had been raised Mennonite, but she'd surmised his parents were deceased. Seeing them very much alive, standing side by side with curious, friendly expressions on their gently lined faces stole her ability to speak.

Fortunately, Adrianna bounced around the corner and rescued her mother. "Hello, Mr. Roper. Hello, people I don't know. I'm Adrianna Amelia Knackstedt, and I'm five. I go to kindergarten, and I can already read. Want me to read you something?"

Light laughter rolled from the adults. Tim's father propped his hands on his knees, bringing himself to eye level with Adrianna. "What is your favorite thing to read?"

"My cat book!" Adrianna's eyes danced. "You wait here. I'll go get it." She dashed off, her giggle trailing her.

Tim's parents exchanged an indulgent look, and then Mrs. Rupp turned to Amy. "Just as Tim said, she's a delightful little girl."

Amy sent Tim a soft smile. "Thank you. She thinks very highly of your son, as do all of my children." She released a self-conscious laugh, gesturing to the furniture. "Please—sit down and make yourselves comfortable. May I bring you something to drink? Coffee or lemonade?"

"No, thank you." Mr. Rupp guided his wife toward the sofa. "We just finished our supper at Tim's place."

Tim and his parents sat in a row on Amy's sofa. The two men hooked their hats over one knee and cupped a hand over the top. Even though they were dressed differently, with different kinds of headwear, their actions were so identical Amy had a hard time not staring. She sank into one of the two chairs facing the sofa.

Mrs. Rupp crossed her ankles and folded her hands in her lap. "We were so happy to learn Tim has Mennonite neighbors. Timothy"—she shifted one hand to her husband's knee, and he automatically placed his hand over hers, stirring a longing in Amy's breast for a man to respond to her in a similar way—"and I have prayed over the years that our son would make friends with people of his faith. He says you haven't lived here for long, but he considers you and your children his friends."

Amy felt as though she was missing a huge piece of a puzzle, but she nodded in reply. "He's been a very good friend to us. We couldn't have asked for a better neighbor."

At that moment, Adrianna skipped into the room with a storybook in her hands. She went directly to Tim and scooted backward, situating herself between his knees. She grinned into Mr. Rupp's face. "Okay, I'm ready." She flopped the book open and began to read about a furry cat named Cindy. While she read, Parker and Bekah inched into the room, obviously wanting to be part of the circle but uncertain whether they should intrude.

Mrs. Rupp's sweet smile of welcome propelled Parker across the floor, and he perched on the arm of the sofa. Bekah slipped into the remaining chair and sat erect, hands in her lap, as ladylike as Amy had ever seen her. Everyone listened as Adrianna read each word in the book, accepting Mr. Rupp's soft corrections when she stumbled.

When Adrianna reached the end of the story, she slapped the book closed and turned a serious look on Tim. "In my class at school, there's a girl named Trista, and her cat had kittens last week. She says if I want, I can pick one. I want a girl one, and I'll name it Cindy, and I'll take very good care of it. But Momma has to say yes first. I won't bring one home unless Momma says yes." She shifted to Amy, her face imploring. "Pleeeeease, Momma?"

The trio on the sofa laughed, and Tim gave her a little nudge away from his lap. "You're pretty smart, asking permission now. How can your mom say no in front of all of us?"

Adrianna hunched her shoulders. "I dunno. With her mouth, I guess." She wrinkled her nose. "It says no pretty good."

Laughter roared, and Tim caught Adrianna in a hug. He set her aside, still chuckling, and she scurried across the floor to climb into Amy's lap.

Mrs. Rupp smiled at Parker. "You must be Parker, and your sister over there is Bekah. Am I right?"

Parker nodded. "Yes, ma'am."

Tim's parents exchanged an approving look. Mrs. Rupp turned back to Parker. "My son tells me you worked very hard for him in his orchard."

Again, Parker nodded. He kept his arms tight at his side, a sign of nervousness, but he spoke clearly. "I helped outside, and Bekah helped inside, but not anymore. He quit needing us." Hurt colored Parker's tone, and Tim lowered his head. Parker went on. "But he's still our friend. You don't quit being friends just because you don't see each other. If you can't see people with your eyes, you can still hold them with your heart." His movements jerky, Parker shifted to look at Amy. "That's what Mom said when our dad died."

Tears glittered in the older woman's eyes. She nodded slowly, her gaze pinned on Parker's sober face. "You have a very wise mother, Parker."

Mr. Rupp cleared his throat. "And I understand you have your own business, is this right, Mrs. Knackstedt?"

"Yes. A quilting business."

"She has quite a machine, Mom." Tim unfolded himself

from the sofa cushion. "Called a long-arm machine. Mrs. Knackstedt, would you mind if I showed it to my mother?"

With Adrianna on her lap, Amy couldn't get up quickly. Bekah bounced up but stood silently, her eyes wide and uncertain. Before she could stop him, Tim slipped his hand through his mother's elbow and aimed her toward the sewing room.

35

Tim stared at the quilt caught in the machine's frame. Although only a small portion of it showed, something about the bright patches seemed familiar. He tipped his head, searching his memory, and then he gasped. His finger reached, brushing across a soft lilac patch while remembering how lovely Julia had looked in the flowing blouse. He shifted his attention to a gray-and-white-striped triangle, and an image of Charlie in his favorite overalls filled his mind. The lines blurred together as tears flooded his eyes. He blinked rapidly and turned away from the quilt, his gaze falling on Bekah, who stood in the doorway, her lower lip caught between her teeth.

The girl inched forward. "M-Mr. Roper, I know you told me to empty the closet, but I kept the clothes instead. And I . . ." She gestured to the quilt, her dark eyes begging him for understanding. "Are you mad?"

Anger was the farthest emotion from Tim's mind. He snaked out one hand, caught Bekah's shoulder, and drew her into his embrace. He held tight, his eyes skipping across the triangles cut from clothes his wife and son had once worn. When Amy had mentioned her business, he hadn't understood why someone would request such a quilt. But looking at the patches—each one releasing a specific memory of either Julie or Charlie—he understood. What a gift Bekah had given him.

He gave her another squeeze and then chucked her under the chin. "Thanks, kiddo. This is . . ." He shook his head, releasing a soft chuckle. "This is amazing." Putting his arm around his mother's shoulders, he gestured his father near and then pointed out a few triangles. They listened intently as he shared how much Charlie had loved wearing overalls, and how cute he'd looked in the little sailor suit he wore to Sunday school, and how ladylike Julia always appeared.

After years of trying to forget, what joy he found in re-membering. He caught Amy's eye, and the tears winking in her very blue eyes brought an answering prick of tears in his own eyes. "Remembrance . . . it's a fine idea."

She nodded, her eyes aglow, and he knew she understood the deeper emotions beneath his simple statement. But did she fully understand everything she'd given him? Tim wanted her to know. He owed her a debt of gratitude, and he didn't want to wait one more second before thanking her.

Shifting to face his parents, he said, "Mom, Dad, would it be all right if I spoke with Amy . . . with Mrs. Knackstedt . . . alone for a few minutes?"

Mom and Dad exchanged a quick look, and Dad answered. "Of course, son. Your mother and me will entertain the chil-dren. You and Mrs. Knackstedt feel free to talk."

Amy's cheeks flooded with pink, but when Tim gestured to the front door, she didn't hesitate to follow him outside. He led her to the edge of the porch. A full moon hung high in the sky, bathing the yard in a soft glow. "It's a beautiful night. Would you like to take a short walk?" She flicked a glance over her shoulder, and he added, "Just to the barn and back. The kids'll be fine with my folks." How odd to speak of his parents so casually, as if they'd never been absent. Yet it felt good. Right.

"Okay."

Together, they stepped off the porch, and even though the moon clearly marked the pathway, he curled his fingers lightly around her elbow. She made no effort to pull away. As they moved slowly across the gravel driveway toward the barn, Tim spoke softly, unwilling to disturb the beauty of this Kansas night.

"Amy, I confess, when you and your kids first moved here, I resented you. I didn't want you here." Her puzzled gaze flicked to his face, and he gave a sober nod. "You served as an unpleasant reminder of the life I tried to escape. Every time I looked at your mesh cap and caped dress, I remembered my mother. Every time I looked at Parker, I remembered my son." He swallowed, his steps slowing. "It hurt me. I didn't want to remember."

She stopped and turned to face him, the moonlight glimmering on her cap and highlighting her heart-shaped face. "We never intended to bring you pain."

The apology in her voice pierced him. "No, no, let me finish. Although a part of me resented you, a part of me—the part I didn't want to acknowledge—welcomed you. Having you and the other Mennonites here in Weaverly forced me to reopen those pages of my life. And in doing so, reawakened the faith I'd tried to bury."

Tears filled her eyes, glittering like diamonds under the

moon's soft glow. She covered her quivering lips with her fingers. "That's exactly what the children and I have prayed—that you would rediscover your faith. God is so good to answer."

Warmth flooded Tim's frame. She'd done even more than he'd imagined. Thinking of her and Bekah, Parker, and little Adri lifting him in prayer even after he'd been resentful and sometimes unkind raised another wave of gratitude. He swallowed the lump that filled his throat. "God is very good to answer. And you're very good to ask Him."

A shy smile curved her lips, and she ducked her head. "Perhaps that's why God brought the Mennonites to Weaverly. It was His way of reaching you."

Tim took her elbow again, and they set their feet in motion. Amazing how nicely their strides matched. They ambled slowly toward the barn, relaxed and at ease with each other. "Maybe. But He'd sent Mennonites before—a long time ago."

"Oh?" Her face held interest.

He nodded. "A group of them came to pick apples." Remembering how Charlie and the other boy had frolicked like a pair of puppies in the orchard made him smile. "There was a boy, kind of like Charlie—with special needs, you know?—and the boy's dad and I had a good talk. I guess you could say we commiserated with each other, wanting to 'fix' our boys but knowing we couldn't. And we agreed when you have a child who needs you especially much, you make sure you're there for them. For the long haul. It was good to talk to the man. To know somebody understood how it felt to raise a boy like Charlie."

Amy's smile grew bigger. "Often I've wished I could talk to others who understand the uniqueness of raising a special-needs child. Do the Mennonites who came live nearby? Perhaps I could find a way to visit with that boy's family."

They'd reached the barn, so Tim paused and leaned against the frame. Bits of chipping paint fell away as his shoulder pressed the worn wood. "I wish I could connect you with them. I know they were from Kansas, but I can't remember which town. I don't remember their names, either, except that the boy's name was kind of strange." He shrugged, dislodging more crisp white paint chips. Maybe he'd round up the Mennonite men and give her barn a good whitewash before winter fell. "Bumper. Or Bugger. Something like that."

She gasped. "Budger?"

Tim pushed away from the barn. "That's it. Budger." Amy's face had drained of color. Tim caught her by the shoulders. "What's wrong?"

Her body quivered beneath his grasp. "Budger . . . that was Gabe's—my husband's—special name for Parker. No one but Gabe called him that. So the orchard they visited was yours . . ." Realization dawned across her white face, the tremble increasing in intensity. "And you . . . you met Gabe . . . and he told you . . ." Her hands whipped upward, her fingers curling around his wrists as if she needed his support to keep herself upright. She stared at him, wide-eyed and almost desperate. "He told you he thought it was important to be there for Parker? For . . . forever?"

"Yes, if the man I spoke to was your husband, that's exactly what he said."

A laugh trickled from Amy's throat. Tim might have thought it maniacal, given her present state, had it not been for the note of joy beneath. She released his wrists and stepped away from his hands, turning her face skyward. "Thank You,

Father. Thank You." She spun to face him again, her hands reaching. He automatically reached back, and she held tight while jabbering a story about her husband's death initially being ruled accidental and then changed to a possible suicide attempt.

She finished, "The insurance agency needs some sort of verification that Gabe didn't choose to end his own life. It could very well be that your conversation with him, in which he indicated a desire to be there for Parker, would be helpful. Would you be willing to contact the agent and share with him what you just told me?"

"Of course I will." Tim pulled one hand free but linked his fingers through hers with the other. He led her toward the house, the fit of her small hand within his comfortable, natural. "First thing tomorrow, I'll give the man a call." Just short of the porch, Tim stopped, drawing Amy to a halt with him. "If my word isn't enough to convince them, what will happen?"

"I'll certainly have to sell the house and my sewing machines to repay the money I was given." Worry briefly creased her brow, but then a smile chased the lines away. "But if I'm forced to do so, I will accept it as God's will. He's met my needs in the past. I have no reason to believe He'll neglect me now."

Tim marveled at her strong faith despite all she'd lost. "You humble me, Amy. And inspire me."

She drew in a slow breath, her expression hesitant. "Tim, may I ask you a question?"

"Anything."

"Was . . . was Julia a believer in Jesus?"

Tim nodded. Julia's faith had been unfaltering. "She led

Charlie to the Lord when he was very young. Sometimes I think Charlie's faith was even stronger than Julia's. With his simplistic way of viewing the world, he was incapable of seeing evil." In some ways, Charlie had been fortunate.

Tears glittered in the corners of Amy's eyes. She squeezed his hand. "Then you'll see them again someday, just as I'll see Gabe. And in Heaven, Charlie is whole, just as my son will one day be fully restored to wholeness."

Something warm and powerful gripped Tim's heart. In his imaginings, although he loved Charlie unconditionally, he always viewed his son as disabled. Amy's words transformed the images, giving him a glimpse of the marvel of eternal glory. A lump filled his throat. "Thank you, Amy."

They stood for long moments, their gazes locked, and Tim felt as though their hearts beat in sync. He hadn't experienced such oneness with another human being since he'd lost Julia. The realization left him breathless and yet completely at peace at the same time.

Finally she sighed, tipping her head toward the house. "I suppose we should go in. They're probably wondering what happened to us."

Tim wasn't ready to abandon their silent communion, but he nodded. He released her hand and followed her inside. They found his parents and the children seated around the kitchen table, sipping tea and playing a game of dominoes. Adri sat in Dad's lap, instructing him on what to play next, and they all looked as if they'd known one another for years rather than minutes.

Amy paused in the kitchen doorway, flicking a warm smile over her shoulder at Tim. He returned it, then shifted his gaze to the group at the table. His mother lifted her face and caught his eye. A secretive smile played on her lips, and Tim's cheeks blazed hot. He jerked his gaze elsewhere, only to collide with Amy's profile.

He examined the soft turn of her jaw, the dark hair smoothed neatly beneath her prayer covering, and her delicate ear framed by the ribbon falling from her cap. His mother had correctly recognized his deep affection for this woman. But if Tim were to act on the feeling, he would have to make some serious changes in his life. Something pinched his chest. After years of living in the outside world, was he willing to be fully Mennonite again?

36

Amy held the telephone receiver tight to her ear, trying to hear the agent's voice over the sound of her pounding heartbeat.

Mr. Corey's voice held a note of apology. "It seems the elevator owner was negligent in allowing your husband to perform a duty that rightly belonged to an elevator employee. By convincing us the fall was intentional rather than accidental, the state would reverse its citations and fines. The investigation is officially closed. You'll receive a full disclosure of our findings in the mail, but I also wanted to tell you personally."

The rush of relief was so strong, her bones turned to rubber. Amy inched sideways and sank into a kitchen chair. "I appreciate your call, Mr. Corey."

"Please accept our condolences once again on your loss."

She disconnected the call, then remained in the chair, waiting for her pulse to return to normal. Songs of praise erupted in her heart. Gabe hadn't chosen to leave her and the children. And they would be able to keep their home. She couldn't wait to tell Bekah when school was out.

She pushed up from the chair. Although pieces of an unfinished quilt lay caught in the needle of her sewing machine, she decided to set aside the project and prepare a celebratory dinner. The past two weeks had been fraught with tension as they awaited final word from the insurance agency. Not knowing whether they'd have to leave their new town and school, where the children had settled in beautifully and made friends, and return to Arborville had kept Amy awake at night. She'd told God repeatedly she would go wherever He led, and she meant it, but knowing they could stay right here in their place of fresh beginnings brought a rush of joy.

"Thank You, Father," she praised aloud.

Bustling to the pantry, she removed the items needed for a pan of chicken-and-cheese lasagna, one of the children's favorite meals. She'd bake bread, too, and toss a salad. Then for dessert, they'd have brownie sundaes. She had everything she needed, except ice cream, and there was time to drive to Weaverly's little grocery store before the bus brought the children home. Envisioning the children's smiles when they found so many treats waiting, her heart gave a happy skip.

And I should invite Tim to join us.

The thought brought her busy hands to a halt midtask. Beneath the modesty cape of her dress, her heart fluttered. What a surprise she'd received last Sunday when Tim had entered the building where the Mennonites gathered for worship. Although attired in pleated brown trousers and a store-bought shirt rather than a Mennonite black suit, he'd sat among the men, joined in the hymns, and followed along in his Bible as if he'd always attended. Then he'd accepted Margaret Gerber's invitation to join the fellowship for the meal after the service. Although he and Amy hadn't exchanged any words, she'd been keenly aware of his presence. Of the way he *fit*. And she'd realized anew just how much she desired him to be a permanent part of her world.

Amy dropped to her knees beside a kitchen chair and rested her linked hands on the vinyl seat. "Dear Lord, I asked You to guard my heart against the growing affection I've felt toward Tim. I didn't want to love a man who didn't live to honor You. But he seems to have changed, Father. I know You've used the children and me to ignite the fire of faith in Tim's soul again, but is our relationship meant to be more than friends? Speak to me, Lord, so I know how to proceed. I don't want to step outside of Your will for me, but . . . I confess to You . . . I love him."

She spent several minutes in prayer, sharing her deepest feelings with the One who already knew them intimately. She finished, "Thank You for the pathways You open to us. Please make clear where I am to walk concerning the children's and my feelings for Tim. Amen." Having given her concerns to her heavenly Father, she rose, ready to complete preparations for the special dinner. But before she returned to the lasagna ingredients, she moved to the telephone and dialed a number she knew by memory. On the second ring, he answered, and she blurted, "Tim, would you like to join the children and me for dinner this evening?"

✢

"Mmm, it smells good in here," Bekah called as she charged through the front door, Parker and Adri on her heels. Her siblings dropped their backpacks and raced back outside, probably heading to the barn to visit the kittens Mr. Roper had brought over in a wicker basket a week ago. The kittens—one black with a white bib and paws and one yellow-and-white striped—were cute, but they were really more Parker and Adri's kittens than hers. They could play with them without her. She tossed her backpack on top of theirs and headed for the kitchen.

Mom stood at the counter, chopping tomatoes. She greeted Bekah with a broad smile. "Hello, honey. Did you have a good day?"

Bekah leaned against the counter, peeking into the big bowl that contained salad makings. Her tummy rumbled. She plucked out a piece of cucumber, stuck it in her mouth, and spoke around it. "Uh-huh. My art teacher said I have a real knack for painting. She encouraged me to take the advanced art class when I'm in high school." She hoped she'd be able to go to the Weaverly high school. Every night since the insurance man had visited their house, she'd prayed they'd get to stay here. Even though she still missed Grandpa and her Arborville friends, she didn't want to go back. Mom and the kids were happy here. And to Bekah, Weaverly had become home. "Can I maybe buy some paints, brushes, and canvasses to practice here at home?"

"I think we could probably fit that into our budget," Mom said. She bobbed her chin toward the table, where their best linen cloth covered the Formica top. "Would you set the table for me? Five plates. Mr. Roper is joining us."

Something in Mom's voice made Bekah pause. The way she'd said "Mr. Roper" sounded different. Softer. A funny tingle tiptoed up Bekah's spine. "He is?"

Mom paused for a moment, giving Bekah a serious look. "Is that all right with you?"

Bekah held her breath. If her suspicions were true, she and

her brother and sister might get more than just a new house to live in. They might get a new dad. Her thoughts tripped through the past weeks and all the kind things Mr. Roper had done for them. She liked him. He was nice. Especially to Parker, who really needed a dad. Bekah blew out the breath she'd been holding. She touched Mom's arm. "It's fine with me, Mom."

The smile that broke across Mom's face made Bekah's nose sting. She reached for the cabinet door. "I'll set the table. And I'll put Mr. Roper's plate next to yours."

❊

"That was delicious, Amy." Tim leaned back and patted his stomach. "The best lasagna I've ever had."

Bekah flicked a quick glance at her mother, a sly smile creasing her cheeks. "Mom's an awesome cook. The best ever."

"Bekah, it isn't polite to brag." Amy rose and began clearing their dishes.

Tim, watching color flood Amy's cheeks, stifled a chuckle. He supposed it would be awkward, having your teenage daughter play matchmaker. Bekah'd been dropping hints ever since he arrived for dinner, praising Amy's cooking and housekeeping abilities. The girl didn't realize he'd already fallen for Amy—he didn't need any encouragement to see her as desirable. But it made him happy to know he'd have Bekah's approval when he finally got up his nerve to ask to court Amy Knackstedt.

Adri wriggled in her chair, tomato sauce smeared across her endearing face. "Momma made brownies for dessert. So lick your fork, Mr. Roper!"

Tim obliged the little girl, grinning when she giggled and snatched up her fork, too. Amy carried a pan of aromatic brownies to the table, and Bekah fetched a tub of ice cream from the freezer. Tim visited with the two younger children while their mother and sister dished up large servings of the dessert. Conversation fell away as they indulged in the treat. Although the brownies were delicious, their flavor couldn't top the sweet taste of belonging that fully encompassed him while he sat at their kitchen table, sharing the meal, talking, laughing. He sent surreptitious glances around the table while he ate, wondering how each of them would react if he suddenly revealed his longing to be a part of their family circle.

When they finished eating, Amy sent the children upstairs to complete their homework. Both Parker and Adri clattered up the stairs, their giggles ringing, but Bekah hesitated beside the stairway opening. "Do you want my help with dishes, Mom?"

Tim rose. "I'll help her tonight, Bekah. It's the least I can do after being fed such a wonderful meal. You go on." He winked, and he could have sworn she winked in reply before slipping around the corner. He turned and found Amy fixing him with a serious look. His pulse stammered. "Is everything all right?"

"Everything is wonderful." Yet she looked so somber. She licked her lips, her gaze zipping to the stairway and then back to him. "I'll tell the children before they go to bed, but I wanted you to know, too. They've dropped the investigation. They'll let the ruling stand that Gabe's death was accidental."

Tim acted on impulse. One step forward, arms stretching outward, and in the next second he held her in his arms. His chin rested on her mesh prayer cap. How perfectly she fit in his embrace. But would she agree she belonged there? "I'm so happy for you, Amy. Such an answer to prayer."

"Yes." She remained nestled against him for several seconds, her warm breath whisking across his collarbone. Then she stepped back, her face flushed. "It's such a relief, for many reasons, the most prevalent being able to put to rest all questions of his state of mind."

Tim scooped up the dessert dishes and silverware and followed her to the sink, where she began running water. "So this means you'll be able to keep your house. Or . . ." Uncertainty gripped him. She'd come here to escape unpleasant speculation. With the question removed, would she return to her former community? He forced a light tone. "Have you decided to go back to Arborville?"

She looked up at him with an inquisitive expression, swishing the soapy rag over a plate. "Why would we do that? The children are happy here." The pink in her cheeks deepened to red. "As am I. This is home now."

He swallowed, fighting a mighty urge to lean down and place a kiss on her sweetly curved lips. But he couldn't do it. Not yet. "I'm glad. I'd miss you if you left." He examined her face, searching for signs of withdrawing. Seeing none, he continued. "I suppose you know, Amy, I've grown very fond of your children . . . and you."

Her hands fell still in the dishwater. She nodded in silence, her blue eyes pinned to his. Although she didn't smile, she seemed to be waiting. He wished he knew what thoughts lurked beneath the bright blue of her unwavering gaze.

"I guess you know I talked to Dillard Gerber last week. About joining the fellowship."

Those blue eyes widened. "Y-you did?"

He'd never heard her voice so squeaky. He swallowed a smile. "I did. I don't know how long it'll take me to get things squared away at my place—get everything approved. I've accumulated a lot of worldly conveniences, although the tornado did its best to steal them from me."

The smile quivered on her lips while her eyes sparkled in response to his teasing.

"And I'm wanting to make a trip to Goshen, to see my whole family. I can't go until after harvest, though." Regret twined through his middle. So much time to wait before he could proceed. "But I'm hoping to be fully restored to fellowship by then, so I can receive permission to"—he drew in a deep breath, gathering courage—"court."

Could her face possibly glow any brighter red? She looked as if she might explode. She spun to face the dishwater and got very busy scrubbing an already clean plate.

"Amy." Tim caught her chin between his finger and thumb, gently lifting her face to his again. Beneath his fingertips, he felt the rapid beat of her pulse. His own was thrumming so madly he found it amazing he could breathe. But he needed to get everything said. "I want to court you." His gaze flicked overhead, where he imagined three youngsters hunched over homework papers. A grin twitched his cheek. "And your children." He returned his focus to her flaming face. "I want us to build a life together. But only if you want it, too."

She swallowed, the sound loud in the otherwise silent room. Shifting aside slightly, she removed her hands from the sudsy water and dried them on a towel. Then, tangling the towel in her hands, she peered up at him again. She licked her lips. "I want it."

The simple statement sent shafts of joy through Tim's soul. He reached for her, and she stepped forward, fully into his embrace. She tipped her head, inviting his kiss, and the sweetness of her lips filled his senses with all things glorious. The kiss was short, agonizingly so, but he knew he shouldn't tempt her. Or himself.

He took a giant step backward and ran a hand through his hair. He released a shaky breath. "Whoa. I think it might be smart for us to avoid being all alone together again."

A fresh blush crept over her cheeks, and she nodded.

Tim stepped to the stairs and called, "Bekah? Parker? Adri? Would you come down here for a minute?"

A raucous clatter sounded on the stairs, and the three kids breezed around the corner, their faces bright with expectation. Adri bounded to Tim's side and beamed up at him. "Whatcha want, Mr. Roper?"

Tim put his hand on Adri's tousled hair and looked first into Parker's and then Bekah's face. "I want to ask your permission to court your mother." Parker's eyes flew wide, and a knowing smile rounded Bekah's cheeks.

Adri yanked on his hand. "What does that mean?"

Tim went down on one knee in front of the little girl. His chest ached with love for the freckled little imp. Would he have the chance to help raise this child to womanhood? *Please, Lord, let them want me as much as I want them.* "It means I want to marry your momma and become your new dad. Would that be all right with you?"

"Yay!" Adri threw herself into his arms.

Tim held her close, looking at the older two over Adri's head. The little one had no memories of her father. But Parker and Bekah might see him as an unwelcome intrusion. His arms clinging to Adri, he waited for the others to express their thoughts. He wouldn't force himself on them.

Parker stepped forward and put his hand on Tim's shoulder.

"I think it's okay." He peeked over his shoulder at Bekah. "Right, Bekah?"

Slowly, her feet sliding across the faded linoleum, Bekah inched forward. She reached her brother's side, and she slipped her arm across Parker's shoulders. "Yes, Parker." She gave a firm nod. "It's more than okay."

Tim rose, lifting Adri with him, and Amy joined them in a five-way hug that left Tim nearly breathless with happiness. After walking away from his family and then losing Julia and Charlie, he never imagined finding a place in another family. But fresh hope blossomed in his heart with the acceptance offered by Amy and her children. God had blessed him beyond his expectation. *Thank You, Lord!*

Bekah's grin grew, bouncing from Tim to Amy and back to Tim. "Does this mean you've decided to be Mennonite again?"

Tim chuckled. "I'm not sure I ever really quit being Mennonite. I just got displaced for a while."

Bekah's grin faded. Her forehead crinkled. "Me too. But . . ." She leaned her head against her mother's shoulder. "It feels really good to know where you belong, doesn't it?"

Tim curled his arm around the girl's shoulders and drew her near. Smiling into Amy's shining face, he nodded. "Yes, Bekah. It's the best feeling in the world."

ACKNOWLEDGMENTS

Writing a book, although a solitary process, is hardly achieved on one's own. I am so grateful for the many people who come alongside and aid me in my attempts to craft a worthwhile story. A few of them are mentioned below.

My family, who give me endless encouragement and support as well as the occasional motivating kick in the seat of the pants. (Yes, Don, those text messages asking "How many words today?" and "Get busy and write!" do not go unnoticed.) I thank God every day for each of you.

My darling little princess, Adrianna, whose name fit perfectly in this book. What a precious gift you are to all of us—grow in Jesus, sweet girl!

My critique group members, who offer suggestions and corrections and who cheerlead more exuberantly than anyone else I know. We've enjoyed a lengthy journey together thus far, and I hope it continues for years to come. Giving a special nod to *Donna* for sending me the article about the Amish starting new communities in Colorado, which sparked the idea for this story. Thanks for thinking of me!

My friend and mentor, Deborah Raney, who helped me brainstorm Amy and Tim's story and got all excited with me right there in the deli. Your "goose bumps" increased my own enthusiasm for this story of new beginnings.

My agent, Tamela, who works behind the scenes always with a smile and a ready word of encouragement. You are appreciated more than you know.

My dear friend Connie Stevens and "beauty consultant" Ammie Claussen, whose remembrance quilts inspired Amy's business. May your quilts continue to bring you comfort and sweet memories.

The community of Waverly, Kansas, which provided a sample setting for my story. Wandering the streets of this delightful town helped bring the imaginary community of Weaverly to life. So thank you, Waverly folk, for sharing your town and its history with me and allowing me to build on it. A special smile and nod to *Jeanne* at the Waverly Library for your friendliness and willingness to provide me with research material for the area.

My friend Kathy, who is always up for a research trip, who listens to me blather on about my make-believe friends without ever making fun of me, and who supports me with her prayers. I suppose you already know this, but I appreciate you muchly.

My editor Charlene and the amazing team at Bethany House, who partner with me in this ministry. My childhood dream came true the day I became a Bethany House author, and I will be forever grateful for the opportunity to be a part of your publishing family.

Finally, and most importantly, *God,* who never leaves me without hope and is able to bring forth new growth in even the most withered soul. You opened this pathway to me, and You lead the way, splashing my footsteps with joy unspeakable. May any praise or glory be reflected directly back to You.

Kim Vogel Sawyer is the bestselling author of more than twenty novels. Her books have won the Carol Award, the Gayle Wilson Award of Excellence, and the Inspirational Readers Choice Award. Kim is active in her church, where she leads women's fellowship and participates in both voice and bell choirs. In her spare time, she enjoys drama, quilting, and calligraphy. Kim and her husband, Don, reside in central Kansas and have three daughters and nine grandchildren.

www.kimvogelsawyer.com
writespassage.blogspot.com

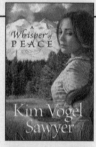